Lynda Chater was b[...]
Ashford, Middlesex. Educated at Twickenham
Girls' School and Leeds Polytechnic, she followed a career in landscape architecture before
becoming a full-time writer. Now living in Suffolk
with her husband and cat, *Makeover* is her second
novel. *That Devil Called Love* was published by
Pocket Books in 1999.

Also by Lynda Chater

That Devil Called Love

MAKEOVER

LYNDA CHATER

POCKET BOOKS

LONDON · SYDNEY · NEW YORK · TOKYO · SINGAPORE · TORONTO

First published in Great Britain by Pocket Books, 2000
An imprint of Simon & Schuster UK Ltd
A Viacom Company

Simon & Schuster UK Ltd
Africa House
64-78 Kingsway
London WC2B 6AH

Simon & Schuster Australia
Sydney

A CIP catalogue record for this book is available
from the British Library

ISBN 0-671-01803-5

1 3 5 7 9 10 8 6 4 2

This book is a work of fiction. Names, characters, places
and incidents are either products of the author's imagination
or are used fictitiously. Any resemblance to actual people,
living or dead, events or locales, is entirely coincidental.

Typeset by Palimpsest Book Production Limited, Polmont, Stirlingshire
Printed and bound in Great Britain by
Caledonian International Book Manufacturing Ltd, Glasgow

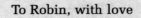

To Robin, with love

With special thanks to Luigi Bonomi of Sheil Land and Clare Ledingham of Simon & Schuster for their invaluable help and support.

CHAPTER 1

If everyone was entitled to fifteen minutes of fame, Carmen Bird had probably cheated an awful lot of people by using up their quota as well as her own. *They ought to resent me for it*, she thought, listening to the rapturous applause as she appeared on the *Makeover* set and stepped forward into the glare of the studio lights. What had she done to deserve such widespread acclaim? But then she reminded herself that fate found its own way of redressing balances. Looking around at the smiling faces of her audience, she wondered what they would think if they knew the truth about her so-called 'perfect life'.

It was such a disturbing idea that she fluffed her opening lines.

'Even the biggest TV stars sometimes get their *mords* in a *wuddle*,' smirked the warm-up man, prompting gales of laughter. He pranced across the front of the set, pretending to trip on a tangle of camera cables as he milked the audience for maximum response.

'Stand by,' sighed Barry, the floor manager, rolling his eyes.

'Roll tape,' said a voice.

'Speed,' called another.

Carmen faced the camera and took a deep breath. 'Welcome to *Makeover!*' she said brightly. 'The show that makes a *real difference* to people's lives! Today we're going to ring the changes for Maureen, a house-wife from Bromley, and . . .'

'We're stopping again,' snapped Barry, striding across the set. 'Who left that Coke can on the counter?'

'Someone's about to get clipboarded,' giggled the warm-up man, as Damien, the makeup expert, hur-riedly gathered up the remains of his lunch. 'Sorry,' he added, ducking behind a cameraman as Barry turned to face him with a thunderous expression. 'Just keeping the folks informed.'

Carmen sat down to let the makeup girl dust her face before they started again. The audience craned their necks to watch, anxious not to miss the smallest detail of their brief excursion into the glamorous world of TV.

They were the kind of people who would do almost anything for the chance to appear on television them-selves, reflected Carmen, as she glanced up at the rows of excited faces. Just to watch her show being made, they were prepared to get up when it was still dark and spend hours travelling on coaches from far-flung parts of the country. Once in Hammersmith, they often doubled their journey time stuck in the traffic sys-tem under the flyover before reaching the Conquest TV studios on Fulham Palace Road and being herded into queues for the indignities of the security search.

She knew about these things because she sometimes eavesdropped on the balcony above the audience foyer, where they milled around guzzling free coffee before they were let in to their seats. *Get to know your audience*, her producer Kevin repeatedly advised her.

They were deliberately kept waiting for at least three-quarters of an hour for two reasons, Kevin had explained. One was to make sure that they all had time to use the toilet – it was a real problem if someone in the centre of Row F decided to make a break for it in the middle of the show. The other was to build up their sense of anticipation – a bit like the ritual of queueing for rides at Disneyland. According to Kevin, television would lose its magic appeal if you could walk straight into a studio from the street. His theory seemed to work, as they were usually quivering on the starting blocks by the time the recording session started, ready to applaud anything that moved.

Their conversations were always the same: they would speculate about the likely broadcast date of the show and compare notes on timing strategies for their video equipment back home. Every so often their talk would circle around to the likelihood of actually appearing on the finished programme. Regular attendees knew the optimum seat positions for getting into the brief shots that raked over the audience once or twice per show, and where to stand in the queue to get these seats. Despite knowing that the shows were planned months in advance, most audiences clung to a fond belief that one of their number might be miraculously plucked from the ranks for an impromptu makeover.

'Better watch out,' they would whisper to each other with knowing nudges as they filed into the studio. 'You never know who might be getting a *makeover* next!'

'Stand by,' said a voice in Carmen's ear. She jumped anxiously to her feet, colliding with a cameraman and sending the audience into gales of laughter.

'Sorry,' she mumbled, struggling to regain her professional poise. But the jolt had set the pain in her forehead throbbing again and, before she could stop them, unwanted thoughts came flooding into her mind. *How long would she be able to go on like this? What fresh punishments would be waiting for her tonight?* With an effort, she forced herself to concentrate on the present. She would have plenty of time to worry about her personal problems on the way home.

The first half of the recording session ran fairly smoothly, if you ignored the delay caused by Maureen from Bromley losing a contact lens on the studio floor. She had also managed to expand by nearly a whole dress size since sending in her measurements and it had taken some ingenious work with double-sided tape to squeeze her into her new outfit. By the time they finished, however, she was scarcely recognisable: the dowdy housewife in sloppy jumper and jeans had been transformed into an elegant creature who looked as if she had stepped from the pages of a glossy magazine.

How appearances can deceive, thought Carmen, not for the first time. But the audience let out a gasp of approval as the new Maureen emerged from the dressing room and sashayed down the catwalk to the show's theme music. Carmen breathed a sigh of relief as applause resounded throughout the studio. These were the moments that made it all worthwhile.

The format for the programme was simple and appealing. The first part was pure makeover – two candidates selected from thousands of applicants would be styled and groomed to perfection, emerging with the 'new look' they felt they needed. The makeover was followed by a short feature from one of their resident experts – Damien on depilation, Sandra on skincare, and so on. The final sequence – the part that Carmen enjoyed most – consisted of an interview with one of the candidates from a previous show. This was her opportunity to ask them what difference the makeover had actually made to their lives.

Today, she was seeing Hazel from Sunbury. The audience clapped and cheered on cue as Hazel appeared through the archway and negotiated the catwalk, a nervous smile plastered on her face.

She had made a good effort, thought Carmen, checking the woman's appearance against the 'before' and 'after' shots on the studio monitors. She wore the same dress that she'd been given on the show, teamed up with a jacket of her own that matched quite well. Carmen worked her way through the mental checklist – shoes, makeup, hair, jewellery, and so on – by which she appraised people's looks both professionally and increasingly, although she tried hard not to, in her private life. As she came closer, Carmen could see that Hazel's makeup was rather uneven, but it wouldn't do to have everyone looking too perfect, she told herself. The shoes were all wrong, but they would be hidden once she sat down.

'Tell me, Hazel,' she began, smiling. 'What made you first decide to come on *Makeover*?'

Hazel wasn't the most forthcoming of interviewees. She seemed content to mumble stock responses to the questions and had an annoying habit of prefixing every remark with a reference to her husband.

'Well, I don't really know, but my husband says . . .'

Doesn't the woman have a mind of her own, wondered Carmen irritably, as they approached the close of the session. She also expected a little more enthusiasm from someone who had been given a free makeover and an armful of designer clothes to take home. This interview, if it was ever used, would be of as much interest to their viewers as the shipping forecast would be to a person in central Mongolia.

Barry was making signals to get things wrapped.

'So, to sum up, Hazel,' she said breezily, 'what were the big highlights of the makeover for you?'

Hazel stared at her blankly. Sometimes the question had to be repeated if they didn't run with it the first time.

'What would you say were the most successful aspects of your makeover? Is there anything you'd like to recommend to the viewers back home?'

Hazel remained silent. Looking at her more closely, Carmen saw a well of moisture forming in the corner of each eye.

'Are you OK, Hazel?' she whispered. Beyond her, out

of the audience's sightline, she could see Barry making a throat-cutting gesture.

'Sorry,' faltered Hazel, wiping her eyes on her sleeve. 'I didn't really want to come on, but the research girl said I ought to. She said it would boost my confidence if I went through with it.'

'So what's the problem?' asked Carmen softly, making a mental note to get the researcher fired. She flashed Hazel a reassuring smile. 'We're not going to eat you, you know.'

This raised an uneasy laugh from the audience, which mingled with a buzz of excited whispering. It didn't take them long to pick up that things weren't going according to plan.

'To tell you the truth,' blurted Hazel suddenly, 'that makeover was the worst thing I've ever done! It's made my life a misery!'

A shocked gasp came from the audience. Barry held up two fingers to his forehead in imitation of a pistol and keeled sideways with a silent groan of despair.

'Why don't you tell us about it, then?' murmured Carmen in an encouraging voice. She was curious now, and wondered what had happened to cause Hazel's tears. This interview would never be aired, Kevin would see to that. This isn't the fucking *Jerry Springer Show*, he would tell her angrily. I need positive feedback if you want to keep that chit-chat slot of yours.

'My husband's been seeing someone else,' announced Hazel dramatically, casting an expectant hush over the audience. 'I thought I could win him back – he was always on about how I was letting myself go. But when I came home all made up, he just laughed at me. Told me I looked like . . .' she glanced doubtfully at Carmen.

'Go on.'

'. . . like one of those daffy women on television. All tits, teeth and shoulder pads.'

Carmen winced. Heads would roll for this and she hoped that hers wasn't going to be one of them. Meanwhile, the audience was loving it.

'I wanted to go back to how I was before,' continued Hazel, suddenly talkative. 'But of course I knew everyone at work was going to see me on the programme and I'd seem stupid if I didn't turn up looking any different. Now I'm stuck with having to spend three hours in front of the mirror every sodding morning, while he's gone off with his tart.'

Carmen stared at her, momentarily lost for words. Then a movement caught her eye and she glanced up to see Barry standing by the autocue with the expression of a man resurrected from the dead. He jabbed his finger at her closing lines, mouthing expletive-strewn instructions to get on with it.

Pulling herself together, Carmen turned to the camera. 'Well, that's all we have time for today,' she said, forcing a warm smile. Thanking Hazel and the audience for coming, she brought the proceedings swiftly to a close.

After a lengthy and unpleasant debriefing session in Kevin's office, Carmen threw on her coat and headed for reception to call a taxi.

'Coming for a drink?' asked Barry, catching up with her in the corridor.

She shook her head. 'I must fly – I'm late.'

'Listen, Carmen.' Barry put his hand on her arm to detain her. 'It wasn't your fault what happened in there. Everyone has bad days.' He swung her round to face him, forcing her to meet his eye. 'It doesn't do any harm to drown your sorrows once in a while.'

'I'm sorry.' Carmen glanced at her watch. 'Gideon's got some business dinner tonight and I have to be there.'

'It's Jessica's birthday today. The new girl in Wardrobe – I don't suppose you've had a chance to meet her yet. Amanda's getting the whole gang together to surprise her in the pub.' He gave her an appealing look. 'They'd be thrilled to bits if you came along, just for half an hour. It would do wonders for morale.'

'Look, I'd love to come if I could, really,' she assured him. 'I know they think I'm stuck-up and everything, but it's not like that. I've just got a lot of things on at the moment and it isn't easy.'

Barry's pale blue eyes searched her face, his brow wrinkled with concern. She looked away, inwardly flinching as he came out with the question she always dreaded.

'Are you OK, Carmen? Is everything all right at home?'

'I'm fine,' she said, shaking herself free of his grasp. 'But I really do have to dash – I've got a taxi waiting.'

Rounding the corner by the lifts and glancing back to check that she was out of Barry's view, Carmen ran into the ladies' toilet and closed the door. She scrutinised her face in the mirror. Had he noticed something?

The swelling on her forehead was scarcely visible beneath her makeup and was, in any case, mostly covered by her hair. One eye was very slightly puffy but she didn't think it really showed. Gideon usually avoided touching her on a Sunday – he preferred to save the big arguments for a Wednesday evening so that she would have four days to recover before she had to return to the public view. Four days for the cuts and bruises to heal. What happened last night had been her own fault really. She'd been nagging again – at least, that's what he called it. She'd made the mistake of questioning his judgement – voicing her doubts about a change in her schedule he'd agreed on her behalf.

She dabbed more powder on to her forehead and patted her hair into place. Taking a lipstick from her handbag, she stretched her mouth into a contorted grimace and applied fresh colour to her lips.

'Be brave,' she told herself.

But the pep talk approach she'd developed lately didn't always work. Feelings of anger and self-pity welled uncontrollably inside her. The lipstick fell into the washbasin with a clatter as Carmen lowered her head and quietly began to cry.

It seemed to Juliet Jennings, newly arrived from Worcester, that there were several different cities called London. They all fitted together like the components of an Escher drawing and you never knew, when you came out of a

Tube station, which part of the picture you would find yourself in.

There was the official 'Visitors' London' with its parks, palaces and blue plaques. On the lavishly illustrated tourist maps, the familiar buildings seemed crammed together, elbowing each other for space as they sprang up in three dimensions from the street plan. In real life, however, Juliet discovered them to be widely spaced and oddly disappointing. All too often they were dwarfed by their everyday surroundings and views of their once-grand façades were cluttered with builders' scaffolding, advertising hoardings, and countless other visual distractions of modern city life.

The other places she'd visited had left her with widely differing impressions: The City hummed with the self-importance of its dark-suited inhabitants, who scuttled back and forth between their temples of Mammon, while Soho and Covent Garden had the relaxed holiday atmosphere of a fairground. Westminster was sober and intimidating, but the echoing grey spaces of the South Bank frightened her more. A brief glimpse of the Docklands made her wonder if she had slipped through a time warp into a future without planning restrictions. Knightsbridge simply made her feel poor.

None of these different Londons fitted in with her preconceptions, which stemmed largely from childhood fantasies inspired by the Monopoly board. She felt a little buzz of excitement each time she recognised the name of one of the squares – Mayfair, Piccadilly, Northumberland Avenue – but discovered that the mental images she had unconsciously constructed while playing the game bore little relationship to the real places.

There was also another London that no one had prepared her for – the London in which people actually lived. The Monopoly board didn't include the suburbs. If it had, and laid them out roughly to scale, the board would cover the whole of the living room floor.

The suburbs didn't make much of an impression when you sliced your way straight into Paddington on the high speed train. Ten minutes of ticky-tacky boxes stacked like rabbit hutches didn't really stick in your mind when you'd just had two hours of rolling countryside flashing by. But when you were out there, on the ground, they seemed to go on forever. It was all a question of relative scale. Siberia probably looked quite dinky from the air.

Juliet had made a few forays into the suburbs during her first week in London. She had given herself a fortnight to find somewhere to live before she started her new job, and had begun, rather naïvely, by setting an unrealistically low maximum price per week, to see what she could get. She hadn't considered herself to be fussy about living conditions – it was only a place to sleep, after all, when she was tired by the cosmopolitan whirl of her new life. But after a couple of long, gruelling journeys to view broom cupboards in places with desperate-sounding names like Neasden, Chingford and Ponders End, she changed her mind. The suburbs were too depressing to contemplate – row upon row of semi-detached nightmares with walls so thin they rippled when the guy next door began to snore. She then drew a circle with an approximately six-mile radius around Charing Cross and vowed not to stray outside it in her search. She would work over-time, if necessary, rather than live in an environment so mean-spirited that people would go to the trouble of painting half a drain-pipe rather than give their neighbour something for nothing.

Juliet believed in getting things done. By the end of the first week, she had viewed several bedsits in the West London area and had one more to inspect before making a final decision.

A middle-aged woman answered the door of the tall, terraced house in Chiswick.

'Mrs Billings?' asked Juliet. 'I've come about the bedsit.'

The woman viewed her doubtfully for a moment, then ushered her inside. 'Frank usually deals with all this,' she said, wiping her hands on her apron. 'He's my husband. It's just that he's been a bit funny ever since . . . I mean, it's on the top floor, you see. He has trouble with the stairs sometimes.'

They climbed three flights to a small landing, where Mrs Billings fumbled in her apron pocket for a key. 'It's all self-contained,' she said, polishing the handle with her handkerchief before opening the door. 'You'd be able to come and go as you please.'

The main room was small, but bright and airy. There was a dormer window offering views across the rooftops and the walls were freshly painted in a shade of off-white. A doorway led through to a tiny kitchenette. Juliet smiled. This was far more to her liking than the other places she had seen. There was even a set of bookshelves that would be ideal for her collection of detective novels.

'Is there a meter?' she asked, glancing around for the tell-tale cupboard. The last place had been stuffed with so many of them, she had half-expected to be charged by the hour for the air she breathed.

'Gas and electric are thrown in with the rent,' said Mrs Billings, bending to pick a piece of fluff from the spotless carpet. She gave a nervous little smile.

Juliet sat on the bed, bouncing gently to test the springs.

'It's a new mattress, of course,' said Mrs Billings hastily. 'Even though there wasn't any blood, it didn't seem proper to . . .' She stopped, silently mouthing an admonition to herself.

'Blood?' asked Juliet.

'I've gone and said it now, haven't I? After I promised Frank and everything.' Twisting her handkerchief into a knot, Mrs Billings gazed at her with an anguished expression. 'I didn't think it was right, mind you. Trying to hush it up, I mean. It was all over the local papers and, besides, someone would be bound to tell you sooner or later. What would you think of us then?'

'Tell me what?' Juliet could contain her curiosity no longer. Had she stumbled on some real-life detective mystery? A murder, perhaps?

Mrs Billings sat down in the armchair facing Juliet and leaned forward. 'He seemed such a bright young man as well,' she continued, tugging at the hem of her apron. 'Jason, his name was. A law student. I'd never have thought he'd have had it in him to . . .' she glanced up at the ceiling and lowered her voice, '. . . to do away with himself.'

Juliet turned her head to follow the direction of her gaze and they both contemplated the large hook fixed in the ceiling directly above the centre of the bed.

'Frank had to cut him down,' she added in a grim tone. 'Horrible, it was. That's why he's so leery of coming up here again.'

'Why did he do it?' asked Juliet, slightly disappointed that there was no murder to solve.

'Your guess is as good as mine,' replied Mrs Billings with a shrug. 'Depression, they called it. He didn't leave no note.'

Juliet sat in thoughtful silence. People didn't just kill themselves for no reason, she told herself. There had to be an explanation. Her imagination went to work, creating unlikely scenarios involving blackmail, murder and espionage. What if he'd discovered some conspiracy, like that law student in *The Pelican Brief*? He might have left a note hidden away somewhere. Maybe she could find it?

'Well, now you know why the rent's so cheap,' said Mrs Billings gloomily. 'I suppose you won't be wanting it now.'

'Is there a bathroom?' asked Juliet, standing up.

'Through there,' she sighed, pointing to another door-way. 'It's a proper flat really. Ought to fetch twice the rent we're asking, by rights.'

The bathroom seemed respectable enough. No mysterious stains in the bath, or traces of dried blood on the walls. Catching sight of herself in the mirror, Juliet experienced the usual jolt of disappointment at her appearance. She turned on a tap to check that Mrs Billings wasn't fibbing about the hot water and stared defiantly at her reflection, taking in the solid country face with its rounded cheeks, thick eyebrows and hint of a double chin. She shouldn't complain, she told herself. She was better off than poor Jason.

Why did people have such strange superstitions about death? The rent was cheap, the location was right and Jason couldn't harm her from where he was now.

She returned to the main room where Mrs Billings was absent-mindedly polishing the mantelpiece with her handkerchief.

'I'll take it,' she said in a confident voice. 'Can I move in tomorrow?'

As she travelled by Tube back to her bed-and-breakfast in Paddington, Juliet congratulated herself on her efficiency. Well-meaning friends and colleagues had warned her how hard it would be to find cheap accommodation in the capital, but she had turned down their offers to make contact with acquaintances who might be able to put her up. At thirty-four, Juliet felt too old to be sleeping on other people's sofas. Besides, she valued her independence – she didn't want her new start in life to be complicated by feeling indebted to strangers for the dubious privilege of sharing their home.

She wouldn't be entirely alone in London. Nick, her manager, was making the transfer from Worcester to the head office of Castlemayne Insurance at the same time. It had been his idea that she should apply to go with him.

'We make a great team,' he had informed her, in a go-getting, dynamic tone that belied his prosaic job title of Regional Deputy Claims Manager (Domestic). 'Why don't we offer them the full package – it might mean a promotion for you.'

'OK, pardner,' she had replied jokingly, going along with the fiction that they operated in a far more exciting sphere than the world of loss adjustment. 'Looks like you've made me an offer I just can't refuse.'

In fact, the decision was easy. Bored and frustrated after nearly ten years in the same job, Juliet had been looking for something to lift her out of her dull routine. The benefits on offer were generous, and there was even a new prefix – Senior – to add to her existing title of Assistant Claims Officer (Loss Adjustment). Ignoring the reactions of her friends and family, who regarded London with the horror of sinners in Limbo peering down into the ninth circle of Hell, she had filled out the necessary forms and kept her fingers crossed.

Now, incredibly, she was here. As the train rumbled out of Earl's Court, Juliet took a small, folded poster from her handbag and smoothed it flat on her lap. It was time, she decided, to face up to her other reason for coming to London – a reason she hadn't yet fully acknowledged, even to herself. She read carefully through the poster, though she already knew its contents by heart. It advertised a play called *The White Devil*, currently being performed at the Lyric Studio, Hammersmith. The cast list included, in the role of the

Duke of Brachiano, an up-and-coming young actor from Worcester called Duncan Swayne.

Duncan had been her close friend since childhood, and occupied a very special place in Juliet's affections. He'll probably never even know it, she thought sadly, gazing through the distorted reflections into the blackness of the tunnel. But she had to admit the truth to herself: Duncan was the real reason why she was here.

Juliet had waited for years to grow out of her hopeless infatuation with Duncan, but it never happened. She had tried everything — making new friends, getting a boyfriend of her own, and forcing herself to wait for long periods before contacting him. The problem was that their friendship had weathered all these trials and she found it hard to resist whenever he suggested a drink or a film. They had continued to meet at regular intervals, much to the annoyance of their respective current partners, who refused to believe that a 'platonic relationship' meant anything other than an excuse for a secret bonk. *If only*, thought Juliet with a sigh.

It had always been evident that Duncan had potential as an actor. His special talent was for mimicry and he had only to spend a short time in a person's company to be able to reproduce their voice and mannerisms with an uncanny degree of accuracy. He was also a natural performer, always happy to be at the focus of attention. Juliet had often watched him silence a crowded pub with his repertoire of celebrity impressions and send-ups of local dignitaries.

But Duncan wanted to be a serious actor. When, after long years of struggling, he finally made the break-through as a professional and moved to London, Juliet had dutifully repressed her emotions and tried to get on with her life. She felt, however, as if a part of her had disappeared with him. Everything she enjoyed became tainted by feelings of loss.

When she was offered the chance to move to London, it seemed as if fate was showing her what to do. Duncan had never actually suggested that she should follow him to the capital, but his letters implied that he also missed her company. This, coupled with the knowledge that he had left his latest girlfriend behind in Worcester, had been enough to encourage her dormant hopes to blossom afresh. Perhaps new surroundings would make all the difference, she thought. Surely a feeling which had lasted all these years deserved one last chance?

Duncan didn't yet know that she was in London. It had seemed best to keep a low profile until she had sorted out the practical issues and found herself somewhere to live. Now, however, she was free for another whole week before she had to start work. She had no more excuses to avoid getting in touch.

Would he be pleased to see her when she called in to surprise him at his flat in Hammersmith? Juliet felt a shiver of nervous anticipation. There was only one way to find out.

When she was sure that Barry and the others had left for the pub, Carmen emerged from the toilet and took the lift down to reception. Seeing that a taxi had just arrived to drop someone off, she pushed open the glass door and signalled for it to wait. It was raining outside. Water splashed against her ankles as she ran across the cobbled courtyard, her high heels skewing precariously on the uneven surface.

'Can we 'ave yer autograph, Miss Bird?' A knot of bedraggled-looking teenagers stood at the gate that led to the main road, trading insults with the security man.

'It's Mrs, not Miss,' said Carmen automatically, scribbling her name on a damp page. 'I'm married.' Gideon hated it when people addressed her that way.

'Aw, you're kiddin', aren't you?' A boy of about sixteen clutched his hands to his chest in mock anguish, then flashed her a cheeky grin. 'An' there I was waiting all this time to grow up so's I could ask you meself.'

As the taxi crawled into the one-way system under the flyover, Carmen willed the traffic to speed up. The day's session had gone on much longer than usual and Gideon was bound to be wondering where she was. She felt guilty for refusing the invitation to the pub but, even if she had been able to go, she knew she wouldn't have fitted in. Barry was all right, but the women — the Jessicas and Amandas who seemed to proliferate at Conquest TV — frightened her with their self-possessed manners and uncompromising attitudes. They were tough, single women, in command of their own lives. How they would despise her if they knew the truth about hers.

Gideon was in his study when she arrived at their house in Holland Park. Carmen had once planned to appropriate the small room over the garage for her own use, but she had returned one day to find that he had filled it with his video-editing equipment and installed a lock on the door. He now spent hours closeted away watching old tapes of *Mangus*, the crime series that had made his name as a producer. The series featured Jack Mangus, a hard-drinking cop with a taste for violence and pretty girls, and had attracted a cult following in the Eighties.

'Where have you been?' Gideon appeared in the doorway, whisky glass in hand, just as she thought she had reached the sanctuary of the kitchen without being heard.

'Nowhere. I mean, we ran late today.'

'How convenient.' He pushed past her into the kitchen and refilled his glass from the bottle on the table. Lighting a cigarette, he leaned back against the cooker and faced her with an expression that mixed polite curiosity with defiance.

Carmen stared at the table. The whisky bottle, which she guessed to be a new one that day, was two-thirds empty. Cigarette butts overflowed from the ashtray into a foil container that also held a half-eaten slab of lasagne. A large brown envelope, addressed to Gideon and torn roughly open, lay at one end of the table. Beside it was a sheaf of typewritten pages, neatly stacked, but crumpled, as if they had been individually screwed into balls and then smoothed out again.

'What are you looking at?'

She inspected her fingernails, then lifted her eyes slowly to meet his gaze. 'Nothing,' she murmured, shifting uneasily from one foot to the other. Her shoes were pinching and she wanted to sit down.

'Don't lie to me,' he snapped, reaching forward to snatch up the papers. He thrust them towards her. 'You were looking at these, weren't you?'

Her heart sank. It was his proposal for a new series of *Mangus*, updated for the third millennium. He had been hawking it around different TV companies for several months now.

'You needn't bother snooping around for the letter that came with it,' he said bitterly. 'Because there wasn't one.' Flinging the papers to the floor, he kicked at them savagely.

Carmen composed her face into a neutral expression and waited to see what came next.

'Television's got no guts anymore,' he snarled, reaching for the whisky bottle and unscrewing the lid. 'It's all namby pamby issues and political correctness — you can't show a guy walking down a street without offending some bloody pressure group or another.' He poured another inch of whisky into his glass, his eyes challenging her to stop him if she dared.

'I've known this Network Plus editor for years,' he continued. 'I've worked with him, eaten with him, even gone out chasing goddamn skirt with him, and the bastard has the effrontery to return my proposal with a *fucking standard rejection slip.*'

Carmen sat down. 'I'm sorry,' she whispered.

'What do you mean, *you're* sorry? Are you part of the conspiracy as well? Keeping the airwaves free for the crap programmes you make at Conquest?'

'I didn't mean . . .' She swallowed. 'You've got a lot of other projects coming up, haven't you? What about the *Flux* commercial?'

She realised her mistake as soon as she had said it. Gideon leaned forward and squashed the remains of his cigarette into the cold lasagne, pressing down hard with his thumb.

'Well, thank you,' he replied slowly, sarcasm dripping from his lips. 'I knew I could count on my supportive little wife to put me in my place. To remind me where my true talents lie – making commercials for fucking chocolate bars.'

Fighting back tears, Carmen made one last effort. 'Look, Gideon, these setbacks happen to everyone. It doesn't mean anything. You just have to keep on trying.'

'Trying?' His voice was cold. 'What would you know about trying? You've never had to make an effort in your whole life.'

'That's not true,' she protested. 'I've done . . .'

'You, my dear little wife, have done precisely fuck all.' He leaned across the table and held his face close to hers, so close that she could see a faint dusting of cocaine on the hairs of his moustache. 'You'd still be doing that crappy Saturday morning kids show if I hadn't come along.' He jabbed at her shoulder with his index finger, seeking out an old bruise on her collar bone. 'You'd be nothing without me – don't you forget it.'

Carmen took a deep breath and stood up. 'I don't have to put up with this . . .'

'Shut up!' He slapped her hard across the cheek and she fell back into the chair with a whimper.

'Yes you do, sweetheart,' he added, his voice softening. He slapped her again, smiling now. 'You, my dear, are going to put up with exactly what I decide you will.'

CHAPTER 2

The bulk of Juliet's possessions were stored at her parents' pub near Worcester, so it didn't take her long to move into the small attic room that was about to become her home.

Cain, Chandler, Dexter. She placed her paperbacks carefully on the bookshelf, arranging them in alphabetical order. One of the Chandlers had a torn cover, courtesy of her last-but-one boyfriend, Keith. She had caught him using it to wedge open a window in the flat they had shared for six months.

Conan Doyle, Hammett, James (PD, not Henry). Her relationship with Keith had ended shortly after that. She had accused him of taking her for granted, of not showing her enough respect. Keith had replied that it wouldn't hurt *her* to make more effort and presented her with a list of her failings, which ranged from lack of sensitivity to not using cosmetics or wearing the right kind of clothes.

Le Carré, Rendell, Sayers. Keith had run off with a platinum blonde who wore black-seamed stockings and enough makeup to furnish a counter at Boots.

Juliet was left to sort out the unpaid bills. *Simenon, Symons, Van Dine*. All her relationships seemed to follow the same pattern, she thought gloomily. Men began by saying they liked her just the way she was, but it was usually only a matter of months before the criticisms started to flow. Why didn't she try to look more 'feminine'? Why didn't she take more interest in fishing/golf/wildlife conservation/current affairs? And why, they asked her, time and time again, was she so obsessed with these silly detective stories? When was she going to give them up and start living in the real world?

Using the tiny kitchen for the first time, Juliet made herself a lunch of boiled eggs, toast and coffee. As she ate, she glanced at the next book she was planning to read, a recent title in the Chief Inspector Dagenham series. It was a gift from her friend Maggie. Opening the front cover, she read the inscription on the fly-leaf:

> *Take care of yourself in 'London, that great cess-pool into which all the loungers and idlers of the Empire are irresistibly drained'. Only joking! Don't worry – I'm sure things have much improved since Sir Arthur's day!*

Smiling, she recognised the quotation from *A Study in Scarlet*. How long had Maggie spent ignoring her customers while she rummaged through the shelves in search of that?

Maggie was the owner of Belfry Books, a tiny secondhand shop in Worcester. A mildly eccentric spinster in her mid-fifties, she had befriended Juliet several years earlier when they discovered a shared interest in crime and mystery novels. Juliet was always amazed that Maggie's shop kept going — it seemed to be under constant threat of closure due to rising rents, pressure from developers and a dwindling supply of regular customers.

Maggie herself couldn't really explain it, she had simply carried on with her old-fashioned methods and trusted to fate. She was interested, nevertheless, in Juliet's suggestions for improvements, and they spent many evenings together discussing the pros and cons of branching into specialist areas or selling books through the Internet. There had even been talk — during late-night sessions over bottles of Maggie's home-made elderflower wine — of Juliet leaving her job in insurance and taking up a partnership in the business.

Brushing stray toast crumbs from the pages, Juliet closed the book with a sigh. She had really wanted to do it, to get out of the corporate rat race and take responsibility for her own life. But the risks had been too great. She had a mortgage to pay. Her flat in Worcester, currently rented out to a carefully vetted non-smoking professional with no pets, represented the one solid achievement in her life. She had scrimped and saved for years to raise the deposit. To sell up at that stage, when the payments were still largely composed of interest, would have been unthinkable.

Joining Maggie would have meant just that — how else would she have found the capital to invest in the business? She would have had to return to live at her parent's pub, exchanging the shackles of salaried employment for another set of more subtle chains. She hadn't even bothered to discuss it with her parents. Their views on these matters were well known to her already — throwing away a well-paid job for an uncertain future would rank high on their list of unforgivable offences, along with murder, devil worship, voting Labour and lighting up in the designated nonsmoking area of the lounge bar. How could she ever have explained to them that her glorious career in insurance hadn't turned out to be as rewarding as she had hoped?

After leaving school at sixteen, she had taken a job as a clerical assistant with a local firm of insurance brokers. She had gradually gained promotions over the years and risen to a senior administrative position by the time she first met Nick. Impressed by her efficiency in handling her firm's dealings with Castlemayne Insurance, he had offered her a job in his department. Juliet's mother proudly announced to all her customers that her daughter had been 'headhunted', and Juliet went to her new employer with expectations of great things.

She had imagined herself as a fearless investigator, tracking down arsonists and uncovering life insurance swindles just like Edward G. Robinson in *Double Indemnity*. But the reality turned out to be much less exciting. She soon found out that her contact with the criminal classes was unlikely to go further than haggling with clients over receipts for stolen clothing or replacement costs for obsolete video machines.

After getting into trouble for exceeding her brief —

having shadowed a client she suspected of planning to bump off a heavily insured spouse – she was removed from outside investigations and placed under Nick's close supervision. If it wasn't for the good working relationship she had found with him, she might have despaired. By making herself indispensable, however, and trying her hardest to succeed with everything she did, she managed to scrape a small measure of personal satisfaction out of her job.

Perhaps she should give Nick a call, she thought, washing up her plate and cup. It might be good for them to meet for a drink before they recommenced work together in a week's time. But as she was reaching for her diary to look up his new London number, she remembered his problematic wife. She had fielded plenty of suspicious telephone calls from Myra in the past. It wouldn't do for her to start getting the wrong idea now.

There was also Duncan to think about, and the need to keep herself free for possible meetings with him.

Duncan. There was nothing to be gained by waiting any longer. Picking up her handbag and coat, she went downstairs to the payphone to find out if he was at home.

'Hello?' A sleepy voice answered after several rings. Juliet hesitated for a moment, then lost her nerve and hung up. If she spoke to him, he might make excuses – putting off her visit to another day. Far better to call round in person and surprise him. He would hardly be likely to turn her away then.

From Chiswick High Road, she caught a bus to

Hammersmith. Duncan's flat was in a street like her own, the houses facing each other across a treeless, litter-strewn canyon clogged with parked cars. Walking slowly, she counted the houses ahead to pinpoint her destination. When she finally reached his number she paused outside, scanning the windows for signs of life and feeling a strange mixture of excitement and guilt. It was too late to turn back now, she told herself, ringing the bell. There was a long silence, punctuated by the whine of a milk float moving up the street. Then she heard the echo of footsteps on uncarpeted stairs, growing louder as their owner descended into the hallway. The door swung open.

'Jules!' Duncan's unshaven face grinned from the darkness inside. 'What are you doing here?' Stepping forward, he enveloped her in a friendly hug that smelled of sweat and a hint of musky scent. 'It's great to see you! Have you come down on the bus for the day?'

'I, er . . . might be here for a bit longer than that.' Juliet backed away in embarrassment, realising that his shirt was undone. 'I've got a new job – I mean, it's the same company and everything, but I've been transferred to London. It's a kind of promotion.'

'You've moved to London?' Duncan's smile dimmed momentarily. 'But I thought you hated the place.'

'Whatever gave you that idea?'

'I, er . . . I don't know.' He turned towards the stairs, buttoning his shirt with one hand. 'Are you coming up, then? I'm just making coffee.'

This was more like it. 'I hope you weren't still in

bed,' she said playfully, following him to the first floor. 'I waited as late as I could.'

'Not really,' he replied, leading her into a darkened sitting room. He pulled back the curtains, letting in a stream of light. 'You caught us just as we were getting up.'

Us? We? Juliet's insides gave a lurch as a door opened and a tall, beautiful, half-dressed creature strolled into the room with the clumsy grace of a young foal.

'Hi!' she drawled, brushing past Juliet and flopping on to the sofa. She turned to Duncan, screwing up her eyes against the light. 'I've been through the laundry bin twice, Dunky, and I still can't find my black knickers anywhere. Are you sure you didn't leave them behind at the launderette?'

Dunky? Juliet stared at Duncan in disbelief. Couldn't he wait five minutes before shacking up with someone? A fragile construction of hopes crumbled to nothing inside her, leaving a dry taste in her mouth.

'This is Sonia,' he said, blushing slightly. 'She's playing opposite me at the Lyric – my Vittoria Corombona.' Introducing Juliet as an old friend from Worcester, he disappeared to fetch coffee.

Sonia yawned and stretched out her legs, revealing several yards of bronzed thigh. 'Wild party after the show last night,' she mumbled, adjusting her short bathrobe. 'Then some pervert woke us up with a bunch of anonymous phone calls.'

Once, thought Juliet irritably, hardly qualified as *a bunch*. She regarded Sonia with disapproval. No prizes for guessing the nature of the relationship between

Vittoria and Brachiano. Why was it that actors were incapable of doing their jobs without dragging them home into their personal lives? Surely the whole *point* of acting was that you were supposed to be pretending?

'What's with this promotion, then?' asked Duncan, returning with coffee. 'I thought you were planning to get out of insurance?'

'That was ages ago,' muttered Juliet defensively. 'I told you at the time that it wouldn't work out.'

'I'll leave you two to get on with it,' said Sonia, unwinding her long limbs from the sofa and padding towards the door. She winked at Duncan. 'I'll be in the bath if you need me.'

When Juliet had outlined the details of the recent changes in her life, he faced her with a look of concern. 'But surely you haven't given up on the bookshop idea? It would suit you so well, Jules – you know you'd be so much happier than in an office full of pen-pushers.'

'The figures didn't add up,' she said, wishing she had never confided in him about Maggie and the bookshop. 'I've got my mortgage to pay, remember?'

'You have to take risks sometimes,' he murmured. 'You can't always get what you want handed to you on a plate.'

Juliet stared at him in confusion. She had expected to be congratulated on her promotion – not given a lecture about her unfulfilled dreams. 'I thought you might be pleased to see me,' she muttered sulkily.

'But of course I am, Jules,' he said quickly. 'I'm sorry

– I didn't mean any of that to sound the way it did. I wasn't thinking – I suppose I was just projecting my own stuff on to you.'

'What do you mean?'

He gave her a sheepish look. 'It's just that I've been a bit worried lately. I took a big risk coming to London and I . . . well, I kind of need to convince myself that it was the right thing to do. The play comes to the end of its run in just over a week. I don't really know what happens next.'

'I thought you were signed up for a big part in some film?'

He shook his head. 'The backer pulled out. It happens all the time in this business.' Glancing at the door, he lowered his voice to a whisper. 'Don't mention it in front of Sonia, will you? I haven't got round to telling her yet.'

'Of course not.' Juliet suddenly felt three hundred percent better. If he kept secrets like that from Sonia, she might not be such a permanent fixture after all.

'I'm sorry, Jules – I didn't mean to be down on you. Don't worry, I'm sure something will turn up.' He grinned, brightening. 'You must come to see the play. I've got some free tickets for Saturday here somewhere.' He rummaged in a pile of papers on the coffee table. 'And we must do things. Give me your phone number and I'll check out some films for us to see.'

An invitation to see a film together could *almost* be counted as a date, thought Juliet, scribbling her number in his address book. They had done all this before, of course, but that had been back in Worcester. And he *had* waited until Sonia was out of the way before mentioning it.

Their fingers touched as she handed back the book. Juliet felt a shiver of excitement as he reached with his other hand and took hers. 'I'm so glad you're here,' he said, squeezing it gently. 'It's great to have a *real* friend around at last.'

He let her hand drop, but his smile seemed to tell her that she really did mean something to him. 'I'm glad I'm here, too,' she whispered, blushing. Might it be possible, she wondered, that her arrival in London would mark the start of a new phase in their relationship?

They talked for another half hour, but she said her goodbyes when she heard Sonia getting out of the bath. She didn't want to put her new-found optimism to the test just yet.

It had been a bad week for Carmen. Gideon had been in a foul temper since the rejection of his *Mangus* proposal on Monday and, as always, things had built to a climax on Wednesday night. She had made the mistake of broaching the question of visiting her aunt in the Scilly Isles, and this had been enough to push him over the edge from self-destructive brooding into violence.

Gideon's ill-treatment of her took a number of different forms. Sometimes his cruelty was verbal – he was capable of spending an entire night tormenting her with insults, waking her up with a fresh bout of abuse each time she drifted into a troubled sleep. Other times he would simply beat her into submission, slapping and punching her until the pain and humiliation became too much to bear. She would curl up, whimpering, wherever he cornered her in the house, not daring to move until he tired of his sport and went to bed. These occasions were, thankfully, rare.

The third and most common form was a short explosion of physical violence, after which he would storm out of the house and disappear, often for days at a time. This was what had happened on Wednesday. It was now Saturday and he hadn't yet returned.

She knew she ought to leave him, but she was afraid of what he might do. It wasn't just a matter of personal retaliation, she had her job to think about. Despite the current lack of progress in his own career, Gideon still had a lot of influence in television circles. If he set his mind to it, he was quite capable of engineering her downfall.

Two full days of solitude had, however, given Carmen a chance to recover her spirits. When she woke that morning to find the sun shining, she decided to make an effort to enjoy herself for a change. Pulling on jeans and a sweater, she embarked on her makeup. She had a bigger task to accomplish than most – not only did she have a fresh bruise on her chin to conceal, but she also had to disguise her appearance as much as possible to avoid the attentions of TV fans.

Until a few years ago, Carmen had coped with the demands of being a minor celebrity without too much difficulty. Then *Makeover* was moved to a prime-time evening slot and she began to be recognised everywhere she went. A six-month stint as a presenter of the National Lottery programme had sealed her fate. It became impossible to lead an ordinary life. Gideon loved the attention, but Carmen found herself becoming increasingly shy and longed for the anonymity she had previously taken for granted. Every small contact with the outside world – with taxi drivers, shop assistants and strangers on the street – was tainted by a single burning question: *Will they recognise me?*

When she had finished applying makeup to her face, she worked on her short blonde hair with mousse and a heated brush, styling it quite differently to the way it appeared on TV. Then she put on a baseball cap, pulling the brim well forward. It all helped to make her look different – to transform her from the glamorous TV presenter into an ordinary woman on the street. She called it her reverse makeover. It wouldn't fool a hardened celebrity-spotter, but it cut down on unnecessary attention from casual passers-by.

Standing sideways, she checked herself out in a full-length mirror. Her size ten jeans fitted snugly – too snugly for her liking. She would have to skip lunch for the rest of the week. The press had torn into her with a vengeance the last time she accidentally gained a few pounds and she didn't want to risk this happening again.

If the press ever found out the truth about her private life, they would have a field day. She imagined the headlines: MAKEOVER MARRIAGE MISERY! BIRDS IN LOVE NEST DRAMA! Did Gideon have a lover? Carmen rejected his sexual advances whenever she could, afraid of where his violence might lead, and he seemed to have come to the conclusion that she was frigid. Although he still forced himself on her from time to time, she suspected that he was satisfying his main urges elsewhere. She didn't like to dwell on the thought. She had no idea where he spent his prolonged absences and had never dared to ask. The one thing she did know was that he never returned on a Saturday. She would have the whole day to herself.

She wasn't going to upset herself by thinking about Gideon now. Setting her cap at jaunty angle, she locked the front door and walked out into the April sunshine.

It didn't take much to put Duncan in a good mood. It was a Saturday – which meant that he could look forward to a day off tomorrow – *and* the morning had started with Sonia bringing him Marmite soldiers in bed. OK, he thought, she had spoiled things a bit by not realising that the bread was supposed to be toasted, and then telling him off for being ungrateful and blaming him for making her late for her aerobics class, but still . . . *Marmite soldiers!* He hadn't had them in years.

Making his way along the Portobello Road, Duncan immersed himself in the bustle of the street life. He had come here on impulse, intending to buy a new hat for his collection. It was an extravagance he couldn't really afford, but he had a superstitious belief that good fortune only came to those who acted as if they deserved it. In his experience, a suitably reckless gesture often brought a whole string of happy coincidences in its wake.

His agent had called the previous day, which was in itself a cause for celebration. Duncan had struggled for years to earn the privilege of being able to drop the magic words, 'my agent', at every conversational opportunity, only to find that it made precious little difference to his actual job prospects. The call had been to advise him of a potential audition for a small part in a TV soap. Losing the words 'potential' and 'small' somewhere in the translation, Duncan daydreamed of achieving fame as the next Grant Mitchell.

Juliet's visit had also cheered him up enormously. She was his oldest friend — someone he knew he could count on when things got tough. He couldn't help feeling that her arrival in London was another omen of good luck.

If he had known that she was coming, he reflected, he would have arranged things so that Sonia was out of the way. Juliet often took a rather dim view of his choice of girlfriends, and Sonia, he realised, was a typical example of the kind of woman he always seemed to end up with: good-looking, great fun in bed, but prone to difficult moods and somewhat limited as a conversationalist.

She also became jealous very easily. In common with all his previous girlfriends, she seemed unable to grasp the concept of a platonic friendship between two people of opposite sex. When Juliet left, Sonia had grilled him mercilessly about the details of their relationship, asking if they had ever slept together and wanting to know precisely how much this 'other woman' meant to him.

Duncan was able to declare, quite truthfully, that there had never been any physical intimacy between Juliet and himself. But the second part was harder; he had to admit that she was 'special', in a way that he couldn't exactly define. 'I've known her since we were kids together, Sonia,' he had explained in a defensive tone. 'That has to count as something special – the fact that she's a woman doesn't even come into it.'

'*Special*?' Sonia had snorted. 'I might just as easily say that Binky Follett was special – I've known him since drama school, after all. But you wouldn't like that, would you? You men don't like it when these things are turned round the other way.'

Duncan couldn't think of anyone less deserving of the word 'special'. As their director, Binky Follett did his job in a professional enough way. As a person, however, with his theatrical affectations and cloying charm, he made Duncan's flesh crawl.

Pausing to admire a display of brightly coloured vegetables, Duncan considered the possibility that Binky and Sonia were having an affair. She had been called in for a lot of extra rehearsals lately, and they seemed to spend hours on the telephone to each other. Then he realised that he was reacting exactly as Sonia had predicted he would. He gave himself a rueful smile. Perhaps she had greater powers of insight than he had thought.

Glancing back as he crossed the junction with Westbourne Grove, he noticed a group of women staring at him. Did they know him, he wondered? Or could they have been in the audience one night? He gave them a friendly smile, but they turned away, giggling among themselves. As he walked on, he felt slightly disappointed. He dreamed that one day he would be famous enough to be recognised on the street.

It was probably just the friendly atmosphere of the market, he decided, grinning at a stallholder who was making strange gestures with a packet of washing powder from his display. It wasn't until a group of teenagers started pointing in his direction, and he noticed a dog following him, that he began to wonder if something might be amiss. When he stopped and turned round, the dog circled behind him – sniffing and pawing at his leg. Twisting to look, he realised with horror that there was something stuck to the back of his trousers.

The events of that morning passed rapidly through his mind – the marmite soldiers, the lingering suspicion when he finished them that there should have been more, and the struggle to get his boots on while sitting on the edge of the bed. It all clicked into place. Blushing crimson, he reached down and peeled a flattened piece of bread covered with sticky brown goo from his backside.

If the trousers had been a darker colour, it wouldn't have been so bad, but he was wearing his pale fawn corduroys that day. He tugged at the back of his leather jacket, but it refused to stretch any lower than his waist. This was his worst nightmare come to life. Everywhere he looked, people seemed to be laughing at him. His only consolation was that it hadn't happened on the stage.

Standing with his back to a wall, he considered his options. He could find a public lavatory and attempt to clean up, but he didn't like the idea of being caught in one of those places with no trousers on. If he bought new trousers, he wouldn't have enough money left for a hat and it would become a pointless journey. He would probably be better off spending the money on a taxi home.

It was then that he saw her. He could scarcely believe the cruelty of the timing. He had spent many Saturdays walking up and down the Portobello Road in the hope of bumping into someone interesting, but it had to be today that he spotted his idol – the woman who always featured in the steamiest of his wet dreams.

It was her, he was certain, sorting through the bracelets on the jewellery stall. She was dressed inconspicuously, with a baseball hat pulled down over her eyes, but he could never fail to recognise that face. *Carmen Bird*. He had her picture pinned to his dressing room wall.

As he saw her moving away, he was faced with a dilemma. Could he miss this opportunity to speak to her? Or would he risk becoming the laughing stock of the entire street? He hesitated, torn between vanity and desire. Then inspiration struck him. Removing his jacket, he knotted the arms round his waist. Checking to make sure that it covered the seat of his trousers, he set off in wary pursuit of his favourite TV star.

'Excuse me, but aren't you Carmen Bird?'

Resisting an impulse to look down at herself and exclaim with shock, *Good God, so I am*! Carmen turned from examining a rack of headscarves to find a tall, good-looking man of her own age facing her with a smile.

'I didn't mean to bother you,' he continued. 'It's just, well, I just wanted to tell you how much I enjoy your show. I think you're a great presenter.'

'Er, thanks,' she muttered shyly. She was about to turn away when an impulse stopped her. He had a friendly look about him. Surely it wouldn't do any harm to talk for a while?

'I'm an actor myself,' he added, as if this explained everything. 'On the stage.'

'Should I have heard of you?' Carmen ventured a smile.

'Duncan Swayne.' He held out his hand and she found herself shaking it, mesmerised by his confidence. He nodded at a nearby pub. 'Perhaps I could buy you a drink?'

Carmen wouldn't normally have taken such a risk, but she was determined to enjoy herself today. Finding a well-screened seat in the pub where they couldn't be seen from outside, she allowed him to buy her a diet tonic water and engage her in conversation. He was rather attractive, she thought, indulging in a brief fantasy where they exchanged telephone numbers and met again. Out of the question in real life, of course. Gideon would kill her if he knew she had been in a pub with a strange man.

As they talked, she checked out his clothes with a professional eye. No designer labels; in fact, his whole outfit could have been put together from an Oxfam shop. But he had an eye for colour and texture, and what might have seemed at first glance to be a random selection of garments worked together to produce a casually fashionable effect. The one thing that puzzled her was the way he wore his jacket wrapped around his waist. Was she missing something here, she wondered anxiously. Had she become so absorbed by her personal problems that she was out of touch with the current street style?

'I used to love *Jackrabbit*,' said Duncan, interrupting her thoughts. 'It hasn't been the same since you left.'

She raised an eyebrow. *Jackrabbit* was the children's programme that had launched her career at Conquest TV. Wasn't he a bit old for that sort of thing?

'I've always wanted to ask you something,' he added with a mischievous smile. 'Do you have shares in Velcro?'

She shook her head, sighing inwardly. How many times had she been asked that question? It was said that *Jackrabbit* did for Velcro what *Blue Peter* had done for sticky-back plastic. Carmen's make-your-own stick-on wall tidy was rumoured to have created a national shortage of the stuff in the early Nineties.

'I tried making the leatherette mobile telephone pouch,' he admitted, grinning at her. 'Even though I didn't have a mobile telephone.'

She couldn't help smiling. 'What about the shampoo bottle mouse-holder?'

'Oh, yes,' he replied with a chuckle. 'I had a go at that one as well. Even though I didn't have a computer.'

'And the pop-up address book . . .'

'. . . even though I didn't have any friends!'

They both laughed. Then Duncan started asking the usual questions about *Makeover:* How did they choose the subjects? Did they get to keep the clothes? What happened if they made a mistake and cut someone's hair wrong? She felt like telling him all about Hazel from Sunbury, but remembered Kevin's warning: Careless talk could cost jobs – especially if the woman decided to sue.

The next time she glanced at her watch, she found that a whole hour had passed. 'I must be going,' she said guiltily, standing up.

'Of course,' said Duncan, jumping to his feet. 'I'm sorry, I didn't mean to keep you. I mean, you must have a lot more important things to do.'

She hesitated. 'It's been nice talking to you,' she said eventually.

'It's been *great* talking to *you*.' He rummaged in the pocket of his jacket. 'I almost forgot,' he said, holding out a slightly crumpled piece of card. 'I'm sure you've got loads of other engagements but, just on the off-chance, here's a free ticket for the show tonight.'

'I don't know if . . .'

'Don't say anything,' he interrupted, holding a finger to his lips. 'If I don't hear you say no, then I can imagine that you *might* be out there in the audience. I'm sure it'll do wonders for my performance.'

Carmen examined the ticket as she walked back towards Holland Park. The Lyric was easy enough to get to – it was close to Conquest TV. She had never heard of *The White Devil*, but she had nothing at all planned for that evening. Why on earth shouldn't she go out on her own for a change?

The week had passed slowly for Juliet. Her enthusiasm for exploring London had begun to subside, but she didn't feel settled enough to do much else until she had started her new job. When Saturday evening finally arrived, she was seated in the Lyric Studio a good half-hour before the performance was due to start. It was smaller and barer than she expected. She had somehow imagined Duncan on a velvet-curtained stage in a large, plush auditorium, but this was more like being in a corner of someone's garage.

She watched with interest as the rest of the audience filtered in, trying to guess things about them from their appearance. It was a game she used to play with Duncan, back home in her parents' pub. The days of being able to deduce a person's history from their hat size might have passed with Sherlock Holmes, but Juliet had occasionally startled passing travellers with an inquiry about their recent holiday or the health of their children. She had never admitted to Duncan that she usually cheated by sneaking outside and peering through the windows of their cars. The domestic detritus people left on their back seats told you a lot about their lifestyles.

'Is anyone sitting here?'

Juliet glanced at the intruder, a well-dressed woman who looked vaguely familiar. She had hoped for the extra leg-room afforded by the vacant seat.

'Er, no. Help yourself.' Reluctantly, she shifted her bag and bundled it out of the way.

As the lights dimmed for the start of the play, Juliet peered sideways to examine the woman's face. She looked to be in her early thirties, like Juliet, but there the resemblance ended. She was pretty — too pretty to be out on her own for want of a date — and wore a lot of makeup. Juliet tried to work out where she might have seen her before, but drew a blank. Perhaps she had simply noticed her in the street, or on the Underground, she thought. A coincidence like that could easily happen, even in a place as big as London.

There was an abrupt flaring of light in front of them and three men in tight black leather and wild eye makeup burst on to the stage. Suddenly remembering why she was there, Juliet scanned their faces in search of Duncan. He wasn't among them, but soon appeared, arm in arm with the dreaded Sonia. Feasting her eyes on her favourite man, Juliet smiled and let out a little sigh. Then she looked sharply sideways. She might have imagined it, but she thought that the woman beside her had just done exactly the same thing.

As the play progressed, Juliet forgot her neighbour as she became caught up in monitoring the body language between Duncan and Sonia. They didn't seem to be able to keep their hands off each other. Was it just acting? It looked too real. She fought back a wave of jealous emotion as she watched a scene where they virtually copulated on the stage. Surely the playwright's directions hadn't called for *that* amount of detail?

Distracted by her preoccupations, she struggled to keep track of the plot. Duncan and Sonia's characters were lovers – that much was simple enough to work out – and they seemed to be conspiring to bump off their respective partners. There was a rather neat murder, where Duncan's wife was killed by kissing a poisoned portrait of her husband, but after that Juliet started to get confused. There were a lot of characters, all dressed in black, and it became increasingly difficult to remember who was who. Why couldn't they have colour-coded costumes, or name tags, even? Their speeches were difficult to follow. Glancing at the programme, she saw that the play had been written in 1612. If they were going to do it all in modern dress, she wondered, why didn't they update the language a bit to make it easier to understand?

The programme promised 'an evening sizzling with intrigue, lust and revenge'. So much for intrigue, she thought with disappointment. This Webster guy hadn't even bothered to conceal the identity of the murderers. Shakespeare was just the same. Think what a brilliant whodunnit *Hamlet* could have been if the story was told from a different angle.

By the time the interval came, Juliet had given up on the plot and was glad of a chance to stretch her legs. Ordering a double whisky at the bar, she leaned on the parapet of the stairwell and watched the crowds returning to the second half of the show in the main house. To judge by their conversations, it was a lot more interesting than the production she was watching. Would anyone notice if she switched to the other one half-way through?

But Duncan would never forgive her. As the crowds thinned out, she saw her elegant neighbour sitting alone at a corner table and impulsively made her way over to join her. Why not satisfy her curiosity about this mysterious woman?

'Do you mind if I sit down?' she asked.

The woman looked up, startled, then shook her head and made a gesture to indicate that the seat was free.

'What do you think of the play?' asked Juliet, unable to think of a more original opening.

The woman stared at her for a moment as if surprised to be addressed, then gave her a hesitant smile. 'I'm not sure really. I rather lost track of things after that silly business with the poisoned painting.'

'Why was it silly?' asked Juliet, with a touch of indignation. It was the only part of the plot that had made any sense to her at all.

'Well, it wasn't very realistic, was it? If your husband told you he was casting you off and never wanted to touch you again, would *you* sit around kissing his picture?'

'I suppose not,' said Juliet. 'But I haven't got a . . .'

'It would never work in my house,' interrupted another woman from the next table, glancing over her shoulder with a laugh. 'It would backfire in the old man's face because the vain bugger would be there in front of me, kissing it himself.' She grinned at one of her friends. 'Perhaps I should try it some day – have the old boy's portrait done and everything.'

'Now that would be getting pretty close to the perfect murder,' said Juliet, wishing she'd thought of it herself.

Her companion faced her with a curious expression. 'I wonder how many women feel like that about their husbands?' she said thoughtfully. 'I'm sure some men treat their wives just as badly as the character in that play.'

Juliet saw the glint of a gold band on her finger. 'Do you?'

'Do I what?'

'Feel like that about your husband?'

The woman blushed. 'I didn't say . . .'

'You could borrow her idea,' said Juliet, nodding at the next table. 'Or there are quite a few other ways of doing it. Have you ever seen *Strangers on a Train*?'

The woman shook her head.

'It's a Hitchcock film. Two people meet by chance, just like us, but on a train. They both have someone in their lives they'd like to see dead. One of them suggests they swap murders, so there would be no motive, or anything else to connect them. The perfect murder, you see. The other guy refuses, but the first one goes ahead and does it anyway . . .' Juliet paused, intrigued by the woman's expression. 'Are you OK?'

'What? Oh yes, fine.' She gave Juliet a questioning look. 'Are you trying to get rid of *your* husband, then?'

'Who, me?' asked Juliet, glancing around with a smile. 'I haven't got one.'

'Then why are you suggesting . . .'

Juliet stared at her and gave an uneasy laugh. 'I was only joking.'

The woman laughed as well. 'Just checking,' she said,

standing up. 'Now, I must find the ladies' room before the play starts again.'

'Me too,' said Juliet, remembering how long the first half had been. Hoping that the woman didn't think she was some kind of weirdo who approached people with murder propositions, she followed her through the swing doors into the lobby.

Carmen had been nervous about going to the theatre alone. She had hoped that a London audience would be sophisticated enough to cope with the odd famous face and, so far, she seemed to be right. One or two people had given her lingering stares, but nobody had bothered her. The woman she had just been talking to hadn't recognised her at all.

Glancing round in the queue for the toilet, she noticed that she was still there.

'I didn't mean to spook you,' said the woman, catching her eye. 'With the murder stuff back there. It's just that it's a bit of a hobby of mine. Reading about it, I mean, not doing it.'

'Of course not,' said Carmen, embarrassed. She had actually been under the impression, for a fleeting moment, that the woman *had* been serious. There was one person ahead of them in the queue, a girl chattering excitedly into a mobile telephone. After they had waited behind her for some time, the girl gave up and departed. It wasn't until Carmen saw her collect a bucket and mop from beside the door that she realised their mistake.

'I think that was the cleaner,' she said, opening the

door to an empty cubicle. 'There's been no one else in here all the time.'

A few moments later, her companion's voice floated over the partition. 'Tell me,' she asked, 'what do you think of Brachiano?'

'He's good,' said Carmen, wondering how this stranger had managed to home in on the real reason why she was here. 'Nice-looking too, don't you agree?'

'He's my friend,' said the voice proudly. 'I could introduce you to him if you like.'

'Well, actually, I've met him already,' replied Carmen. 'He bought me a drink at lunchtime.'

'He did what?' There was a spluttering noise and the rest of the reply was drowned by the sound of a flushing toilet.

When Carmen emerged from her cubicle, the woman was vigorously washing her hands. 'I don't know him *that* well,' she said, with a trace of bitterness in her voice. 'We just come from the same place. Went to school together.'

'Really?' Carmen watched with interest as the woman dried her hands. She was tall and generously proportioned – you couldn't call it fat – with clothes that made her look dumpier than she really was. Her sense of style was non-existent – baggy jeans with turn-ups over chunky boots, a checked shirt in brown and cream (where *had* she managed to find such an appalling garment?) and a green cardigan. Her long brown hair was clean, but badly out of condition, and her face was bereft of makeup.

She would be an ideal subject for *Makeover*, thought

Carmen. They were going to be selecting candidates for the new series over the next few weeks.

She touched the woman's arm. 'We've been talking all this time,' she said, 'and I don't even know your name.'

'Juliet,' she said. 'Juliet Jennings. I don't know yours either.'

So she hadn't been pretending – she really didn't recognise her. 'Haven't you ever watched *Makeover*?' asked Carmen with a smile.

'Makeover?' Juliet shook her head with a puzzled expression.

Carmen paused. 'It's a TV show,' she said eventually. 'I present it. My name's Carmen Bird.'

'Oh,' said Juliet, looking strangely uncomfortable. 'That wasn't why I was . . . I mean, I don't watch much TV, so I didn't realise . . . Only the detective programmes – Inspector Morse and so on.' She frowned. 'You do look kind of familiar, though. I can't quite work it out.'

'Have you heard of *Jackrabbit*?'

Her face lit up with comprehension. '*That's* where I've seen you! Duncan used to watch it all the time.' She laughed. 'Would you believe, he used to record it so that he could see the same programme over and over again?'

Carmen pushed open the door to the lobby with a smile. It seemed that Duncan hadn't been exaggerating his fondness for the show.

'I mean, it's incredible,' continued Juliet. 'You'd think a guy of his age would have grown out of that kind of cra . . .' She clapped her hand to her mouth. 'Oh, shit, I didn't mean . . .'

'That's OK,' said Carmen. It was refreshing to meet someone without a hidden agenda, someone who spoke their mind without playing sycophantic games. 'To tell you the truth,' she added, 'I often thought that programme was pretty shoddy myself.'

They entered a deserted foyer. 'Oh God,' wailed Juliet. 'Duncan will never speak to me again if I miss the second half.'

'I'm sorry,' said a smug attendant, as they scurried towards the studio door. 'We can't interrupt the performance once it has started.'

'But surely . . .' Carmen gave him a pleading look. 'We could go in ever so quietly.'

'House rules, ma'am,' said the attendant, moving to block their passage. Recognising her, he gave a little smirk. 'We don't make exceptions for anybody, I'm afraid – not even if you were Sir Peter Hall himself.'

'What do we do now?' asked Juliet with a distraught expression.

'At least we won't have to worry about keeping up with the plot any more,' said Carmen, privately relieved to be absolved from another two hours of boredom. She risked a smile, hoping that Juliet wasn't one of those intellectual types who took Webster to the beach for light holiday reading.

'Well, it was a bit dull, I suppose,' said Juliet with a giggle. She glanced expectantly at Carmen, then looked away, thrusting her hands in her pockets and shifting awkwardly from one foot to the other.

Remembering who I am, thought Carmen, wishing now that she hadn't told her. People treated you differently when they knew you were famous, freezing off at the slightest conversational lull and expecting you to take the initiative. She didn't want to go home yet, that was for certain. She was just beginning to enjoy herself.

'I know,' she suggested with great daring. 'Why don't we get out of here and have a drink in a pub?'

Juliet brightened immediately. 'Hey, that's a good idea.'

As the two women left the theatre, Carmen experienced a feeling of optimism for the first time in months. She had met two new people that day – two potential friends. Perhaps it might be possible for her to lead a normal life after all.

CHAPTER 3

Gideon Bird enjoyed his 'holidays' from his wife. They ought to be written into the marriage contract, he thought grimly, chopping out two neat lines of cocaine on Angie's smoked glass coffee table. A man could only take so much before he needed a break.

It wasn't as if she'd ever shown him any gratitude. Carmen Hughes had been a nobody when he met her at the BBC, eight years earlier, wasting her time in some dead-end educational programme for backward kids. In the space of a year he'd courted her, married her and lifted her out of obscurity – negotiating a tough new deal for her with Conquest TV. *Jackrabbit* had launched her as a mainstream children's presenter, as he'd intended it to. He'd neglected his own work to promote her career, building her confidence and choosing the right time for her to make the move into adult programming. She made an instant hit with *The Dressing Room*, the groundbreaking fashion show, before moving on to become a household name with *Makeover* and *Conquest Lottery Live*.

What had she done for him in return? Nothing. He'd

thrown all his efforts into creating a wife who matched up to his own reputation and now, predictably enough, she thought that *she* was too good for *him*. His only reward was the constant irritation of having to live with the self-righteous bitch.

Extracting a crisp twenty-pound note from his wallet, he rolled it into a tube. His hands were trembling slightly with anticipation and it took a couple of attempts to get it right.

A wife like his was enough to turn you into a junk head. These days she gave him nothing but complaints. Telling him he should *work on the relationship*, for Christ's sake. What did she think he'd been doing all these years? She also seemed to expect him to drop everything to satisfy her ridiculous little whims. Wednesday's argument had been typical. Did she think the creator of *Mangus* had nothing better to do with his time than hold his wife's hand while she visited her boring relatives? He was damned if he was going to travel all the way to some God-forsaken place like the Scilly Isles to hang around at fucking tea parties.

He was poised over the table with the rolled note at his nostril when a voice came from the bathroom.

'Giddy, darling? Aren't you coming in?'

'In a minute,' he growled impatiently, shielding the white powder with his hand and reflecting that mistresses could sometimes be just as tedious as wives. Their only real advantage was in their ignorance. Gideon maintained a strict policy of secrecy with his lovers and Angie had no idea he that was married, or who he was married to. He was able to come and go as he pleased.

A waft of perfumed steam drifted into the room, making him want to gag. God only knew what she was doing in there with all those candles and music and aromatic crap. She made out that it was supposed to relax her, but it wouldn't surprise him if it turned out to be some kind of goddamn fertility rite.

You can count me out on that one, he thought, checking the pack of condoms in his pocket. AIDS had never bothered him much – he was sure the statistics were rigged by the Government – but there were worse things a guy could catch. Like a palimony suit.

His nerve ends were screaming with longing when he finally swooped on the two lines of powder, sucking them deep into his nasal cavities. The first stinging rush made him feel as if his eyeballs would pop out, then the good feeling started to kick in and he threw his head back with a sigh of pleasure. It was always better when he waited those extra few moments, pushing the craving right to the limit to remind himself who was in control.

'Giddy?'

Why couldn't the stupid bitch ever call him by his proper name?

'The water's gone cold. I'm going to have to get out now.'

Bingo! He smiled, realising that he'd kept out of the way for long enough to escape the ritual. He could never understand why she always wanted to drag him into the bathtub with her. As far as he was concerned, bathing was something you did in private, like having a crap, or cleaning the wax out of your ears. If he went anywhere near the bathroom when she was in one of these moods, she would be straight at him with her so-called 'essential oils' and bottles of goo she wanted to massage all over his genitals. She thought it was sexy. He thought that kind of stuff should be left to the fucking witch doctors.

He heard the bedroom door open and knew she was getting ready. Making a special effort, no doubt, as it was their last night together before he went back home. It was also Saturday. Angie belonged to the culture that believed in throwing all its efforts into one great orgy of excess on a Saturday night and was happy to spend the rest of the week in abstinence and self-denial for the sake of it. The poor, brain-washed sods couldn't see that the other days were there for the taking, if only they could open their eyes to the world that existed beyond their humdrum little lives.

He paced the tiny living room, impatient now for some action. He was actually rather touched by Angie's eagerness to please. She would invest huge amounts of time in shopping for a particular garment that she thought might titillate him in some way, and was happy to comply with his requests for less than conventional sexual positions. He had once casually mentioned that he was turned on by the idea of a shaved pussy and, lo and behold, the next time he saw her she'd gone and done it. There it was, all clean and pink and plump like a goddamn peach, laid on especially for him. Angie was a girl with a real generous spirit.

And there she was in the doorway, her flimsy bath-robe hanging open to show black bra and suspenders, stockings and high heels — just the way he liked her. She'd gone to town on the makeup, and her hair was piled up in a casual looking style that he knew she'd have been fussing over for hours.

It was an effect any woman could throw together for a few quid and, frankly, she looked cheap. Funnily enough, this did more for his sexual appetite than any of the sophistication Carmen might throw at him. He loved the way Angie asked for sweet sherry as an aperitif, couldn't pronounce Versace, and thought Stolichnaya was a Russian pop group.

A red-taloned finger beckoned him towards the bed-room. Gideon followed, as ready as he was ever likely to be for his command performance as Saturday night stud.

He opted for light bondage that night, just the hands tied loosely behind her. It was the best method he had yet found to avoid the cloying embraces and the tell-tale scratch lines on his back. He liked to be a little rough with her — to frighten her into thinking that he was going to hurt her. He loved to watch the expression in her eyes as it changed, first from eagerness to doubt, then on through varying degrees of fear, and then to blissful relief as he suppressed his baser urges and got on with the conventional part of the job.

Afterwards they lay in silence. He knew exactly what she was thinking: *What would he say if I tell him I love him?* It seemed to be all that was on most women's minds — except for his wife's, of course.

His thoughts were heading in another direction: *How would she react if I ended it now? Would it be safer to wait until the next time?* The problem was that he'd been repeating these same thoughts for the last three and a half months and hadn't quite got round to doing anything about them. Gideon's affairs were generally one night stands, occasionally extending to a week or so in special circumstances. He'd made a lot of excuses for Angie, granting her several stays of execution and last-minute reprieves as the weeks stretched into months. Sooner or later he was going to have to face up to the truth. If he didn't take action soon, Gideon Bird was going to find himself hooked.

Angie began to stir. 'Can we go out now?' she asked, sliding out of bed and opening the wardrobe in anticipation.

'Soon,' he muttered, gazing in fascination at her naked bottom. She was ten years older than Carmen, though you wouldn't guess it by her behaviour, and holding up remarkably well. She rummaged through a rack of brightly coloured garments and turned to face him, coyly holding a pair of dresses in front of herself.

'Shall I wear the pink one tonight, Giddy, or the green?'

'The green,' he said firmly, wincing at the sight of what looked like a tutu bedecked with magenta sequins and frills. He strapped on his watch. She would be a good half hour messing around at the mirror. Time for a quick fix of news and a look at the latest detective serial on ITV.

Gideon loved television. Once he had satisfied himself that *D for Dogberry* was no rival to *Mangus*, he began to channel hop, soaking up the soundbites with the obsessive intensity of an addict. It was a shame that *Makeover* wasn't on that night, he thought wistfully, punching the buttons on the remote control. It gave him a very special thrill to watch his wife perform while he fucked Angie doggy-fashion on the living room floor.

He would have been happy to stay there for the rest of the evening, but it was Saturday. With Angie, there was no laid-back, middle-class option of a quiet Saturday night in front of the TV. He would have to come up with the goods as far as the promised meal out was concerned, or suffer the consequences.

When she was finally ready, they took a taxi to a cheap bistro chosen by Gideon for its virtue of being located in the opposite direction to Holland Park. It was both exciting and convenient to have a mistress who lived in Notting Hill – less than a mile away from the marital home – but even Gideon drew the line at parading her in his local restaurants.

Angie was none the wiser, he thought, smiling to himself. She was pathetically eager to swallow the lies he told her and considered it a social triumph of the highest order to be seen with him in some sleazy eatery in Kilburn or Kensal Green. She was under the impression that Gideon was a big wheel in the movie business, on first name terms with all the major stars. When she pressed him for details of his personal life he simply refused to tell her anything, making the excuse that he wasn't ready for commitment. 'That's the way it is, baby,' he would say in a stern voice. 'Take it or leave it.'

Angie took it. It didn't seem to have occurred to her that, if all he said was true, she was a rather unlikely choice of consort. Why should a man with a casting couch at his disposal want to attach himself, even temporarily, to a nobody like her?

Gideon had no appetite for food. He sat through the meal, fighting off boredom and getting steadily drunk while Angie chomped her way through what she thought was a gourmet supper. Idly, he wondered what Carmen was doing. Sharpening the knives, no doubt, ready for his return.

He was going to have to do something about Carmen, soften her up somehow, because he was going to need her help. He had been counting on getting the *Flux* commercial but, contrary to what she believed, the project was still a long way from being his.

That day, while Angie thought he was out clinching movie deals and Carmen thought about whatever prissy nonsense filled her head when he wasn't there, he had been busy networking in the watering holes of Soho and had at last come up with a contact. Crispin Scrope wasn't the kind of guy Gideon would normally befriend but, once he had revealed his connection with the agency producer dealing with the *Flux* account, Gideon was ready to hand him the keys to his house and offer him the free run of his drinks cabinet, his wife, and even his cocaine stash, if he would put in a word for him in the right place. At the very least, the situation called for a dinner party. Would he be able to persuade Carmen to come up with the goods?

His best chance, he thought, gazing blearily out of the taxi window on the way back from the restaurant, was to dump Angie and concentrate on buttering up Carmen for a week or so. Once he had the *Flux* commercial under his belt, he could focus his energies on the new *Mangus* project again and make some real progress towards the comeback he so desperately needed.

He could do it right now. Drop Angie off at her flat and disappear from her life forever. She would never track him down; she didn't even know his real name. But as the taxi turned into Ladbroke Grove, he remembered the new underwear she had mentioned and his resolve began to weaken. Tomorrow would do just as well, he told himself. Although his finer sensibilities might incline him to return to Holland Park, his loins were pulling him inexorably toward Notting Hill. How could he disappoint a sweet girl like Angie on a Saturday night?

Juliet was woken by the sound of the telephone ringing downstairs. Squinting at her watch on the bedside table, she sat up in alarm. Twelve o'clock! So much for her plan to get up early and go to the launderette. Reaching for her dressing gown, she staggered out of bed and made her way unsteadily into the kitchenette. Strong black coffee, she thought, fumbling in the cupboard. Aspirins. Orange juice. Breakfast. She leaned dizzily against the cooker, her stomach churning. Forget all that, she corrected herself. Bathroom first.

The telephone rang again as she returned from a half-hearted attempt at vomiting, the sound reverberating insistently through the house. Was nobody else going to answer it? Unable to bear the thought of missing a call that might be for her, she tied the belt of her dressing gown tightly around her waist and stumbled downstairs.

'Wurghh?' she mumbled, struggling to get the receiver the right way round.

'Jules? Is that you?'

'Duncan.' She spoke with difficulty, gulping back a mouthful of saliva.

'Caught you at last,' he chuckled. 'Come on Jules, spill the beans. Tell me what happened to you last night.'

'Last night?' The events of the previous evening crowded into her mind. Where should she begin?

'I didn't notice your empty seat until the middle of my death scene – it's the only chance I get to have a look round the audience. Where did you go? Have you met a new bloke, or something?'

Juliet felt another bout of dizziness coming on but, when she told Duncan that she had been out drinking with Carmen Bird, it took a long time to get him off the telephone.

'Why couldn't you have stayed in the theatre?' he kept asking in petulant tones. 'Why didn't you bring her round to my dressing room afterwards? You could have come to our little party.'

'It wasn't my idea,' replied Juliet, pleased to think that, for once, she had been able to turn down one of Duncan's 'little parties' because she had something more interesting to do. She and Carmen had stayed talking in the pub until long after closing time, accepting free drinks from the landlord on the strength of Carmen's fame. It had been approaching two in the morning when Carmen dropped her home in a taxi.

'I've got to go now, Duncan,' she said eventually, interrupting a long anecdote about something that had happened to him in the Portobello Road. Her head was calling out for the aspirin that her stomach had rejected earlier. It wasn't until she hung up that she realised she hadn't made an arrangement to see him again.

Back upstairs, when she had dosed herself with various hangover remedies, she attempted to recall the details of what had happened in the pub. She realised with embarrassment that she had done most of the talking – rattling on about her new job, her favourite detective stories, and even about her thwarted plans for Maggie's bookshop. Carmen had used her interviewing skills to draw her out, while at the same time revealing very little about herself.

The only consolation was that she had managed to keep quiet about Duncan. She didn't want to spill *all* her secrets to someone she had just met. Searching through her handbag, she found the torn piece of beer mat on which Carmen had scribbled her telephone number and address. She probably didn't mean to give it to me, thought Juliet. She'll be regretting it right now, sitting in her big expensive house in Holland Park with her family and friends all round her and hoping that the weirdo she met at the theatre doesn't turn up in the middle of Sunday lunch.

Not that Juliet saw herself as a weirdo. It was just an assumption people seemed to make in London if you approached them with anything less than an introduction, a list of references, and a certified copy of your family tree. These show-business types were the worst of the lot, she thought bitterly, reflecting on past experiences with Duncan's friends. They were happy enough to have you around as an audience while they were showing off but, as soon as you tried to engage them in normal conversation or tell them anything about yourself, their eyes would glaze over. The next thing you knew, they'd be on the other side of the room schmoozing with their pals and you'd be left talking to the potted plants.

Carmen hadn't seemed like one of these people. But why should she want to spend time with someone like me, thought Juliet. It didn't add up. If this was a story in a book or a film, she reflected dreamily, they would become best friends – running away to have an adventure together like Thelma and Louise.

Meanwhile, back in the real world, the launderette was waiting and she needed to get herself ready for starting work the next day. Dropping the beer mat into the drawer of the bedside table, she tipped out the contents of the cardboard box which acted as her laundry basket and began to hunt for large carrier bag.

The London headquarters of Castlemayne Insurance were situated in a vast office building near Cannon

Street. Glancing up at the forbidding exterior as she arrived, Juliet felt a pang of uneasiness. It was hard to imagine this place becoming a familiar feature in the landscape of her daily life.

After announcing herself at the front desk and submitting to various security checks, she waited for twenty minutes in the reception area before the personnel officer came down to meet her. The look of anxiety on the woman's face was the first indication that something might be amiss.

'We were trying to get in touch with you all last week,' she explained, ushering Juliet into the lift. 'But there was no contact number for you in London. Nobody knew where you were.'

'Is there a problem, then?' asked Juliet in a guarded tone. Inside, her stomach tightened with fear as possibilities raced through her mind: One of her parents was ill? Her flat in Worcester had burned down? Someone had bungled the transfer and her new job had fallen through?

'Not as far as your contract's concerned, we've seen to all that,' she replied briskly. 'It's just that Nick . . .' She paused and faced Juliet with a questioning look. 'I wasn't sure if you knew already. He's, well, he's not coming. He put in his resignation a week ago.'

Stunned, Juliet fell silent as she tried to make sense of this unexpected news. 'But why?' she asked eventually, as the lift lurched to a halt on the fifteenth floor. 'I didn't . . . I mean, I thought . . .'

'That he was keen to make the move? So did we.' Leading Juliet out of the lift into a long corridor, the woman lowered her voice. 'Domestic problems, I believe. I was hoping you might be able to fill us in a bit. I gather you two worked very closely together.'

'We never discussed our personal lives,' lied Juliet, anxious to protect Nick from gossip in spite of his desertion. Poor Nick. She could imagine just what had happened: Myra would have brewed up a storm at the last moment in her usual way, confronting him with threats and promises in a last, desperate attempt to wreck all his plans.

'Of course not,' said the woman hastily. 'Now I'd better fill you in on the situation here. It was lucky that we were able to do some restructuring at short notice. We've created a position for you under Rowena Hawthorne, our Senior Claims Manager, which is more or less the same as what you were expecting in terms of salary and, er, responsibilities. You don't need to worry that you might be losing out.' Turning a corner, she led Juliet into a large, open-plan office. 'You'll be based in this section,' she said, indicating an empty workstation in an exposed position by the door. 'Make yourself comfortable and I'll let Rowena know you're here.'

Juliet sat down, smiling weakly in response to curious glances from the occupants of adjacent desks, and gazed around the bustling office. It was a very different kind of working environment to the one she was used to in Worcester. The people looked busier, smarter and more intimidating. Everything seemed to be on a much grander scale. Seized with panic, she realised that she would never have applied to work in a place like this if she had known she was coming to London on her own. How on earth was she going to survive without Nick?

Rowena Hawthorne was a slim, well-dressed woman in her forties whose features seemed to be fixed in a permanent expression of displeasure, as if she had accidentally bitten into a lemon. 'So, you've come in from one of our *provincial* branches,' she remarked, when she finally deigned to acknowledge Juliet's presence later that morning. 'I hope you're ready to hit the ground running – you'll find things happen a lot faster here than they do in the country.' Fetching a large pile of folders from a nearby shelf, she placed them on Juliet's desk. 'We'll start with these accident reports. I want detailed summaries by lunchtime tomorrow. You'll find the format in the office manual – I take it you've familiarised yourself with our QA procedures?'

Juliet shook her head. 'In Worcester we . . .'

'Never mind,' interrupted Rowena with a sigh of impatience. 'We'll just have to re-educate you.' Disappearing briefly, she returned with a set of bulging ring-binders. 'They should have told you to read these this morning. There's a form to fill out in Appendix S when you've finished. I think you'll find the report procedure somewhere in D or E.'

She turned, as if to leave Juliet to her task, then swung round and inspected her with a thoughtful frown. 'While we're on the subject of company policy,' she murmured, 'I hope you won't mind if I mention this. Your clothing, to be frank, isn't appropriate. They might bend the rules in Worcester, but we have a strict no-trouser policy here for our female staff.' She leaned forward with a conspiratorial whisper. 'See if you can find a smarter blouse as well. There's a good girl. We don't want the managing director thinking he's wandered into a country barn dance.'

With a twitch of her lips that might have been intended as a smile, she departed. Juliet stared after her with loathing. She had purchased her trousers, an inoffensive pair of dark blue slacks, especially for office wear. And what was wrong with her carefully washed and ironed gingham shirt? Opening the first volume of the office manual, she leafed through the closely typed pages with dismay. It would take weeks just to read it — let alone to make sense of its obscurely worded demands.

Turning to the first page, Juliet willed herself to concentrate. After a few moments, however, she was overwhelmed by a feeling of longing for her cosy little office in Worcester. But she couldn't go back; it would be seen as an admission of failure. Besides, Nick wasn't even there any more. Everything had gone horribly wrong, she thought miserably, fighting back the urge to burst into tears. She hadn't expected her bright new future in London to turn out like this.

Carmen faced the wreckage of her dressing table. The mirror was cracked in one corner and the surface was strewn with broken trinkets and jars, gathered up hastily from the floor the previous night. A damaged powder compact had leaked its contents, covering everything with a fine, shimmering dust. A pile of splintered china fragments were all that remained of her favourite vase.

It was Thursday morning. The day before had not only been the last *Makeover* recording session for that week, but also the end of a series. With a sense of occasion befitting a man of his habits, Gideon had marked the event with an Armageddon of a row.

Things had been quiet at home in the earlier part of the week, lulling her into a false sense of security. When he returned on Sunday, Gideon had been in a friendlier mood than she had known for some time. He soon lapsed into his customary withdrawn silence, but there was less hostility in his manner than usual. Thus, by Wednesday night, Carmen felt bold enough to make a reference to her evening at the theatre. As she removed her makeup in preparation for bed, she casually mentioned that, in his absence, she had been to see a play.

He had led her on, asking for details in an interested voice. Buoyed by a sense of achievement in having shown so much independence, she had gabbled on carelessly, revealing more than she intended. Somehow she let slip that she had been given a ticket by one of the actors. That they had talked to each other in a pub. When she had finished, there was an ominous silence. Then she saw Gideon in the mirror, towering over her with the expression that she had learned to dread.

At least he hadn't marked her where it showed, she thought, wincing as she touched the cigarette burn on her upper arm. He had probably remembered the forthcoming *Makeover* party, laid on to celebrate the wrap of another series. Apart from this event, at which they would be forced to display a façade of domestic felicity, she would have no further contact with her colleagues until the new season's recordings began. It seemed that her fame and her relationship with Gideon had conspired together to isolate her from the rest of the world. She had no real friends, no one in whom she could confide. How was she going to cope with her life for the next three weeks?

Opening a drawer to find a home for the contents of a smashed jewellery box, Carmen caught sight of the frame that held their wedding photograph. She kept it face-down under her tights and knickers, unable to cope with the hypocrisy of having it on display.

She took it out now and gazed at it, feeling only numbness where once there had been emotion. Why hadn't she listened to the warnings, seen the signs? How could she have mistaken for passion the violence that had always been part of his nature?

Her face, eight years earlier, was a picture of inno-cence. Carmen's childhood had been happy and, until she married, the course of her life had been smooth and predictable. When Gideon began to abuse her, it was as if the bottom had fallen out of her world. Not having the faintest idea how to deal with it, she did nothing. Stunned into passivity, she suffered his brutal treatment in silence and hoped that things would improve. They didn't.

She had been afraid to confide in her parents, who had disliked Gideon from the start. She had ignored their warnings when she married him and they would have been certain to take the view that she had brought it on her own head. Her mother was unlikely to be sympathetic in any case. She had old-fashioned values and believed that a woman should be subservient to her husband. *There's no smoke without fire*, she used to say. If a man mistreated his wife, she must have done something to deserve it. In her view of the world, domestic violence only happened on council estates and branded its victims in the same class as those who practised adultery or petty theft.

Her father wouldn't have understood, either. He had blundered through life getting his own way in everything and wondering why people made such a fuss about 'relationships'. He had never suspected that his own trouble-free marriage was almost totally due to his wife's compliant behaviour.

Carmen had kept up the pretence of being happy for so long that it would be unthinkable to shatter her parents' rosy image of her life. Despite their differences of opinion, she was fond of them and wanted them to be proud of her. If she told them the truth, she would feel as if she had let them down. Her Aunt Bridget might have provided a more sympathetic ear, but she now lived in the Scilly Isles and had never even met Gideon. They had once been close – Bridget was different to her parents and treated her more like a friend. They kept in touch by letter, but Carmen felt unable to commit her troubles to paper. It would require too much analysis of her own feelings – too much probing into matters that she didn't want to confront.

She regretted not making more effort to arrange a visit, especially now that Bridget was widowed and living on her own. But all her attempts to persuade Gideon had come to nothing and it somehow seemed that it was now too late.

In the early days of their marriage, Gideon was the star and she was his protégée. After his success with *Mangus*, his confidence had known no bounds. Leaving the BBC, he set up his own production company and was, for a time, fêted by the media as a maverick talent who could write his own rules. As Carmen's career prospered, however, Gideon's fortunes began to wane, and she realised that his aggressive behaviour was not restricted to home. Projects were cancelled without explanation, usually following one of his mysterious absences. Rumours circulated. Acquaintances shunned him. Contracts fell through.

Midianite Productions went into liquidation. The house was in Gideon's name, but it was Carmen who paid the mortgage now. Clinging to her career as the only part of her life that made sense, she had cut herself off from her feelings and concentrated on papering over the cracks in the image she presented to the world. The strain was beginning to show.

She slid the wedding photograph out of sight beneath a jumbo size box of Tampax and closed the drawer. Continuing with her salvage operation, she came across a scrap of paper inscribed with two telephone numbers and a name.

Juliet Jennings. Carmen thought wistfully of the odd-looking woman with the warm, if somewhat eccentric, personality. She had enjoyed her night out with Juliet. It had taken a while to get over their initial awkwardness but, once they had downed a few drinks in a backstreet pub, they had found plenty to talk about. Juliet had treated her as an equal — something that was rare in Carmen's experience. She was used to people being so much in awe of her TV fame that they couldn't relate to her as a human being. Juliet had made her laugh. It had been a glimpse of what she imagined proper friendship to be like.

Crumpling the paper into the wastebasket, she thought with a sigh how carefree Juliet's life must be in comparison with her own. She would have liked to get to know Juliet, but she knew that Gideon would never allow it to happen. He had managed to drive away every other woman she had tried to befriend.

A door slammed downstairs, making her start. Holding her breath, she heard the clinking of bottle against glass in the kitchen. Gideon's footsteps moved along the hall, pausing at the foot of the stairs. She waited. The footsteps continued towards the study. After a moment, the theme music to *Mangus* drifted through the house.

She felt a surge of contempt. When was the self-pitying fool going to stop living in the past and get himself a life? Then she looked in the mirror. Who was the bigger fool, she wondered. Him or her?

Feelings welled up inside her, threatening to break through her carefully constructed barrier of reserve. She fought them back with action. Retrieving the ball of paper, she smoothed it out and went downstairs to the telephone. To hell with the consequences, she thought angrily. Why shouldn't she take this chance to participate in an ordinary social life?

As the end of her first week drew near, Juliet was growing increasingly dissatisfied with her new job. Rowena was impossible to please – reprimanding her for showing any signs of initiative. 'A summary is meant to be objective,' she had snapped, handing back Juliet's first assignment for her to do again. 'I'm not interested in your opinions. Just stick to the facts.'

Juliet tried to point out that she had been used to making decisions on Nick's behalf, but Rowena was unimpressed. 'If he'd paid a little more attention to proper procedure, he might not have got himself into such a mess,' she said darkly. 'Have you filled out your self-audit and QA compliance assessment forms yet?'

Anxious to avoid further criticism of her appearance, Juliet had acquired a sensible-looking skirt. It was uncomfortable to wear – biting into her waist and producing angry red marks on her skin – and also precipitated a further problem, that of what to wear on her legs. Socks were out, she discovered, finding herself to be the subject of much amusement on her second day. Reluctantly, she submitted herself to the torments of tights – the continual need to hitch them up as the crotch worked its way towards her knees, the itchy sweating between the legs and the painful blisters as her shoes chewed into her unprotected toes. Inspecting her new appearance in a mirror, she felt foolish and resentful. She hadn't looked half as ridiculous in the clothes she had been wearing before.

The position of Juliet's workstation was clearly the least popular in the office. A constant stream of people passed back and forth, frequently parking their backsides on the end of her desk while they stopped to chat with a colleague. It was impossible to concentrate for any length of time.

She also discovered that she was sitting on the edge of the typing pool, and that the self-possessed women who had so intimidated her on her first day were, in fact, junior administrative staff. They all had names like Tracey, Barbie, Jackie, Kerry or Terry, and Juliet found it extremely difficult to tell them apart. Their talk was exclusively centred around boyfriends, make-up and clothes, and what they had seen on TV the previous night. Juliet was forced to listen to detailed accounts of hot dates and new outfits, together with interminable discussions about the plot of *Southsiders*. Occasionally, hearing mention of *Makeover*, she was almost tempted to join in. What would they think if they knew she had been out drinking with Carmen Bird?

But they seemed to regard her as something of an oddity, pointedly excluding her from their company as they departed for washroom or wine-bar in whispering huddles. Juliet was left to make her own entertainment at lunchtimes. She often ended up in a nearby outlet of Big Boy's Burgers, finding secret consolation in the comforting calories of a Double King Boy.

Late on Thursday morning, Juliet received her first telephone call at work. Not having been given the dignity of her own extension, she was obliged to take it at Tracey's desk.

'They said it was *personal*,' commented Tracey, handing her the receiver. 'Better not let old Lemon-Lips catch on.'

'Perhaps it's her boyfriend,' giggled someone, possibly Jackie. The typing pool girls were all in their early twenties and probably saw Juliet as an ancient spinster who had as much chance of finding her way off the shelf as flying to the moon.

'Hello?' asked Juliet cautiously, wondering if Duncan might have finally made the effort to get in touch. But it was Carmen Bird, inviting her for coffee at her house on Sunday morning.

'Are you sure you want . . . I mean, yes, I'd love to.' Juliet found herself blushing with pleasure and surprise to learn that Carmen had remembered her. She had thought a TV star would be far too busy hobnobbing with the rich and famous to spare time for socialising with the likes of her.

When she had finished making the arrangements, she replaced the receiver and looked up to find a row of faces watching her with ill-concealed curiosity.

'Well?' squealed Jackie, spinning her chair in excited circles. 'Who's the lucky guy, then?'

'It was only a woman,' whispered Tracey loudly.

A ripple of amusement travelled around the room. 'Probably the best she can get,' murmured Barbie, in a voice she obviously hadn't been meant to hear.

Juliet glared at her, determined to hold her ground. 'Actually,' she said frostily, 'it was Carmen Bird. She's a friend of mine.'

'Sure it was,' said Barbie, her lips curling into a mocking sneer. 'I'm best pals with Oprah Winfrey myself. I was out with her just the other night.'

Kerry and Terry burst into fits of uncontrollable giggles, which quickly spread to those around them. With as much dignity as she could muster, Juliet turned and made her way back to her desk. She was about to sit down when a further whispered comment from Barbie reached her ears. '. . . must be going ga-ga, if you ask me. Why on earth would *Carmen Bird* want to be talking to a old bag like her?'

'Shhh, she'll hear you. You shouldn't . . .' It sounded for a moment as if Tracey was going to stand up for her, but she caved in to peer pressure. 'Maybe she wants her to go on *Makeover*,' she finished lamely.

'They'll have their work cut out there,' squeaked Kerry, still giggling helplessly. 'Do you think they're doing a special edition for hopeless cases?'

Juliet fled for the door, biting her lip in a fruitless attempt to hold back her tears. How could they be so cruel? She spent the next twenty minutes locked into a cubicle in the ladies' toilet, crying miserably and wondering why she had chosen to come to such an awful place as London. She was lonely and unloved, her job was a nightmare and she had no friends to confide in. As far as Duncan was concerned, she might as well not even exist.

Returning, red-eyed, along the corridor, she saw

Rowena approaching. Unable to face another dressing-down, she darted into an empty room and crouched behind the door. It was an extension of the boardroom, separated from the main area by a set of folding screens. As she waited, she could hear the drone of voices; some kind of management meeting was about to commence.

A door clicked open and Rowena's voice joined the others. Good, thought Juliet. *Lemon-Lips*, as Tracey had called her, would be out of the way until well into the afternoon. Straightening up, she was about to leave the room when she saw what was in it. An eyewateringly delicious-looking buffet was spread out on a large table. The boardroom lunch. Quietly, Juliet closed the door.

Half an hour later, she was feeling much better. Checking carefully to make sure no one saw her, she emerged into the corridor and headed off for her lunch break. Rowena was bound to be on a diet, she reasoned, wiping her mouth with her sleeve. The rest of the senior management – all men – were probably far too high-powered to pay much attention to the details of what they ate. They wouldn't miss the odd smoked salmon vol-au-vent, Parma ham twist, or even the bottle of wine. Juliet let out a small burp of satisfaction. She was sure that they would never notice the other missing item. She had hidden the empty tray on a ledge outside the window. Even if they did, it would have been worth it for the sheer pleasure of the experience. It was no mean achievement, she told herself proudly, to have single-handedly demolished a conference-sized serving of breadcrumbed king prawns.

CHAPTER 4

It was Sunday morning – the day after the end-of-run party for *The White Devil* – and Duncan was feeling terrible. Clutching a glass fizzing with soluble aspirin in one hand, he made a second attempt at dialling Juliet's number. She was the only person he knew who could possibly cheer him up at a time like this.

It had been a disaster – one of those evenings that rocketed straight to number one in his personal chart of all-time bad experiences. It would probably stay there for weeks before it faded in his memory and found its rightful place in the lower reaches of the top ten. He knew, of course, that it would ultimately be deposed by long-running classics such as *Failing the Eleven-Plus*, *Missing the Audition for* Hamlet, or *Getting an Erection at the Swimming Pool*, but that didn't make him feel any better right now.

Juliet wasn't answering her telephone. He listened to the ringing tone one more time, then replaced the receiver with a sigh. It wasn't like her to be asleep at midday on a Sunday.

A picture of the Hammersmith Tandoori flashed

immediately into his mind like the opening shot of a home video. He made several attempts to abort the viewing by thinking about other things, but the cut-off mechanism refused to operate. Watching in his mind's eye, he saw his innocent self of the previous day appear on the scene. He was walking, hand-in-hand with Sonia, into the venue for the break-up of their relationship.

He had expected a more salubrious setting for the end-of-run party. The Lyric counted as a West End theatre, after all, even if their production hadn't been in the main house. Surely they could have rewarded their hard-working actors with something a little more classy than a trip to the local curry house?

In a truculent mood, he had ordered the most expensive things on the menu. Didn't he deserve a little pampering? He *was* the male lead, after all. Later in the evening, however, he found out that the Lyric management had nothing to do with the event, which had all been arranged by Binky Follett, their director. He also discovered that they were expected to pay for themselves.

Things began to go downhill when everybody started talking about their forthcoming roles on stage and TV. Duncan realised that he and Sonia were the only members of the cast who didn't have new work lined up. People kept rubbing it in by asking about his filming schedule, and each time he was forced to admit that the project had been cancelled.

Sonia had been strangely quiet for much of the evening, but he soon discovered that she was merely waiting for the moment when her announcement would have the most impact. With no more than a whisper of apology for her secrecy, she told the assembled company that Binky had cast her in the lead role of his next production, *Miss Julie*.

Then she divulged, in front of everyone, that she was looking forward to her new life south of the river. With all the lager he had consumed, it had taken a few mental spins of the compass before Duncan worked out that she couldn't be planning to stay in Hammersmith. Why hadn't she told him she had found them another flat?

Soon after this, the drift of her conversation suggested that there were further details about which he was unaware. The next thing he knew, she had casually informed him that she was *moving in with Binky bloody Follett*.

It wasn't Duncan's habit to make a scene in public places, but the ensuing argument had caused quite a stir. Drinks had been hurled at various people, adding even further to his share of the bill. After this, he had been ejected from the restaurant and found himself continuing his denunciation of Sonia and her duplicity on the pavement outside.

It had all ended with Sonia flouncing off in a huff, leaving him to pay for her meal as well as his own. The final humiliation consisted of having to negotiate his settlement of the bill in sign-language through the window, watched by an assortment of passers-by. The proprietor refused to let him back into the premises, so he had been left with no option but to write out a cheque in the street and post it through the letter box.

A series of banging noises from the bedroom brought him back to the present with a start. He didn't know where Sonia had spent the previous night, but she had returned that morning to collect her things.

She wasn't wasting any time, he thought despondently. Earlier on, before his prospects as a film star had been dashed, she had implied that she saw their relationship as something more permanent. He hadn't wanted anything *too* permanent, but it would have been useful to have someone to share the rent for the next few weeks – not to mention the bills that would, no doubt, arrive as soon as she had gone.

There was another banging noise, this time in the hallway. 'I'm taking the hat stand,' she said, appearing briefly at the living room door. 'Seeing as I paid for it.'

'All right,' he muttered. 'Suit yourself.' He had been under the impression that it had been a gift for him – his birthday present, in fact.

'Leave the birdcage, then,' he added gruffly. They had paid half each for the elaborate bamboo structure, shaped like a small pagoda. He had been the one who spotted it, in an obscure side street off the Portobello Road.

'But Dunky . . .' She reappeared in the doorway. 'Didn't I explain? I promised it to Binky for the play – you know, for the bit where Jean strangles Miss Julie's pet bird. I can't go back on it now.'

It was the first Duncan had heard of this. It was a good thing, he reflected, that they hadn't got round to purchasing an occupant for the cage. The bloody woman would probably have offered it to Binky to wring its neck on stage as part of the package.

Duncan hated being dumped. It had happened to him more often than he cared to admit, and it hurt like hell every single time. The fact that the women who dumped him, like Sonia, were usually totally unsuited to him in the first place didn't make it feel any better. Somehow, Duncan seemed destined to attract, or be attracted by, unsuitable women – and he could never quite work out exactly where he was going wrong.

Each time, he would turn to his career for consolation, telling himself that if only he was more successful, he would be sure to have better luck. But his career wasn't looking too bright at the moment, with few job prospects on the horizon and no definite future work lined up.

Sometimes, in his loneliest and most depressed moments, he would wonder if he had set his sights too high. Despite his efforts to live by the actors' creed: *Believe in yourself, keep on trying and never, ever, give up*, the reality of the situation often seemed bleak. In the competitive world of the London theatre, talent alone offered little guarantee of getting you to the top. Luck had its part to play, together with a good network of contacts, but the truth of the matter was that the best qualification for success was to be successful already.

For every big name lauded by the critics, how many talented hopefuls had sunk without trace? What happened to them all? Did they admit defeat and go back to their day jobs? Or did they linger on in the twilight world of non-speaking parts, progressively lowering the standard by which they judged their achievements? After the fiasco of the *Southsiders* audition, attended by every unemployed actor in London and their dog, Duncan's agent had suggested that there might be a part available in the forthcoming *Flux* commercial. Was this the direction his career was now going to take? Was he, Duncan Swayne, destined to earn his living by dressing up as a giant raisin and leaping into a vat of molten chocolate?

'Do you want these old videos?' Sonia had finished plundering his CD and book collection and was now making a final sweep through the living room.

'Hey, put those down!' He jumped to his feet and knocked the stack of tapes from her hand, scattering them all over the floor. Duncan wasn't a materialistic person – he was proud of the fact that he could take a relaxed attitude to the division of the spoils. But there was a limit. Frantically checking the labels, he gathered the cassettes into a neat pile. He wasn't going to let the grasping little bitch start ransacking his classic film collection, painstakingly recorded from the TV over a number of years.

'No need to lose your temper,' snapped Sonia, slamming out of the room.

One of the labels was missing. He slipped the tape into the video player to check its contents, but he couldn't find the remote control and the television came on instead. He was treated to a glimpse of Carmen Bird, winding up proceedings on the Sunday morning repeat of *Makeover*. Duncan sighed, remembering his exhilaration after their meeting. He had been full of excitement when she had appeared at the theatre that night, wondering if she too had felt the chemistry of attraction between them. It had been a big disappointment to discover that she had left without seeing the second half.

Too soon, the *Makeover* signature tune started up and the closing credits began to roll. What had Juliet been up to, he wondered, dragging her away like that? She had been uncommunicative on the telephone last Sunday, and he had been too busy with the play to make contact with her during the week. Lifting the telephone receiver again, he dialled her number for the fifth time that day. But there was still no reply.

As Sonia dragged her last suitcase through the hallway, Duncan succumbed to a wave of self-pity. Where the hell *was* Juliet? Why did his friends never seem to be there for him when he needed their help?

Juliet was, at that moment, sitting at Carmen Bird's kitchen table. 'Why don't you leave him?' she asked, scarcely able to believe what she had just heard.

'It's not that simple,' said Carmen, shaking her head. 'Gideon knew what he was doing when he married me. I sometimes wonder if he planned the whole thing this way.'

The last hour's conversation had turned Juliet's preconceptions about Carmen Bird on their head. She had thought her to be the woman who had everything – a successful career, money, a happy home and a loving husband. Nothing had prepared her for the revelation that Carmen's life was dominated by horrors that made the shortcomings of her own existence seem trivial and absurd.

Juliet had been nervous about coming. A peculiar feeling had gripped her stomach for the last few days, though she couldn't be sure if this was simply the result of her overindulgence in king prawns. Expecting some kind of formal occasion, possibly with other friends of Carmen in attendance, she had dreaded fumbling her way through a minefield of social etiquette. When she arrived, however, Carmen answered the door in a shabby tracksuit and led her into an empty kitchen.

Waiting for the kettle to boil, they exchanged a few comments about their previous meeting. Carmen seemed preoccupied, adjusting the positions of appliances on the work surfaces and wiping invisible marks from the handles of cupboards and drawers. Juliet wondered uneasily if she had somehow mistaken the invitation and come on the wrong day.

Eventually, they were both sitting at the table with mugs of coffee. Embarrassed by the silence, Juliet gazed around the well-equipped kitchen in search of a conversational opening. Gleaming saucepans hung from the walls like trophies. A collection of old-fashioned glass jars contained layers of dried pasta in different colours and shapes. Beside the cooker was a rack of shiny gadgets – the kind of things you never actually bought but were always drawn to, magpie-like, in kitchenware shops.

'What does that one do?' she asked, pointing to a device that looked like an instrument of medieval torture.

'It's for taking the stones out of olives,' replied Carmen tonelessly. 'Gideon buys that stuff – it's not mine.' Lowering her eyes, she stared into the corner of the room with a troubled expression. Juliet looked round and saw a heap of glass fragments on a sheet of newspaper beside the waste bin. They were coated in beige-coloured gunk and looked like the remains of a mixing bowl.

'I was going to make a cake.' Carmen's voice faltered, catching in her throat. 'Can you think of anything more ordinary and harmless than that?'

'But why . . .' Juliet turned back to face her, noticing the puffiness around her eyes for the first time. 'What happened?'

Rolling up the sleeve of her tracksuit, she held out her arm. 'I can't put up with this any more,' she whispered. Juliet stared at the angry red swelling, just above her elbow. It looked as if someone had gripped the skin and twisted, in just the same way that Chinese burns were doled out by the playground bullies at her old school.

'I'm frightened.' Carmen was on the verge of tears. 'I don't know what he might do next.' She took a deep breath, composing herself. 'I need to talk – I need to let someone know what's happening to me.'

Juliet listened in astonishment as Carmen began to describe the horrific treatment she suffered at the hands of her husband. 'I can't sleep at night,' she confessed in an anguished voice. 'It's driving me mad. I can hear him creeping around the house in the dark and I never know when he's going to start smashing things up.'

She told her about Gideon's drinking, his emotional

cruelty, and his draconian system of rules and punishments. Juliet was appalled to learn of the regular beatings – outbursts of physical violence that sometimes stopped only just short of necessitating hospital treatment.

Bewildered by Carmen's motives, Juliet wondered why she had chosen to reveal such intimate details of her personal life to someone she barely knew. Could such a terrible story really be true? She had always imagined domestic violence to be the weapon of the impoverished and the unemployed. Things like this didn't happen to TV stars.

'But why don't you just leave him?' she repeated, struggling to grasp how there could be any other alternative. 'You must have friends you could stay with.'

Carmen burst into tears. 'But I don't *have* any friends,' she cried. 'That's the whole point. Every time I try to make friends with anyone, he ruins it somehow – frightens them away.' She covered her face with her hands and let out a series of muffled sobs. 'I expect it'll be just the same with you,' she added quietly. 'People don't like getting involved when they sense there's violence around.'

'But I'm not . . .'

'I'm sorry.' She wiped her eyes on her sleeve and looked up, blinking. 'I didn't mean to sound so ungrateful. You're the first person who's treated me decently for a long time.' A shadow of doubt fell across her face. 'You won't tell anyone about this, will you?' she asked anxiously. 'The scandal would finish me off.'

'Of course not,' said Juliet indignantly. She fell silent,

struck by the contrast between Carmen's world and the one she had left behind in Worcester. Back home, everyone in her circle knew all about everyone else's business. They had grown up together, sharing confidences and fighting over boyfriends, and now knew all the interesting details of each other's marriages or divorces. They were all too eager to learn of a disaster in somebody's life – all too ready to pile in with gossip and advice.

That was another reason why she had wanted to leave, she reminded herself, remembering how friends and neighbours had gloated and picked over the remains when she split up with Keith. Faced with the loneliness of London, however, Juliet was beginning to realise how much she had taken friendship for granted. Now, she needed it just as much as Carmen did.

'You really ought to leave him, you know,' she said eventually. 'It sounds like he's out of control. He could go too far one day – hurt you worse than he intended.'

'It's not as simple as . . .'

'You could stay with me,' she added impulsively, wanting to help. 'I'd make sure he didn't come after you.'

'You don't know what Gideon's like,' said Carmen in a weary voice. 'He'd follow me everywhere, make my life even more of a misery than it is now. He'd never let it rest until he'd got me back again.'

'But why? Why would he want you back if he hates you so much?'

'He can't let me go because he needs me. He's so used to being in the limelight with the celebrities that he couldn't cope with being a nobody again.' A flash of anger came into her eyes. 'That's what he'd be without me, you know. His talent's all been pissed away with the drugs and whisky. He couldn't even produce a bloody wedding video these days, much less a TV programme.'

Carmen pulled a tissue from her pocket and blew her nose noisily. 'He's trying to punish me now,' she continued. 'Just because he helped me when I was starting out – fixed up a few lousy contracts for me – he thinks all the success I've had is due to him. He's got some idea in his head that he's sacrificed himself for me – that it's my fault his career's gone down the drain.' She paused and looked at Juliet with a despondent shrug. 'Who knows? Maybe it *is* my fault.'

'But that's ridiculous. How could it be?' Juliet felt a rush of indignation on Carmen's behalf. Had Gideon broken her spirit so much that she was trying to blame herself for his outrageous behaviour?

'I don't know.' Carmen sighed and leaned forward at the table with her head in her hands. 'I don't know anything anymore. I just feel like I'll never be free of him for as long as I live.'

They sat in silence for a few moments. Juliet's mind was racing – she was imagining the horrors of Carmen's situation and desperately trying to think of a constructive suggestion to make. Her thoughts kept circling back to their first meeting at the theatre – to the expression she had glimpsed on Carmen's face when the woman at the next table had joked about murdering her husband.

'It's a shame you haven't got a poisoned painting knocking about the place,' she murmured abstractedly.

'What do you mean?'

Juliet blushed. 'Sorry,' she muttered. 'I just keep remembering that play we saw. All those murders. I suppose that's how they dealt with things in those days.'

'I wish somebody *would* murder him,' said Carmen thoughtfully. 'That would be the answer to all my problems.' Then she sat up and stared at Juliet. 'You're not suggesting . . .'

'Of course not,' said Juliet hastily. 'Besides,' she added, trying to lighten things up with a joke, 'if you really wanted to get rid of him, it would be far easier to do it yourself. Poison his coffee or something.'

Carmen stared at her for a moment, then let out a nervous laugh. 'If only it were that simple . . .'

'It's easier to kill someone than you might think,' murmured Juliet, drifting into a private fantasy where she solved all Carmen's problems by orchestrating the perfect murder. There were plenty of ways to do it without getting caught, she reflected. She read about them in fiction all the time.

There was a sudden noise in the hallway – the sound of a key being rattled in a lock.

'It's him,' gasped Carmen, her face flushing pink. She jumped to her feet and began to rinse the coffee mugs with frantic movements. 'I thought he'd be out for the rest of the day.'

A door slammed shut, its echoes reverberating through the house. Footsteps moved towards the kitchen. Juliet looked up as the door opened and saw a tall man with an expensive-looking raincoat draped over his shoulders. There was something sinister about his appearance. Even if she had known nothing about him, Juliet would have felt uncomfortable in his presence. His hair was slicked back in a distinctive style and the slopes of his smooth, olive-tanned features were broken only by a prominent moustache.

'Hello, ladies,' he said, pronouncing his words with the slow deliberation of a man who had been drinking. 'Having a nice coffee morning, are we?' He glanced round the kitchen with raised eyebrows. 'I'd have expected there to be more of you. Considering all the fuss we had earlier.'

He turned to address Juliet. 'Did you know that my wife was going to bake a cake specially for the occasion?' he asked, with a sneer in his voice.

Juliet glared at him, unable to think of a suitable response.

'It's a shame she lost her temper and decided to decorate the walls with it,' he added, settling his gaze on the pile of broken glass beside the bin. 'Still, I'm sure you've had a lovely time gossiping about all the terrible things your wicked husbands have done to you.'

He lifted his eyes to meet Juliet's. 'You know your way out, don't you? When you're ready to leave us to our privacy, that is.'

'Gideon . . .' Carmen spoke hesitantly.

'Some of us have lives to get on with,' he snapped, whirling on his heels and stalking out of the room.

'Gideon!' Carmen ran down the passage after him

and they both disappeared from view. There was the sound of a door slamming and muffled voices raised in argument.

If somebody did murder Gideon, thought Juliet fiercely, they would be doing the world a huge favour. She waited for some time, listening to the angry voices and wondering whether she ought to leave. If this was what marriage was like, she reflected, she was glad she had never been asked.

The following day, Carmen stood in Barry's garden in Richmond, sipping a glass of chilled white wine. The sunny weather had allowed Barry to avoid the embarrassment of having his domestic arrangements laid open to public scrutiny by holding the *Makeover* party outdoors.

She watched the activity around her, feeling isolated from the event, trapped in the quiet place at the eye of a storm. Food and drink were being consumed in large quantities, as everyone connected with the pro-gramme – from the producer right down to the most junior assistant – reacquainted themselves with each other's partners and celebrated getting another series of *Makeover* in the can.

Gideon was ensconced by the drinks table, dividing his attention between talking shop with Kevin and star-ing down the front of the low-cut dress worn by Jessica from Wardrobe. Nothing unusual about that. Imagine a life, thought Carmen wistfully, where such token infidelities were the only source of discord. Imagine what it must be like to have a normal marriage.

'Hi, Carmen.' Amanda, the assistant producer, picked her way unsteadily across the lawn on spiked heels. She sounded slightly the worse for alcohol. 'Shame about Barry, eh? He's got the garden looking so nice and everything, but I suppose he'll have to sell the place now.'

Carmen made a non-committal noise. It was, by now, common knowledge that Barry's wife had left him, but she felt it was an abuse of hospitality to gossip about it in his own garden.

'Have you been inside?' continued Amanda in a conspiratorial whisper. 'There's hardly any furniture left downstairs. It looks as if the poor sod's really being taken to the cleaners.'

Carmen glanced guiltily towards the patio where Barry was tending the barbecue, dishing out sausages to a throng of hungry guests. 'Perhaps we should give him a hand with the food?' she suggested.

'Oh, but I'm a vegetarian. Didn't you know?' Amanda wrinkled her nose. 'I can't stand being around the smell of meat.'

'I'll go and offer myself, then,' said Carmen, turning towards the house. 'He looks as if he's having trouble coping on his own.'

'That's a good idea,' murmured Amanda in a bitchy tone. 'You'd better get some practice in, because it's going to be your turn next.'

'What did you say?' Carmen whirled round in alarm. Had Gideon said something she didn't know about? Had people started to gossip about *her* marriage as well?

'No need to get touchy.' Amanda gave her a truculent smile. 'I heard your husband telling Kevin what a lovely big garden you've got.' She giggled loudly, attracting glances from people standing nearby. 'So I told them I was going to put you down on the list to host the next party. It's about time you took your turn with everyone else.'

Carmen made her way to the patio, narrowly avoiding being knocked over as a series of small children hurtled across the lawn towards the tree house at the far end.

Barry accepted her offer with alacrity. 'If you could be an angel and chop up a bit more salad, I'd love you forever,' he said with a grin. 'The stuff's all laid out ready in the kitchen, but I've been so busy feeding these gannets here that I haven't had a chance to nip in and do it.'

In the kitchen, Carmen let out a sigh of relief to find herself alone. The basic layout of the room was similar to her own kitchen and the only obvious difference was that most of the movable contents had been stripped out. A series of gaping holes under the worksurfaces testified to the former presence of major appliances such as washing machines and cookers. It appeared that Barry had been left to fend for himself with little more than a kettle and a microwave.

Finding the salad ingredients, she set to work with a smile. She rarely experienced the pleasure of preparing food. Gideon hardly ever turned up for meals if she cooked them, and it never seemed worthwhile to go to the trouble just for herself. She existed largely on a diet of ready meals, supermarket sandwiches and occasional snacks of dried fruit, crackers and cheese.

Slicing a cucumber into thin disks, she thought back to her conversation with Juliet the day before. She felt she had messed things up – that she had rushed in and told her too much, too soon.

The main reason for asking Juliet round had been to offer her a chance to appear on *Makeover*. She hadn't intended to divulge anything more than the slightest of hints about her problems with Gideon. If he hadn't come in beforehand and upset her, she might have kept to her resolve. As it turned out, however, it looked as if she had ruined her chances of friendship with Juliet for good.

After Gideon had returned and insulted them both, things had gone rapidly downhill. When Carmen finally got round to broaching the subject of a makeover, she managed it clumsily. What had been meant as a gesture of friendship had ended up sounding patronising. No wonder Juliet had been offended. She had refused the offer without explanation and departed almost straightaway.

Carmen had been left to face Gideon. She hadn't really thought that inviting another woman to their house for coffee was a cardinal sin, but he had been angrier than she had seen him for some time. It was as if he *knew* what she had said about him. Why hadn't she thought twice before betraying their secrets to a stranger? Why was it that she didn't know the first thing about how to make friends?

Returning to the patio with a huge bowl of salad,

she helped organise the buffet table into a semblance of order.

'Thanks a million,' said Barry, tipping a tray of barbecued ribs onto a serving dish as a fresh wave of hungry-looking people approached. 'You deserve a big kiss,' he continued, removing his oven gloves and catching her by the hand.

'No! Stop it, Barry,' hissed Carmen, backing away in alarm. She had seen Gideon moving towards the patio.

'What's the matter?' asked Barry with a look of surprise. 'I wasn't going to eat you, I was only going to give you a peck on the . . .'

'What the fuck do you think you're playing at?' A shocked silence fell over the gathering as Gideon pushed his way drunkenly to the table. Carmen felt a sharp pang of fear. Gideon usually kept up an act in front of other people, but it looked as if the drink had undermined his capacity for self-control.

'Hey, what's the problem?' asked Barry, dropping Carmen's hand as if it had burnt him. 'I was only saying thank you.' He let out a nervous laugh, attempting to turn it into a joke. 'I do have a *droit du seigneur* as your host, after all.'

'I don't care whose host you are! Just don't you ever lay a finger on my wife again, you ugly little slimeball!'

'Gideon, that's not fair . . .' Carmen trembled with embarrassment. 'He was only . . .'

'Shut the fuck up, you little whore!' He moved round the table, knocking plates to the ground as he went, and grabbed her by the arm.

Carmen didn't move. Everybody waited in silence to see what was going to happen. Then there was a distant scream as somebody's child fell out of the tree house. Heads turned eagerly in search of a distraction and the crowd began to disperse.

'You're coming home with me now!' snapped Gideon. Taking advantage of the confusion, he marched Carmen straight through the house and out of the front door.

Carmen gripped the steering wheel with shaking hands and stared blankly at the road ahead. Gideon had shown her up in front of everyone, had made her look like a complete fool by dragging her away from the party, and now he expected *her* to drive *him* home. She felt a rush of nausea as a bilious anger rose inside her and threatened to overflow.

As they crossed Barnes Common, her vision became blurred with tears. She couldn't put up with any more humiliation. Something had to give.

She pulled the car into a layby. 'Gideon,' she said in a trembling voice. 'I want a divorce.'

'You're drunk,' he replied in a contemptuous tone. 'I'm the one who should be saying that, after the way you've behaved.' He glanced at her with an expression of disgust. 'Now would you just shut up and drive us home please? I've got things to do.'

'I'm serious. I've had enough of all this.' She unclipped her seatbelt and opened the door of the car. 'I'm leaving you.'

'Are you crazy?' He seized her by the arm, dragging

her back into her seat. 'What the hell do you think you're doing?'

'Let me go!' She struggled to get out, but he leaned across her and pulled the door shut with a dull crunch.

'My handbag . . .'

'Fuck your handbag!' He yanked at the strap, which was caught in the door, and it snapped in two. Hurling the bag onto the back seat, he slapped her clumsily across the face. 'I'll see you rot in Hell before you get a divorce out of me, you bitch! Do you think I'm going to let you screw things up for me now, after all I've done for you?'

'I can't take any more violence!' screamed Carmen, releasing the pent-up tension that had been brewing inside her for weeks. Feebly, she swung her arm in retaliation, but he caught her by the wrist. Her elbow banged painfully against the steering wheel.

'Violence?' he snarled. 'What about the emotional violence you inflict on me? You'd drive most men to worse things than I've ever done – the way you behave. Can you imagine what it's like living with a woman who's snivelling and complaining all the time? You're so wrapped up in yourself, you can't see what you're doing to other people. It's about time somebody told you – it's no picnic being around an ego as big as yours. You're probably the most selfish person I've ever met!'

Carmen sank back into the seat, her head throbbing, and closed her eyes in resignation. He was turning the whole thing back on her, making *her* take the blame for it all. Nothing she said ever seemed to make any difference.

'I don't suppose you've ever stopped to wonder what it's like for *me*, have you?' he continued bitterly. 'After all the sacrifices I've made, you might think I'd deserve a little support from my wife. It's not easy living with constant rejection.' He tightened his grip on her wrist. 'Especially when it extends to the bedroom as well. What do you expect me to think?'

Carmen said nothing. She wasn't falling into the trap of letting him turn this into an argument about their sex life.

'Now you just listen to me.' His tone became one of stern admonishment. 'I don't think you realise just how much you need me, Carmen. I've been talking to Kevin about your next series and, quite frankly, he thinks you may not be up to it. He thinks . . .'

'How dare you!' burst out Carmen. 'How dare you gossip about me with my producer!'

'I think you're forgetting who manages your precious career, my dear.' Gideon's cheek twitched as a smile of victory crept across his face. 'Now, as I was saying, everyone thinks you're heading for a nervous breakdown if you carry on with this foolish behaviour of yours. I've heard that you keep turning up late with shadows under your eyes, and I gather you have an attitude problem with your colleagues. You didn't tell me about the fiasco with that interview you messed up, either.'

Carmen stared at him with loathing. He was deliberately setting out to ruin her, both professionally and socially, and there seemed to be nothing she could do to stop him.

'You know as well as I do that you can't carry on like this,' he continued. 'As for all this nonsense about divorce, well, you can take it from me that you'll be out of a job if the management of Conquest TV hear about it. Have you any idea what damage a scandal like that would do to the programme?'

Carmen's anger had by now taken her far beyond a state where she could think rationally. In a blind fury, she restarted the car and drove in silence towards Hammersmith Bridge.

Fuck you, Gideon. The phrase circled repetitively in her head. As they entered the Hammersmith one-way system, she missed a red light and they found themselves slewing across a stream of oncoming traffic.

'Watch out, you stupid bitch!' bellowed Gideon as a screech of hastily applied brakes announced the convergence of their path with that of a fast-moving lorry. Glancing to her left, Carmen saw a huge set of wheels looming within inches of the passenger window.

Her stomach churned with fear. For a split second, she imagined what would happen if she failed to act. Then instinct took over and she wrenched the wheel round to the right. They clipped the front bumper of the lorry, cut across the path of several other cars and mounted the kerb on the inside of the roundabout. A cacophony of horns drowned out the crunch of metal on concrete as they came to rest against one of the pillars supporting the flyover.

'You stupid fucking bitch!' Gideon's face was purple with rage. 'Are you trying to kill me?'

Carmen stumbled out of the car and collapsed, sobbing, on the litter-strewn patch of tarmac under the flyover. *Yes*, she screamed silently. If only she hadn't lost her nerve at that crucial moment, he would be dead now. All her pain and misery would be over.

She would probably be dead as well, of course. Even in her present state of confusion, she couldn't pretend to be sorry that she had survived. She was only thirty-three, for Christ's sake. She had a whole life ahead of her.

Her head felt as if it had been wrapped in cotton wool. Drawing her knees up under her chin, she rocked herself gently back and forth. As she watched the disrupted traffic sort itself back into a regular flow, it occurred to her that this was the first time in her memory that she had seen this stretch of road unencumbered by a traffic jam.

A police car arrived. She watched Gideon waving his arms as he entered into a self-righteous explanation of how the incident had been everyone's fault but their own. She couldn't hear what he was saying, but she knew that, for once, he wouldn't be pointing the finger of blame at his wife. He was too afraid of bad publicity that might reflect unfavourably upon himself.

She thought back, once again, to her conversation with Juliet. *Poison his coffee, or something.* It had taken a brush with death to convince her, but she now knew that Juliet was right

'Are you OK, miss?'

She looked up to see a policeman standing over her. 'I expect you've had a bit of a shock,' he said, draping a blanket over her shoulders. He glanced at her face and did a double take. 'Hey, aren't you . . .'

'Carmen Bird,' she said with an automatic smile. She struggled to her feet. 'Don't worry, I'm fine.'

Poison his coffee, or something. She would just have to work out the best way of doing it. The next time, she told herself firmly, she wasn't going to lose her nerve.

CHAPTER 5

Carmen woke up the next morning to find her name in the newspapers. Their regular broadsheet had a small item on the second page: *Carmen Bird treated for shock after car accident*, it said, in its usual matter-of-fact tone. The tabloids, however, must have been short of material that day: 'MAKEOVER STAR IN NEAR-DEATH SMASH', screamed *The People's Probe*. 'BIRD CLIPS WING ON FLY-OVER', sniggered *The Daily Dog*, picturing a close-up of their damaged car. A third publication seemed to have its wires crossed: CARMEN IN CRITICAL CONDITION', it reported earnestly. 'TV STAR FIGHTS FOR HER LIFE AFTER HIGH-SPEED CRASH'.

'Look what you've done now,' said Gideon, marching angrily into the kitchen and throwing a further bundle of newsprint onto the breakfast table. 'I've just phoned the hospital,' he added. 'Apparently there was a pile-up on the M4 last night and some fuckwit got their press releases muddled up.'

Carmen leafed through the bundle, pausing to read a column that informed her that she was currently languishing on a life-support machine, her condition deteriorating by the minute. She had, in fact, spent no more than an hour at the hospital before being told to go home and rest.

'I'm going to the garage to see about the repairs,' snapped Gideon, heading for the front door. 'Try not to smash up anything else while I'm gone.'

As soon as he had left, Carmen pushed the papers to one side. She felt slightly dazed by what she had read, but reminded herself that inaccurate reporting was nothing new. It was a rare event when an article published managed to get even half its facts about her correct. She had more important things to worry about that day. Like how she was going to get rid of her husband.

It was difficult to know where to begin. This was one field of activity where being famous didn't buy you any favours. How were you supposed to commit the perfect murder if you were a household name?

For a moment, Carmen wondered if she should confide in Juliet – it was she who had given her the idea in the first place, after all. But then Juliet had only been joking, carried away with her talk of detective stories. Real murder was a serious business, and she couldn't take the risk of getting anyone else involved.

But she needed more information. Disguising herself carefully, she set off for the local library to do some research.

Carmen had thought at first that she might get some ideas from fiction – that she might find the inspiration for the perfect murder in a detective story. When she saw the dozens of shelves filled with crime novels, however, she realised that this was scarcely feasible.

She had no idea which ones to look at. Gideon would die of old age before she managed to read them all.

The Health section didn't offer much promise. It was full of books telling you how to stay alive. Glancing through a slim volume on the subject of euthanasia, Carmen learned that it was actually very difficult to kill someone effectively. There were numerous case histories of elderly invalids who had recovered from overdoses of barbiturates and survived attempts at suffocation carried out by impatient heirs.

Feeling somewhat discouraged, Carmen sat down at the computer terminal which gave access to the library catalogue. Checking that nobody was watching over her shoulder, she typed in the word *murder* and hit the search button.

A pair of unsavoury-looking youths who were huddled over the nearby Internet terminal began to stare in her direction. 'Hey,' whispered one of them, nudging his friend. 'Isn't that Carmen Bird over there?'

The other shook his head. 'Nah. Can't be,' he muttered, frowning thoughtfully. 'She's in hospital, ain't she? After that car crash. Didn't you see it in the papers?'

Overhearing this, Carmen smiled to herself. Then a long list of entries flashed up on the screen, directing her to the 'True Crime' shelves. They were hidden away in the 'Government and Law' section, possibly to discourage casual browsing by would-be criminals in search of ideas.

After trawling through endless sensationalist biographies of serial killers, she found exactly what she needed — a whole shelf of DIY murder books. They weren't called that, of course, but masqueraded under serious titles such as *An Advanced Dictionary of Forensic Science*, or *The Criminologist's Guide to Toxicology*. Glancing through their pages, she saw detailed descriptions of a variety of murder methods, including poisoning. *Poison his coffee, or something*. There were even tables showing the quantities required for a lethal dose.

She was about to go to the counter when she realised that it wouldn't look too good to have these titles on her library record, especially if Gideon was soon to expire in suspicious circumstances. Remembering a trick she had learned in her schooldays, she wandered through to the fiction department and picked out a couple of innocuous romances.

'Oops, sorry!' she exclaimed, as the alarm went off at the exit. 'I completely forgot!' Discreetly placing her bulging bag on the floor and sliding it under the barrier with her foot, she presented the librarian with her selection from Mills and Boon.

'Please try to remember in future,' said the woman huffily. 'It upsets the system if you keep setting it off.' Reading the name on Carmen's card, she gave her an unfriendly glare which told her that she couldn't expect special treatment just because she was famous. 'They'll be due back on the 17th,' she added pointedly, brandishing her date stamp. 'There's a fine to pay if you return them late.'

She obviously didn't read the tabloids, thought Carmen, passing through the barrier and retrieving her bag of what was now stolen property. She looked the kind of person who would make extra trips to the dentist so that she could finish the *Hello!* magazines in the waiting room, but who would die rather than admit to an interest in such vulgar matters as the private lives of TV stars.

Back home, Carmen spent the afternoon learning about recent developments in forensic science. Solving a murder was no longer the simple matter of deduction it had been in the time of Sherlock Holmes. The modern police detective could, it seemed, reconstruct the events of a crime with such accuracy that the criminal might just as well have sent him a gift-wrapped home video of the whole thing.

You could hardly walk into a room without leaving a trail of evidence behind you. Everyone knew about fingerprints, but there were a host of other things – dust, hair, dead skin, fibres from your clothing and a variety of bodily secretions – which, to an expert, would confirm your presence as clearly as if you had signed your name on the wall.

The time at which somebody died could be calculated with ease from body temperature, and the effects of rigor mortis and putrefaction. The actual cause of death could be established beyond doubt by an autopsy, and any attempt to tamper with the body was sure to be swiftly found out.

It didn't make encouraging reading. *Do not try this at home*, thought Carmen gloomily, remembering the warnings she had issued on *Jackrabbit* when reporting on any dangerous activity. Perhaps she should forget about murder and simply persuade Gideon to take up skydiving.

Opening another book, Carmen turned to the section on poisoning. The introduction looked daunting with its liberal use of technical terms but, as she read, she decided that this was a far better method. According to the author, a conviction of murder could only be made if it was proved that the person accused had actually administered the fatal dose. Obviously, she couldn't just dump a spoonful of arsenic in Gideon's coffee and expect to get away with it. But if she could find an appropriate substance – something which Gideon, in one of his befuddled states, might accidentally mistake for something else . . .

Cocaine? It was there on the list, in between chloroform and cyanide. It was well known that unscrupulous dealers sometimes mixed it with other things. How she would get her hands on his supply was another problem but, if she had the substitute ready, she could bide her time until the right opportunity came.

What should she use? She needed something which was easily available and looked like cocaine, but how could she find out? She could hardly go down to the local chemist and ask for samples. Glancing out of the window, she remembered Amanda's remark about their garden. It was the time of the year when weeds were beginning to sprout. What could be more natural than to attempt to tidy things up with the aid of some chemical control? Turning back to the book, she made a short-list of substances that were mentioned as being a constituent of weedkiller or pesticide. Arsenic, cyanide, paraquat, phosphorous, strychnine – any of these could do the job if contained in a white powder. It was time to check out the labelling at her local hardware store.

Angie crossed her legs carefully, aware of the dangers of sitting on a bar stool in a short skirt, and looked at her watch. Where the hell was Ronco?

'All right, Ange?' asked the barman, ambling lazily past. Two dark-suited businessmen had appeared at the end of the bar, grinning like schoolboys who had been let out early to play.

'Fine, Trev,' she replied, instinctively patting her hair and turning her head so that her profile would show to its best advantage. Her local pub seemed to be going up in the world, attracting a better class of customer than when she had first moved to the area ten years earlier. Back then, she couldn't have picked up a man like Gideon without making a special trip into the centre of town.

She threw a coy smile towards the end of the bar, but the businessmen were occupied with their drinks and didn't appear to have noticed her. With a frown, she turned back to her newspaper. She might be in semi-retirement these days, but she didn't want to think she was losing her touch.

'MAKEOVER MIX-UP,' said a small heading in the corner of the front page. 'TV STAR ALIVE AND WELL'. There were few people who had been more relieved than Angie to learn this news. Gazing at the familiar article, which she had read several times already, she pondered over the problem that had been occupying her mind for most of the week. How was she going to reap the maximum profit from her discovery that Carmen Bird was Gideon's wife?

Gideon thought she was stupid. Had he really imagined that she would accept his mysterious comings and goings as the actions of a man who had nothing to hide? Angie had played along with the role of dumb bimbo to keep him happy, but she had recognised from the start that Gideon had the haunted eyes of a married man.

A routine search of his wallet while he was sleeping had given her the basic information she needed: his address, his telephone number and his real surname. She hadn't made the connection with the famous name at first, but a few afternoons spent lurking behind a tree in a well-heeled street off Holland Park Avenue had eventually rewarded her with a glimpse of the TV star coming out of the front door. *Carmen Bird!* Angie felt like a small-time pickpocket who had unsuspectingly lifted a winning lottery ticket. All she had to do now was to work out how to cash it in.

Blackmail was the obvious solution. She was sure that Gideon would pay good money to keep his affair secret. Even if he didn't care about his wife finding out, Angie was certain that he wouldn't want the news-papers to get wind of her story. If she followed the few simple steps she had observed in TV thrillers, she could soon be the lucky recipient of a large plain brown envelope bulging with cash.

But there were drawbacks to this approach. Gideon would hardly be likely to keep her on as his mistress.

She would miss out on the free meals, the kinky sex and the kudos of having a good-looking lover. Most importantly, she would have severed the slender thread that connected her, via Gideon, to the glamorous world inhabited by TV stars.

Angie had always dreamed of meeting somebody famous. In her youth, she had spent long evenings hanging around the stage door at rock concerts, missing the actual performance so that she could be first in line for a chance to get close to the star. Her only lasting achievement, however, had been to contract herpes after getting laid by the drummer of an obscure punk band.

She imagined the life Gideon and Carmen must lead, feeding on caviar and sipping champagne at glittering parties as they mingled with household names. Could there be a chance, if she applied pressure to Gideon in the right way, that she might somehow gain entry into their world? Gideon must have plenty of contacts, she thought. Perhaps he could even get her on TV?

She wasn't quite sure how to go about this. It would require delicate handling. But if things went wrong, she reassured herself, she would always have the first option as a fall-back. All she needed was some hard evidence to back her up.

Luckily, this matter was already in hand. At least, she hoped it was. Tipping back the dregs of her brandy and lemonade, she checked her watch again. Where there hell *was* Ronco?

At that moment, a pale moon-like face appeared at the glass panel in the street door.

'Come inside,' she mouthed, beckoning impatiently.

The door opened slowly and Ronco's shambling figure edged its way inside. He was clutching a carrier bag and glancing nervously from side to side, as if he had never been in a pub before.

Ronco had lived in the flat downstairs from Angie for as long as anyone in the building could remember. She had worked out that he must be in his early forties, like she was, but he had a look of plump youthfulness which made it impossible to tell his age from his appearance. There was something peculiar about Ronco — something which Angie didn't care to investigate too closely. Angie wasn't in the business of getting involved with other people's problems.

Unfortunately, she had made the mistake of getting blind drunk with Ronco one night, about a year ago, when her man of the moment had stood her up. Things had led from one to another in their clichéd and predictable way, and Angie had, in a moment of panic-stricken loneliness, allowed Ronco to screw her.

She had never forgotten the look of sheep-like adoration in his eyes when she woke the next morning to find him standing at her bedside with a cup of tea. The next few weeks had been difficult, with Ronco following her everywhere and lying in wait on the stairs every night with proposals of marriage. Eventually, she had managed to explain to him that it wasn't on, that he couldn't be her boyfriend, and that she was going to carry on with her own life and sleep with other men. Surprisingly, he had accepted it all. He had continued, nevertheless, to act as if he was her devoted slave. He had helped her out when she was short of rent money, and had tended her injuries when one of her clients had turned nasty and beaten her up. Ronco, funnily enough, was now the only person Angie felt she could trust.

'Have you got the photographs, then?' she asked eagerly, when he had completed his cautious progress to the bar.

He nodded, holding up his carrier bag. 'I'd like a drink first,' he said slowly.

Angie sighed with impatience, but decided to humour him. He could get himself in a bit of a state when he was flustered and she knew he didn't like to be rushed. Signalling to Trev, she ordered a round of drinks.

She had set things up with Ronco as soon as she found out about Gideon's true identity. Calling in all the favours she could think of, and a few she had invented, she persuaded him to learn how to use her pocket camera and stay at home for a while.

She never knew when Gideon was likely to turn up but, luckily, they didn't have to wait too long. Towards the end of the week, he called round for an afternoon quickie and they swung their plan into action. At the signal of three sharp raps on the bathroom floor, Ronco was to climb the fire escape with her camera. Angie had left the bedroom window slightly open, so that he would be able to reach inside and twitch the net curtains out of the way. As far as she knew, it had all gone according to plan.

Trev placed a half-pint of lager and blackcurrant at Ronco's elbow, then turned with a conspiratorial wink to recharge Angie's glass.

'Have you got them?' she whispered again, scarcely

able to contain her impatience. Waiting as Ronco fumbled with maddening slowness in his carrier bag, she wondered how he had ended up with such a stupid name. Had his mother spent long hours toying with alternatives such as Acme and K-Tel?

Ronco made a low rumbling sound in his throat. With a theatrical flourish, he produced a brightly coloured envelope and laid it on the bar. '*Da daaah!*'

'Shit . . .' Angie drew a sharp breath of annoyance. 'I told you not to take them to Fotorola! I go past there a lot – someone might recognise me.'

'They had a special offer on,' he said apologetically. 'And look, I got you a free film.'

Angie tore open the packet and began to leaf through the pictures. There were several views of the local children's playground and some close-ups of the flowers in somebody's garden. 'What's all this about?' she asked suspiciously, holding up a shot of Ronco pointing the camera into his bathroom mirror.

'I was just finishing up the film,' he muttered, embarrassed. 'I meant to take those ones out.'

Eventually, she came to the pictures she was interested in. 'Blimey!' she gasped, staring at a candid shot of Gideon straddling her naked bottom. 'I didn't mean you to get that close!'

'You said you wanted them dirty,' sniggered Ronco, blushing.

'I didn't tell you to climb in through the bloody window,' she spluttered, turning to another which showed Gideon mounting a frontal assault. 'How on earth did you do manage this without us seeing you?'

'I go badger watching sometimes,' he admitted shyly. 'It's not that different really. Except that people aren't as sensitive as badgers. They don't notice you when you move slowly.'

Angie blinked with surprise. It was the most sophisticated thought she had ever heard Ronco express. Then she smiled and let out a sigh of satisfaction. He had done a far better job than she had expected. She would have preferred to see herself in some slightly more dignified positions, but these photographs were going to mark a change in her fortunes.

'Things are looking up,' she told Ronco, sliding from her bar stool. 'I'll see you around.'

'Are you going already?' His pale features melted into an expression of disappointment. 'I haven't even finished my drink.'

'Must dash,' said Angie breezily, heading for the door. Soon, she told herself, she would no longer have to depend on the society of weirdos. If things went the way she wanted, she would be able to choose her friends from the TV guide.

Gideon's telephone number was smouldering in her pocket. She wasn't yet ready to reveal her intentions. That would require some careful planning. But there was no harm in dialling the number. She hoped it wouldn't be Gideon who answered, but his wife. She wanted to hear her voice – the voice of the woman who had everything. Who knows, thought Angie. Perhaps we could even become friends.

* * *

As Carmen stood in the hardware shop and glanced through the instructions on a packet of *Weedogone*, she became aware of a presence at her elbow.

'Good afternoon, Mrs Bird,' said an unctuous voice. 'How refreshing to learn that our local celebrities aren't above tending their own plots.'

Turning guiltily, she found herself facing a bald-headed man in a brown overall. 'Perhaps I can be of some assistance?' he suggested, peering at her through the dusty lenses of his horn-rimmed glasses.

'I was, er . . . just looking.'

'Dear, dear,' he murmured, taking the packet from Carmen's hand and examining it with a frown. 'I don't think you'll find this very effective.' He let out a little laugh. 'Unless you're fond of couch grass, of course.' Replacing the offending product on the shelf, he blocked her exit from the narrow aisle and regarded her with the supercilious gaze of an expert. 'Perhaps the first question we should ask,' he said, 'is whether we are mounting our hostilities against annual or perennial weeds?'

'I, um . . . don't really know.'

'Oh dear,' he sighed. 'This could be a problem. It wouldn't do if we were to let our prize dahlias become the victims of friendly fire.' He rubbed his hand over the shiny dome of his head, as if polishing it. 'Perhaps you could describe them? It always helps to know your enemy in cases like this.'

About six foot tall with a moustache, thought Carmen. 'They're kind of big and green,' she said.

'Aaah,' he said knowingly, unwilling to admit defeat. His face took on a thoughtful expression. 'I think, in the circumstances, we might try a post-emergent herbicide with translocating properties,' he said eventually. 'Do you have an applicator?'

This was getting too personal, thought Carmen irritably. If she went to the chemist for tampons, she didn't expect to be grilled about her menstrual cycle or whether the size she had chosen would fit.

'Look, I think I'll just leave it for now,' she said, backing away. As she left the shop she saw him pounce on an elderly woman who was examining a packet of flower seeds.

'I wouldn't expect too much from those, madam,' she heard him say in a gloomy voice. 'Not unless you have a calciferous soil with good drainage and an exceptionally high nitrogen content . . .'

Outside, Carmen hailed a taxi and asked to be taken to the nearest DIY superstore. It had been a mistake to go to a small local shop, she told herself reproachfully. She needed to make her purchases in a more impersonal place where nobody would remember her.

The superstore seemed to fulfil these requirements admirably. Entering the cavernous space, she felt strangely light-headed, as if a massive dose of tranquillisers had been pumped into her veins. After a few moments, she realised that it was the effect of the piped music. Other shoppers passed her with glazed expressions, their feet moving in time with the slow, but compulsive rhythm as they pushed their trolleys through the wide aisles.

Feeling like an extra in a Sixties' film, Carmen wandered in search of the gardening section. She was soon lost in an endless corridor of lurid wallpaper samples and ghastly lampshades, and began to wonder if she could simply frighten Gideon to death by redecorating the house. Eventually, scenting the acrid smell of gardening products, she turned a corner and found herself in fairyland. A half-timbered wishing well stood on a hillock of Astroturf, flanked by clusters of garden gnomes. It looked like a stage set for an amateur production of *Snow White and the Seven Dwarfs*.

The serious products were kept on the higher shelves against the back wall, out of the reach of marauding gnomes. A notice hung over the section for weedkillers and pesticides: *Our policy is only to stock products that are environmentally friendly and safe for use in households with children and pets.*

Carmen inspected a number of preparations that invited her to *Take the Organic Challenge*, promising that they would *gently eliminate unwanted weeds the safe and natural way*. A note at the bottom of one of the labels warned her that it *could take up to four weeks for death to occur*, and that *repeat applications may be necessary*. If it was that difficult to kill a weed, she wondered, how much of the stuff would it take to finish off a fully grown man? Glancing at the price tag, she concluded that the whole thing was a clever marketing strategy to make people spend twice as much money on something that was only half as effective.

Eventually, she selected a large packet of *Weedogone* and headed for the checkout. To avoid drawing attention to her purchase, she picked up an assortment of other items on the way.

At the till, the bar code reader got stuck.

'Eileen!' bellowed the checkout girl. 'What's the code for *Weedogone*?'

'It doesn't matter,' said Carmen, panicking. 'I'll leave it.'

'That's *W-e-e-d-o* . . .' The girl paused, frowning, as a flicker of recognition came into her eyes. 'Hey, aren't you . . .'

'No, I'm not,' muttered Carmen in embarrassment, pushing the remaining items forward on the counter. 'And I'll leave it. I'll just take these.'

'Suit yourself,' said the girl, shrugging as she began looking up codes for a selection of purchases that Carmen didn't even want.

Returning to Holland Park in another taxi, Carmen had to admit that her shopping expedition had been a failure. How was she going to murder her husband with a pair of gardening gloves, a make-your-own hanging basket kit, and a set of 'Victorian-style' plant labels that came in a blister pack with a free trowel?

Back home, it occurred to Carmen that there were probably plenty of poisonous substances in the house already. Surely the elusive white powder she needed could be found somewhere in the medicine cabinet or the kitchen cupboard?

Half way through an inventory of the cleaning products under the sink, she picked up a bottle festooned with orange warning labels. Drain cleaner. Unscrewing the lid, she sniffed experimentally at the contents. A sharp smell penetrated her nostrils, causing a burning sensation inside her head. Her eyes began to water. *What am I doing?* she thought. For the first time, she considered the actual consequences of poisoning – imagining the pain as the caustic liquid ate its way through living tissue. *How could I inflict this on another human being?* she asked herself.

But Gideon wasn't a human being, he was a monster. Contemplating the bleak horror of their life together, she was overwhelmed with misery. What other choices did she have? Leaning against the draining board, she began to cry – softly at first, but then releasing the pressure on her emotions with sobbing howls of anguish. The bottle of drain cleaner slipped from her fingers and fell to the floor, quietly gurgling its contents over the smart linoleum tiles.

When Gideon returned an hour later, Carmen was on her hands and knees with a bucket of water and a scrubbing brush. She had recovered her sense of purpose and was struggling to remove the discolouration caused by her research.

'You're looking at a winner, baby,' he announced in a slurred voice. 'Crispin Scrope's promised me a meeting with the main man at the agency. The *Flux* commercial's as good as in the bag.'

Pushing *The Toxicologist's Handbook* out of sight under the cooker, Carmen stood up and wiped her hands. 'That's great,' she said cautiously, smelling the whisky on his breath. Gideon didn't usually volunteer details of his business affairs unless he wanted something in return.

'I had to invite him to dinner,' he added casually.

'With his girlfriend Elvira. You don't mind rustling up a little something for Saturday, do you?'

Carmen was about to tell him that she had better things to do than entertain his sleazy bar-room acquaintances, when it struck her that a dinner party was one of the few occasions when Gideon was likely to eat whatever she put in front of him without complaint. She had been put off the idea of using chemicals, but further reading had suggested that more 'natural' methods would be harder to detect.

'What sort of food did you have in mind?' she asked in an ingenuous voice. 'They're not vegetarians, are they?' Rabbit meat could sometimes cause poisoning, according to the book, if the animal had eaten deadly nightshade. Quail were known to feed on hemlock seeds.

Gideon looked at her with surprise, as if he had expected more opposition. 'Good God, no,' he said. 'Crispin's as carnivorous as they come.' He let out a menacing chuckle. 'Crispin likes his meat rare. He'd probably eat it straight off the cow if you gave him the chance.'

Carmen briefly pictured herself bribing a backstreet butcher to sell her a carcase riddled with CJD. Then she reminded herself that she was only trying to get rid of one person, not three. No matter which poison she chose, it was bound to look suspicious if only one of the portions was contaminated.

'I need some coffee,' grumbled Gideon, lurching unsteadily across the kitchen. Picking up the kettle, he turned and tripped over the bucket of water. 'You stupid bitch!' he roared, kicking the scrubbing brush across the room. 'I'm soaked! Don't you know it's dangerous to leave stuff lying around like this?'

Carmen stared at the scene in front of her. It was just like one of the pictures you get in books about safety in the home – the scene showing you the things you *must never* do. She looked at the pool of water on the floor, at Gideon's wet feet, and at the frayed cord on the electric kettle. You could almost see the arrows in the diagram marking the route the current would take through his body to reach the earth.

Forget poisoning, she told herself. This was so much easier. Holding her breath, she willed him to plug the kettle into the socket.

He stood there for a moment, apparently lost in thought. Then he banged the kettle down on the worksurface and reached for the whisky bottle instead. Carmen tensed in preparation for a blow.

But the blow didn't come. Slumping into a chair, Gideon began to remove his wet shoes and socks. 'We should invite some other people as well,' he said. 'Pull out the stops and make a party of it – Crispin likes to have a good time.'

Realising that he was too preoccupied by his courtship of the bloodthirsty Mr Scrope to bother with her, Carmen fetched a mop and cautiously began to clear up the mess. People got drunk at parties, she thought. Sometimes, they became careless and did stupid things. That was how accidents happened. Opening a cupboard, she inspected the armoury of electrical gadgets which Gideon had brought home over the years. Coffee and spice grinders, food whisks and blenders, a mincing machine, an electric carving knife. These things only ever got used when they had company – when Gideon wanted to show off his culinary prowess to his friends.

'Who else do you want to invite, then?' she asked, wondering if there was anyone left who hadn't been alienated by Gideon's offensive behaviour. There would be no harm in having a few reliable witnesses around.

'I don't know,' he muttered, taking a swig of whisky from the bottle. 'We don't want anybody too pushy who might steal Crispin's thunder.' He gave her a belligerent stare. 'Can't *you* think of someone, for Christ's sake?'

Carmen felt like pointing out that he had insulted and driven away every single person she had ever known but, instead, bit her lip and waited. Any suggestion that came from her was sure to be shot down in flames.

Eventually Gideon spoke again, his mouth curling into a sneer. 'What about that friend of yours from the other day? You know, the ugly one with the bad hair.'

'You mean Juliet?' asked Carmen quietly, hardly daring to believe her luck. Juliet would be the ideal accomplice for what she had in mind.

'*Juliet?*' Gideon laughed maliciously. 'Is that her name? I'd have thought Lassie was more appropriate.' He took another swig from the bottle. 'She'll do,' he said decisively. You two can play at coffee mornings and keep out of trouble while I concentrate on my business with Crispin and Elvira. I don't want you poking your nose in and screwing up this deal for me.'

'Fine, I'll ring and ask her,' snapped Carmen, struggling to control her temper. Parking her mop in the bucket, she left the room quickly before he could change his mind.

Juliet switched off the television and checked her watch. Time to get ready. The promised trip to the cinema with Duncan had finally evolved into a firm date and he had even suggested taking her for a meal beforehand. She knew it was more likely to be a quick snack at the local fast food joint than a candlelit dinner in intimate surroundings, but she didn't mind. Now that Duncan had confided that Sonia was out of the picture, she felt that the chances of progressing their relationship were greatly improved.

She had just watched *Makeover* for the first time. As the ugly ducklings were transformed, with a wave of Carmen Bird's magic wand, into glamorous and worldly looking swans, Juliet had felt a stab of insecurity. Had Carmen been right, after all? Was this what she needed if she wanted Duncan to see her as a woman rather than just a friend?

Carmen's behaviour the previous weekend had left Juliet thoroughly confused. After listening for over an hour while the TV star poured out the horrific story of her marriage, Juliet had looked forward to sharing her own problems – to confiding in someone about her feelings for Duncan. But she had been disappointed. When Carmen returned from her argument with Gideon, her manner had changed. She seemed to have made the assumption that Juliet was only being friendly because she wanted to get herself on TV.

Juliet felt that she would rather die than submit herself to the public humiliation of appearing on a programme like *Makeover*. She wanted people to accept her the way she was. Why should she have to paint expensive muck all over her face to win their approval? Why should she be expected to throw out her comfortable clothes and parade herself in short skirts and high heels? Appearances weren't everything, she told herself. Carmen Bird might look like a fashion model, but Juliet now knew that the glossy image was a lie. The insincerity of her TV smile only served to emphasise the difference between the public persona and the unhappy woman inside.

With a pang of guilt, it occurred to Juliet that Carmen's confession had probably been a cry for help. But what could she have done? Uneasily, she remembered her joke about disposing of troublesome spouses by poisoning their coffee – hardly the most tactful remark in the circumstances. It wasn't really surprising that Carmen hadn't called her again.

Pushing these thoughts of her social inadequacies to the back of her mind, she faced herself in the bathroom mirror. What she really needed wasn't a concealing layer of makeup, but an injection of self-confidence to drive away her uncertainty and bring out the happier person she knew was inside. All this pining over Duncan, she told herself, was doing her no good.

When she had cleaned her teeth and brushed her hair,

she went back into the living room to pour herself a glass of wine. Why was she keeping up this charade of not caring? Why didn't she just come out with it and tell him how she felt?

The possibility of rejection was terrifying. Could she risk losing the one friend she had in London? Filling her glass to the brim, she took a large gulp. Was it such a terrible crime to love someone more than they loved you?

By the third glass of wine, she had made up her mind. She was tired of playing games and this was a rare opportunity to catch Duncan between girlfriends. She needed to do something to win back her self-respect. If he didn't return her feelings, she would just have to learn to live with it. The sooner she got it over with, the sooner she could pick up the pieces and get on with her life.

She had reached this same decision on a number of occasions in the past, but she had never had the courage to follow it through. This time, she resolved, it was going to be different. She wasn't going to allow herself to chicken out.

The issue, she decided, was best confronted over dinner. That way, if they needed more time to talk, or whatever, they would have the option of postponing the film until another day. *Or whatever*. With a shiver of anticipation, she checked to make sure that the sheets on the bed were clean, and that her secret supply of condoms was still in its hiding place. The odds might not be in her favour, she told herself, but there was no harm in being prepared.

She was opening a second bottle of wine when the doorbell rang. Duncan was waiting on the step outside surrounded by a haze of savoury smells.

'I thought we'd eat in,' he said, holding up a plastic carrier bag from the Hammersmith Tandoori with a grin. 'I hope you fancy a curry.'

Juliet didn't, but she consoled herself with the thought that it would be much more intimate than going out. 'We'd better go upstairs then,' she said with a smile. 'I'll find us some plates and things.'

She was juggling the hot cartons of food in the kitchen when the telephone rang downstairs. After several rings, it became apparent that nobody else was going to answer it. 'Duncan,' she called, unwilling to let him take over and make a mess. 'Could you get the phone?'

While he was gone, she arranged cushions on the floor and lit some candles. Expecting him to return at any moment, she laid out the plates of food on the coffee table and poured two glasses of wine.

After about five minutes, she felt a stirring of irritation. It was typical of Duncan to get into a long conversation with some stranger. Why couldn't he just take a message like anyone else? Opening the door, she went to the top of the stairs and leaned over the balustrade. The sound of his voice drifted up, chattering away in animated tones.

'I'll have to check my diary,' he was saying. 'But I'm sure Saturday night will be fine.'

How dare he give her telephone number to some girlfriend? Finishing her wine with a gulp, she refilled her glass. It had better not be that bloody Sonia, she thought angrily. She had already caused more than enough heartache for both of them.

When Juliet finally heard him returning up the stairs, nearly an hour had passed. The food was cold and the wine bottle was empty.

Duncan burst into the room, his face flushed. 'Hey, Jules!' he began excitedly. 'You'll never guess . . .'

'We've missed the film,' said Juliet, stony faced. She was by now too drunk to have watched it anyway, but that wasn't the point.

'I'm sorry, Jules,' he said, looking embarrassed. 'I should have called you down, but . . .'

'But what? Who the hell have you been talking to all this time?'

'I was trying to tell you,' he said in a flustered voice. 'It was for you really, it was Carmen Bird! She wanted to ask you to dinner!' He swung his arms back and forth, unable to suppress his excitement. 'We kind of got talking, and she ended up inviting me as well! Isn't that great?'

'Great,' said Juliet. The sarcasm in her voice was lost on Duncan. A small part of her was secretly delighted that Carmen had apparently decided to give her a second chance, but she wasn't going to let him see it after the way he had behaved. Her plans for the evening forgotten, she faced him with an angry glare.

'I can hardly believe it,' he continued enthusiastically. 'She's my absolutely favourite TV star!' He sat down and reached across the table towards her. 'Hey Jules?' he asked dreamily, breaking off a cold piece of bhaji and popping it into his mouth. 'Do you think she fancies me?'

Juliet struggled to retain her self-control and failed. 'How dare you!' she exploded. 'How dare you interfere with my private telephone calls and accept invitations on my behalf?'

Duncan stood up and backed away from the table in alarm. 'I'm sorry,' he mumbled, struggling with a mouthful of food. 'I didn't mean to . . .'

'Didn't mean to leave me waiting here for hours while you were busy organising your next seduction?' Juliet swayed unsteadily to her feet and pointed her finger at the door. 'Get out!'

'But Jules . . .' Duncan stared at her wide-eyed. 'We're friends, aren't we? I thought you'd be pleased . . .'

'But I don't want to be your *friend* . . .' Juliet clenched her hands in frustration, unable to finish what she really wanted to say.

'Well, if that's how you feel . . .' With a hurt expression, Duncan stalked out of the room.

Juliet held her breath as she heard him descending the stairs. Surely he wasn't really going to leave? But the front door slammed shut behind him and his departing footsteps echoed in the street outside.

Throwing herself on the bed, she burst into tears. 'Oh, please come back,' she sobbed into the pillow she had hoped might be a resting place for Duncan's head. 'Can't you see I didn't mean it like that?'

Why was it, she asked herself bleakly, that men never understood that you sometimes meant the opposite of what you actually said?

CHAPTER 6

It was six o'clock on Saturday evening. While Gideon was at the off-licence replenishing the alcohol supplies, Carmen was making the final preparations for their dinner party. The beef was in the roasting tray, ready to go in the oven, and all the vegetables had been peeled and chopped. Taking a screwdriver, she opened the back of the plug on the electric carving knife and examined the neatly arranged wires. She had spent the last few days in a dream-like state, repeatedly running over her plans in her mind and carefully avoiding any thoughts that might weaken her resolve.

'Blue for neutral, brown for live,' she murmured to herself. 'Yellow and green stripes for earth.' Loosening a tiny brass screw, she pulled out the striped wire and tucked it to one side. Carmen knew very little about electricity, but she had studied a list in a DIY manual that warned you of all the things you mustn't do. This was one of them. Replacing the cover on the plug, she took the whole implement and immersed it in a bowl of water. This was another.

When the bubbles had stopped rising to the surface, she lifted out the knife and gave it a good shake. Then she carefully dried the outer casing and placed it on the breakfast counter. Humming softly to herself, she returned to the sink and began to wash a lettuce. The DIY book recommended regular safety checks for kitchen appliances. Wiring could easily get damaged. Electrical contacts could become damp in a steamy atmosphere. If Gideon couldn't be bothered with a few simple precautions, she told herself, it would be just as much his fault as hers if something went wrong.

On the rare occasions when they had company, Gideon always made a fuss about the ritual of carving the joint. The electric knife was one of his favourite toys. Not content to wield a sharpened Sabatier like everybody else, Gideon liked to assert his status by presiding over the dinner table with the domestic equivalent of a chainsaw. Sometimes, when he had been drinking, he was like a demented circus performer. You could almost hear a roll of drums as he embarked on cutting each slice.

The front door rattled, announcing his return, and she heard the clink of bottles in the hallway. 'Don't put the joint in the oven too early,' he said, poking his head through the kitchen door. 'I want it to be nice and rare – so that it's still bloody in the centre. Crispin's something of a gourmet, I'll have you know. He doesn't hold with any of this nonsense about mad cow disease.'

Crispin Scrope would be no different from the others

Gideon had brought home – dissipated Soho has-beens, like himself, who clung to fading media careers and held out promises of favours they rarely had the power to bestow. One thing was certain, thought Carmen blackly. He would have plenty to gossip about in his drinking clubs next week. When Gideon carved the joint tonight, he would give the performance of his life. It would be electrifying.

Carmen was still in the kitchen when the guests began to arrive. Juliet and Duncan came first, precipitating a minor crisis.

'Who the hell's this bloke?' hissed Gideon, appearing at her elbow as she lifted the roasting tray into the oven. 'I didn't tell you to invite anyone else. Is this your idea of a joke?'

'She asked if she could bring her boyfriend,' lied Carmen, dropping her voice to a whisper. The last-minute invitation she had made to Duncan on the telephone had completely slipped her mind. 'Keep your voice down, they'll hear you.'

'I don't care what they hear! I'm not having some jerk poking his nose into my business discussions with Crispin . . .'

'Is anyone there?' Juliet's voice interrupted them from the hallway.

'We're in the kitchen,' called Carmen, wiping her hands on her apron. 'Do come through.'

Juliet wasn't looking her best. Her face remained defiantly bare of make-up and she was wearing clothes that were, in Carmen's view, more suited to a walk in the country than a dinner party. Glancing warily

at Gideon, who was pouring himself a large whisky,
Juliet crossed the room and handed Carmen a wrapped
bottle. 'We've brought some wine,' she said shyly. 'I
hope we're not late.'

'Hello there!' Duncan breezed into the kitchen with a
cheerful smile. Reaching inside his jacket, he produced
a small bunch of flowers. 'For our charming hostess,'
he said, presenting them to Carmen with a flourish.
Before she could stop him, he leaned forward and
kissed her on both cheeks in full view of Gideon. 'You
look divine!'

There'll be hell to pay for this afterwards, thought
Carmen, flinching as she caught sight of her husband's
outraged expression. Then she remembered that there
wasn't going to be any 'afterwards' as far as Gideon was
concerned. Not ever again. Staring at the carving knife
on the counter, she felt her stomach lurch queasily.
Was she really going to have the strength to carry this
through?

The doorbell rang. Shooting Carmen a venomous
look, Gideon hurried out to greet his friends.

'Dinner smells good,' said Duncan, sniffing like a
character in a gravy commercial. 'What is it?'

'I hope you're not a vegetarian, or anything,' said
Carmen apologetically. 'It's beef.'

'Not me,' he replied with a laugh. 'I'll eat anything!'
Glancing sideways at Juliet, he gave her a conspiratorial
nudge. 'As long as it's not curry, eh? I always seem to
get into a fight when I have Indian food.'

Voices echoed in the hallway. 'Come in here, darling,'
called Gideon, his manner abruptly transformed to one

of genial bonhomie. 'Crispin and Elvira are dying to meet you. Bring the others with you and I'll pour us all drinks in the front room.'

Crispin Scrope looked like a middle-aged public schoolboy. He wore white trousers and a navy-blue blazer with gold buttons that strained to cover his generous paunch. His sleek features glowed in testimony to a pampered life and the redness of his facial extremities betrayed his dedication to the fruits of the vine. His girlfriend, Elvira, appeared wraith-like beside him, as if he had sucked all the goodness out of her and added it to his own. The whiteness of her face was emphasised by pale makeup, and her slender figure was sheathed in a tight black dress. Her only concession to colour was in her scarlet lipstick, which fought a closely run competition for brightness with Crispin's nose.

Handing round glasses of wine, Gideon made an elaborate fuss of introducing Carmen. Then, pointedly ignoring Juliet and Duncan, he turned to Crispin and launched into television talk. They began to discuss the production values of *D for Dogberry*, comparing various sequences with long-forgotten episodes of *Mangus*. Elvira appeared to be listening with rapt interest, but Carmen could see her eyes wandering inquisitively around the room. Duncan gazed in fascination at Elvira. Juliet, standing slightly apart, directed hostile glances towards them both.

Gideon moved on to outline his ideas for a new series of *Mangus*. Crispin listened impassively, slurping his wine. 'It's no more than a proposal at present, of course,' concluded Gideon modestly, refilling Crispin's glass. 'But with the *Flux* commercial behind me, who knows?'

Crispin let out a short, braying laugh. 'Ah yes, that *Flux* business. Weren't we talking about that the other day?'

'I was hoping we could discuss it later,' murmured Gideon. 'That meeting you were going to set up . . .'

'I did make a few inquiries,' said Crispin in a casual tone. 'I can't make any firm promises, of course, but my contact tells me that the field's still wide open. They're still trying to get agreement on the concept for the new campaign.'

'*Flux*? Is that the chocolate bar?' Duncan roused himself from his reverie. 'I thought they were shooting the commercial right now. I went to an audition for it only the other day.'

'What did you say?' Gideon stared at him with a horrified expression, publicly acknowledging his existence for the first time.

'I think you must have your facts wrong somewhere, young man,' said Crispin smoothly. 'There are quite a few different chocolate bars around. I expect you've got the names mixed up.' He turned back to Gideon. 'Let's leave the business for later, old boy. I wanted to tell you all about this wonderful new restaurant I've found . . .'

'But I'm sure it was *Flux*,' protested Duncan. 'It was the one with the raisins and . . .'

'Are you an *actor*, then?' interrupted Elvira. Her voice was deep and syrupy, sounding as if it couldn't possibly emanate from somebody so thin. '*Do* tell me all about your work. Should we have *heard* of you?'

'I had the most marvellous *goujons* of wild salmon, each one wrapped up in a tiny parcel of filo pastry,' continued Crispin. 'One of my friends in the business tells me they poached the chef from a place in Burgundy with *three* Michelin stars.'

Carmen, who had been listening in a kind of daze, suddenly remembered that she was supposed to be producing food. 'Shall we sit down,' she said, indicating the table by the window laid with six place settings. 'I'll go and fetch the first course.' Pausing in the doorway, she glanced back at Crispin. 'I hope you don't mind prawn cocktail.'

'Carmen doesn't cook very often,' said Gideon with a patronising laugh. 'She's too busy being a famous TV star.'

In the kitchen, Carmen struggled to open a jar of *rose-marie* sauce. When she was first married, she had dreamt of hosting elegant dinner parties, of creating gourmet menus for select gatherings of famous names. In reality, however, she found that she lacked both the time and the inclination to spend long hours slaving in the kitchen. Even if Gideon had been different, she doubted whether her culinary skills would have progressed much beyond their present basic level. People expected too much, she thought irritably. Besides, how were you supposed to murder your husband and produce perfect *filo parcels* at the same time?

Six bowls were lined up on the counter, each containing a bed of soggy lettuce and a small heap of peeled prawns. It had only occurred to her late in the afternoon that more than one course was needed for a dinner party. She could dispense with the dessert – the guests were hardly likely to be screaming for cheesecake and gâteau with Gideon's body slumped over the table – but some kind of *hors-d'oeuvres* were certainly required.

She had been lucky to find the prawns in the freezer. Spooning out sauce in untidy dollops, she wondered if she should have come up with something more filling. Not only was dessert off the menu, but there was also very little prospect of anyone getting a chance to begin the main course.

'Are you OK, Carmen?' She started, hearing Juliet's voice behind her. 'Do you need any help?'

'I'm fine,' she replied abstractedly. She tugged open a second packet of prawns, this time still in their shells. Tiny crystals of ice skittered across the worksurface and melted into little pools.

Juliet gave her an anxious look. 'Are you sure?' She glanced towards the doorway. 'He hasn't been, um . . . you know . . . hurting you again, has he?'

Carmen shook her head. 'I'm all right, really,' she said, hooking prawns over the rim of each bowl. She looked up, smiling for Juliet's benefit. 'Don't worry, I've got everything under control.'

Better than you imagine, she thought, counting the prawns to check that they were evenly distributed. Part of her longed to share her plans with Juliet, but she knew it would be much safer to keep them to herself. She had an instinct that Juliet would know how to behave when the crisis came.

'Hey, this looks like a dangerous weapon,' said Juliet with a laugh. Leaning over the counter, she picked up the electric carving knife and fingered the blade. 'How does it work?'

'Put that down!' shrieked Carmen, dropping a bowl of prawns with a crash. 'Sorry,' she added, seeing Juliet's startled expression. 'I didn't want you to cut yourself. It's very sharp.'

'For Christ's sake,' snapped Gideon, appearing at the door. 'What's going on in here? Where's the bloody food?'

Carmen scraped up the prawns and dressing from the kitchen floor and reassembled them in another bowl. Juliet helped her take the things through to the front room, which resulted, quite by chance, in the dishes being rearranged so that the mismatched portion ended up in front of Elvira.

Duncan was talking about his recent role in *The White Devil*. Suppressing a yawn, Elvira glanced across at Crispin, who was deep in a name-dropping session with Gideon and didn't respond until she made a sharp movement under the table with her foot.

'Have you told Gideon about our trip to Paris?' she murmured, dipping her spoon into her bowl.

'What did you say?' Crispin paused, rubbing his leg with a frown. 'Oh yes, I was just coming to that.' He looked round the table to make sure that everyone was listening. 'Elvira's in television, too,' he announced with a note of pride in his voice. 'She works as a free-lance researcher and presenter. She's putting together a documentary about famous graveyards at the moment.'

'That sounds interesting . . .' began Juliet.

'I've been joining her on her travels,' he continued with a broad grin. 'Tax-deductible expenses and all that. We were in Paris last month, checking out locations.'

'The programme's called *Bleeding Stones*,' explained Elvira, sliding a spoonful of prawns through the bright red opening of her mouth. 'We're going to film a large part of it in Père Lachaise.'

'Such a lovely cemetery,' murmured Crispin, depositing a rigidly frozen king prawn on his side-plate with a clunk. 'We had a wonderful picnic there, right next to Oscar Wilde's tomb. Freshly baked *croissants, saucisson à l'ail, fromage de chèvre*. And a rather memorable bottle of Pouilly-Fuissé.'

'We even poured a glass for Oscar,' added Elvira solemnly.

'What did you do with it?' asked Gideon. 'Chuck it over the headstone?'

'Good God, no,' said Crispin with a shudder. 'I drank it for him. No sense in wasting a good vintage.'

'Do you know a lot about wine, then?' asked Carmen, hoping to steer them away from the subject of graveyards. She was uncomfortably aware that she would soon have to be making funeral arrangements herself. The knife in the kitchen kept pushing its way to the forefront of her thoughts, weighing her down with guilt. Would she be haunted by this feeling, she wondered, for the rest of her life?

'I know enough to get by,' replied Crispin with a hearty laugh, holding out his glass for a refill. 'Now when we did Highgate Cemetery last week, for example, we had the most delicious, full-bodied Barolo, which simply had to be given enough time to breathe. It was a touch on the cold side going round some of those vaults, so I opened the bottle, wrapped it in my jumper, and hid it in the bushes behind the Rossetti headstones. By the time we were ready for lunch, it was perfectly *chambré*!'

'And, the Egyptian necropolis was so *atmospheric*,' said Elvira in a dramatic tone. 'I'm just *fascinated* by the culture surrounding death.' Chewing thoughtfully, she picked a piece of grit from her tongue. 'These prawns have remarkable flavour,' she added, turning to Carmen. 'You must let me know where you get them. The ones from our local shop always taste like blotting paper.'

'Isn't Highgate where the victims of Jack the Ripper are buried?' asked Juliet, making another attempt to join in the conversation.

'We found this marvellous little Italian delicatessen in Highgate Village,' continued Crispin, ignoring her, 'where we picked up *prosciutto di Parma, mozzarella di bufalo* and a whole bagful of their home-made *bruschetta al pomodoro*.'

'I suppose you'll be mentioning the grave of Karl Marx,' said Duncan, trying to regain Elvira's attention. 'He's buried in Highgate, isn't he?'

'Oh, we won't be bothering with any of those boring political types,' said Elvira dismissively. 'This is going to be an *arts* programme. Besides, his grave is on the eastern side. Only the *tourists* go there.'

'You must tell them about the exploding coffins, darling,' said Crispin, grinning. He nudged Gideon. 'You'll like this bit.'

'When above-ground burial came into vogue with the Victorians,' pronounced Elvira in the emphatic tones of a TV presenter, 'regulations stipulated that the caskets had to be encased in lead. As the bodies began to decay, the build-up of noxious gases caused the lead to expand and . . .'

'Bang!' said Crispin, waving his arms graphically. 'Just like that scene in *Mangus* where they had the big shoot-out at the funeral.'

'The problem was solved by drilling small holes in the coffins and inserting . . .'

'I was thinking of that scene only the other day,' murmured Gideon thoughtfully. 'How I could do a Tarantino-style, Nineties' take on it.' He turned to Elvira, interrupting her discourse. 'This sounds like my kind of graveyard, honey. What do you have to do to get in?'

'Die, of course!' roared Crispin, slapping his thigh.

Carmen shuddered. It was all starting to feel like a bad dream. Did they somehow *know* what she was planning?

'I think you'll find that the permanent residencies are fully subscribed,' said Elvira, with a prim smile. 'But if you were just thinking of making a visit, I could give you the number for the guided tour.'

Carmen stood up and began to collect the empty dishes with trembling hands. The spectre of the knife loomed in her imagination, mocking her.

'When *I* die,' continued Elvira, 'I want to be buried in a glass casket, dressed entirely in white.'

'I think I'd rather be cremated . . .' began Crispin.

Elvira interrupted with a tinkling laugh. 'In a traditional, wood-fired pizza oven, no doubt, if you had your own way.'

'Good God, darling!' Crispin looked shocked. 'How unspeakably common. I was thinking more along the lines of being flambéed in brandy at the Savoy Grill.'

'I want a green funeral,' said Duncan. 'With a cardboard coffin. It's a lot cheaper, and you make virtually no impact on your surroundings.'

'Why do things any differently just because you're dead?' muttered Gideon in a low voice.

'What about you, Carmen?' asked Duncan, not hearing him. 'What do you want to happen to *your* body?'

The room fell silent as everyone waited for her answer. 'I . . . I don't know,' she whispered. 'I've never really thought about it.' But she was thinking about it now. A feeling of horror began to grow inside her as she realised how much she herself was frightened of death.

'She'll probably live forever,' said Gideon bitterly. 'She's much too famous to get old and die.'

Carmen turned and stared at him, wide-eyed. It was as if she had noticed his presence at the table for the first time. Gradually, with the sensation of waking from a dream, she recognised the enormity of the crime she was about to commit. However much she despised him, Gideon was still a living, breathing human being, like herself. How could she dispatch him to an oblivion whose terrors she couldn't even begin to contemplate? Death was forever – there would be no second chances, no room for forgiveness. How could she face up to the consequences of such a terrible deed?

'Have you ever made love on a tombstone?' asked Elvira unexpectedly, addressing nobody in particular. 'When we were at Kensal Green the other day . . .'

Leaving the plates on the table, Carmen fled into the kitchen. She clutched the edge of the sink for support and began to retch violently. What had possessed her to think that she was the kind of person who could carry out cold-blooded murder? Fighting back waves of nausea, she looked round for the knife. Where was it? She had to get rid of it before anyone found out what she had done.

A thin plume of smoke was rising from the edge of the oven door. Shifting her gaze to the control dial, Carmen saw that she had forgotten to make the necessary adjustments after pre-heating. The oven temperature was still set to maximum. With a whimper of alarm, she snatched up a handful of tea towels, threw open the oven door and pulled out the roasting tray. Acrid smoke billowed into the kitchen, accompanied by a frantic sizzling of fat.

'What's that smell of burning?' Carmen trembled as she heard Gideon's footsteps quickening in the hall. 'Christ Almighty!' he exploded, rushing through the door. 'What in hell's name have you done with that beef?'

'I don't know how it could have happened,' she

faltered, peering at the blackened joint. 'There must be something wrong with the oven.'

'I don't know what's wrong with you tonight,' he hissed. 'Are you deliberately trying to make a fool of me in front of Crispin?'

'I'm sorry,' she mumbled, backing away in alarm as she caught sight of the thunderous look on Gideon's face. 'I've got some chops in the freezer. They wouldn't take long to cook.'

'Serve frozen chops to Crispin Scrope?' said Gideon scornfully. 'Over my dead body, you will!' Picking up a large fork, he poked it experimentally into the joint. 'Leave this to me,' he muttered. 'It might not be as bad as it looks.'

They both watched as a trickle of blood ran from the puncture. 'It seems to be all right,' he said in a relieved tone. 'It's only burnt on the surface. I can serve those bits to your friends.' Hefting the joint onto the serving dish, he carried it towards the door.

To her horror, Carmen saw him pause at the counter and pick up the electric knife. 'But Gideon . . .' she wailed, rushing towards him. 'You mustn't . . .'

'Stop whining and bring in the vegetables,' he snapped. Pushing her roughly to one side, he strode out of the kitchen with the deadly implement in his hand.

Carmen followed him silently to the door of the front room and watched with an increasing sense of desperation as he placed the dish on the table. Four pairs of hungry eyes gazed at the joint.

'Looks a bit well-done, old boy,' said Crispin, wrinkling his nose.

'Looks delicious to me,' said Duncan, catching sight of Carmen in the doorway.

'I'll just take off a few slices to get the knife warmed up,' said Gideon, licking his lips and throwing a glance at Crispin. 'Why don't you come round here and watch – you'll see that it's still quite rare inside.'

Carmen stood helplessly in the doorway as Gideon rolled up his sleeves and unwound the electric cord from the instrument of his impending doom. Draining his wineglass, Crispin pushed back his chair and stood up.

Then she realised there was an obvious solution. Why on earth hadn't she thought of it before? 'I'll be right back,' she yelped, retreating into the hallway. Diving into the cupboard under the stairs, she fumbled with the lid of the fuse box. Where the hell was the trip switch?

As the house was plunged abruptly into darkness, there was a hoarse scream from the front room followed by a loud crash.

'Oh bugger,' wailed Crispin. 'I think I've just knocked something on the floor.'

'What the bloody hell's going on?' bellowed Gideon. 'I've just cut my finger on this goddamn knife!'

A few minutes later, when Gideon had reset the trip switch and the lights came back on, Carmen was seated at the table. The electric knife had vanished, buried by Carmen in the depths of the kitchen waste bin, and an ordinary steel Sabatier lay in its place.

Gideon returned from the hall cupboard, blinking.

'I can't understand it,' he muttered, shaking his head. 'I don't see why the circuit breaker should have gone when . . .' He stopped, staring under the table with a horrified expression.

Everyone shifted back in their chairs to see what he was looking at. The joint of beef lay on the carpet in a pool of reddish-brown juice, close to Crispin's feet. A spattering of similarly coloured splashes could be seen on Crispin's white trousers, and there was a bloody handprint on the tablecloth next to the empty serving dish. Juliet let out a squeal of laughter, then clapped her hand to her mouth. Elvira gave a shocked gasp. Duncan coughed.

Crispin blushed deep crimson. 'It was an accident,' he muttered. 'I tripped and put out my hand to stop myself falling – I couldn't see what I was doing in the dark.'

'I've had enough of this,' snapped Gideon. 'We're going to a restaurant.' Striding to the telephone, he flipped open the address book and dialled a number.

'Is that Foccaccio's? Listen, I know this is rather short notice, but have you got a table for four right away? It's for Carmen Bird.'

'Doesn't he mean six?' asked Duncan.

'I think we'd better be going,' said Juliet, kicking him.

'You'd better make that three,' muttered Carmen weakly, attempting to stand up. 'I don't feel very well.'

'Are you all right, Carmen?' asked Juliet, approaching her with a concerned expression.

'I'm just a bit dizzy . . .' Taking a deep breath, she clutched the edge of the table and fought against the approaching blackness.

'Somebody help her,' called a distant voice. 'I think she's going to pass out.'

CHAPTER 7

When she had finished lighting candles around the bathroom, Angie lowered the bamboo blind to cut out the bright, Sunday morning glare. She switched on the mini CD-player in the hallway, checked her bottles of essential oils, and placed her breakfast tray within easy reach on the lavatory seat. Then, scattering a handful of dried rose petals into the water, she climbed into the bath.

As the gentle strains of her *Mystic Moments* compilation CD drifted through the steam, Angie closed her eyes and lay back in the water. The bathroom was her private sanctuary — the place where she could live out her dreams. Today, she imagined that she was the wife of a Hollywood producer, floating in the pool of their Beverly Hills mansion. She was rich, famous and beautiful. When she opened her eyes, she would see the butler approaching with champagne in a bucket of ice.

Instead, she saw chipped tiles and mildewed grout. Despite the candlelight, and her efforts at cosmetic enhancement with tastefully hung Indian print drapes, it was apparent that the bathroom of her tiny flat was in dire need of renovation.

Gideon could take me away from all this, she thought, sitting up and reaching for her coffee and toast. She hadn't yet decided what approach to take with her blackmail plans, but she knew that a certain amount of subtlety would be required to get what she wanted. She had resolved to wait until she saw him again – that way, she could check out his reaction and play it by ear. But she hadn't heard anything from him for nearly two weeks. What could have happened to keep him away for so long?

Her financial situation was starting to get desperate. The rent would be due before long but, with the risk of Gideon turning up unexpectedly at any time, she could scarcely pursue her regular employment. Ronco was happy enough to police the front door, turning away unwanted clients with the story that she was visiting her sick mother in Hull. If she didn't get this thing with Gideon sorted out soon, however, she would have to go back to work. It was looking as if her plans for 'early retirement' as a kept woman might have been premature.

With a stab of jealousy, she thought of the big, white house in Holland Park where Gideon lived. In her mind, it had a special quality that distinguished it from its neighbours – an aura of warmth and homeliness like the house in the gas advert on TV. She could imagine the interior, with deep, fitted carpets and sleek cats curled in front of warm fires. Why should a spoilt creature like Carmen Bird have all that luxury when

Angie had nothing? Surely a man like Gideon would prefer to have a mistress who could entertain him in style?

Keeping a mistress was hardly a big deal these days, after all. You only had to look in the papers to see that the people who counted were doing it all the time. All she needed was a nice flat in Kensington, an account at a designer boutique, invitations to the right parties and a large bouquet of flowers delivered at least once a week. This was Angie's impression of how such matters were usually arranged.

When she had completed her various cleansing rituals, she climbed out of the bath and dried herself in front of the mirror. The rose petals weren't such a good idea after all, she realised, peeling off several reddish-brown spots that had glued themselves to her skin. Neither, she discovered, picking gritty, brown crumbs from her nipples, was the toast.

Opening a bottle of scented oil, she rubbed it into the parts of her body she could easily reach. She had often longed for Gideon to do this for her – massaging her into a state of heightened sensuality – but he made no response whatsoever to her increasingly blatant hints. Occasionally, desperate to get her back oiled, she would summon Ronco upstairs to carry out the task. Issuing strict instructions as to the boundaries he must not overstep, she would lie face down on her bed and imagine that he was somebody else – abandoning herself to his surprisingly dexterous touch. It worked well enough as long as he didn't get over-excited. Sometimes, listening to his grunting noises and short, rasping breaths, she felt as if she had invited a badger into her bed.

Her limbs were gleaming with oil as she stood in front of the mirror and admired her well-proportioned figure. She had no doubts that her body was her most lucrative asset – its high-earning capacity had always enabled her to make a living without the effort of having to exercise her brain. But it wasn't going to last forever. Now was the time, she told herself, to bring her mental capabilities into play. She could be just as clever as the next person if she tried.

Wrapping herself in a grubby, towelling robe that she never used when Gideon was around, she applied her thoughts to what her next move should be. She needed to progress things – to contact him and remind him that she was still there. It had to be done in a way that didn't seem threatening, but would make it clear that she knew more about him than he thought. Then it would be up to him to draw the right conclusions. If he had any sense, he would swiftly realise that he should be treating his mistress more generously and come up with the goods without the need for unsavoury words like 'blackmail' to pass anyone's lips. Ronco's photographs were purely for back-up purposes, she reminded herself, just in case anything went wrong.

How should she get in touch? The telephone was no good. She didn't want to run the risk of blowing everything with a single careless word. A letter, on the other hand, seemed too formal, and there was nothing to be gained by exposing her literary inadequacies to Gideon's eye. A greetings card with a short note seemed the most promising option. Wasn't that the way people kept in touch with each other in his world?

She had a large collection of cards, accumulated from impulse buying over a number of years, but was unable to reach a decision as to which one she should send. Eventually, she spread them out on the smoked glass table in the living room and called Ronco up to give her the benefit of a man's point of view.

Ronco appeared in the doorway wearing a shellsuit and furry, novelty slippers. His face lit up with expectation when he saw that she wasn't fully dressed.

'That wasn't exactly what I meant . . .' she began, tightening the belt of her dressing gown. She stopped, staring at his slippers. Two little badger faces peeked up at her with beady, knowing eyes. The creatures were eerily realistic – she almost expected them to leap up and scuttle across the floor on their own.

'Do you like them?' he asked shyly. 'I got them half-price at the market because they only had two left feet.' Without warning, he took one off and thrust it towards her. 'The markings are quite realistic,' he added. 'Look, you can tell it's the native British badger by the arrangement of the stripes.'

Angie backed away, wrinkling her nose in disgust as she caught a whiff of Ronco's feet. Was this his idea of a seduction technique?

It took her some time to make him understand the true purpose of her invitation. In an attempt to soften his disappointment that she didn't want a massage, she agreed to let him take her for a lunchtime drink if he helped her select the right card. Once this was settled,

Ronco launched himself into the task with enthusiasm – comparing the offerings of Hallmark and Athena, and debating the merits of soft-focus photography and cartoon teddy bears. Eventually, he discovered the solution to her problem wedged inside an old Valentine's card. It was a reproduction of an oil painting of a woman bathing in a stream, surrounded by flowers. This was *classy*, thought Angie, peering at the caption inside. *Ophelia*, by John Everett Millais. Wasn't she some character from Greek mythology? This would show Gideon that Angie had educated tastes.

Sending Ronco away to change his footwear and put on his best anorak for the pub, she struggled to make up her mind what to write on the card. This was the hard bit, she realised, furrowing her brow. What should she say? *I know where you live?* That sounded too sinister, and was also rather superfluous as the fact would be evident from the address on the envelope. What about a joke, based around the picture? *My bathtime is lonely without you?* But Gideon didn't have much of a sense of humour, as far as she could tell. Eventually, she decided to keep it simple. *Thinking of you, love Angie*, she wrote. After a moment's thought, she added *xxxxx*.

As she slipped the card into the envelope, she took another glance at the picture. The flowers floating in the water reminded her of her earlier experience in the bath. Maybe she should try using fresh ones like Ophelia, she reflected, instead of recycling her old pot-pourri. She was sure to be able to pick some up cheaply in the Portobello Road.

*   *   *

When Carmen woke on the Sunday morning after the dinner party, her first thought was one of regret that Gideon was still alive. Why, after so much careful preparation, had she lost the courage to go through with her plan? Her second thought, feeling the throb of her bruises and the soreness between her legs, was one of determination that she would let nothing stand in her way the next time. The brute who had inflicted this on her deserved to die.

Her fainting spell the previous night had frightened her badly. She had regained consciousness to find herself in bed, not knowing how she had got there. When she called out, there was no response. Where had everybody gone? Too weak to get up and investigate, she had drifted into a delirious half-sleep until Gideon's return.

He had woken her with a barrage of invective, yelling accusations about how she had deliberately ruined the evening and sabotaged his career. Then he demanded sex. When she turned away, protesting that she was unwell, he tore the covers from the bed and dragged her round to face him. He started hitting her – harder than usual – until she no longer had the strength to fight back.

Carmen shuddered as she remembered how he had raped her, muffling her screams with a pillow and pinning her to the mattress with his weight. A cold, hard anger was growing inside her. Any lingering doubts she might have had were now dispelled.

The house was silent. She had no idea where Gideon had spent the rest of the night but, as she crossed the landing to the bathroom, she saw that the door of his study was slightly open. Usually, he kept it securely locked, even when he was inside. Cautiously, she peered through the opening. He was sitting in his high-backed leather chair, his head and arms slumped forward onto the desk. An empty whisky bottle stood in front of him. She retreated in alarm as he shifted position and let out a loud, rumbling snore. Juliet had been right, she told herself anxiously. Gideon was out of control. If she didn't stop him soon, he would go too far.

Downstairs, the wreckage of the dinner party remained just as she had left it. Washing the dishes, which were considerably fewer in number than one would normally expect from a meal for six, Carmen tried to work out exactly what had gone wrong with her plan. Her method, she now realised, had been badly flawed. Electric shocks weren't always fatal. Gideon might have escaped with nothing more than a few burns, but there was also a chance that he might have been brain-damaged, or crippled in some way. Carmen was glad she had now avoided that particular risk — she couldn't imagine a fate more terrible than being condemned to nurse a bedridden Gideon for the rest of his days.

Having other people present had also been a mistake, particularly the two ghoulish individuals who had been Gideon's guests. Apart from the fact that, next to the ghastly Crispin and Elvira, Gideon hadn't seemed quite as monstrous as usual, it had been all their talk about graveyards and death that had made her feel too squeamish to carry on. If she was going to succeed the next time, she concluded, she would need to find a way of killing him from a distance, with nobody else around.

Hearing footsteps on the stairs, she composed her face into a neutral expression and concentrated on the washing up. Gideon slammed his way into the kitchen, made himself a cup of coffee with irritating slowness, then stalked out again — all without a word. As far as she could tell from a few furtive glances, there wasn't anything wrong with him that couldn't be cured by a good night's sleep and a month at a drying-out clinic.

Seeing him asleep in the study had, however, given her an idea. In her book on poisons, she had read that accidental deaths were often caused by carbon monoxide fumes leaking from a garage. Gideon's study was directly above the garage. It seemed that the properties of this particular gas were worthy of further research.

Carmen spent the rest of the day quietly, keeping out of Gideon's way. As soon as he went out, early in the evening, she retrieved her stolen library books from their hiding place and began to read. Carbon monoxide, she learned, was a colourless, odourless gas which could, if breathed in sufficient concentrations, cause a relatively quick and painless death. It was mentioned as a popular choice for suicides, if 'popular' was an appropriate term to apply to something that killed you. An ordinary car running in a closed garage could generate a lethal level of the gas in a very short time.

Opening her purse, Carmen took out the spare key to Gideon's study. She had discovered it several months previously, quite by chance, and had kept it hidden away with the vague idea that she might need it some day. Now, she realised, was the time to use it. Moving quietly, so that she could listen for sounds of Gideon's return, she went upstairs and let herself into his private sanctum. She needed to check the condition of the floorboards and work out a method of getting the sash window to jam.

Gideon spent most of Sunday and Monday in an alcoholic haze, cursing the treachery of his false friend, Crispin Scrope. After the fiasco over the power cut on Saturday night, Gideon had somehow lost his appetite for food. His guests had to be wined and dined, however, so he had accompanied them to Foccaccio's and picked at *antipasto* while they feasted lavishly at his expense. It wasn't until the bill had been paid, and they were lingering over brandy and cigars, that Crispin had finally admitted his discussions with the agency producer for the *Flux* commercial had been a complete fiction.

'I was hoping to catch up with him before they settled the deal,' he had explained in an offhand manner. 'It just seems that the negotiations were moving faster than I thought.' Gideon had watched in disbelief as Crispin pocketed the Havana that Elvira had chosen, but neglected to smoke. 'It's just the way the cookie crumbles, old boy,' Crispin had added, patting him on the shoulder as he stood up to leave. 'It looks as if we might have to pass this one by.'

The vile couple had disappeared into a taxi, leaving

Gideon fuming in frustration. They knew, no doubt, that he valued his reputation at Foccaccio's too much to create a scene.

By Monday night, Gideon sobered up enough to wonder what had happened to the rest of that evening. He dimly recalled having asserted his rights as a husband, but what had come after that? He would have to ease up on the drink, he told himself firmly, before he did something foolish that he would regret.

The future looked bleak, but Gideon felt sure there had to be a way out of the mess he was in. Things might not be as bad as they seemed. If he went directly to the agency, using Scrope's name to get him through to the main man, there might still be a chance of muscling in on the *Flux* deal. Once they had heard his pitch, they were bound to recognise that his vision for the new campaign was far superior to any of that rubbish with actors dressed up as giant raisins. 'Think Milk Tray meets *Pulp Fiction*,' he murmured to himself. 'On the set of *Apocalypse Now* . . .'

There was also his *Mangus* proposal. Refusing to be deterred by rejection, he had sent it out again – this time to Cloud Eleven, a newly formed satellite company who were known to be looking for fresh ideas. He had at first been hesitant about offering a high quality product like *Mangus* to a company with no track record, but he had now convinced himself that this was the best way to go. He was sure to get a call from them in the next few days.

Meanwhile, he would have to clean up his act with Carmen. He couldn't risk having her walk out on him at this crucial juncture. Preproduction work demanded huge amounts of energy and he would need the backing of a supportive wife. Ultimately, he realised, Carmen would have to be traded in for a newer model. Her fame wouldn't last forever, and he didn't want to find himself shackled to a fading has-been. But now was not the time. Once his career was back on the rails, he would be free to get rid of her whenever he chose.

Carmen had been acting a bit strangely lately, he reflected. There seemed to be no rational explanation for her hysterical behaviour on Saturday night. As for the food she had produced – he would be the laughing stock of the media world if it got around that Gideon Bird had offered his dinner guests frozen prawn cocktail and burnt beef. It was lucky that the electricity had failed when it did.

Tuesday morning's post contained two items for Gideon. The first was a slim package from Cloud Eleven, returning his proposal and declining to take further interest in *Mangus*. Gazing at the familiar document in despair, he noticed that someone had pencilled a comment on the cover and failed to erase it properly. *He must be joking*, read Gideon, angling it towards the light. *What planet has this guy been living on for the last ten years?*

What the fuck did these upstarts know? They had probably still been in nappies when he was making a name for himself at the BBC. Crushing the accompanying standard rejection letter into a ball, he threw it across the study with a howl of rage. Cloud Eleven had been his last real hope.

The second envelope contained Angie's card. He had forgotten about Angie over the last few days, but he felt a stirring in his loins as it occurred to him that a good fucking was just what he needed to relieve his misery. He was about to toss the card in the bin and set off for Notting Hill, when its significance suddenly dawned on him. *She had his address.* With a sense of foreboding, he reread her message, searching for some clue. Then he flipped the card over and stared at the picture. It was one of those sentimental, Pre-Raphaelite eyesores that pretentious types liked to hang on their walls. The death of Ophelia, by Millais.

What was the scheming bitch up to? Reaching for the telephone, he dialled her number. A male voice answered.

'Who's this?' demanded Gideon.

'Just a friend,' replied the voice slowly. 'If you're called Gideon, she's left a message for you.'

'What is it?'

'She's gone shopping. She said you were to come at seven if you wanted to see her.' There was a pause and a series of scuffling sounds. 'You'd better be there on time,' added the voice in a more sinister tone. 'You'll find that it'll be *worth your while.*'

'I'll come when I bloody well like!' spluttered Gideon. 'Who the hell are you?'

There was a click as the line went dead. Gideon's stomach tightened. If Angie knew his address, he realised, she must have been checking him out. The chances were that she had discovered more about him than he wanted her to know. It was only nine-thirty in the morning, but he found himself reaching for the bottle of scotch. It was the worst possible time for something like this to happen. If Angie told Carmen — or anyone else in his circle — about their affair, he could end up being shunned by the contacts whose goodwill he so desperately needed right now.

Whether or not it turned out to be blackmail, he couldn't afford to take any more risks. Angie would have to go. It had been his own fault, he told himself, for keeping her on for so long. Women always began to get greedy after the first couple of weeks.

As the level of the scotch crept down the bottle, Gideon began to feel sluggish and disorientated. He reached to open the window, but it had somehow jammed. After several abortive attempts to get it open, he felt a rush of nausea and realised that what he really needed was a fix of cocaine.

Rummaging through his desk drawer, he paused, remembering that he had used up the last of his supply in a lonely orgy of excess the night before. Then his hand brushed against something cold and hard, and a smile flickered on his lips. Wrapping his fingers around its familiar contours, he lifted out his most treasured possession.

'Hello, baby,' he murmured, feeling the thrill that always came to him when he handled his gun. It was a Smith and Wesson .38 revolver, and it had been a gift, complete with bullets, from a wealthy eccentric who was an avid *Mangus* fan. As there were no records to trace it to him, he had never bothered to get it licensed.

Pressing the latch forward, he pushed the cylinder sideways out of the frame. The cartridges were in another drawer. Feverishly, he extracted six from the carton, dropping them into the empty chambers. The cylinder went back into position with a satisfying click. Now he was ready.

He began his ritual, manoeuvring around the room with practised movements. Taking sight on imaginary targets, he felt the resistance of the trigger against his quivering finger. He was in control now. *He was Mangus*. One little squeeze was all that was needed to blast the opposition away.

He felt his erection swelling and reached with his free hand to unzip his fly. Sweating heavily, he worked his way towards a climax. As he was approaching the moment of release, however, he found himself thinking of Angie and her duplicity. At the same time, the nausea kicked in again – a sharp reminder that his addiction needed to be fed.

His erection wilted abruptly. With a sigh, he put the gun back in the drawer and refastened his trousers. Then he considered his options. There was a small emergency stash that he kept at Angie's flat for when his supplies ran out, but he couldn't possibly wait until seven that evening. He would just have to make a trip down to Soho to stock up.

He passed Carmen in the hallway. 'Going out?' she enquired.

'Mind your own . . .' Gideon stopped himself, remembering that he had to be nice to her. 'Just for a couple of hours,' he said in a friendly voice. 'See you in a while.'

*   *   *

Gideon didn't return until five-thirty that afternoon. To Carmen's astonishment, he came into the front room and apologised for being late.

'Ran into a contact in Soho and stopped for a couple of drinks,' he gasped. His pupils were dilated and he was wheezing slightly, as if he had been running. He took a deep breath. 'I'm going to be doing some editing upstairs for the rest of the evening,' he added, with a note of warning in his voice. 'I don't want to be disturbed.'

'Fine,' said Carmen in a neutral tone. 'See you later.' She listened to his progress upstairs and waited for the sound of the key turning in the lock. This was it, she thought, trembling. The best opportunity she was likely to get. With the cocktail of drink and drugs he already had inside him, it probably wouldn't take much more in the way of poisonous substances to finish him off. After a few moments, she heard the familiar sounds of gun-shots and music as Gideon started to butcher another episode of *Mangus* on his editing machine. Switching on the television to create additional background noise, Carmen went into the garage to prepare.

She had already positioned the garden hosepipe. It ran unobtrusively up behind the shelves on the end wall and disappeared through a small hole in the ceiling. This had been carefully measured to line up with a gap in the floorboards above, where the heating pipes entered the study. It had been a simple matter, while Gideon was out that afternoon, to slip into his room and pull the hose through, threading it up the back of the radiator where it couldn't be seen.

The other end of the hose was curled innocuously on the garage floor, close to the rear of the car. Taking a handful of old rags from a shelf, Carmen wrapped strips of cloth around the hose until she had created a plug that fitted tightly inside the exhaust pipe. When everything was ready, she went quietly upstairs and listened at Gideon's door. *Mangus* was still blaring away, but she could hear no other sounds inside. With a bit of luck, he would have fallen asleep.

She paused, realising that the next step would commit her to going through with the rest of the plan. Did she really want to do it? Remembering the look of sadistic pleasure in his eyes when he was raping her, she assured herself that she did. She had suffered his violence for eight long years and she simply couldn't take anymore.

Taking a deep breath, she wedged a bent paperclip into the lock. She had practised this earlier, testing it with her own key. It would now be impossible to open the door from the inside. Later, when she had removed the obstruction, the whole thing would look like suicide. It might not even be so very far from the truth, she reflected. His recent consumption of whisky had given the impression that he was doing his best to drink himself to death.

Downstairs, she started the car, waiting for a moment or two to make sure the engine was running properly and wasn't going to cut out. Then she escaped into the hallway and closed the connecting door. Taking the telephone off the hook to prevent any calls being made from the study extension, she left the house. It was time to establish her alibi at the local late-night store.

She walked along Holland Park Avenue in a daze. Everything seemed so relentlessly normal – so much the same as when she had last come this way – that she began to wonder if the last half-hour had really happened. People scurried past her, dodging through the rush-hour traffic as they hastened home to their families on an ordinary Tuesday evening. Why weren't they stopping and pointing their fingers with cries of accusation? How could they be so cheerfully oblivious to the terrible thing that was happening only a few streets away?

In the supermarket, she tossed items into her basket with automatic movements. It wasn't until she hesitated over the choice of salad dressings that the reality of her situation began to sink in. *Gideon prefers blue cheese to mustard mayonnaise*, she found herself thinking. *He'll kill me if I get the wrong one* . . .

Overcome by a sensation of dizziness, she leaned against a cabinet of cold drinks and began to shed silent, frightened tears. It was too late to go back now, she realised. This time, she had really done it. By the time she arrived home with the shopping, Gideon would be dead.

CHAPTER 8

Far from being dead, Gideon was at that moment striding purposefully through the streets of Notting Hill. Checking his watch as he turned into Ladbroke Grove, he congratulated himself on having slipped from the house unnoticed. He had locked the door of the study behind him and made his escape while Carmen was messing about in the garage. The tape on the editing machine would last for a good three hours, giving her every reason to believe that he was still inside.

He had reached the conclusion that his carelessness had made him vulnerable. He would have to modify his behaviour if he wanted to get Carmen on his side. In the future, he resolved, he would take greater care in choosing his mistresses and put a lot more effort into covering his tracks.

As he drew closer to his destination, he was struck, as always, by the abrupt change in his surroundings. He had passed through a rapid transition, in the space of a few streets, from a leafy, well-heeled neighbourhood to a menacing slum. It had been a mistake, he now realised, to come so far down-market in search of his pleasures. Women of Angie's class were never to be trusted – they would always be ready to betray you if they sensed there was money to be made. Even so, he felt a twinge of regret that it had to end so suddenly. Sex with Angie had been good, and he would now suffer the inconvenience of having to search for a replacement at a time when he had other, more pressing, concerns.

When he reached the front door of the run-down house where she lived, he was surprised to find it open. He thought he heard a scuffling in the hallway as he climbed the stairs but, when he stopped and looked round, there was nobody there. Probably a rat, he decided, given the dilapidated state of the building. Moving to one side to avoid a patch of green mould on the wall, he continued his ascent.

The door of Angie's flat was also slightly ajar. He hesitated on the landing, belatedly remembering the male voice that had answered her telephone. Was he walking into some kind of trap? Then he pulled himself together. People didn't mess with the creator of *Mangus* and get away with it. Pushing the door fully open, he stepped inside.

The flat was in semi-darkness, with all the curtains tightly drawn. A trio of candles burned on the table inside the door, casting long, dancing shadows along the hallway, while another faint flickering of light was visible through the bathroom door. A sweet, sickly smell hung in the air, making him feel nauseous. Distant wailings and ululations – the kind of New Age crap that people like Angie called music – floated through from another room.

As Gideon moved across the hall, he felt a soft rustling beneath his feet. Looking down, he saw that the carpet was strewn with flowers. What was the crazy bitch playing at? He kicked angrily at a spray of carnations as he felt the itch of pollen in his cocaine-ravaged nostrils. Hadn't he made it clear to her that he hated flowers?

It wasn't until he opened the bathroom door that he made the connection with the card she had sent. 'Christ Almighty,' he breathed, peering through the steam in disbelief. Angie was stretched out naked in the bath, surrounded by floating garlands of limp flowers. It was Millais's *Ophelia*, complete with special effects.

For a horrible moment, he thought she might have gone the whole hog and topped herself. Then, seeing the rise and fall of her breasts in the water, he realised that she was asleep. He was about to wake her, and was debating whether to dump her straightaway or have sex with her first, when it occurred to him that this was an ideal moment to retrieve his secret stash of cocaine. Striding into the bedroom, he stood on the bed and reached for the top of the wardrobe. It didn't take long to find the small polythene bag taped to the inside edge but, as he took it down, his fingers brushed against a flat, rectangular package that hadn't been there before.

'What's this?' he murmured, turning over the Fotorola envelope and inspecting it with a puzzled frown. 'Holiday snaps?'

Angie opened her eyes with a start, realising that she must have dozed off. Sniffing the heady vapours rising from the water, it occurred to her that a whole bottle of 'relaxing' seaweed bath oil might have been overdoing things. She would have to be more careful in future. It could be dangerous to fall asleep in the bath.

She glanced at the clock on the shelf. If Ronco had passed on her message correctly, Gideon would be arriving soon. Idly stroking her breasts with a daffodil, she tried to imagine his reaction to her new style of bathing. Inspired by the picture of Ophelia, she had spent the day searching the market for bargains and eventually picked up a whole carton of mixed flowers for next to nothing from a stallholder who was clearing his stock. What was a mistress for, she asked herself, if she couldn't come up with imaginative new ways to stimulate a jaded sexual appetite? Gideon was sure to be aroused by the erotic combination of ripe floral blooms and naked flesh.

Hearing a sudden crashing noise in her bedroom, she sat up in alarm. Was she being burgled? But Ronco was supposed to be watching the front door, with instructions to let no one but Gideon upstairs.

'Giddy?' she called softly. 'Is that you?' There was another crash, then she heard his voice, cursing. What on earth was he doing? Climbing reluctantly from the bath, she wrapped herself in a towel and went to find out.

She stopped at the bedroom door, her mouth dropping open with surprise. It was Gideon and he appeared to be having some kind of fit. At first, she thought he might have stubbed his toe on the wardrobe. Then she saw the Fotorola envelope in his hand and realised, with a sinking heart, that her carefully laid plans had gone horribly wrong.

She was attempting to back away unnoticed when he looked up and saw her. 'What the fuck do you think you've been playing at?' he snarled in a choked voice.

'I could ask you exactly the same,' she retorted angrily. 'What are you doing going through my private things?'

Taking a deep breath, Gideon recovered himself. 'Private?' he asked. Flicking disgustedly through the stack of prints, he showed her a picture of himself thrusting between Angie's splayed thighs. 'This doesn't look very private to me,' he hissed in a savage tone. 'What were you planning? Blackmail?'

'But I didn't . . .' Angie floundered, searching for an alternative explanation but finding none. Her stomach tightened with fear. She hadn't prepared herself for this, but there seemed to be little point in pretending any more. 'I've got the negatives,' she said eventually in a shaking voice. 'You're going to have to pay me . . . pay me some money . . .'

'Got the negatives?' Gideon laughed, opening a side pocket in the envelope and taking out a handful of orangey plastic strips. 'You won't mind if I take these, then?' he sneered, dangling them just out of her reach.

She clenched her hands in frustration. Why hadn't she thought to hide them away somewhere else? 'I've had other prints done,' she began unconvincingly. 'They're in a safe place . . .'

Returning his booty to the envelope, Gideon thrust it into his coat pocket. 'Let's get something straight, shall we?' he said in an icy tone. Angie backed away, trembling, but he reached out and took hold of her towel, pulling her towards him. 'If you even think about trying to blackmail me again,' he said, 'I'll fucking kill you!' He slapped her viciously across the face. As she flinched and stumbled, his hand shot out with a violent movement and seized her by the throat. 'Get out of my life, bitch,' he hissed, slamming her against the wall. 'I don't ever want to lay eyes on you again.'

Speechless with shock, Angie watched as he turned and strode out of the flat. Gideon had never hit her before. As she heard his footsteps crashing down the stairs, she sank to the floor with a moan of despair. It looked as if she could kiss goodbye her flat in Kensington. Her career as a blackmailer seemed to be over before it had begun.

There was a scuffling noise on the landing and Ronco appeared at the door, wide-eyed. 'Are you all right?' he asked anxiously.

'The photographs,' she whispered hoarsely. 'He's taken the photographs. I need to get them back.'

They both flinched as the front door slammed shut. Ronco became suddenly alert, cocking his head to one side as he listened to the departing footsteps. His nose twitched briefly, as if picking up a scent. 'He's turned to the left,' he murmured decisively, zipping up his anorak. 'If I take the side alley, I can catch up with him by the launderette.'

'Be careful,' Angie warned him. 'He's not in a very good mood.' But Ronco had already departed, vanishing silently into the street in pursuit of his prey.

*   *   *

Passing the open door of a pub, Gideon stumbled inside and ordered a double scotch. He had badly miscalculated Angie's capabilities, he realised. She had turned out to be far more dangerous than he had thought.

When his drink arrived, he downed it in one gulp and ordered another. How could he be sure that Angie hadn't already made copies of her photographs? If they fell into the wrong hands, Carmen would have the excuse she needed to leave him and his reputation would be dragged through the tabloids. Not only would his career would be over, but he would also be faced with the humiliation of becoming the laughing stock of people like Crispin Scrope.

Taking his second drink to a table in a quiet corner, Gideon took the Fotorola envelope from his pocket for another look. She must have used some kind of hidden camera, he decided, gazing at a close-up of his own genitals. A person couldn't possibly have taken a shot from that angle, even with a zoom lens, without being right there beside them in the room.

'Gideon? Is that you?'

He started, spilling his drink, and hastily jammed the photographs back into their envelope. A woman was standing in front of him, facing him with an accusing glare. She looked vaguely familiar, but he couldn't remember where he had seen her before.

'What in hell's name happened to you?' she asked in an aggressive voice. 'At the jewellers, remember? Two years ago. You were supposed to meet me there to choose the ring.'

Christ Almighty. Gideon had thought he was through with his quota of nasty surprises for one day. With a feeling of desperation, he recognised the woman as one of his ex-mistresses. He dimly remembered having proposed to her on their last night together, just before ditching her for someone new. It was one of the games he enjoyed playing – seeing how far he could stretch the credulity of women who were stupid enough to believe his blatant lies.

'You turned out to be a right bastard, didn't you?' she continued angrily. 'I hope you're proud of yourself for messing up my life like that. I've spent the last two years on Prozac because of you.'

'Keep it down,' hissed Gideon, glancing around in alarm to see if anyone had heard. In any other circumstances he would have told the crazy bitch to fuck off, but he didn't want to draw attention to himself by making a scene in Angie's local pub. Thinking rapidly, he turned back to face his persecutor. 'Why don't you sit down and have a drink?' he suggested, forcing a smile. 'I'm sure we can sort out the misunderstanding if we talk it through.'

She stared at him suspiciously, but eventually took a seat. 'You can get me a double vodka and tonic then,' she conceded in a grudging tone. 'With a twist of lime.'

At the bar, Gideon struggled to recollect which of his stories he had given her. Was he supposed to be the hot-shot movie producer or the high-flying entrepreneur? This was ridiculous, he told himself angrily. He couldn't even remember the bloody woman's name.

The open door beckoned invitingly. If he made a quick dash for it, he thought, he could probably be several streets away before she realised he had gone. He glanced back at the table, preparing to make his move.

But something stopped him. A hidden corner of his memory unexpectedly yielded its secrets and he felt a stirring of excitement as he remembered how accommodating this particular mistress had been in bed. There was a part of Gideon that could never resist a challenge. He had seduced plenty of women in his time – leading them on with false promises before he vanished from their lives without trace – but he had never before had the opportunity for a repeat performance. Could he pull it off with the same woman twice?

Returning to the table, he felt the familiar surge of adrenalin as he caught his victim in his sights. 'When I saw you walk into the pub tonight,' he began, 'I realised what a terrible mistake I made two years ago.'

She faced him with a stony stare. 'Do I look as if I was born yesterday?' she asked scornfully. 'Do you seriously think I'm going to fall for a line like that?'

'I was in a pretty bad way myself, back then,' he continued, ignoring her response. 'I didn't have much confidence, and when you didn't turn up to meet me that day, I thought . . .'

'What do you mean, didn't turn up?' she interrupted. 'I waited for three sodding hours outside Goldsmith's.'

'Goldsmith's? I thought we were supposed to meet at Samuel's.' Gideon watched with satisfaction as a flicker of doubt crossed her face. 'Anyway, when you didn't turn up,' he went on, 'I started thinking – you know

– wondering if you had really meant all the things you had said. It somehow seemed better that I didn't call you again.' Looking straight at her, he fixed her with a gaze of mournful longing. 'It was always hard to imagine what a beautiful woman like you could possibly see in me.'

'Beautiful?' The ghost of a smile began to play around her lips. 'Are you trying to tell me that all this happened because I waited for you in the wrong place?'

As she started wittering on about how she might have mixed up the names of the two jewellers, Gideon gave a secret smirk of triumph. He had her. It was only a matter of time now before he was ready to move in for the kill.

Angie had just finished getting dressed and was making a start on clearing up the flowers when Ronco telephoned. He seemed to be in a state of excitement, and it took her some time to worm out of him that he had tracked Gideon down in the local pub. Warning him not to do anything until she got there, Angie grabbed her handbag and hurried out of the house.

Everything had happened so suddenly that she could hardly bring herself to believe her affair with Gideon was over. Might there be some chance, she wondered, of persuading him that it had all been a misunderstanding? That the blackmail photographs had only been intended as a joke? Wiping away an unexpected tear as she approached the door of the pub, she realised that she had been more fond of Gideon than she cared to admit.

The interior of the pub was dark and crowded and it took her a few moments to locate Gideon on the far side of the room. She was about to rush over and beg his forgiveness, when she saw that he wasn't alone. He was talking to a tarty-looking woman. As she watched, he reached across the table and took the woman's hand, pressing it to his lips. Angie started forward with a jealous cry, but found herself restrained from behind.

'Come in here,' hissed Ronco, pulling her through a door into the other bar. 'Don't let him see you.' Manoeuvring her through the crowd, he found her a seat at the end of the bar and placed a drink in front of her. 'Don't make any sudden movements,' he said in a low voice. 'If you turn your head slowly to the left, you should be able to see them through the gap between the Bell's and the Famous Grouse.'

'Who's that tart he's with?' she demanded angrily, swivelling her head and craning her neck for a better view. Gideon now seemed to have his hand up the woman's skirt. 'What the hell's going on?'

'I don't know,' replied Ronco in a hurt tone. 'I was only trying to help. Do you want me to get those photographs back or not?'

'Can you?' asked Angie eagerly, forgetting her earlier mood of repentance. Ronco nodded. Standing up, he pressed a finger to his lips and made a sign that she should stay where she was. Then, with a rapid shuffling motion, he vanished into the crowd.

If she recovered the pictures, thought Angie, she would teach that two-timing bastard a well-deserved lesson. It was one thing to share Gideon with his TV star wife, but there was no way that she was going to tolerate a usurper from her own class. Leaning across the bar, she peered through the gap to watch Ronco's progress in the other room.

He seemed to be able to move quite invisibly from one place to another. At one moment he was lurking unobtrusively by the door, at the next, he was leaning nonchalantly against the fireplace. In the blink of an eye she lost him again, only to see him reappear magically behind Gideon's chair. Gideon was too busy sticking his tongue down his bimbo's throat to notice the swift movement at his side. Angie smiled, took a sip of her drink, then jumped back in surprise as a familiar-looking Fotorola envelope appeared on the bar in front of her. Whirling round, she found Ronco sitting placidly beside her as if he had been there all the time.

'Blimey,' she gasped, taking another gulp of her drink. 'That was quick.'

'That was nothing,' murmured Ronco modestly. He gave her an uncharacteristic wink. 'You should have seen me back in the old days, working the crowds on Oxford Street.'

When Carmen realised that she had no choice but to go through with her plan, she determined to wait until a full hour had passed before she returned to the house. The whole thing could easily backfire on her if she went home too soon. Finishing her shopping, she wandered the streets of Holland Park and worried about the performance she would shortly have to give. She might be a success as a TV presenter, but she wasn't sure that her acting skills were up to much. Would she be convincing in the role of the distressed wife who had 'popped out' to get the supper and come back to find that her husband was dead?

She made a long circuit of the side streets, but found herself back on Holland Park Avenue more quickly than she expected. She whiled away the last twenty minutes pretending to wait for a bus, staring uncomfortably at a poster that urged her to donate blood. *It only takes an hour of your time*, it said. Carmen reflected that, in the same short period, she had rendered a whole eight pints of the stuff unfit for further use. By now, she thought, glancing at her watch – if the information in her library book was correct – Gideon's carboxyhaemoglobin levels would be off the end of the scale.

As she let herself into the house, she could hear the car engine chugging away in the garage. An unpleasant smell had already begun to spread into the hall. She wasted a few moments trying to decide what an innocent person would do first, before realising that, if she didn't stop the engine soon, she would become the second victim of her own devious plot.

When she had switched off the ignition and opened the garage door to let in some air, Carmen stood outside Gideon's study and braced herself for the ordeal ahead. Everything seemed just as she had left it. She could still hear the sounds of the *Mangus* video playing in the room. With trembling hands, she removed the paperclip from the keyhole. Now, she told herself, she would have to spend a good few minutes shouting

Gideon's name in hysterical tones and struggling with the door before she went to call the police. She took a deep breath.

Then she let it out again. Not the police, she thought confusedly. That would look suspicious. She ought to call an ambulance first. Or would the fire brigade be a more obvious choice, to break down the door?

She hesitated on the landing, unable to bring herself to act. Eventually, she decided that she couldn't go through with this charade until she had seen with her own eyes that Gideon was actually dead. A quick peep wouldn't do any harm, she reassured herself, taking out her key and inserting it in the lock. She needed to be absolutely certain that nothing had gone wrong.

A cloud of evil-smelling fumes greeted her as she opened the door. Holding her breath, she stepped inside. The first thing she saw was Gideon's empty chair.

'Make my day, sucker,' said Mangus, pointing his gun at her from the video screen. She flinched, then turned and stared around the room. Gideon wasn't on the floor, either. In fact, she quickly realised that, unless he had somehow folded himself into the desk drawer, Gideon wasn't in the room at all.

Staggering dizzily to the window, she saw that the screws she had inserted earlier were still in place. He couldn't have escaped that way. Gideon seemed to have vanished, magically, into thin air.

With a choked gasp, she remembered that she needed to breathe. Leaving the room, she ran to the window in the hallway, threw it open, and took in deep gulps of air. Conflicting feelings of anger, disappointment and relief surged up inside her as she admitted to herself that she had failed once again.

The sounds of gunfire from the video drew her back towards the study. Standing in the doorway, she watched in frustration as Mangus coolly dispatched half a dozen villains without ruffling a strand of his blow-dried hair. If murder was supposed to be that easy, she asked herself angrily, what was she doing wrong? What was it about Gideon that made him so damned difficult to kill?

Gideon was having trouble getting an erection. He had been in a state of high excitement on the drive back to the woman's flat, nearly causing an accident when his hand invaded her knickers half-way round Shepherd's Bush Green. Now that he had his victim naked and panting beneath him, however, the urgent throbbing in his groin had mysteriously ceased.

'Oh baby,' he whispered, rubbing his limp member against her thigh in an attempt to resuscitate his desire. If only he could remember her name, he thought irritably. How could he count this as a proper victory if he had no label to attach to the spoils?

The woman moaned and shifted her position, reaching between his legs. Gideon backed away, rapidly checking through his mental list of past mistresses. *Irma*? *Norma*? It was something to do with the name of a film, he remembered, frowning. Suddenly, it came to him. It was the one where those two crazy bitches drove off the cliff-top at the end.

He felt the woman's cold hand close around his genitals. 'Thelma,' he murmured, breathing heavily into her ear.

Her grip tightened for a moment, then she let go and abruptly moved away. 'Actually,' she said in a icy voice, 'it's Louise.'

When he opened his eyes, he saw that she was standing at the side of the bed. 'What are you doing?' he asked indignantly.

'I don't think this was such a good idea after all,' she muttered, pulling on her dressing gown. 'I think you'd better leave.'

He stared at her in shocked disbelief. No woman ever rejected Gideon Bird. 'Come back here, you silly bitch,' he said gruffly, snatching her by the wrist and pulling her back towards the bed. He slapped her lightly across the face. 'I haven't finished with you yet.'

'Take your hands off me,' she yelped, jerking away. 'Who the hell do you think you are?' With a sudden movement, she twisted from his grasp and rounded on him with a furious expression. 'You bastard,' she hissed. 'Is this the thanks I get for taking pity on you?'

'Taking pity on *me*?' echoed Gideon in an incredulous tone. 'What are you talking about?'

'Have you seen yourself lately?' she asked with a sneer. 'You looked in a pretty bad way sitting there in the pub, getting pissed all on your own with your dirty photographs. I felt kind of sorry for you. I didn't have anything on tonight, so I thought I'd let you have a quick one for old times' sake.'

'But you said . . .' Gideon couldn't believe what he was hearing. Was the woman completely mad?

'You didn't really think I'd been pining for you all that time, did you?' she asked, letting out a gasp of surprised laughter. 'Couldn't you tell I was winding you up with all that stuff about Prozac and waiting at the jewellers?' She faced him with a look of amused contempt. 'Christ, you really are a sad case!'

'How dare you!' spluttered Gideon. He stood up, trembling with anger.

She glanced down at his shrivelled penis. 'I see you're still having the same problem as before,' she added scornfully. 'Not that it was ever much use when you did manage to get it up.'

Lunging at her with a cry of rage, he seized her by the shoulders and hurled her onto the bed. No woman had ever dared to criticise his sexual performance. Climbing on top of her, he pinned her down with his weight. He'd show the little bitch just what he could do.

'Let go of me!' she shrieked. 'Get off me this minute, or I'll call the police!'

He clamped his hand over her mouth. Images of Carmen and Angie flashed into his mind, taunting him. These bloody women were all the same, he thought, fighting to hold her down as she tried to escape. They were all out to get him. A bilious anger rose up inside him and he felt a pounding in his temples as his blood pressure soared.

'Bitch!' he screamed. Wrapping his fingers around her throat, he began to squeeze. The woman stared up at him, her features frozen with shock. There was a roaring in his ears and darkness filled his vision, as if he was plunging into a black void.

When he recovered himself, he found that she wasn't struggling any more. Releasing his cramped fingers from her windpipe, he watched in dismay as she fell back limply onto the bed. What was the wretched woman playing at? He slapped her face several times, telling himself that she was only messing around, but there was no response.

Eventually, he was forced to acknowledge that he was dealing with a corpse. 'Christ Almighty,' he gasped, reaching for his trousers with a surge of panic. He had enough problems on his plate right now without having to defend himself against a murder charge.

Nobody had seen him come here, he thought, wrestling with his tangled shirt. If he could make a clean getaway, there would be nothing to link him with the scene of the crime. Picking up the rest of his clothes, he edged towards the door, trying not to look at the dead eyes staring from the bed. He needed to get home as fast as possible and sneak back into his study. Carmen could be his alibi, he told himself desperately. If she didn't hear him come in, she would be under the impression that he had been there all the time.

CHAPTER 9

When the air had cleared in Gideon's study, Carmen sat in his chair and took a swig from the half-empty bottle of whisky on the desk. Her thoughts circled disjointedly as she puzzled over the enigma of his disappearance. With the window screwed shut, the only way out of the room was through the door. But he couldn't have unlocked it without disturbing the paperclip – and she had found this, undamaged, exactly where it had been left.

The only logical explanation was that he hadn't been in the room from the start. But why had he gone to the trouble of fooling her into thinking he was there? He had never bothered to conceal his absences from her before.

Carmen was certain that Gideon had no idea she was trying to kill him. The smallest hint of disloyalty on her part was usually enough to trigger a full-scale eruption of violence, but he had, in fact, been uncharacteristically civil to her that day. She frowned, taking another sip of whisky. Now that she thought about it, Gideon had been acting very strangely. There was something peculiar going on.

Without any clear sense of purpose, she began to look into the drawers of his desk, one by one. Catching sight of a glint of metal in the second drawer down, she opened it fully and found herself staring at a gun. *A gun?* Trembling, she picked it up and turned it over in her hands. It was cold and heavy, instilling her with a feeling of dread. Where had he acquired it, she wondered, and for what purpose? Had Gideon secretly been planning to kill *her*?

She placed the gun on the desktop and returned her attention to the drawer, where she found his Filofax and a folder containing his *Mangus* proposal. Taking these out, her attention was caught by a greetings card tucked into the folder — one of those smug reproductions of well-known paintings that were supposed to show off the sender's superior education and taste. It wasn't like Gideon to keep things like this, she thought, opening it to have a look. She had given up sending him birthday cards because she was sick of finding them screwed up in the bin the next day.

Her stomach gave a lurch as she read the message inside. Who the hell was Angie? And what kind of relationship did she have with Gideon that gave her the right to use the word *love* and put a row of *x*'s after her name?

She crumpled the card in an angry gesture and threw it on the floor. Of course Gideon was having an affair — had probably been doing so for years. The trouble was, she had never properly confronted the reality of what this actually meant. She had coped with the idea of him sloping off on a regular basis to perform sordid acts with some tart or another, but it had somehow never crossed her mind that he might be involved in a *relationship*.

With a shudder, Carmen imagined them together. She could picture this *Angie* as being like one of the Amandas or Jessicas at the TV studio — younger, slimmer and much more confident than she was. Did Gideon confide in this woman? Did he talk about his marriage — complaining about his wife's failure to satisfy his needs?

Carmen had always thought it would be the answer to all her problems if Gideon got involved with another woman, but she had never anticipated the emotions it would arouse. She knew there was no logic to it, but she felt a stabbing pain of betrayal. Anger and resentment welled up inside her, blotting out any attempts at rational thought.

Distracted by another outburst of gunfire from the video, which was still running, she turned and stared at the screen with a glazed expression. It was the sequence in the final episode that Gideon was always talking about, where Mangus tracks down the villains to a graveyard and precipitates a full-scale gun battle as a gangland funeral takes place.

She watched Mangus step forward, raising his weapon with both hands. Then, scarcely aware of what she was doing, she took Gideon's gun from the desk and copied his movements. Closing her eyes, she tightened her grip on the trigger and imagined Gideon standing in front of her. How would he feel, she wondered, to be treated with Mangus's brand of justice? Had it ever occurred to him that his hero was just as much of a murderer as the villains he hunted down?

There was a noise on the landing outside. Opening her eyes, she swung round as the door creaked open. Gideon stood there, looking like a ghost. His clothes were crumpled and disarrayed, and his face was contorted with surprise.

'What the fuck are you playing at?' he roared, lurching drunkenly towards her.

Carmen flinched involuntarily, jerking her finger against the trigger. A deafening explosion filled the room and she was thrown back into the chair, which swivelled itself around to face the other way.

She crouched there, rigid with fear, dreading and at the same time hoping for the inevitable retaliation. It had somehow never occurred to her that the gun might have been *loaded*. What if she had hit him, or wounded him in some way? The consequences were unthinkable. If his past conduct was anything to go by, he would be quite capable of killing her in a drunken rage.

But nothing happened. After what seemed like a very long time, she unwrapped her bruised fingers from around the gun and put it back on the desk with shaking hands. Then she looked round.

She caught her breath with a gasp. Gideon was stretched out on the floor with blood all over the front of his shirt. A pool of darker red was slowly expanding beneath him, soaking into the handmade designer rug. As she watched, his head moved slightly and he let out a final, gurgling moan. With an uncanny precision of timing, the closing credits of the last-ever episode of *Mangus* began to roll up the screen. And that, she realised after a few more moments had passed, was that.

Faced with a choice between news, three different kinds of sport, or a documentary about woodworm, Juliet switched off the TV and made an effort to concentrate on her book. Chief Inspector Richard Dagenham was making heavy weather of his latest case – he had spent the last two chapters indulging in flashbacks to his childhood, and it still hadn't been established whether or not a murder had actually taken place.

When she realised that she had just read the same paragraph three times, she threw down the book and poured herself another glass of wine. Just one more before bedtime, she promised herself. It was past eleven and she didn't want to be late for work again this week.

That day had been the worst she had yet experienced at Castlemayne Insurance. Arriving late, she had missed a staff meeting that had been called at short notice to discuss the problem of office pilfering.

'It wasn't just paperclips and envelopes they were talking about,' Tracey reported breathlessly to Barbie, who had also missed the meeting. 'They said it was getting to be a serious matter. Someone stole half the director's dinner the other week.'

Eavesdropping guiltily, Juliet was relieved to learn that the person responsible for the missing king prawns was yet to be found. According to Tracey, however, the management had called in a forensic expert, and rumour had it that traces of prawn shell had been detected in the mail room. With a smile, Juliet remembered taking Rowena's post there that very afternoon. Discovering a scrap of food caught inside her sleeve, she had flicked it into the desk drawer of the loathsome individual who operated the franking machine.

Her triumph was short-lived, as Rowena emerged from her office at that moment – demanding to know where Juliet had been. 'You should allow extra time to cover delays in your journey,' she pronounced, waving aside Juliet's protests that her train had been held up by a suicide at Gloucester Road. 'If you can't even get to the office on time, I don't know how you expect me to take your employment here seriously. I intend to speak to the department manager about this.'

Anxious to make up for her lateness, Juliet had set to work in earnest. Grappling with the intricacies of the office manual, she filled in the endless forms that seemed to need to accompany each task and dispatched them in the internal mail. These forms, she had noticed, took up far more of her time than the actual work itself.

A few hours later, puzzled by the responses that were piling up in her in-tray, she re-read the relevant section of the manual and discovered, to her dismay, that she had turned over two pages at once. She had completed a form in the section reserved for the duties of the office manager, unwittingly activating an emergency cross-departmental procedural review.

Rowena dismissed her explanation out of hand, giving her a dressing-down in front of the entire typing pool. 'If you can't follow simple instructions,' she concluded, 'I don't know how you expect to be trusted with the responsibilities of your position. Your colleagues might have covered up for you out in the *provinces*, but we don't have any room for passengers at the *London office* of Castlemayne.'

Juliet endured this tirade in silence, afraid that she might lose her temper if she opened her mouth. It was bloody ironic, she thought, remembering the number of times she had covered up for Nick's mistakes. Each time Myra precipitated a marital crisis, she had found herself looking after Nick's responsibilities as well as her own. She had handled them well, and that was part of the reason why Nick had wanted her to go with him to London. But he had let her down, leaving her stranded with the vile Rowena. And the woman seemed determined to break her spirit – as if she bore her some kind of personal grudge.

It was only a job, Juliet told herself miserably, staring through the window of her bedsit. But what else did she have going for her right now? Refilling her glass of wine, she felt a pang of loneliness. It was supposed to be bad to drink on your own, but what was a single person expected to do? She had tried going to a nearby pub one evening, but had been frightened away by the aggressive behaviour of the local youths. They wouldn't have got away with acting like that in her parents' pub, she thought wistfully. Her mother would have banged their heads together and sent them home.

She wasn't about to give up and return to Worcester. It would be far too humiliating to admit defeat at this early stage. But why weren't things happening for her? In a city of seven million people, she had thought it would be easier to make friends. She knew that there were plenty of single people about – she had seen them down at the late-night supermarket, filling their baskets with frozen meals for one. Her attempts to strike up a conversation, however, had been met with muttered excuses and suspicious glares. No one seemed willing to risk so much as an exchange of smiles.

Philip Marlowe had made it sound cool to live alone, but then you probably needed a little peace and quiet at home if you were out chasing villains and being seduced by beautiful women all day long. Juliet wished she could have the self-confidence of her fictional heroes, but was aware that her lifestyle didn't quite make the grade. She might be able to match their consumption of coffee and alcohol, but she had never killed anyone or solved a crime. She had no exotic drug habit, didn't smoke, hated opera and poetry, and thought it would be cruel to keep a cat in such a small flat. And she was also a woman. Why was it, she asked herself, that single men were somehow dignified by their lone status, while women who lived on their own were regarded as sad?

Duncan seemed to manage all right. He didn't even have a job at the moment, as far as she could tell, but he never called her up to tell her that he was lonely or miserable. She hadn't seen him since Carmen's dinner party and felt that their friendship had somehow changed – that he was trying to keep a distance between them. He had apologised for walking out on the night of Carmen's telephone call, but Juliet sensed that this had been more to do with his desire to remain included in the invitation than with any belief that he had been in the wrong.

She had been puzzled to learn that Carmen was giving a dinner party. It hadn't seemed consistent with the picture she had painted of her troubled domestic life. Hoping that it meant there had been some kind of improvement, Juliet had decided not to tell Duncan anything about Gideon's violence. She *had* made a promise to keep Carmen's secret, after all.

The events of that evening were now a hazy and unpleasant memory. She hadn't imagined that Gideon would be particularly friendly towards them, but Carmen's strange behaviour had come as a complete surprise. Juliet had tried to talk to her several times, but found her distant and uncommunicative. Did TV stars always treat their friends in this offhand way?

She had tried not to let her disappointment show. When Carmen fainted, Juliet had even offered to stay and look after her while the others went out. Gideon, however, had completely ignored her, carrying his wife upstairs to the bedroom. When Juliet attempted to follow, she and Duncan were more or less forcibly ejected from the house.

Duncan was incensed at not being included in the restaurant invitation and spent most of their walk back to Hammersmith ranting about Gideon's rudeness. While Juliet fretted about Carmen's well-being, Duncan performed an impersonation of 'The Host from Hell'.

Looking back, she had to admit that he had been rather convincing – he had frightened the wits out of three nasty-looking skinheads on Shepherd's Bush Road with an improvised diatribe on the virtues of bloody red meat.

After this incident, he had walked her home in silence. He seemed to be in a filthy mood, but Juliet couldn't tell whether this was due to something she had done, or to the way the evening had turned out. If he had expected Carmen's invitation to be his entrée to the celebrity world, he was bound to be feeling a little let down. Refusing her invitation to come in for coffee, he had vanished into the night with a vague promise that he would keep in touch.

Three days had now passed, and he still hadn't called. She raced downstairs each time the telephone rang, but it was always for one of the other occupants of the house. Mrs Billings was starting to give her funny looks, as if she was worried that the influence of the previous top-floor tenant might be having some kind of effect.

She glanced at the hook in the ceiling. There was no way that she was going to give in to poor Jason's brand of despair, she told herself sternly. Life without Duncan might be pretty bleak, but it was too precious a commodity to be so thoughtlessly cast aside.

As if to taunt her, the telephone started ringing at that moment – its sound echoing distantly from the hallway below. In an effort to pretend that she didn't care who it was, she took a swig of wine and forced herself to stay put. When she heard Mrs Billings call her name, however, Juliet reached the door almost as soon as the last syllable had died away.

Her landlady intercepted her at the foot of the stairs, clad in dressing gown and slippers. 'I wouldn't get your hopes up, love,' she warned with an uncharacteristic flash of insight. 'It isn't your young man.'

Trying not to show her disappointment, Juliet shrugged and reached towards the telephone, but Mrs Billings put out a hand to detain her. With a cough, she glanced meaningfully at her watch. 'I don't know where you young people get your energy from, staying up half the night and calling each other at all hours, but Frank says it's going to have to stop.'

Then her expression softened. 'You'd better talk to your friend this time, though,' she whispered. 'It sounds like she's in a bit of a state.' She patted Juliet on the arm and gave her a conspiratorial smile. 'I wouldn't be surprised if she's got boyfriend troubles as well.'

As the taxi turned into Holland Park Avenue, Juliet struggled to imagine what could have happened to make Carmen want to see her at this late hour. She had protested that she was about to go to bed, but Carmen was insistent. 'You must come now,' she had repeated in tones of evident distress. 'I need your help. I can't explain on the telephone, but you'll understand when you get here.'

Juliet had pressed her for more details, but Carmen refused to be drawn. 'It's not what you think,' she had added cryptically. 'Gideon won't be making a nuisance of himself tonight.'

Belatedly, Juliet realised that she should have put up more resistance. Just because Carmen was a big name in television, it didn't give her the right to start ordering people around London in the middle of the night — even if she had promised to pay for the taxi at the other end. But her curiosity was aroused and she was secretly rather flattered that Carmen had chosen to turn to her. One more late night, she told herself, couldn't really do her any harm.

By the time she was sitting at Carmen's kitchen table and listening to her story, however, she began to wish that she had followed her better instincts and gone to bed.

'You've done *what*?' she asked in a horrified tone, taking a large slug from the glass of whisky Carmen had placed in her hand.

'I've killed him,' repeated Carmen in a flat voice. Her face wore the blank expression of someone in a state of shock. 'It was an accident, at least, the bit with the gun was. I tried to gas him with carbon monoxide first, but it didn't work out. And the knife — at the dinner party — that didn't work either. It all turned out to be much harder than you said it would be.'

'Hold on,' said Juliet, unable to believe what she was hearing. 'What do you mean, *I* said it would be? What's all this got to do with me?'

'But it was *you* who gave me the idea,' said Carmen with a look of surprise. '*Poison his coffee or something* — don't you remember? I knew you only meant it as a joke, but then we had a car accident coming home from a party, and it all started to make sense. I realised that it was the only thing left for me to do.'

'But I didn't . . .' Juliet fell silent as she recollected that these *had* been her exact words.

'I need your help, Juliet.' Carmen's voice took on a note of urgency. 'You said you knew all about these sort of things. At the theatre – remember? You have to tell me what to do next . . .'

'Now just a moment,' she interrupted, confused. 'I don't know what you're expecting from me here. The way you described it just now, it sounded like an accident. The only thing to do is go to the police and tell them the truth. Nobody's going to accuse you of murder if you were defending yourself against a violent bastard like Gideon. The British system of justice isn't as corrupt as you think.' Draining her whisky, she placed the empty glass on the table. Inspector Dagenham would be proud of me, she thought.

But Carmen didn't seem to share this optimistic view. 'What if they don't believe me?' she protested. 'I could easily end up in prison. And think of what the tabloids would do to me if I was up in court. It wouldn't make any difference to them whether I was guilty or not. They've been waiting for a chance to drag my reputation through the gutter for years.'

Losing her apparent self-possession, she dissolved into a flood of tears. 'You know what Gideon was like,' she whimpered. 'I thought you were my friend – that you would be on my side.' She faced Juliet with a look of abject misery. 'You've got to help me – there's no one else I can turn to. You've no idea how empty my life is.'

It was hardly likely to be as empty as hers, reflected Juliet, struggling to collect her thoughts. Carmen Bird had everything that most people dreamed of – drop-dead good looks, money, fame, and a big house in Holland Park. But that was all on the surface, she reminded herself. It was easy to fall back on pre-conceptions – to forget the things Carmen had told her and ignore the unpleasant details of what her life was really like. Beneath the veneer of worldly success, Juliet had caught glimpses of a lonely, fright-ened woman who wasn't all that different from her-self.

She had always seen herself as being on the side of the good guys, rooting for the likes of Inspector Dagenham in their intrepid fight against crime. Sud-denly, however, she wasn't so sure who the good guys were, or whether they would see things her way. It was all very well to talk about justice, but what if Carmen didn't get away with it? There were plenty of women who had been sent to prison for killing their violent husbands while acting in self-defence.

And some kinds of murder *were* justified. Who would be complaining now if someone had succeeded in assassinating Hitler? Would anyone in this country grieve if Saddam Hussein was mysteriously bumped off? Even Sherlock Holmes had approved of murder in certain circumstances, as anyone would know if they read *The Adventure of the Abbey Grange*.

Carmen had rid the world of a monster. She didn't belong in prison, whether her act had been premedi-tated or not. Leaning across the table, Juliet touched

Carmen's hand. 'Don't worry,' she whispered. 'I'll think of a way to sort this out.'

As she said it, she realised that, deep down, she had intended to help all along. How could she resist the challenge? She had always dreamed of working out the plot for a perfect murder, and of being involved in the investigation of a real life crime. She hadn't quite anticipated that both things would come in the same package, but she wasn't about to pass up the chance of adventure because of a minor detail like that.

The problem was made somewhat harder by the fact that the murder had already taken place. But Juliet was convinced that, with all the knowledge she had stored up from years of reading detective stories, she could overcome this difficulty. If she could solve locked-room mysteries, she told herself, she would be equal to this.

Germs of ideas were already coming together in her mind. First of all, she needed to acquaint herself with the full details of what had happened. There was also the matter of dealing with the body. Action would have to be taken before rigor mortis set in.

'Er, Carmen,' she asked, in what she hoped was an appropriate tone for dealing with such a sensitive matter. 'What have you, er . . . actually done with him?'

CHAPTER 10

Juliet stood in the doorway and gazed at the scene in the study. Gideon lay motionless on his back, his eyes gazing blankly towards the ceiling. She flinched as a fly landed on his forehead, half-expecting him to lift his hand and brush it away. But he didn't react. The fly walked casually across his eyeball, pausing to wash its feet in a droplet of moisture before buzzing its way towards the bloody patch on the front of his shirt for a late-night snack.

'I haven't tried to move him or anything,' whispered Carmen, squeezing past her into the room. 'I can't quite believe that he's really dead.'

'He's dead all right,' said Juliet, stepping closer and bending to stare at the hole in his chest. 'It looks as if you got him in the heart.' Looking at the position of the wound, she could see that suicide was an implausible explanation. A ballistics expert would probably be able to tell straightaway that the angles and distances were all wrong.

Glancing up, Juliet saw the gun on the desk. 'Is it still loaded?' she asked.

'I don't know,' said Carmen. Juliet picked it up, dangling it awkwardly by the handle. What did it feel like to shoot someone – to turn another living being into a lump of dead flesh? To judge by Carmen's expression, it wasn't at the top of her list of fun things to do in Holland Park on a Tuesday night.

Taking care to point the muzzle away from them both, Juliet fumbled with a latch on one side of the casing. It sounded so easy when it was described in detective stories, but it took her several minutes to work out how to operate the thing. Eventually, the cylinder fell open with a sharp *clink*, disgorging five cartridges and an empty case into her hand. She let out a sigh of relief.

'We're going to have to get him out of here pretty soon,' she said, nudging Gideon's body experimentally with her foot. 'What kind of car have you got?'

To her surprise, Carmen let out a snort of amusement. 'Now I know why we chose a Mitsoki Freeloader,' she muttered.

'Chose a what?'

'It's a bit like a Range Rover. I think Gideon only wanted it because Crispin Scrope had one.' She grinned. 'He always said the extra luggage space would come in handy one day.'

An hour later, the two women struggled down the stairs with a long, bulky package and manoeuvred it through the garage door. Neatly wrapped in polythene bin liners, string and sacking, it contained Gideon's body, the bloodstained rug and the gun. Despite their efforts to disguise the shape, it looked – to their eyes, at least – distinctly humanoid.

When she saw the Freeloader, Juliet began to worry about how they would conceal this incriminating cargo from view. It seemed to have windows everywhere, as if to taunt would-be car thieves with glimpses of the goodies inside.

'Wait,' said Carmen, opening the rear hatch and fumbling around on the floor. She lifted a large carpeted flap which seemed to run the full length of the vehicle. 'The high-capacity underfloor storage bin,' she announced with a mocking note of pride. 'I think it's meant for skiing equipment and stuff like that, but I reckon it should be just about the right length to fit him in.'

It was almost as if it was specially designed for their purpose, thought Juliet, grunting with exertion as they heaved their load into the back of the vehicle and rolled it into the shallow recess. Had Mitsoki found themselves an unpublicised market niche in providing the wheels for freelance undertakers, illegal immigrants and prison escapees?

'Where are we going to take him?' asked Carmen, pushing the concealed floor flap back into place.

'I don't know yet.' Juliet walked round the vehicle, checking that nothing was visible from outside. 'I'll need a bit of time to work out a plan.'

Carmen glanced at her watch and yawned. 'It's nearly two o'clock,' she murmured sleepily. 'Are you going to stay the night?'

'Looks like it,' said Juliet. 'But we can't go to bed yet. There's still a whole lot of cleaning up to do.'

'Cleaning up? Can't we do it in the morning?'

'We don't want to take any chances, do we? What would we do if the police turned up on the doorstep first thing?'

'The police?' Carmen looked frightened. 'But how . . .'

'I'm sure they won't,' said Juliet in a reassuring tone. 'But it'll be easier to get rid of the bloodstains if we don't leave them overnight.'

As they locked the car and went back into the house, Juliet wondered if Carmen was going to have the stamina for what lay ahead. To judge by most of the books she had read, covering up a murder was a task that didn't have an end. There would always be a possibility of discovery at any time. She was taking a huge risk in getting involved. Even if they succeeded in the initial stages of the deception, there was nothing to guarantee that Carmen wouldn't break down and confess to everything several years hence.

To avoid such unpleasant thoughts, she began to compile a mental list of cleaning jobs. Carpet, walls, door, stairs, Carmen's clothes and shoes. Was it possible to beat the forensic experts? These days, they could tell you your grandmother's maiden name from a single strand of carpet fibre. It seemed that the best chance of fooling them would be to get them looking in entirely the wrong place. But before she could come up with any kind of plan for this, she needed a lot more information about Gideon and his habits. There was a great deal of work to be done before either of them got any sleep that night.

The cleaning took until four in the morning, after which she sat Carmen down with a cup of coffee and grilled her about life with Gideon. 'I need to build up a complete picture,' she said, pacing back and forth in the kitchen. 'Don't leave anything out, however trivial it might seem. The tiniest detail might be the key that tells us how to deal with the problem.'

'You sound like a psychoanalyst,' muttered Carmen, rubbing her eyes sleepily. Reluctantly, she began to speak, sketching an outline of what seemed to Juliet to be a bleak and lonely existence. They had few friends or relatives who kept in touch – even Carmen's parents seemed to have lost interest in their only daughter. The only person she spoke of with any warmth was an aunt in the Scilly Isles. As Carmen talked on, Juliet noticed that she was avoiding any mention of events in the recent past.

When pressed on this subject, Carmen looked up at Juliet with a forlorn expression. 'Do we really need to go into all that?' she asked. 'Can't we just get rid of the body and pretend he's gone off on one of his jaunts?'

'*Just* get rid of the body?' echoed Juliet scornfully. 'How do you suggest we do that, then? Put him out for the bin men?'

'I meant bury him or something. Where he won't be found.'

Juliet sighed. 'It's not as simple as that, you know. You'd have to go down at least six feet if you didn't want every dog in the neighbourhood sniffing around and digging him up again. How would you manage that without anyone noticing what you're doing? Then you'd still have the problems of settlement – a freshly-dug grave is harder to conceal than you might think.'

'How come you're such an expert?' asked Carmen sulkily. 'I'm sure there must be places out in the country where nobody goes.'

'It's not just a matter of hiding him,' said Juliet impatiently. 'If he disappears without trace, you'll be the most obvious suspect, and the police will be round here searching for bloodstains in no time at all. They'll find them if they look hard enough. It's impossible to remove them completely. Our only hope is to think laterally, to divert their attention somewhere else.'

As she said this, the broad principles of the solution began to come together in her mind. Nobody else knew that Gideon was dead. If they could somehow pretend for a while that he was still alive, they could dispose of him in a far more appropriate way. The 'perfect murder' could still take place.

Running through the plots of various books and films in her head, she kept returning to *Double Indemnity* – the film that had made her imagine the world of insurance to be so much more exciting than it actually was. She had always secretly dreamed of looking like Barbara Stanwyck in her role as Phyllis Dietrichson, the murderous wife. The story involved a life-insurance swindle, with the husband's death being fixed to look like an accident on a train. It failed in the end, because villains always had to get their come-uppance in those days. But Juliet was sure that the idea could be adapted to fit their present dilemma.

Carmen was almost asleep at the table. Realising that she needed more time to think, Juliet sent her upstairs to bed and settled herself on the sofa to work things out. Forensic science had progressed somewhat since *Double Indemnity* was made in 1944, and it was no longer possible to fake an accidental death by simply dumping a dead body on a railway track.

Once the police got their hands on Gideon's body, they would easily be able to establish the time and manner of his death. They could probably also work out that the body had been moved, and all kinds of inconvenient details about how and where from. The more she thought about it, the more she was convinced that the actual body was too much of a liability to incorporate in her plan. The best thing to do would be to get rid of it as soon as possible.

She had laughed at Carmen's suggestion of burial, but what were the alternatives? Burning it? Chopping it up into little pieces? She shuddered, imagining the feats of butchery likely to be involved. Her dissecting skills didn't go a lot further than cutting a chicken into portions for a stew. Eventually, after pondering her way through a series of increasingly gruesome options and rejecting them all, she realised Carmen had been right all along. Of course they should bury the body, and she knew the perfect place to do it. It was some distance away, but it was a place where nobody would ever think of looking, or be likely to find anything if they did. The journey there might have been a problem if they didn't have the Freeloader but, with the body safely concealed in the underfloor storage compartment, they should be able to transport it to any part of the country they chose. The further away the better, in fact, thought Juliet. If anything went wrong, they needed to be sure that no one would be able to make a connection with the actual location where Gideon had been killed.

Once she had satisfied herself that she knew how to get rid of the body, Juliet moved on to the question of how they could make it look as if Gideon was still alive and, just as importantly, how they were going to fake his accidental death. They needed witnesses, she decided – people who could be tricked into thinking they had seen Gideon and would vouch for his continued existence without suspecting that it might not have been him. Going back over the information she had gathered earlier, Juliet remembered the aunt in the Scilly Isles. Carmen had told her that this aunt had never met Gideon. With a smile, she realised that the Scilly Isles were in exactly the same direction as the place she had earmarked for the disposal of Gideon's remains. If Carmen was willing to deceive her aunt, Juliet was beginning to see how her idea for the 'perfect murder' could be made to work.

Without a body, the options for faking Gideon's death were limited to methods in which it was reasonable to expect that the body would never be found. Drowning at sea was probably the safest bet, and the Scilly Isles were an ideal location – twenty-eight miles into the Atlantic from the mainland. You could take a proper sea journey to get there, without the need for any of the administrative hassles of going abroad.

Juliet had always believed that it must be fairly easy to make it look as if someone had fallen overboard from a ship. The clichéd view was that there was always a witness – someone to rush around the decks shouting *Man Overboard!* But what if someone slipped through the railings unnoticed in bad weather? And what if their travelling companions believed them to be elsewhere on the ship? Surely there must have been cases, thought Juliet, where a person's disappearance at sea hadn't been discovered until reaching port, after the rest of the passengers had disembarked.

All that was needed, apart from some good acting on the part of the distraught companion, was to concoct some evidence to show that the person in question had actually been on board. A ticket could be purchased in their name and someone could impersonate them, changing their disguise to take on a different identity once the 'accident' had occurred.

The weak point in applying any of this to the present situation was the problem of finding someone to play the part of Gideon. Carmen was hardly likely to want to take a stranger into her confidence about what she had done. Sleepily, Juliet searched for a solution. Before long, however, she had exhausted herself with her mental efforts and drifted off to sleep.

She dreamed she was trapped in a distorted version of *Double Indemnity* in which the murder was being acted out on board a ship instead of on a train. Gideon had come back to life and was chasing her along a narrow corridor lined with portholes. Turning a corner, she came out onto the deck and ran straight into Barbara Stanwyck, who was aiming a revolver at her pursuer. 'Goodbye Baby,' murmured the film star, pulling the trigger. Turning, Juliet saw a figure lying slumped against a railing. But it wasn't

Gideon any more – it was Duncan. As she watched, he began to get up again and lunged towards her, dripping with blood.

She woke with a shiver of horror. In the real version of *Double Indemnity* it was Phyllis's lover, Walter Neff, who disguised himself as the dead husband so that he could fake his death falling from a train. Carmen didn't have a lover, but there was, she now realised, an obvious candidate to impersonate Gideon. Duncan. He was approximately the same height and build, and she had already seen him practising for the part in Shepherd's Bush Road on Saturday night. With a touch of make-up and a false moustache, he would have a good chance of fooling anyone who hadn't known Gideon very well.

But how could she persuade Duncan to do it? It wasn't exactly the sort of favour you asked of a friend – *Hey mate, would you mind impersonating someone who's dead to help out this murderer I happened to meet the other day? Don't worry, it won't be much more than a couple of years inside if you get found out.*

If you put it like that, it sounded preposterous. Duncan was certain to refuse. But what if they could carry out part of the deception without telling him about Gideon's death? People often went to great lengths to keep up appearances, attempting to convince relatives that they were happily married when, in reality, they were in the middle of some acrimonious divorce. If Gideon was constantly disappearing without explanation when he was alive, Carmen might well have decided to hire a stand-in to accompany her on a visit to her aunt.

There was a good chance that Duncan might swallow this, thought Juliet, especially if they told him that his acting skills had played a part in sowing the seed of the idea. She was completely caught up in her plan now, oblivious to the dangers she was creating for herself. If Duncan agreed to help them, she concluded, there was a possibility that it might actually work.

When Carmen woke that morning, she was relieved to find that Gideon wasn't beside her. He must have got up early, she thought, listening to the sounds of him moving around downstairs. Then she remembered that Gideon was dead. It was Juliet she could hear clattering about in the kitchen. Gideon was in the garage, jammed into the luggage space of the stupid car he had bought to impress his friends, and he wasn't likely to be making very much noise.

It was hard to believe that it was true. She felt a rush of panic and confusion as she struggled to make sense of what had happened the day before. Her tired brain kept delivering the wrong message: *Gideon will kill me when he finds out what I've done.*

If she was suffering from shock, it wasn't doing much to cushion the effects of her hangover, which made itself felt as she pulled on her dressing gown and stumbled downstairs. Wincing at the sight of the empty whisky bottle on the kitchen table, she rummaged in a drawer for aspirins.

'Coffee?' asked Juliet, glancing round from the cooker and holding out a mug. Taking it, Carmen slumped into a chair and struggled with the child-proof lid of a pill bottle. Her life had changed dramatically since the previous day and she was beginning to feel as if she had stepped over the threshold to a different world.

The lid flew off the bottle and rolled across the floor. It wasn't going to be an easy world to live in, she realised, shaking tablets into her hand. Although she would never suffer from Gideon's cruelty again, a new shadow would always hang over her. Because of the simple action of pulling a trigger, she had become a fugitive – a person condemned by society. She might be caught and punished at any time.

Miserably, she swallowed several aspirins and sipped at her mug of coffee. She was grateful to Juliet for taking control and telling her what to do, but she didn't really believe that she would be able to cover up Gideon's death. How long did she have left, she wondered, before justice caught up with her? With a shock, she realised that the new series of *Makeover* would begin in less than a fortnight. Would she be presenting it, as planned, or would she be sending Kevin a note of resignation from a prison cell?

As Juliet handed her two boiled eggs and a plateful of toast, Carmen glanced at the clock on the wall and saw that it was half past nine. 'Aren't you going to be late for work?' she asked anxiously, unsure whether she could cope with the horrors of being left alone.

'Work?' Juliet grinned. 'You don't think I'm going to work at a time like this, do you? I'm sure the insurance business can manage without me for a day or two.'

'What are we going to do, then?' asked Carmen, relieved. 'Have you got any ideas?'

'One or two,' replied Juliet. 'In fact, I've almost got a plan worked out. I just need to sort out a few more details.' Taking a slice of toast, she buttered it and cut it into strips. Carmen watched as she dunked one of them into her egg, causing a stream of yolk to run down the side of the shell and collect in a yellow pool on the plate.

'This aunt you mentioned last night,' continued Juliet, chewing noisily. 'The one in the Scilly Isles. How would she feel if you turned up to visit her unexpectedly?'

'Aunt Bridget?' Carmen carefully sliced the top off one of her own eggs. 'She'd be pleased, I should think. She's invited me to stay with her often enough. Why do you ask?'

'That's good,' murmured Juliet thoughtfully. She pointed a finger of toast towards Carmen, dripping egg on the table. 'And what if you had taken Gideon with you? When he was still alive, I mean.'

'Well, she did keep saying she wanted to meet him.' Carmen scooped out a neat spoonful of egg and sprinkled it with a tiny pinch of salt. 'It was Gideon who refused to go. He had this excuse about not liking flying, and it was always far too complicated to go by boat.' She put the spoon in her mouth and felt the familiar comforting sensation as the egg slid down her throat. It was a surprise to discover that she could still enjoy the taste of food. Weren't murderers supposed to live in some kind of torment, their appetites permanently tainted by the bitter flavour of their guilt?

She was about to ask what Aunt Bridget had to do

with their current predicament when Juliet finished her egg and began to speak. 'I'd better explain my plan,' she said. 'First of all we need to bury the body . . .'

'Bury it? But I thought you said we couldn't do that.'

'I've changed my mind,' she replied with an enigmatic smile. 'I've thought of the perfect place.'

'Where's that?'

'All in good time. Let's deal with the broad strategy first, shall we, before we get bogged down in detail.'

Carmen listened with an increasing sense of disbelief as Juliet described her plan to get Duncan to impersonate Gideon. 'But that's a ridiculous idea,' she interrupted eventually. 'We're not in one of your Agatha Christie stories now, you know. This is real life. We'd never get away with it.'

'Murder happens in real life, doesn't it?' Juliet's tone was unexpectedly harsh. 'If you wanted to stick with your rose-tinted version of what it's all about, then you shouldn't have started killing people. Quite frankly, we'll never get away with this if we *don't* do something pretty extreme.'

'I'm sorry,' muttered Carmen. 'It's just that I can't see how it could work. Surely nobody's going to believe that Duncan is Gideon. He's too nice, for a start.'

'I wasn't exactly planning to take him round to schmooze with all Gideon's friends,' retorted Juliet. 'That's the whole point about visiting your aunt. She's never met him before, has she? She'd have no reason to suspect a thing and she'd be the perfect witness to say that Gideon's still alive. Then, when we bump him off, we can make it look just like an accident.'

'Bump him off?' echoed Carmen, confused. She had thought that Duncan was Juliet's friend. Surely she wasn't planning to commit *another* murder to cover up this one?

'I don't mean really bump him off, you idiot,' said Juliet, laughing. 'We fake it, don't we?' She launched into an explanation of her idea about the drowning at sea. 'But I can't work out the final details until we've done the trip and checked how they handle things like boarding cards,' she added. 'That's why we have to wait until the return journey, after we've visited your aunt.'

'But how on earth are you going to persuade Duncan to help us?' asked Carmen, uncomfortably aware that she didn't want Juliet's attractive friend to see her as a murderer. 'Surely you're not intending to tell him what really happened?'

'Well, not exactly,' admitted Juliet. 'I had this idea for a cover story about your aunt. It would do for the first part of the plan, at least. Once we're down on the Scillies, I'm sure it'll be easier to explain the rest.'

Carmen listened to Juliet's story about persuading her elderly aunt that she was happily married. 'I suppose it might just work,' she said thoughtfully. 'Though I wouldn't call Aunt Bridget *elderly* – she's only in her fifties.' Then she frowned. 'But what happens after that? We'll have to tell Duncan what's going on eventually. It's all very well to conjure up these fancy stories, but how's he going to react when he suddenly finds out he's mixed up in a murder plot? Surely it would be much safer to tell him the truth from the start?'

'I'm not so sure,' said Juliet. 'Look at it this way: If we tell him straight off, and he refuses to have anything to do with it, we're going to be pretty well stuck. I can't see how we're going to find another way out of this mess. Now if, on the other hand, we spin him the story and wait until after we've seen your aunt before we tell him the truth, then we can be certain of achieving at least half of what we're aiming for. We'll have made everybody think that Gideon's still alive.

'Listen,' she continued, 'if anything goes wrong, we're actually protecting Duncan. He can't get into trouble over a murder he knows nothing about. But the important thing is that, even if he washes his hands of us once we've told him, we can *still get away with it*. As long as we can persuade him to keep his mouth shut, Gideon can just 'disappear'. It won't be as good as faking his death, but at least it means that no one's going to be rooting around looking for bloodstains in Holland Park.'

'But how do you know Duncan won't go straight to the police when you tell him the truth?' asked Carmen doubtfully.

'I don't think he will,' said Juliet. 'I think he'll actually help us when it comes to it. He's one of these guys who just needs to be pushed a little. If you give him the option of settling for a quiet life, then he'll go for it every time, but if he's forced to choose between being the sneak who goes off to the police or the lawless adventurer, he'll go for the heroic role. He's an actor, remember – always wanting to play the lead. And I've known him all my life. I'm certain that he'd stand by me if I was in trouble. I really think we'd be risking much less if we do it my way.'

'But what if he does go to the police?' asked Carmen anxiously. 'Just supposing.'

'He won't,' said Juliet firmly. 'I'll make sure he doesn't. If it comes to it, I can always threaten to reveal how I forged a reference to help him get his Equity card.'

Later that morning, Duncan was walking along Holland Park Avenue with a spring in his step. Juliet had just called and invited him to lunch with Carmen Bird.

He was in need of something to cheer him up. The last week had been one of the worst since he arrived in London. The bills had come in, as predicted, after Sonia's departure, and his emergency funds were getting alarmingly low. He had heard nothing about the *Flux* commercial and none of his other enquiries for work had produced the slightest response.

His only recent outing, in fact, had been to Carmen's disastrous dinner party. He couldn't remember all the details of that evening too clearly, as he had consumed a considerable amount of alcohol on an empty stomach. The main thing that stayed in his mind was the unpleasant shock of being sent away without a proper meal, especially after he had just spent most of his available cash on flowers and wine. The walk home had seemed to last forever, and he had been anxious to get rid of Juliet so that he could sneak off and splurge his remaining funds on dealing with his hunger pangs. He hadn't been in touch with her since then, as he was worried that he might have offended her. He just hoped that she hadn't ventured out again that night, or she might have spotted him on the pavement outside the Hammersmith Kebab House, mingling with the late-night drunks as he wolfed down a king-size doner and chips.

But the telephone call that morning seemed to have put everything to rights. Juliet really was a good friend, he thought, fixing things up for him so that he could get to know Carmen better. As he approached the front door, he was aware of two hopes pressing in his mind. The first was that lunch might be a little more substantial than his last meal at that house, and the second was that Carmen's obnoxious husband wasn't going to be around.

Two hours later, he returned through the same door in a state of confused euphoria. He had a job! OK, so it was a little unorthodox – not the kind of thing you could put on your CV – but he was going to be paid for it, and it was with Carmen Bird.

Lunch had been somewhat basic: jacket potatoes cooked by Juliet, who appeared to be hanging around at Carmen's house rather a lot these days, followed by fruit, biscuits and cheese. The wine had flowed freely, however, and Duncan had been in a receptive mood when the suggestion that he could help out with a family problem was made.

It seemed that Carmen had an elderly aunt in the Scilly Isles who intended to bequeath her a substantial inheritance, but insisted on meeting Gideon before she finalised her will. The arrangements had all been made to travel down for a visit, but Gideon had disappeared. He had walked out after a big argument the previous night and, to judge by his performance on other occasions, wasn't likely to return for at least a week.

Carmen explained that the trip had already been cancelled several times for similar reasons. Her aunt was beginning to lose patience, and she suspected that this was her last chance. What she needed was someone to act as a stand-in for Gideon. Turning to Duncan with a look that made him go weak at the knees, Carmen had asked him if he would pretend to be her husband for a few days.

Did Shakespeare write plays? Was Macbeth a Scot? Duncan would have turned down the role of the Dane himself for a chance at this part. Amazingly, she was also prepared to pay him, at a rate that was well above the Equity minimum, and to reimburse him for any expenses incurred on the trip. It looked as if his financial worries could be temporarily put to rest. He was a little anxious about what might happen if Gideon turned up unexpectedly, or somehow found out what he had done, but the two women seemed strangely certain that this wasn't going to happen. Was it possible, he wondered hopefully, that Gideon might already have left Carmen? At the very least, it sounded as if he was having some kind of an affair.

When they insisted on testing out a disguise to make him look more like Gideon, Duncan had been happy to sit back in a chair and let Carmen set to work on him, applying makeup and a false moustache, and altering the style of his hair. The result was surprisingly convincing. Even though he was used to stage makeup, Duncan felt a shock when he glanced at the mirror and thought, for a split second, that he was looking at Gideon's face.

He was just beginning to enjoy himself, feeling his way into the role and experimenting with his posture and speech, when the afternoon was brought to a hurried conclusion. Instead of opening another bottle of wine, as he had hoped, Carmen produced a large tub of cleanser and scrubbed off his make-up with brisk movements. Then, before he had a chance to enter into any further conversation, or even thank Carmen for the lunch, Juliet bustled him towards the door.

'Here's a list of the things you need to bring with you,' she told him, handing him a piece of paper.

The list seemed straightforward enough – items of clothing and suchlike – but was oddly specific in places. 'Why does it matter if my trousers are light-weight or not?' he asked, puzzled.

'I'll explain that bit later,' Juliet said, planting herself firmly in the hallway and blocking his access back into the house. 'Just make sure you don't forget anything, and get yourself here on time in the morning. We need to set off by ten o'clock.'

There was something rather strange about this whole business, he reflected, walking away from the house. For one thing, he couldn't see why was it necessary for Juliet to come on the trip as well. In fact, she seemed to have become remarkably intimate with the

TV star in the space of the last few days, and gave the impression that she knew more about what was going on than Carmen did herself.

Juliet was definitely up to something, he decided, heading towards the hat shop on Portobello Road for a celebratory browse. But he wasn't going to ask any awkward questions for the time being – there was too much at risk. When would he ever get another chance to realise his fantasy of sharing a bed with Carmen Bird?

As soon as they had got rid of Duncan, Carmen telephoned her aunt. 'She's a bit surprised,' she told Juliet half an hour later, 'but she said we could come and stay for as long as we like.'

Juliet was ecstatic that Duncan had agreed to help. It had been worth telling a few lies, she thought, just to get the opportunity of spending some time with him at last. Now was her chance to show him that she could be just as good company as Sonia and her kind.

Returning to Chiswick to pick up some clothes and a toothbrush, she left Carmen with strict instructions to act normally if anybody telephoned or called at the house. 'If they ask for Gideon,' she said, 'tell them he's out and you don't know when he'll be back. But make sure you mention that he's going to the Scilly Isles with you tomorrow – it'll add a lot of credibility to our story if people think they know where he is.'

It didn't take long for her to collect the few things she needed from the bedsit. Her Chief Inspector Dagenham book was lying open on the coffee table where she had left it the night before, together with her empty glass and wine bottle. 'Eat your heart out, Dagenham Dick,' she murmured, replacing the book on the shelf. 'This time I'm going to have the adventure and you're going to be the one who stays at home.'

Before she left, she telephoned Castlemayne Insurance and told Tracey (or was it Jackie?) that she had a bad case of food poisoning. 'The doctor says I have to stay in bed for a while,' she added with a groan. 'You'd better tell *Lemon-Lips* to find someone else to bully for a few days.'

When she returned to Holland Park, Carmen handed her a crumpled greetings card. 'I should have shown you this before,' she muttered with downcast eyes. 'It's just that I kind of pushed it out of my mind. It upset me too much to think about it.'

Juliet opened the card and looked inside. 'Who's Angie?' she asked.

'Gideon's mistress, I suppose,' said Carmen with a contemptuous snort. 'Beating me up obviously wasn't enough for him. He had to humiliate me with this as well.'

Flattening out the front of the card, Juliet gazed at the picture of the drowned Ophelia. It seemed an odd choice for an adulterous *billet-doux*. It was also an unwelcome complication to their plans. What if this Angie, whoever she was, turned up looking for Gideon? What if he had made some arrangement to see her in the next few days. 'Does, I mean, *did* Gideon have a diary?' she asked anxiously. 'Or an address book . . . anything like that?'

'Don't ask me,' replied Carmen bitterly. 'I'm the last

person to know about these things.' But she relented
after a moment and led Juliet up to the study, handing
her a black leather Filofax from the drawer of Gideon's
desk. 'I've already checked,' she said in a flat voice.
'There's nothing in it.'

Juliet flicked briefly through the pages and saw that
this appeared to be the case. But then Gideon hadn't
seemed the sort of person who would meticulously
write down his appointments, or need reminding when
to turn up for his next illicit bonk.

'I'll leave you to it,' said Carmen, moving towards the
door. 'Carry on looking, if you think it's important, but
I'd rather not hear about the details. It makes me feel so
bloody stupid, not to have realised that he was having
an affair with some floozy right under my nose.'

When Carmen had gone downstairs, Juliet went
through the Filofax more carefully, but found nothing
incriminating. She was about to give up, when she
came across an extra pocket at the back that she
hadn't spotted the first time. Inside was Gideon's
driving licence. Useful for Duncan's false identity,
she thought, pulling it out to check the details. As
she unfolded it, something fluttered into her lap – a
small, passport-sized photograph of a brassy-looking
woman. This *had* to be Angie, she decided, inspecting
the made-up features and provocative pout. 'Floozy'
was the most apt description that sprang to mind.

Juliet slipped the photograph into her pocket, noticing,
as she did so, that there was a telephone number
scribbled on the back. Best not to mention this discovery at present, she decided. In a way, she could

understand how Carmen felt. She could remember, only too clearly, her own reaction when she discovered that her ex-boyfriend Keith was cheating on her.

She was also obscurely reminded of all the times her hopes had been dashed with Duncan. He hadn't mentioned his love life the last time she saw him, and she hoped there had been no further developments. She wasn't sure that she could bear it if another Sonia came along right now.

CHAPTER 11

Duncan arrived at nine-thirty the following morning. Opening the front door, Juliet was alarmed to see a camera dangling around his neck.

'Come in, quick,' she hissed, stepping to one side to let him pass. 'We don't want the neighbours thinking the paparazzi have turned up.'

Taking her literally, Duncan breezed into the kitchen to greet Carmen, leaving Juliet to bring in his rucksack and bags. 'Are we setting off straightaway?' he asked, perching on the edge of the table. 'I'm really looking forward to getting out of the smoke for a few days.'

'Not until we've done some work,' said Juliet briskly. 'This isn't a holiday, you know. You're being paid to do a job here.' Dropping Duncan's bags on the floor, she reached out and unhooked the camera strap from around his neck. 'I think we'd better get a few things straight before we start. Number one. No photographs.'

Duncan opened his mouth to protest, but Juliet continued without giving him a chance to speak. 'If Gideon finds out about any of this, there'll be a lot of trouble. The less evidence there is to prove anything, the better.'

She handed the camera to Carmen. 'You'd better put this away somewhere safe until we come back.'

She turned back to Duncan. 'The other thing to remember is that you must stay in character as Gideon the whole time. You must be on your guard whenever other people are around. Now, Carmen's going to sort out your moustache and stuff, and you . . .'

'Hang on a minute,' said Duncan, interrupting. 'I thought this disguise business was just for the aunt. Why do I have to pretend to be Gideon for anyone else?'

'I think it's best to be consistent,' said Juliet. 'It's going to look rather strange if you suddenly acquire a moustache overnight. People do tend to notice these things. Besides, you need the practice. You wouldn't go on stage without rehearsing a part, would you?'

'But what if we run into someone who knows Gideon? They'd see straightaway that something funny was going on.'

'That's not very likely to happen where we're going,' she said firmly. 'If it does, Carmen will be able to warn you, and you'll just have to keep out of the way for a while.'

'I'm sure it won't be necessary,' added Carmen. 'Gideon's never been to the Scilly Isles in his life.'

Leaving Carmen to apply her *Makeover* skills to Duncan, Juliet went into the garage and loaded a pair of garden spades into the car. When she returned, he was sitting patiently in a chair with a towel draped around his neck. Frowning with concentration, Carmen was squeezing latex glue onto a dark, furry caterpillar of a moustache.

'How did you learn to use all this stuff?' asked Duncan, inspecting the contents of Carmen's makeup box. 'I mean, you only *present* the programme, don't you? I've never seen you doing any of the actual makeup sessions yourself.'

'I wish more people were bright enough to work that out,' she murmured, positioning the moustache on Duncan's upper lip and clamping it into place with her hand. 'Don't worry,' she added, catching sight of Juliet's anxious expression. 'I'm not going to mess this up. When the programme got popular, I had so many requests to do demonstrations that I went on a special course to learn the tricks of the trade.' She smiled. 'A typical example of the back-to-front way things happen in the world of entertainment, don't you think?'

'Mmmff,' said Duncan, in agreement.

The telephone began to ring in the hallway. 'I'll get it,' offered Juliet, not wanting to interrupt the moustache-glueing operation. As she lifted the receiver, however, she belatedly realised how odd it might sound that a stranger should be picking up Carmen's calls.

'Hello?' she asked warily.

'Uh . . . Hi. Can I speak to Gideon, please?' There was a distinctive nasal whine to the woman's voice.

'He's out,' replied Juliet briskly. 'Who is it?'

'Uh . . . just a friend. Do you know when he'll be in again?'

'He's on his way to the Scilly Isles with his wife,' said Juliet, remembering the strategy she had agreed with Carmen. 'He set off this morning and he won't be back for at least a week.'

There was a pause. 'Do you want to leave a message?' she added, hoping the caller wasn't about to ask who *she* was. But there was no reply, just a click as the line went dead.

Strange, she thought, dialling 1471. When she learned that the number had been withheld, it suddenly occurred to her that it might have been the mysterious *Angie*. Searching her pockets, she retrieved the photograph and dialled the number written on the back.

'Hello?' It was the same voice.

'Shit,' muttered Juliet, slamming down the receiver. Why hadn't she been more careful? Gideon's mistress was the one person who shouldn't have been told where they were going.

'Who was that?' called Carmen from the kitchen.

'Just a wrong number,' replied Juliet in a casual voice, not wanting to admit to her mistake. The woman was hardly likely to follow them, she reasoned, especially if she thought that Gideon was with his wife.

When Carmen had finished with Duncan, he looked so much like Gideon that Juliet wondered for a frightened moment if he had come back to life and escaped from the garage. Instead of the scruffy jeans and sweatshirt he had arrived in, Duncan was kitted out in Gideon's expensive-looking designer wear. The moustache was now firmly in place, and Carmen had darkened his hair with spray-on colour and trimmed it into an exact copy of Gideon's style. Make-up subtly altered the contours of his face: his eyes now had deep shadows around them and he looked a lot older than his thirty-four years.

'What do you think?' he asked, pausing in the task of transferring his luggage into Gideon's sleek leather suitcases. The moustache gave him an unfamiliar and faintly sinister air.

'Not bad,' replied Juliet in a matter-of-fact tone. 'Except that your moustache is on upside-down.'

'But it can't be . . .' Dropping an armful of clothes, he flew to the mirror for reassurance.

'Only joking,' she murmured, slipping past him with a torch and a pair of wirecutters. She didn't want him getting too suspicious about the equipment this trip was going to require.

Eventually, they were ready to go.

'Hey, I've always wanted to have a ride in one of these,' said Duncan, catching sight of the Freeloader as they took the bags into the garage. 'Aren't they supposed to have an on-board computer to tell you where the traffic jams are?'

'Only as an optional extra,' said Carmen. 'I'm afraid I put my foot down when I found out how much Gideon had spent on the car itself.'

Duncan looked disappointed. 'What about the satellite telephone and the secret storage compartments?'

'It doesn't have any of those either,' said Juliet firmly, opening the rear door. 'Now are you going to put your stuff in there or not?'

Duncan peered into the luggage space, hesitated for a moment, then picked up his bags and hefted them inside. Turning back to face them, he winked at Carmen. 'Seeing as I'm supposed to be your husband,' he said, 'are you going to let me drive?'

*   *   *

Angie paced back and forth in her flat, seething with frustration. Why hadn't she tried to make contact sooner? She had recovered her blackmail material, but she was now unable to use it because Gideon had chosen this, of all times, to go on holiday.

The voice that had answered the telephone was unfamiliar – some secretary or housekeeper, she supposed. It just didn't seem fair, she thought angrily, that some people were rich enough to have minions to do everything for them when she couldn't even afford to pay the rent on her flat at the end of the month.

Flicking through the photographs, which were by now getting rather grubby, she began to wonder if she was approaching the whole thing in the wrong way. Might it be better to go straight to the newspapers and see what they would offer? It would be a much safer way of obtaining money than risking a repeat performance of Gideon's wrath.

She didn't know how to go about getting in touch with a newspaper, so she went out to buy one to see if they had telephone numbers inside. But once she was in the local newsagent's, she completely forgot the purpose of her trip. 'LONDON SEX MURDER!' screamed the headlines of the tabloids. 'WOMAN FOUND STRANGLED IN SHEPHERD'S BUSH FLAT'. With a shock of recognition, Angie stared at a photograph of the victim. She never forgot the face of a rival – and this was undoubtedly the woman who had been enjoying Gideon's favours in the pub on Tuesday night.

Returning home with copies of all the papers, Angie

soon learned that the murder had taken place on that very same evening. When she had finished reading the various reports, there was little doubt in her mind that Gideon was to blame. She had watched the pair go off in a car together only an hour before the estimated time of the woman's death. With a shudder, she tried to imagine what might have happened at the woman's flat to change Gideon from a lusty admirer into a cold-blooded killer. How close had she come, she wondered, to getting the same treatment herself?

But she didn't waste time mourning the fate of her mysterious rival. It wasn't so much a tragedy, she realised, as an incredible stroke of luck. She could forget about the photographs now, and the rest of the small-time blackmail she had planned. This was the big stuff. How much would a man be prepared to pay to avoid spending the rest of his life in jail?

Gideon's unexpected 'holiday' now made perfect sense. He was running away. If she moved fast, she might be able to catch up with him and cash in on a big payment. The important thing was to find him before the police or anybody else did. At least she knew where he was going, she thought with satisfaction. That housekeeper of his had really screwed up.

She would have to be careful about how she approached him, now that she knew he was capable of murder. His reaction to her first blackmail attempt had been frightening enough. But she would be safe, she reassured herself, if she only saw him in public places. He could scarcely bump her off in broad daylight with other people around.

Folding up the newspapers, she went downstairs to ask Ronco where the Scilly Isles were. With a bit of luck, she might be able to persuade him to let her borrow his car. But she stopped herself in the hallway before she reached his door. If she was going to risk her neck to blackmail Gideon, she didn't want to have to share the proceeds with anyone else. It would be better if she didn't give Ronco the option of deciding to come along as well.

Instead, she went to the local travel agents, where she was surprised to learn that the Scilly Isles were twenty-eight miles off the tip of Cornwall. She had always been under the impression that they were somewhere near Scotland. To judge by the cost of getting there, however, they might have been halfway across the Atlantic. It looked as if she would have to break into the last of her savings if she wanted to track Gideon down.

The boat was the cheapest method of travel, departing early each morning from Penzance. Remembering that Gideon had told her he hated flying, she decided that this would be the best bet. If he had only set off that morning, she thought excitedly, he wouldn't be able to make the crossing until the following day. He was probably staying overnight in Penzance. If she left straightaway, she could intercept him on the quayside the next morning when he tried to embark.

Returning to her flat, she packed some clothes and left a note for Ronco telling him not to worry. Then she slipped quietly out of the house and down to the end of the street, where he kept his car. It was an ancient Volkswagen Beetle, with moss growing out of the window seals and spiders inhabiting the air vents. The vehicle supported more wildlife than the pet shop across the road.

In case of emergency, the spare key was kept in a large rust hole under the edge of the bonnet. Wincing as something scuttled across her hand, Angie picked it out and gingerly opened the door. The engine started first time. Opening the window to throw out a snail that had attached itself to the gearstick, she pulled away and drove quietly to the junction with the main road.

She would call Ronco from a telephone box, she decided, just as soon as she was outside London. With a bit of luck, he might not have any badger-watching trips planned for that weekend.

Peering over Duncan's shoulder as the motorway rolled past, Juliet watched anxiously for the service station sign. Biting her nails, she fretted that she might have forgotten to turn off the water heater in her bedsit. She knew it was pointless to worry, as she couldn't do anything about it, but it served the useful purpose of distracting her from other, more serious, concerns.

Instead of feeling the usual excitement at the prospect of a long journey, she was beginning to wake up to the enormity of the crime in which she had let herself become involved. Each time they were passed by a police car, she broke into a guilty sweat. With an effort, she forced herself to concentrate on the navigation. If she didn't pull herself together, they would miss the garage, and the last thing they wanted right now was to run out of petrol on the hard shoulder of the M4.

Carmen was at the wheel, keeping to a steady speed on the inside lane. They had started the journey that morning with Duncan driving but, after he had raced round Shepherd's Bush Green like Damon Hill – narrowly avoiding being stopped by the police – he had been demoted to the front passenger seat. Juliet would have preferred to sit there herself, but decided it would be safer if she kept an eye on things in the back. Each time they turned a corner, there was a dull thud beneath her feet as their illicit cargo rolled sideways. She didn't want Duncan getting curious about the contents of the Freeloader's storage space.

At the service station, they filled up with petrol and went into the cafeteria for lunch.

'Oh great, I could murder a hamburger,' said Duncan gleefully, making a beeline for the Big Boy's Burgers concession.

'Yeuch,' muttered Carmen, wrinkling her nose. 'I can't stand those things, they're full of additives and stuff.'

Juliet, who had secretly been looking forward to a Double King Boy with all the trimmings, found herself being dragged across to the Country Granary for a lettuce-filled baguette coated in gravel chippings.

'I have to be careful about the calories,' confided Carmen. 'I don't think they'd let me present *Makeover* if I went any bigger than a size ten.'

As they sat down to eat, a coach party of pensioners straggled slowly into the cafeteria. 'Look Mavis,' squawked a woman with hair like purple candy floss. 'Isn't that *Carmen Bird* from the telly over there?'

Carmen whipped out a pair of dark glasses from her handbag, but it was too late. Heads swivelled with clucks of recognition and a bevy of elderly fans began to advance purposefully in their direction.

'I don't know if I can handle this,' whispered Carmen, cowering. She glanced at Duncan, whose face was temporarily hidden behind the ketchup-dripping layers of a Triple Boy Racer. 'What if they realise that he's not Gideon?'

'Think laterally,' replied Juliet. 'It's *you* they're interested in. They don't know Gideon from Adam, but they'll assume he's your husband because he's with you.'

The candy floss woman bore down on them, brandishing a pen. 'Can I 'ave yer autograph, Miss Bird?'

With a lukewarm smile, Carmen scribbled her name on a napkin and handed it over. A queue quickly formed and Juliet was forced to go in search of more paper to satisfy the demand. After about half a dozen signings, however, Carmen muttered an apology and fled in the direction of the toilet.

'What's wrong?' asked Juliet, catching up with her in the doorway.

'I'm sorry,' she whimpered, bursting into tears. 'I just can't do this at the moment, not while we've still got the . . . you know, the body . . . out there in the car park.' She faced Juliet with a look of desperation. 'Do you think they might go away if you tell them I'm not feeling well?'

'I doubt it,' murmured Juliet, glancing back at the table. Duncan had now finished his burger and was busy wiping ketchup and chunks of gherkin from his false moustache. She watched him chatting to one of the remaining autograph hunters, then let out a cry of dismay as she saw him reach for a pen. 'No!' she wailed, darting back towards him. She arrived just in time to stop him signing Gideon's name on the back of the woman's bus pass.

'What do you think you're playing at?' she hissed, dragging him out of the cafeteria and into the car park.

'But I was only trying to help, Jules,' he protested. 'Let me go back in – I haven't even finished my chips.'

'Your signature doesn't look anything like his,' she told him angrily, imagining what the police might discover if they began to investigate 'Gideon's' last movements. 'You'll get us into trouble.'

Duncan glowered at her. 'I don't see why you're making such a fuss. Nobody's going to find out, are they?'

'I wouldn't be so sure,' she muttered darkly, scanning the rows of cars for the Freeloader. For a moment, unable to spot it, she forgot her concerns about Gideon's handwriting. What would happen, she wondered with a surge of panic, if somebody stole the car with his body inside?

Then, with a start, she saw it parked only a short distance away. It was surrounded by a small group of people, some of whom were crouched on the tarmac and peering underneath. She had visions of the dead body dangling from the underside of the vehicle. 'What's wrong?' she cried, rushing forward in alarm.

A woman in pink leggings and a baggy jumper

embroidered with pictures of sheep was crawling around on her hands and knees at the side of the car. 'Tarquin!' she called. 'Come back to Mummy!' Bending to look underneath, Juliet saw a plump toddler sprawled on the tarmac, just out of arm's reach.

'Would you mind pulling him out of the way?' she asked the woman. 'We have to leave now.'

'Pull him out of the way?' echoed the woman. 'I don't think that's very wise, do you? He'll never develop a sense of independence if he isn't forced to find his way out of difficult situations on his own.' Tarquin let out a delighted gurgle and began to bang on the underside of the Freeloader with a toy hammer. 'Oh, look,' she added fondly. 'Isn't he clever? He's showing us how cross he is with the nasty car.'

'We're in a bit of a hurry, I'm afraid,' added Juliet. 'Perhaps we could just drive very slowly out of the parking space while you keep an eye on him?'

'Are you mad?' exclaimed the woman with a horrified expression. 'That's far too dangerous! I can't possibly allow you to move your vehicle!'

'What do you expect us to do then?' asked Juliet irritably. 'Catch the bus?'

'I don't know that you'll find any buses running on the motorway,' said the woman, oblivious to Juliet's sarcasm. 'It's far better to wait patiently, don't you think? I'm sure that whatever it is you're in such a hurry to get to can't be as important as the miracle of a child's life.' Unpacking a large bag of brightly coloured toys, she began to spread them around the parking space. 'Now, I wonder if he'll be more attracted to the Tellytubbies or the building blocks,' she murmured thoughtfully. 'It's always fascinating to see how his little mind works.'

'What's going on?' asked Carmen, appearing at Juliet's shoulder. Her face was pale. 'Why are all those people looking under our car?'

'Don't ask,' muttered Juliet, 'or this madwoman will keep us here all day. Just let us in quickly and get the engine started.'

'But Jules,' began Duncan, 'you can't . . .'

'Can't what?' asked Juliet, pushing him inside. 'Keep quiet, it'll be all right.'

As Carmen started the engine, the woman leapt to the window with a look of horror. 'Stop! Wait! My child . . .' she began, hammering on the window. Then she recognised Carmen. 'Goodness me,' she exclaimed. 'You're Carmen Bird!'

'I can't face any more bloody autograph hunters,' muttered Carmen, gripping the steering wheel. 'What should I do?'

Juliet peered through the back windscreen. As she had predicted, little Tarquin had crawled out as soon as the engine started. He was now playing happily with the litter on the grass verge. 'Just drive away,' she said, grinning.

As Carmen gunned out of the parking space, the woman screamed hysterically and tried to throw herself in front of the car. There was a satisfying crunching noise as they drove over Tarquin's Tellytubby Activity Centre.

'What was all that about?' asked Carmen, as they left the service area and rejoined the motorway. 'I've never seen anyone that desperate for my autograph before.'

After they had been travelling in silence for several miles, Duncan leaned forward and began to fiddle with a plastic flap next to the dashboard. 'What's in here?' he asked. 'Are you sure there isn't an on-board computer?'

'It's only the stereo,' said Carmen, tapping a number into a small keypad beside it. The flap slid open to reveal a gleaming array of buttons and dials.

'Hey, let's have some music, then,' said Duncan. 'Cheer us all up.' He pressed a button and the car was filled with the sounds of an orchestra playing a funeral march.

'Gideon must have been the last to use it,' said Carmen apologetically. 'He always likes to keep it tuned to Radio Three.'

'Well, he not here now, is he?' said Duncan, pressing another button with a grin.

They were swamped in a burst of canned laughter. '*Now we move on to round five,*' honked a jolly, overeducated voice, '*where our celebrity contestants tell their favourite anecdotes while balancing buckets of live piranha fish on their heads . . .*'

'Damn,' he muttered, stabbing the buttons repeatedly. 'How do I get any music on this thing?'

'*Police have launched a murder hunt for the killer of . . .*'

'Wait,' said Juliet. 'Stay on that one a minute – I want to hear the news.'

'*. . . 37-year-old Louise Cooper, who was found strangled yesterday in her Shepherd's Bush flat . . .*'

'Yeuch,' said Duncan, glancing back at Juliet. 'Shepherd's Bush isn't far from us, is it?'

'. . . *police are appealing for witnesses who may have seen the victim on Tuesday night . . .*'

'I don't want to hear about murders,' said Carmen with a shudder. Reaching into the glove compartment, she passed a booklet across to Duncan. 'That's the instruction manual for the Freeloader,' she said. 'It'll tell you how to reset the channels somewhere in there.'

After several further attempts, Duncan succeeded in retuning the radio to Conquest Gold, which was playing an old hit by Johnny September. 'That's better,' he sighed, leaning back in his seat and gazing at Carmen. 'This feels just like being in a film,' he added. 'You know, one of those road movies like *Thelma and Louise.*'

No prizes for guessing who reminded him of the younger, prettier one, thought Juliet sulkily. He, presumably, had allocated himself the Brad Pitt role.

'*I guess I'm gonna break your heart tonight, baby . . .*' he warbled, flicking idly through the Freeloader manual.

'Shut up, you berk – you're out of tune,' she grumbled, attempting to hit him on the head with the road atlas.

'Aw, Jules, that hurt,' he protested, ducking out of reach.

He listened to the radio in silence for a few moments before he spoke again. 'Hey, look at this,' he said, pointing at the manual. 'Did you know that the back of this thing converts into a double bed?'

'You're kidding,' said Juliet.

'Listen,' he continued, reading from the booklet. '. . . *simply slide rear seating unit into fully-extended horizontal position, retract high-capacity underfloor storage bin cover flaps, rotate by one-eighty degrees and lock into place on adjustable runners.*' He looked up with a grin. 'Anyone want to give it a try?'

'No!' said Carmen and Juliet in unison, having both realised that this would expose Gideon's hiding place. Juliet reflected gloomily that it was the first time Duncan had ever invited her to share a bed with him. How ironic that she should be forced to refuse in this way.

'I bet they call it the Freeloader Bonkmobile,' said Duncan, chuckling.

'So *that's* why Gideon was so keen to buy it,' burst out Carmen angrily. 'No wonder the people in the showroom were laughing at me.'

'Oh my God . . . I'm sorry . . .' Duncan turned to her with a look of anguish. 'I wasn't thinking. I didn't mean it like that.'

'It's all right,' said Carmen flatly. 'I'll get used to the idea eventually.' Juliet shifted uncomfortably on the rear seat, unable to stop herself from checking the upholstery for stains.

'Look, I know this is none of my business,' he continued, 'but I just don't understand how that bastard can screw around when he's got a beautiful wife like you. He must have something wrong with him.'

'If he didn't then, he certainly has now,' muttered Juliet under her breath.

'You see, I can't help wondering . . .'

'Oh, put a sock in it, Duncan,' interrupted Juliet, exasperated. 'Can't you see Carmen's upset?'

'I beg your pardon,' he said huffily. 'I was only trying to help.'

The journey continued in silence. Gideon must be getting to know the back of his car pretty well by now, thought Juliet. For the next hundred miles, she struggled to banish a mental picture of him romping naked with his mistress in the back of the Freeloader. He would never have suspected, she thought blackly, that he was fornicating in his own hearse.

As they approached Okehampton, on the edge of Dartmoor, she began to concentrate on more pressing matters. They would soon be arriving at the place where she intended to dispatch Gideon from their lives once and for all. Glancing at the map, she leaned forward and began to whisper directions in Carmen's ear. Before they could do anything, she needed to undertake a reconnaissance mission to check out the final details of her plan.

'Why are we stopping here?' asked Duncan, as they pulled into a layby on a deserted stretch of road.

'I need to, er, spend a penny,' muttered Juliet coyly, opening the door and indicating a nearby clump of trees. 'I won't be long.' She forced a smile, trying to dispel a sudden feeling of depression. 'Don't go anywhere without me.'

Setting off down a narrow footpath, she broke into a jog as soon as she was out of sight of the car. The distant screeching of seagulls reassured her that she was going the right way. She had been to this place only once before, a few months previously. As soon as the rich, rotting smell began to seep into her nostrils, memories of the visit came flooding back into her mind.

After Keith ran off with his blonde, Juliet had found temporary consolation with a boyfriend called Eric. He worked as some kind of environmental engineer, and was keen to interest Juliet in his subject. She had, in the early days of their relationship, dutifully accompanied him on trips to see wind farms, power stations, and even, on one occasion, a sewage plant. He had completely failed to grasp, however, that she might not share his enthusiasm for the details of waste treatment processes. Neither did he seem to appreciate how they might affect her appetite for a slap-up meal afterwards at one of the dubious curry houses he liked to frequent.

Juliet had been desperate to hang on to any kind of relationship at that time – if only to prove to herself that she was capable of attracting a man. But the landfill site had been the last straw. Dressing it up as a day trip to Devon, Eric had suggested that she might like to accompany him on one of his site visits. When they arrived, Juliet found that he expected her to tramp around in wellington boots and a hard hat, holding his ranging rods while he checked the levels of effluent outlets. It had taken her days to wash the smell out of her clothes and hair.

Just past the clump of trees, the footpath met up with another road. This would be the best place to stop the Freeloader when they returned later that night, she thought. On the left, a chain-link fence ran along the base of a steep bank. She was pleased to see that the mesh was torn or missing in several places. It looked as if the wire-cutters wouldn't be needed after all.

She had finished with Eric shortly after their visit to this place, explaining to him, over dinner at the Three Counties Tandoori, that it took more than common interests to ignite the spark of romance. As soon as he started drawing parallels with methane combustion processes, Juliet knew she had done the right thing. But she had learned a lot about landfill management, and about this site in particular. Slipping through a gap in the fence, she found the path she had taken with Eric on her previous visit. Following it, she climbed the bank on a shallow incline and reached a vantage point where the current activities could be observed.

The smell was much stronger at the top of the bund and there were loud beeping noises from lorries that were tipping waste only a short distance away. Watching the work in progress, she tried to determine the best place to deposit Gideon. If it was close to where tipping would recommence the next day, they would only need a shallow covering to prevent him being spotted by the operatives. The bulldozers would do the rest. By the end of the day, he would be buried beneath several tons of waste; by the end of the year, he would be deep in the centre of a new hillside. According to Eric, there were risks of environmental pollution if the landfill was disturbed and stringent measures would be applied to protect the capping layers. It was one place where they could be certain that he would never be dug up.

After making a mental map of the route they would take when they returned in the dark, Juliet went back to the Freeloader. A short time later, they were driving into Okehampton in search of a place to stay.

'I can't see why we don't just carry straight on to Penzance,' said Duncan, looking at the map. 'It would only take another couple of hours at the most.'

'There's no point in getting overtired,' said Carmen, yawning ostentatiously. 'I've been driving all day, you know.'

'But I could take over if you want,' he offered eagerly. 'You'd be perfectly safe – I'd drive much more carefully this time. You could even open out the bed thing and have a sleep in the back.'

'We have to stop here so that Carmen can meet someone,' said Juliet, improvising as she realised they had forgotten to work out a cover story for what they were doing that night. 'She's, er, interviewing people for a new project at Conquest TV.'

Duncan looked crestfallen for a moment, then brightened again. 'Will I be going, too?' he asked hopefully. 'Do I have to pretend to be Gideon?'

'Er, well, not exactly . . .' began Carmen.

'She means no,' said Juliet, as they pulled up outside an imposing looking building on the main street. It announced itself in gold lettering as 'The Black Dog Hotel' and displayed a bewildering array of stars, crowns, and other cryptic symbols after the name.

'Shall we go in here?' asked Carmen, nodding at a 'Vacancies' sign in the window.

'It looks a bit expensive, doesn't it?' ventured Juliet.

A picture flashed into her mind of Duncan and Carmen ensconced in double-bedded luxury. 'Couldn't we try the youth hostel?' she suggested.

'You must be joking,' said Carmen, looking shocked. 'I'm not staying in one of those places. I need an *en suite* bathroom and room service the way I feel tonight.' She opened the door of the Freeloader. 'Are you coming? Since I'm paying for all this, I think I should be allowed to choose where we stay.'

Juliet waited in the background with Duncan while Carmen booked the rooms. The receptionist, recognising the TV star as she walked through the door, fawned over her in a manner that Juliet found quite repulsive. Carmen didn't exactly ask for the honeymoon suite, but the Lady Howard Room on the first-floor front sounded like the next best thing. Juliet was allocated an unnamed single in the Coachman's Rest Annexe.

'Do you think there'll be a television?' asked Duncan. 'I don't want to miss *Southsiders* tonight.'

'I don't know,' muttered Juliet. Carmen might at least have asked for a twin-bedded room, she thought, feeling a pang of jealousy as they fetched the luggage from the Freeloader. She had somehow failed to anticipate the possible consequences of pushing Carmen and Duncan together like this. But it had been her own idea to get Duncan involved, she realised miserably. If anything happened between them, she would only have herself to blame.

CHAPTER 12

Angie drove into Penzance that evening feeling as if she had spent the whole day on a white-knuckle fairground ride. Ronco's car seemed to have been designed long before the word ergonomic was invented, or before anyone had thought of the need to conserve oil resources. It was the only car she had ever driven where the needle on the fuel gauge moved faster than the speedometer, racing towards empty as she pulled out of the garage. If she had known how much the journey was going to cost her in petrol, she would have applied for a bank loan before she set off.

Her first attempt to explore Penzance was short-lived. Sucked into the centrifuge of the one-way system, she was spun round and hurled back out in the direction she came. By the time she realised what had happened, she was trapped on a dual carriageway with signs saying 'No U-Turns' and 'London 300' flashing past. Luckily, a roundabout allowed her a second chance. This time, she managed to escape from the circuit into a huge car park that occupied much of the seafront.

Glancing across the harbour, she could see a ship coming in, presumably the return crossing from the Scillies for that day.

When it sailed again the next morning, with or without Gideon on board, she hoped to have a large cheque in her pocket. How much should she ask for, she wondered dreamily? Ten thousand? Twenty? It would be a small price for Gideon to pay for his freedom, after all. She smiled, relishing the power her knowledge had given her. Her only regret was that she wouldn't be able to share what she knew with his wife.

It would have given Angie enormous pleasure to watch the smile disappear from Carmen Bird's face when she realised that she was married to a murderer. There was too great a risk, however, that the TV star might denounce her husband and leave him – wiping out Angie's opportunities for further blackmail at a later date. There was also the matter of the photographs she had retrieved on the night of the murder. If Gideon and Carmen stayed together, there was no reason why these couldn't be brought back into play as well. On the whole, it seemed best to keep quiet at this stage in the game.

Her immediate task was to find a place to stay overnight that wouldn't blow the remainder of her funds. A glance at the list in the window of the Tourist Information Centre soon told her that the hotels and guest houses in the town were beyond her means. Except for one. At the bottom of the list, the Harbour Lodge Boarding House (DSS welcome) was so cheap that even Angie was hesitant about going there. To make any profit at the rates they were charging, they would almost be obliged to creep into your room at night and steal everything you owned.

It didn't look any more enticing than its description. Facing the railway tracks on what appeared to be the least desirable stretch of the seafront, it was in dire need of repainting and a forest of weeds inhabited its front lawn. A garden gnome was padlocked to the basement railings, as if to stop it escaping. Stepping over a drunk who lay asleep on the pavement in front of the entrance, Angie went inside.

A grim-looking woman with a tattoo on her arm relieved her of the necessary cash and showed her to a gloomy room on the first floor. It had a sea view, just visible through the vertical sliver of window that remained after partitioning the front of a standard Victorian semi into three separate rooms. Pressing the light switch, Angie discovered that electricity wasn't included in the price. A grubby handwritten notice taped to the wall informed her that she would have to insert a coin into the meter if she wanted the luxury of artificial light. A second notice warned that it was forbidden to eat takeaways in the room, while a third requested her '*not to steel the towls please*'.

Remembering that she hadn't called Ronco, she went downstairs to find out if there was a telephone. With a shrug, the woman pointed out of the window to a public call box on the other side of the harbour. Even from this distance, Angie could see that there were at least half a dozen people queueing outside.

When she finally got through to Ronco and he said

nothing about the car, she decided not to mention that she had taken it. If she finished her business here tomorrow and took it straight back, she thought hopefully, he might not even notice that it had gone. She needed to tell him her location, however, as insurance in the event that Gideon turned nasty and tried to do her in.

'That's a long way away,' he remarked. 'How on earth did you get there so quickly?'

Angie muttered something noncommittal about the train.

'I'd have lent you my car if I still had one,' he continued. 'It would have been so much easier than . . .'

'What did you say?' interrupted Angie. 'About your car?' He had obviously missed it already, she thought despondently. How long would it take for him to work out where it had gone?

'Didn't I tell you?' he said, sounding surprised. 'I decided to get rid of it. I sold it last week to a bloke who lives down the end of our road.'

The centrepiece of the Lady Howard Room was an ornate four-poster bed. 'Wow,' said Duncan, bouncing experimentally on the mattress. 'I've never slept in one of these things before.'

Watching him, Carmen felt mildly alarmed at the prospect of spending the night with him. Was he attracted to her? She hadn't shared a bed with anyone but Gideon for over eight years.

Dragging her suitcase into the bathroom, she filled the tub with hot, scented water and locked the door.

She was tired and sticky from the journey, and needed a long soak. Later, when she had finished, she dressed carefully and reapplied her makeup. Just because they were going to bury Gideon that night, she thought defiantly, there was no reason why she shouldn't look her best.

Dusk was falling when she came out of the bathroom. It was time to go and meet Juliet. Duncan was engrossed in *Southsiders* on the wide-screen TV, and scarcely glanced up when she reminded him that she was going out for a few hours.

The Coachman's Rest Annexe turned out to be a shabby-looking building at the back of the car park. Juliet came to her door dressed in black fatigues and heavy boots, needing only a red beret to be mistaken for a member of a crack commando unit. 'Haven't you got anything more suitable to wear?' she hissed, seeing Carmen's flimsy designer clothes. 'Those shoes won't get you very far.'

'What's wrong with them?' asked Carmen indignantly, glancing down at her flat, sensible sandals.

'We're not going to a fashion show, we're going to be scrambling across a rubbish tip. You need something to protect your feet.' Juliet held open the door of her narrow room. 'You'd better come in and I'll see if I can lend you something,' she added, glancing at her watch. 'We don't want you going back and making Duncan suspicious.'

Carmen emerged, ten minutes later, with several pairs of socks and Juliet's size 8 trainers on her tiny feet. Her stylish blazer had been replaced by a nylon waterproof jacket in a nasty shade of green and she wore a pair of enormous jeans, which reached almost to her arm-pits and had to be belted with Juliet's dressing gown cord. As they crossed the car park to the Freeloader, she turned up the jacket collar and tried to look as inconspicuous as possible. It wouldn't be much of an advertisement for *Makeover* if anyone saw her dressed like this.

Driving towards the landfill site for the second time that day, Carmen tried to summon up courage to get through what came next. While Gideon had been safely stowed away out of sight, she had been able to avoid thinking about him. Now, she had to confront the question of how they were going to dispose of his body without getting caught.

'Slow down a minute,' said Juliet suddenly. 'I'm a bit lost.'

Carmen felt a rush of panic. What if they never managed to find the place again in the dark? They would be stuck in the middle of nowhere with a rotting corpse in the car.

'Take a left here,' muttered Juliet, indicating an unlit side road with high banks on either side. They turned into it, descending a steep slope that looked as if it was going to deliver them straight into the jaws of hell. At the foot of the hill, there was a sharp bend. 'Pull over now,' she said as they rounded the corner. In the moonlight, Carmen could see an area of grass at the side of the road with a fence and a steep bank beyond.

'This is it,' said Juliet as they rolled to a halt. 'I

checked it out earlier. It's much closer than the place we stopped before.' Clambering into the back of the vehicle, she began to struggle with the fastenings of the storage compartment. 'What are you waiting for?' she asked, glancing back at Carmen. 'Come on, let's get on with the job.'

Getting Gideon out of the back of the Freeloader turned out to be a lot harder than putting him in. There was no space to obtain a proper leverage once the cover flaps were opened, and the high-capacity underfloor storage bin seemed strangely reluctant to surrender its load. Eventually they managed to claw him out, inch by inch, and tip him through the rear door onto the grass. As they did so, the glow of a pair of headlights appeared at the nearby bend in the road.

'Shit,' muttered Juliet, jumping out behind him and slamming the door. 'Quick,' she hissed, grabbing Carmen by the arm. 'Hide!' They both dived to the ground beside the Freeloader as the headlights raked across the grass, briefly illuminating the body. Instead of driving past, however, the car pulled off the road and drew up right next to them. Trembling, Carmen could hear the blood pounding in her veins as the sound of its engine died away.

There was a squeaking noise as the window of the car was rolled down. 'There's somebody here already,' whined a woman's voice. 'I'm not doing it if there's anybody watching.'

'I can't see anyone,' replied a man gruffly. 'It just looks like an empty car to me.' A lit cigarette end flew out of the window. Stifling a yelp of pain, Carmen shook it off her hand. 'Come on, love,' continued the voice in a more encouraging tone. 'I've been waiting for this all week.'

'Well, I want to go somewhere else. It smells funny here.'

'But we haven't got time, love. I told you it would have to be a quick one. I'm only supposed to have nipped out to the petrol station to fill up the car.'

'Why does it always have to be a *quick one*. I bet that's not what you say to your wife.' The woman's voice became angry. 'I'm fed up with always being second best,' she continued. 'When are you going to tell her about us?'

'Look, we've been through all this before, haven't we? Didn't we agree that we'd wait until the children finished school?'

'I've had enough of waiting!' wailed the woman. 'I want to get on with my life!'

'So do we,' hissed Juliet under her breath.

'But what about tonight?' asked the man. There was the sound of a brief struggle. 'Come on, love, you know you want it as much as I do . . .'

'There's somebody out there, Brian,' insisted the woman. 'I'm sure I saw a movement in that car. I don't like this place. I want to go somewhere else.'

'OK, OK,' he muttered, starting the engine. The car moved forward slightly, then stopped again. 'Hang on a sec,' he said, making a rummaging noise. 'Might as well clean this out while I'm here,' he muttered, shaking something out of the window. Carmen let out a gasp as the contents of an ashtray were strewn in her face.

'Bloody litter lout!' she spat, wiping her face on Juliet's jacket as the car pulled away.

'Look on the bright side,' said Juliet. 'At least they never got round to doing what they came here for. Who knows what might have come out of the window then.'

The next few hours were a nightmare for Carmen. She had never realised quite how heavy Gideon was. By the time they had struggled, a few feet at a time, to the top of the steep bank, she was convinced she could go no further. After a rest, however, they still had to carry him down the other side and across the uneven surface of the landfill to the place where tipping would begin the next day. The stench was horrific, and Carmen kept losing her footing and slipping in puddles of unspeakably squishy substances. Protruding pieces of metal and glass threatened to cut her to ribbons if she fell.

'Are you sure no one's going to see us?' she asked, as Juliet switched on a torch to check out the most suitable place to deposit their burden.

'I shouldn't think there's a night watchman, if that's what you're worried about,' replied Juliet. 'There isn't much here that anyone's going to want to nick.'

When she had chosen a burial site, wedged between a rotting mattress and a crushed set of plastic garden furniture, they had to go back to fetch the spades from the car. It took them some time to find enough loose material to cover Gideon's body but, eventually, he was completely hidden from view.

'How do we know he won't be dug up again?' asked

Carmen doubtfully. She could scarcely believe that she had seen the last of Gideon – that she and her tormentor were about to part company for good.

'Trust me,' said Juliet. 'I've watched this place in operation. Once they've tipped a few lorryloads of rubbish where we're standing right now, I don't think anyone's going to want to dig it up again on a whim. By the end of tomorrow, he'll be about ten feet under – that's ancient history in archaeological terms.' Throwing a final spadeful of debris to cover any traces, she took Carmen by the arm. 'Let's get out of here now,' she whispered. 'There is such a thing as pushing your luck.'

When they finally returned to the Freeloader, Carmen was exhausted but, at the same time, felt a lightening of spirits. Infected by Juliet's confidence, she was starting to believe for the first time that they might actually get away with it. With Gideon out of her life, she would have a future again.

Back at the Coachman's Rest Annexe, Carmen took a shower in Juliet's tiny bathroom and changed into her own clothes. Juliet seemed keen to accompany her to the main hotel, but Carmen dissuaded her, explaining that she was tired and wanted to go straight to bed.

As she returned to her room, crossing the foyer towards the stairs, a peal of female laughter came out of the half-closed door of the Coach & Bones bar. It was followed by a voice which stopped her in her tracks.

'So who are you spending the night with, then?'

asked Duncan in a jovial tone. 'I've got a woman who murdered her husband.'

With a premonition of horror, Carmen pushed open the door. Duncan was sitting at the bar with an attractive blonde in her twenties. She was peering at some kind of tourist leaflet. 'Mine doesn't sound half as exciting as yours,' she replied in a husky American drawl. 'Just some local politician who got caught with his fingers in the till.'

Glancing up, Duncan saw Carmen standing in the doorway and waved. 'I thought you'd abandoned me here,' he said with a laugh, beckoning her to join him. 'Have you met Martha? She's staying in the hotel tonight as well.'

'What on earth are you doing?' she whispered, noticing that the American had her hand on Duncan's arm. 'I thought you were going to stay upstairs.'

'We're comparing notes on our rooms,' he replied. 'Did you know they're all named after local ghosts?' Taking the leaflet from Martha, he held it out to show her. 'Look, it tells you all about them in here. We've got Lady Howard, who apparently murdered four husbands. It says that she turns into a black dog every night and rides from Tavistock to Okehampton in a coach made of their bones.'

'Say, are you guys married?' asked Martha suddenly, withdrawing her hand.

Smiling weakly, Carmen nodded, then turned to Duncan with a look of entreaty. 'Isn't it time for bed, Dun . . . er, Gideon? Shall we go up now?'

Martha yawned and stood up, gathering her purse

and room key from the bar. 'I'd better turn in myself,' she said with a yawn. 'We're heading back to the States tomorrow, and I have to get up early to get around the Town Trail before we go.'

Carmen watched her leave, wondering what might have happened between Duncan and this woman in other circumstances. Swallowing the remains of his drink, Duncan followed her up to the room, where they both tried to act as if the huge four-poster bed wasn't there.

'Don't worry,' said Duncan. 'I pretended to be Gideon just like you wanted. I didn't say anything that's likely to mess up your plans.'

He had played the part better than he realised, thought Carmen bitterly. It was just the sort of thing Gideon might have done – attempting to seduce another woman while staying in a hotel with his wife. Opening the mini-bar she discovered a generous supply of spirits and mixers. 'Do you want another drink?' she asked uncertainly.

'Hey, that sounds like a good idea,' he replied, peering over her shoulder to inspect the gleaming rows of miniatures. 'You look like you need one, too. What on earth happened tonight to get you so stressed out?'

For a moment, Carmen felt like telling him everything. *I've just killed my husband and buried him down at the local dump. That's probably the reason why I'm feeling a little low.*

When she didn't answer, Duncan went into the bathroom and emerged with a pair of beakers. 'I've found some glasses,' he said, placing them on the table with a clink. Reaching into the refrigerator, he picked out a handful of miniatures and faced her with a grin. 'What do you want to start with?' he asked. 'Vodka? Whisky? Gin? Or would you prefer all three?'

As she watched him concoct a pair of deadly-looking cocktails, Carmen wondered how her life might have turned out if she had been married to someone like Duncan – a normal sort of person who was capable of warmth and humour, and had no hidden agenda of violence. She had no experience, she realised, of what an ordinary relationship was like.

'Cheers,' said Duncan, handing her a glass.

She drank gratefully, savouring the warm glow of the alcohol. When she finished it, Duncan made her another. As the mini-bar began to empty, the atmosphere became much more relaxed. Duncan was easy to talk to, and seemed happy to converse about trivial matters. They were soon sitting side by side on the bed, chatting away like old friends.

Halfway through the third 'Lady Howard Cocktail', as Duncan insisted on calling them, Carmen noticed that the curtains were still open.

'I do hope nobody's been spying on us,' she said, crossing to the window with a laugh. One of the curtains closed with a heavy swishing movement, but its twin refused to budge.

'Let me try,' offered Duncan, appearing at her side. 'I expect there's a knack to it.' He gave the recalcitrant curtain a sharp tug, but nothing happened.

'I think there's something stuck in the runner,' he muttered eventually, dragging the armchair over to the window and climbing onto it. I'd better see if I can pull it out.'

The Lady Howard room had an unusually high ceiling and Duncan found that he couldn't quite reach the top of the curtains from the seat of the armchair. Eventually, with one foot on the backrest and the other braced against the wall-mounted trouser press, he managed to remove the obstruction. He was just about to descend, with Carmen's assistance, when the trouser press fell open with a crash. Duncan toppled forward and there was a sound of cracking plaster as the whole thing parted company with the wall.

'Are you OK?' asked Carmen, kneeling beside him.

Duncan gazed at the wreckage. 'Damn,' he muttered, shaking his head. 'Just when I was looking forward to putting a crease in my jeans for tomorrow.' Then he turned back to face Carmen, reaching out and catching her by the hand.

'Did you know that I've adored you for seven years,' he said, his voice suddenly serious. 'Ever since I first saw you on *Jackrabbit*.'

Carmen stared at him, confused. With a shock, she felt her body responding as he drew her closer. This was all wrong, she thought, willing herself to pull away. But she couldn't quite bring herself to do it — something inside her was yearning for the comfort of his embrace.

Then the telephone rang, making them both hesitate. Carmen prayed for it to stop, to be a wrong number of some kind, but the ringing persisted until the intimacy of the moment could no longer be sustained. 'I'll get it,' she said eventually, scrambling to her feet. 'It's probably someone wanting to complain about the noise.'

'Carmen? Just checking to make sure everything's OK,' said a familiar voice. It was Juliet. 'Listen, I've had an idea,' she continued. 'Why don't I swap with Duncan, now that everyone's gone to bed? It'll save you the embarrassment of having to share a room with someone you don't really know.'

Carmen felt a rush of disappointment mingled with relief. 'You'd better come over, then,' she replied softly.

'I didn't disturb you, did I?' asked Juliet in an anxious tone. 'I mean, wake you up, or anything?'

'Not at all,' she murmured. She glanced across at Duncan, who was struggling, with little success, to wedge the trouser press back in position. 'We hadn't even got as far as thinking about going to bed.'

CHAPTER 13

Despite the fact that the sign outside the Harbour Lodge Boarding House advertised Bed & Breakfast, Angie was unable to discover the slightest trace of the latter. Exploring the ground floor and basement in search of an eating area, she found only locked doors. The tattooed receptionist seemed suddenly unable to speak English when Angie questioned her, simply shrugging as if to say, *What do you expect at this price?*

Her quest for bathing facilities was similarly unrewarding. After spending an uncomfortable night in itchy bedclothes and waking to find someone's used corn-plaster stuck to her leg, she was desperate to immerse herself in hot water. There didn't seem to be a bath in the house, however, and her hopes were soon dashed when she opened the door on the landing marked 'shower'. The grime-encrusted cubicle looked and smelt like a public urinal. If any water had passed through it in recent years, it certainly hadn't been the kind that came from a tap.

Cleaning herself as best she could with a damp flannel in her room, she focussed her thoughts on the reason she was there. Her first attempt at blackmailing Gideon had failed because she wasn't properly prepared, but she had no intention of letting that happen again. She had everything worked out in her mind now, right down to the smallest detail. When Gideon tried to board the ship to the Scillies that morning, he was going to be in for a nasty surprise.

Down at the quayside an hour and a half later, as the gangplank of the *Scillonian III* was raised, Angie realised that something had gone wrong. There had been no sign of Gideon, nor his wife, among the boarding passengers. Could they have travelled by plane or helicopter after all?

But she knew that he didn't like flying. It was the reason they'd never spent a romantic weekend abroad together – the classy destinations he favoured were too far away to reach by land or sea in a short enough time. He had told her that he wasn't going to insult her by taking her somewhere tacky. They would just have to make do with spending their weekends in Notting Hill.

Remembering that he had run back to his wife and wouldn't be spending weekends or any other kind of time with her again, she felt a pang of confused anger. How dare he dump her like this, without the pay-off she deserved? But she mustn't give up at the first hurdle, she told herself. If blackmail was easy, then everybody would be doing it. Gideon would have been cleaned out long ago and there would be nothing left for her.

The mooring ropes were cast off and the ship moved

slowly away from the quay. Watching a row of people waving from the deck, Angie fought an impulse to wave back. What was it about ships, she wondered, that made you act so dumb in front of people you didn't even know? She retraced her steps along the quay, keeping her eyes open in case Gideon should arrive late. *He's on his way to the Scilly Isles*, his housekeeper had told her yesterday. *He set off this morning.* So why the hell hadn't he turned up?

The only explanation she could think of was that he might have decided to stop overnight on the way. If so, she realised, he would have to spend a night in Penzance as well, as there wasn't another crossing to the Scillies until the next day.

The best thing, she decided, would be to search the hotels. She hoped that there weren't too many. In the light of the unexpected discovery that she was in possession of a stolen car, it seemed prudent to carry out her investigations on foot. The last thing she needed right now was to be arrested for a completely different crime to the one she was trying to commit.

She wasn't too happy at the prospect of a second night at the Harbour Lodge, either, but it would be worthwhile if it gave her the time to track Gideon down and conduct her negotiations properly. If all went well, she reminded herself, she would soon be able to afford a suite in the smartest hotel in town.

Juliet was somewhat disconcerted to wake up and find herself in the same bed as Carmen Bird. Remembering how she had got there, she felt a surge of embarrassment. What must Carmen have thought of her for barging in like that?

She had spent a long time battling with her emotions as she emptied the mini-bar in her narrow cell the previous night. Feeling lonely and rejected, she had been plagued by thoughts of what Carmen and Duncan might be doing in their luxurious double room. Her imagination had worked overtime, conjuring up the scenes that might have been taking place behind their closed door.

She had tried to divert her thoughts by reading the hotel leaflets, but only succeeded in frightening herself. Her annexe, she learned, was named after Lady Howard's coachman, who had been killed in mysterious circumstances. His ghost was reputed to haunt that very site, rattling chains and lamenting his mistress's crimes.

Eventually, unable to bear any more, she had tried to vanquish her demons by taking action. But it hadn't really helped. Now, she couldn't stop wondering what she might have interrupted. They must have been doing something pretty kinky to break that trouser press, she thought, gazing at the heap of rubble in the corner of the room. She knew Duncan well enough by now to be certain that he wouldn't have been trying to iron his trousers in the middle of the night.

After breakfast, Juliet returned to the annexe for her things while Carmen closeted herself with Duncan and attended to his disguise. They all seemed to be in a subdued mood that morning, as if aware of having gone too far the previous night. It wasn't until they left Okehampton, and the sun came out from behind the clouds, that Juliet began to feel more cheerful. They had succeeded in getting rid of Gideon's body and nobody had any cause to suspect that he was dead. There were plenty of difficulties ahead, she reminded herself, but they were on their way to the Scilly Isles and, most importantly, she was spending time with Duncan. There was no reason why she shouldn't relax a little and enjoy the rest of the day.

Now that the body was gone from the high-capacity underfloor storage bin, Carmen had decided that it would be safe for Duncan to take the wheel of the Freeloader. He drove at a restrained pace, even managing to refrain from his Damon Hill impersonations on the faster stretches of the A30. His curiosity about the gadgets in the car, however, had not subsided. As they entered the Penzance one-way system, he pointed to a large red button under the steering wheel. 'What happens if I press this?' he asked.

'I don't know,' said Juliet abstractedly, studying the map. 'Why don't you just do it and find out?'

'Wait,' said Carmen, reaching for the manual with a note of alarm in her voice. 'I've got a funny feeling . . .'

But Duncan had already pressed it. There was a loud metallic clanging sound from the base of the vehicle. Looking round, Juliet saw two spades and a pair of wire-cutters bouncing into the road.

Carmen stared at the manual, white-faced. 'It's the auto loadspace ejector,' she explained in a quiet voice. '*Handy for agricultural supplies and difficult loads.* I didn't know we had one of those.'

'Pull over, quickly,' gasped Juliet. As Duncan went to retrieve the accidentally jettisoned tools, she exchanged a horrified glance with Carmen. They both sat in thoughtful silence for a moment, contemplating what might have happened if Duncan had pressed that same button yesterday on the M4.

After a short battle with the one-way system, they found their way to the harbour and pulled up next to the quay. 'It's not very pretty, is it?' observed Carmen, as they gazed at a landscape of building sites, car parks and industrial sheds. 'It doesn't even seem to have a beach.'

'What do you expect from a working port?' asked Juliet, feeling an inexplicable urge to defend this shabby-looking town. 'I suppose you'd like to see it all tarted up like Brighton, would you?'

'I didn't say that,' replied Carmen. 'I was just thinking that a few trees and a coat of paint here and there wouldn't do any harm.'

In the offices of the quaintly named Isles of Scilly Steamship Company, they discovered that there was only one sailing to the islands each day. The next didn't leave until the following morning.

'Couldn't we go by helicopter?' asked Duncan in a hopeful voice. 'I saw the heliport as we drove in.'

'I don't think we can do that,' said Juliet. She nudged Carmen, who was immersed in studying an accommodation list. 'Can we?'

'What?' Carmen looked up, confused. 'Er . . . no, we can't,' she added quickly, as Juliet jabbed her in the ribs a second time. 'Gideon hates flying. Aunt Bridget would be dead suspicious. It's the main reason I've given for not visiting her all these years.'

'We'll have to stay overnight in Penzance and go on the boat tomorrow,' said Juliet firmly, ignoring Duncan's protests that he was prone to seasickness. She should have remembered that, of course, but it was too late to restructure her plan now. He would just have to grin and bear it with everyone else if the weather got rough.

'Actually,' whispered Carmen as they booked tickets for the next morning, 'I don't think Gideon really hated flying at all. I'm sure it was just his excuse to get out of taking me on holiday. He used to say that all the places worth visiting were too far away to justify the hassle of going by land or sea.'

The Mount Imperial Hotel was the only establishment on the accommodation list with a large enough collection of stars and rosettes to interest Carmen. 'I don't understand why you're so fussy,' grumbled Juliet as they circled the one-way system trying to find it. 'We passed a perfectly decent looking place on the last street.'

'I'm paying, aren't I?' retorted Carmen. 'Besides, you get more privacy in a good hotel.'

When they finally located it, perched high on the hill above the town, the Mount Imperial Hotel looked imposing enough to satisfy Carmen's requirements. At the reception, however, she discovered that privacy might be harder to come by than she had thought.

'Just a moment,' gasped the receptionist, handing them a registration card. 'I'll fetch the manageress.' Opening a door behind her desk, she disappeared from view. '*Mrs Mountjoy!*' they heard her calling excitedly. '*Come quickly! You'll never believe who's just arrived – it's Carmen Bird!*'

Over the next few minutes, a succession of faces appeared briefly at the gap in the doorway and stared at them, wide-eyed.

'Perhaps we should clear off while the going's good,' murmured Juliet uneasily.

'We can't,' hissed Carmen, looking embarrassed. 'They've recognised me already. They'll make a big fuss if we leave now.'

Mrs Mountjoy swept in, a smartly dressed woman in her fifties with hair piled up in a bouffant style. 'Mr and Mrs Bird, how delightful!' she exclaimed, ignoring Juliet. 'We're almost full, as usual, at this time of the year, but we always keep one of our best rooms in reserve for old friends.' Leaning over the desk, she crossed out some names on a chart and turned to the receptionist. 'Make some excuse if they turn up,' she whispered. 'Tell them there was a problem with their credit card validation, or something like that.'

'I don't think we ought to stay in this place,' said Juliet in a low voice, feeling a premonition that things were about to go wrong.

'It's not going to be much different anywhere else,' replied Carmen, looking suddenly weary. 'At least we'll be comfortable here.'

'We do hope you'll join us for dinner this evening, Mrs Bird,' continued Mrs Mountjoy eagerly. 'You'll find that we're quite informal – we try to offer the friendly atmosphere of a country-house party rather than being like just another hotel.' She made several swift changes to another chart behind the reception desk. 'I've put you down for eight o'clock,' she announced firmly, ringing a bell. 'I think you'll agree that's the best time to dine.'

Juliet opened her mouth to protest that they didn't want dinner, but a gaggle of porters appeared, clustering around Carmen and Duncan and bearing them off with their luggage to a suite of the best rooms on the first floor. Juliet, who seemed to have been taken for some kind of minion, was shown to yet another narrow cubicle, this time in the attic.

Carmen was losing touch with the purpose of their journey, thought Juliet fretfully, dumping her bags on the single bed. Now that Gideon had been buried, she was neglecting to take the rest of their plan seriously. She didn't seem to be aware of the dangers. Couldn't she see how easily Duncan might inadvertently give them away? Washing her hands in the tiny basin provided in the room, Juliet stared unhappily at a sign requesting in copperplate lettering that she refrain from stealing the towels. She had hoped this trip would bring her closer to Duncan, but she hadn't found a single opportunity to be alone with him yet.

Glancing at her watch, she realised that it was still only early afternoon. How on earth were they going to get through the rest of the day in this place? Then she had an idea: she would see if she could persuade Duncan to go out sightseeing with her. Not only would it give her some quality time with him, but it would also keep him away from Carmen and reduce the chances of anything going wrong.

Downstairs, she knocked on the door of the luxury suite and tentatively went in. Duncan was adjusting his moustache in front of a huge mirror, while Carmen had taken off her shoes and was stretched out on the vast double bed in the next room. Fighting back a pang of resentment at the contrast to her own quarters, Juliet made her suggestion.

'Hey, that would be great,' said Duncan, touching up the shadows under his eyes. 'I've always wanted to see Land's End.' He pushed back his hair with his fingers, casting her an uncannily Gideon-like look that was completely at odds with his demeanour. There's an open-air theatre I've heard of that's round here somewhere, as well. Can we go there? It's supposed to be built right on the edge of a cliff.'

Juliet waited for Carmen to insist that she wanted to come, too, but she raised no objections. 'Actually, I'm feeling a bit tired,' she murmured. 'I think I'll stay here and rest.'

Carmen wasn't, in fact, particularly tired, but was simply longing to spend some time on her own. Glancing out of the window, she waited until she was sure that Juliet and Duncan had left the hotel, then took a magazine from her bag and went downstairs. She didn't want to waste a sunny afternoon like this holed up in a hotel room. Darting through the reception, she opened the door of the lounge in search of a way through to the garden and found herself gazing across a sea of crocheted wraps and white hair. The smell of lavender water hung thickly in the air.

'Have you heard?' quavered a woman in a pink-quilted cardigan. 'The porter told me that *Carmen Bird's* staying here. You know, the one from the telly?'

'Perhaps she'll give us all a makeover,' giggled her companion, peering over the top of a large-print book.

'Fat lot of good that would do me,' a woman with a complexion like blue Stilton squawked cheerfully. 'We could have done with having someone like her around thirty years ago.'

'I don't know about a makeover – I could do with a complete rebuilding,' cackled another. 'I hope she's remembered to bring her concrete mixer and trowel.' Brandishing a pair of walking sticks, she attempted to stand up. 'Where's that waiter gone with my sherry?'

'I must get her autograph for my grandchildren,' said the first woman gleefully. 'They'll be sick with envy down at the day centre when they hear about this.'

'Now's your chance,' hissed her friend loudly, poking her with the handle of her magnifying glass. 'She's over there.'

They all turned their heads with gasps of recognition. Forcing an embarrassed smile, Carmen backed hurriedly out of the room. Finding another route out to the garden, she sat on a bench under a tree and attempted to read her magazine. But it didn't take long for the hotel bush telegraph to spread news of her whereabouts. She watched with amusement as the garden, previously deserted, became suddenly populated with elderly guests who didn't look as if they'd walked further than the distance between their armchairs and their TV sets for years. Mrs Mountjoy decided to carry out some unseasonal pruning to an unlucky rose bush close to where Carmen was sitting, while the porter took it upon himself to start sweeping non-existent leaves from the path.

Before long, one or two of the guests plucked up the courage to approach, brandishing pieces of paper for her to autograph and requesting snippets of makeup advice. As their confidence grew, some of them began to loiter nearby, talking loudly in tones she was obviously intended to overhear.

'Of course, when we stayed in the same hotel as that nice man from the antiques programme, he looked at all our jewellery for us,' said a woman with a long face like a horse. 'He gave us each a free valuation on a selected piece.'

'I wonder if she's down here to find volunteers for her programme?' suggested her friend, checking her face in a compact mirror. 'I daresay they've never had anyone from Penzance on their show before.'

Eventually Carmen stood up and went over to the rose bush. 'Look, I'm supposed to be on holiday,' she said in a low voice. 'Can't you do anything to make them leave me alone?'

Mrs Mountjoy put down her secateurs with a smile. 'I think we both know what they're after, don't we?' she said softly.

'A makeup demonstration,' offered Carmen, admitting defeat.

'They'll be so thrilled,' said Mrs Mountjoy in a conspiratorial tone. Patting her hair, she turned back towards the hotel with a look of satisfaction. 'I'll make an announcement, shall I? The lounge at three o'clock?'

With a sigh, Carmen nodded her agreement, then rolled up her magazine and followed her. It was lucky, she thought, that she had brought her makeup kit with her for Duncan's disguise.

'Who are you going to use as a model?' asked the horsey-faced woman, intercepting her at the door.

'Whoever you like,' said Carmen. 'You, if you want.'

'Oh, I couldn't possibly,' she said blushing. 'You wouldn't be able to do a *thing* with an old fright like me.'

'Neither could I,' added her friend, catching up with them. 'It would be *so* embarrassing – I'd just simply *die*.'

'Well, you'd better find someone by the time I come back,' said Carmen, heading upstairs to fetch her things. 'I can't do a makeover on thin air.'

After Angie had been laughed out of three hotels on the promenade for suggesting that Carmen Bird might be lurking unnoticed among their guests, she realised that there might be an easier way to find out where she was staying. Obtaining a phonecard and an accommodation leaflet from the tourist office, she closeted herself in the telephone box near the harbour.

'Hi, I'm from *Hello!* magazine,' she said to the receptionist at the first hotel on the list. 'I'm supposed to be doing an in-depth interview with Carmen Bird. Have I got the right place?'

'Oooh, blimey, I wish you had,' she replied wistfully.

'But she's actually up at the Mount Imperial. The old bat – I mean Mrs Mountjoy – who runs it has been ringing all over the town to brag about it for the last hour.'

Angie replaced the receiver and checked her street map. *Gotcha*, she thought with a smile. She was about to set off to find the place, when it occurred to her that it might be sensible to call Ronco again. Gideon wasn't exactly going to be pleased to see her, and she would feel safer if someone else knew where she was.

He answered after a single ring, as if he had been waiting by the telephone. 'Listen,' she said excitedly, 'I've found out where he is. I'm going to see him about . . . well, you know, the photos and things.'

'Found out where who is?' asked Ronco slowly.

'Gideon, you idiot. Who do you think? Now listen, he's staying at the Mount Imperial Hotel. Make a note of the name in case anything happens to me. I'll call you straightaway as soon as I get back.'

Her insurance thus arranged, Angie took her bearings from her street map and set off. Toiling up the steep hill that led to the hotel, she realised that she was entering a different world to that of the Harbour Lodge. In this part of town, the gardens were well tended and the hedges neatly clipped. The inhabitants wore smug expressions to show how satisfied they were with their lives, and even the garden gnomes looked plump and well-fed.

Approaching the front entrance of the Mount Imperial Hotel, Angie felt intimidated. A silence hung in the air, broken only by the distant whine of a vacuum cleaner and the crunch of the gravel driveway under her feet. A row of wide bay windows gazed down at her, their frilled blinds furled up like eyebrows in expressions of disdain. Entering the foyer, she fixed her eyes straight ahead and braced herself for the dreaded words: *May I help you*? The last thing she wanted was to announce her presence to Gideon by enquiring for him at the desk.

It wasn't until she had crossed the foyer unchallenged that she looked back and realised that the reception was unmanned. The whole place, in fact, seemed deserted. Then she heard the sound of a door opening at the rear of the building. Footsteps accompanied by a babble of conversation began to approach. Rounding a corner, Angie found her path blocked by a horde of elderly women who were slowly flooding in from the garden and crowding around the door to the lounge.

'Well, I'm not going to be the model,' quavered a reedy voice in her ear. 'I'm not letting her loose on my broken veins.'

'But I want to be able to see what she's doing,' replied another. 'Besides, I've got so many wrinkles and lines that she'd need a map to find her way around my face.'

Crumbly city, thought Angie disgustedly as they swarmed around her. What on earth was Gideon doing staying here? As she turned and attempted to retreat, however, a walking stick rapped her ankles and a claw-like hand descended on her arm.

'Here's our answer,' said the woman with the wrinkles, holding her in a surprisingly firm grip. 'I'm sure this young lady wouldn't mind helping us out.'

'Would you like a makeover, my dear?' asked another,

whose flaring nostrils and long face made her look like a horse. 'We're having a bit of a problem finding a suitable model for *Carmen Bird*.'

As comprehension gradually dawned, a broad smile spread across Angie's face. 'Sure,' she said happily. 'I'm not in any hurry. In fact, I'd simply *love* it.' Following them into the lounge, she took a seat on a makeshift podium in front of several rows of hastily arranged chairs.

Before long, there was a flurry of excitement at the door and Carmen Bird came into the room with a large plastic toolbox under her arm. 'Well,' she said brightly, placing it on a table and opening it out to reveal a vast collection of makeup. 'Who do we have here?'

Your husband's lover, thought Angie, staring in fascination at her rival. *Just wait until he comes in and finds me here with you.*

Carmen usually managed to establish some kind of rapport with her *Makeover* subjects, but she knew straightaway that it wasn't going to happen with the tarty-looking woman waiting for her in the lounge. Wrinkling her nose in distaste as she surveyed her cheap clothes and badly dyed hair, Carmen wondered where on earth Horseface and her friend could have found her. She certainly didn't look the type to be staying in a hotel like this.

Her audience were still tottering in, but Carmen decided that she'd better get started. Pulling the woman's hair gently back from her face, she secured it with a hairband. Some people never learned, she thought, feeling how dry and brittle it was. Didn't she realise that her hair would eventually fall out if she carried on dyeing the whole lot instead of just doing the roots?

'Is this OK?' she asked, noticing how the woman flinched at her touch. The woman nodded, glancing up at her with a curious expression. It was funny, thought Carmen, how makeup brought you into such intimate contact with strangers. If you attempted to touch someone like this in any other circumstances, they would think you were some kind of pervert. As soon as you had a makeup brush in your hand, however, everything became all right.

'The first thing to do,' she began, moistening a cotton wool pad with cleanser, 'is to remove all traces of previous cosmetics.' Wiping the pad gently across the woman's cheeks, Carmen glanced at the results and frowned. It looked as if she had slept in her makeup for several days, applying a new layer each morning on top of the rest. Rolling up her sleeves, Carmen reached for another piece of cotton wool. This was going to be a bigger job than she had thought.

'The key to healthy skin is to follow the cleanse–tone–moisturise routine every single day,' she continued, glancing round to see if there was anyone in her audience who was actually young enough to benefit from this advice. 'Use an alcohol-free toner, especially if you have an . . . er . . . an *older* skin. Look for a moisturiser with some kind of UV protection built in, as exposure to the sun can cause premature wrinkles and other signs of . . . er, ageing.'

The audience nodded sagely, wondering, no doubt,

why no one had told them this when they were all
tanning themselves to a crisp in their back gardens forty
years ago. Embarrassed, Carmen scrubbed impatiently
at her model's face and wished that the standard spiel
she had learned was less blatantly youth-orientated. It
would be easier once she had got past the foundation,
she told herself. It was far safer to talk about the details
of covering things up than to dwell on the inadequacies
of what lay beneath.

When the grime of the old makeup had finally been
removed, Carmen took a closer look at her model, who
faced her with a defiant stare. She appeared to be in
her early forties and her skin was dull and lifeless,
testifying to a poor diet and overindulgence in alcohol
and smoking. Looking carefully, Carmen could see the
places where further lines and wrinkles would form
in the next few years. It was easy to imagine the kind
of life she must lead – the badly paid menial job,
the nights at the pub and the Bingo hall, the other
nights slumped dejectedly on the sofa in front of the
TV. Carmen could picture this woman queueing up
twice weekly for lottery tickets and being angry and
disappointed each time she failed to win.

'It's worth spending money on a good quality foundation,' she said brightly, picking out a bottle and
mixing the colour on the back of her hand. 'If you
get the basics right, you can afford to experiment with
cheaper brands for eyes and lips.' Was she being a snob,
she wondered, judging this woman by her appearance?
People told you it was the one thing you should never
do – that it was what was on the inside of a person

that really counted. Carmen couldn't help thinking, however, that this woman's face showed you everything you needed to know. Written across her forehead in big letters you could read: *The world owes me a favour.* Beneath this, slightly smaller but still clearly legible, was the warning: *Don't get in my way.*

There was something else as well, something in the way the woman kept looking at her, but Carmen couldn't pin it down. 'Use a sponge, rather than your fingers, to get even coverage and avoid smearing,' she continued, spreading a generous layer of foundation over the woman's face. 'A liquid foundation is best for this type of complexion and helps create the natural look most women are aiming for today.'

The 'natural' look was what she was going to get, Carmen decided. She would hate it, of course, but it would be interesting to see the effect. Could an attractive woman be moulded from such unpromising clay? Sealing the foundation with a light stippling of powder, she launched into her little speech about 'natural' and 'synthetic' colours and how you shouldn't mix them. She couldn't do anything about the hair, she thought, but it might work out if she tied it back using the scarf the woman was wearing wrapped choker-style around her neck.

As she reached to loosen the scarf, however, the woman's hands flew to her throat in a defensive gesture. Too late, Carmen realised that the flimsy material was there for a purpose other than decoration. It concealed a large purplish bruise around the base of her neck.

'I'm . . . I'm sorry,' she gasped, letting go and backing

away in confusion. She had seen bruises exactly like this one before, many times, inflicted by Gideon on herself.

Mutterings could be heard in the audience. 'What's the matter with her?' Horseface asked her friend loudly. 'Did you see that? She looked as if she'd seen a ghost just then.'

Carmen shuddered as visions of the horrors of life with Gideon rose up to confront her, and she had to force herself to remember that he was dead. Pulling herself together, she took a large brush and swirled on a dusting of bronze blusher. She must concentrate on the moment, she told herself, resisting the temptation to look into the past or the future. How else was she going to remain sane?

It was time to do the eyes. 'You don't need to use many colours to get a sophisticated effect,' she said, remembering a magazine article she had read about eye make-up for older women. 'Soft, natural colours are the thing to wear right now and single shadow tones are simpler and kinder to . . . er . . . crease-prone lids.'

She had resolved to get through this ordeal as quickly as possible, without getting into conversation with anyone or taking risks. As she bent closer to apply a warm beige to the woman's upper lids, however, curiosity overcame her. 'Do you mind if I ask what you do?' she asked softly. 'For a living, I mean.'

'I help people,' replied the woman, smiling for the first time. 'People with special needs.'

'You mean like disabled people?' suggested Carmen,

puzzled. It didn't fit in at all with what she had imagined.

'Did you hear that?' burbled Horseface to anyone who was listening. 'Working with the *disabled*. What a kind and caring young girl she must be.'

'No, I *don't* mean "like disabled people",' hissed the woman. Glancing around, she beckoned Carmen closer. 'I mean like men whose wives won't screw them anymore,' she added in a low voice that nobody else could hear.

Shocked, Carmen stared at the woman. '*What* did you just say?'

'Nothing,' she replied, smiling sweetly. 'I just love your programme on the TV.'

Carmen was beginning to wonder if she had imagined the whole thing, when there was a commotion by the door.

'Out you go, young man!' squawked the woman with two walking sticks who had been at the sherry earlier. 'This is a girls-only gathering! We don't want any men in here!'

Looking round, Carmen saw Duncan standing in the doorway with a confused expression. As she watched, Juliet appeared beside him, tugging at his sleeve.

'What's all that noise?' asked the woman, twisting in her seat to see round Carmen. 'What's going on? Who's the man that's just come in?'

C H A P T E R   14

When Carmen looked round a second time, Duncan was gone. A moment later, Juliet reappeared in the doorway, gesturing urgently, and seemed to want Carmen to go over and talk to her straightaway. 'Would you mind holding on a moment?' she asked her bemused-looking audience. 'I've just got to have a word with my friend.'

As soon as she reached the doorway, Juliet grabbed her by the wrist and pulled her out into the corridor. 'What's wrong?' asked Carmen, alarmed.

'Where did that woman come from?' hissed Juliet, dragging her into the empty dining room and closing the door behind them. 'How on earth did she get in here?'

'I don't know,' said Carmen, confused. 'Why? Who is she?'

Juliet hesitated. 'I know I should have shown you this before,' she said, rummaging in her shoulder bag. 'It's just that I didn't want to upset you.' Producing a small piece of glossy paper she handed it to Carmen. 'It's *Angie*. You know, Gideon's . . .'

'*Angie*?' repeated Carmen stupidly, staring at a photograph of the woman she had just left in the lounge. 'But how . . .'

'I found it in Gideon's diary,' admitted Juliet. 'It was folded up in his driving licence. I . . . I kind of guessed that it was her – that she was Angie, I mean. But there didn't seem to be any point in telling you at the time.'

Angie? The significance of the woman's identity quickly sank in. 'But how did she find us?' asked Carmen, puzzled. 'Surely nobody else knew that we were coming here.'

'I don't know,' mumbled Juliet, blushing.

'But if she had seen Duncan just now . . .' Carmen shuddered, realising how close it had been. 'Where is he, anyway?'

'It's all right,' said Juliet. 'He's out of the way for the moment. The thing is . . .'

'And what does she want from us?' A note of panic crept into Carmen's voice. 'Do you think she knows what we've done?'

'I don't really see how she could,' replied Juliet with a frown. 'But listen, we've got to get her out of here before she realises there's anything wrong. It's going to take me a few minutes to think of something, so you're going to have to go back in there and keep her occupied until I'm ready. We mustn't let her find out that we know who she is.'

'Go back in there?' echoed Carmen faintly. 'I don't know if I can.'

'But you must!' Juliet stared at her with an expression of disbelief. 'If she thinks we're on to her, she could blow this whole thing apart. Do you want to end up in prison?'

'But that's Gideon's *lover* you're talking about,' said Carmen unhappily. 'She's been screwing my husband. She must be *laughing* at me.'

'Surely you're not planning to give up now, after all the risks I've taken for you?' Juliet was beginning to sound angry. 'If you don't pull yourself together, I'm not going to help you anymore. I'll just leave you to sort this out on your own.'

'But I can't . . .' Carmen's voice tailed away as she heard a loud rattling at the french windows. With a crash, one of the doors flew open and Duncan appeared in the room.

'Hey, what's going on with you two?' he asked, glancing from one woman to the other with a look of confusion. He settled his gaze on Juliet. 'Why did you lock me out just now? I've been trying for ages to get back in, but no one's answering the door.'

'Is everything all right in here?' squawked another voice, as Horseface appeared with her friend. 'Are you coming back soon?' she asked, looking at Carmen. 'They're getting a bit restless in there, I'm afraid.'

'Oh, you must be *Mr* Bird,' squealed Horseface's friend, spotting Duncan for the first time. 'You must come and see what a lovely job your wife's been doing in the lounge.' Reaching for his hand, she began to lead him in faltering steps towards the door.

Juliet stood in silence, watching them.

'Please,' whispered Carmen. 'I'm sorry, Juliet. I'll go back in.'

Juliet waited until Horseface's friend had almost reached the door before she made up her mind. 'Oh hell,' she said eventually, throwing Carmen a frustrated glance. 'I can't bear to watch you mess it all up now that we've come this far.'

Snatching Duncan by the arm, she whisked him deftly from the clutches of Horseface's friend. 'Sorry,' she said, dipping her head to meet the old woman's querulous gaze with a sweet smile. 'It's just that *Gideon*'s already promised to come and talk to me for a while. I'll let you have him back as soon as I've finished with him.' Leading a surprised-looking Duncan back out through the french windows, she turned on the threshold and faced Carmen with a quizzical stare.

'Well?' she asked. 'What are you waiting for?' Raising an eyebrow, she nodded in the direction of the lounge. 'Get back in there quickly and carry on with what you were doing,' she hissed in a low voice. 'Don't let her guess that you know who she is, but just keep her there until something happens. I'll think of a way to get her off our backs.'

In the lounge, Carmen's audience was rapidly approaching the limit of its attention span. The level of conversation had risen to a chattering hubbub, and the gathering threatened to break up at any moment as thoughts began to turn towards TV schedules and afternoon tea.

'Sorry to keep you all waiting,' said Carmen nervously, as they acknowledged her return with loud shushing noises and a sprinkling of applause. Approaching the woman she now knew to be Angie, Carmen wondered how she was going to be capable of putting on her eyeliner with a steady hand.

Rummaging in her toolbox as a delaying tactic, she reminded herself that this was hardly the time to be wallowing in her emotional insecurities. She had to pull herself together, as Juliet had told her, and get on with what needed to be done.

The thing that was hardest to come to terms with was that Angie probably knew all kinds of details about her marriage – about her failure to make the grade as a wife. What Angie *didn't* know, however, Carmen considered with some confusion, was that *she knew* that Angie knew. *And that was one thing that Angie mustn't find out.*

She made the first contact, smudging a thin line of pale mushroom beneath Angie's lower lashes. Then another thought dawned on her: *Angie didn't know that her lover was dead.*

Somehow, this made all the difference, giving Carmen the confidence to continue. She could almost feel sorry for this woman, she decided, remembering the bruise she had seen on her neck. In a sense, Angie was just another victim of Gideon, not so very unlike herself.

When the eyeliner was in place, she applied mascara in three separate coats. When was Juliet going to do something, she wondered, glancing at her watch. She wasn't going to be able to spin things out for very much longer. Selecting a taupe lipstick, she loaded a brush and prepared for the final part of the makeover.

'I don't want *brown* lips,' said Angie suddenly,

snatching the lipstick tube from Carmen's hand. Elbowing Carmen out of the way, she began sorting through the trays of the makeup box, twisting open the sticks of colour in search of something she liked better. 'I always have red,' she announced in a petulant tone. 'Not dingy old colours like these.'

Eventually, she came across a bright scarlet that Carmen kept in reserve for fancy dress parties. 'That's more like it,' she muttered, pulling a face and slicking the colour around her lips straight from the tube. The effect was startling – Carmen's 'natural look' was slashed in two by a bright, gaping wound of a mouth.

Applause rippled through the room. Carmen faced her audience with an uncertain smile, wondering how she was going to prolong the event any further. 'Before we finish,' she said, clearing her throat, 'I'll give you a few tips about choosing the right type of makeup . . .'

She spoke slowly, keeping her eyes on the door and hoping for some sign of rescue. How on earth was Juliet going to get them out of this mess?

Walking up and down in the hotel garden with Duncan, Juliet had been asking herself the same question. This was all her own fault, she realised. If she hadn't blabbed out their destination on the telephone, Angie would never have had the faintest idea where they were.

'I don't know why you've dragged me out here like this,' muttered Duncan. 'Why can't I go in and watch Carmen? There's something funny going on around here, if you ask me.'

Turning to face him, Juliet suddenly remembered

how he had impersonated Gideon in Shepherd's Bush Road on the night of Carmen's dinner party. He had mimicked his voice perfectly, capturing the sneering and arrogant tone to a T. Duncan might not *look* sufficiently like Gideon to fool someone who knew him, she thought, but maybe he could *sound* enough like him to be mistaken for the real thing.

'I need you to make a telephone call,' she said, realising that the answer was not to remove Duncan from the scene, but to get Angie out of the way. If Duncan could be persuaded to impersonate Gideon on the telephone, arranging to meet her in some suitably distant place, they would be able to continue with their plan. But how the hell was she going to explain all this to him without giving the whole story away?

'What do you mean, a telephone call?' asked Duncan, gazing at her suspiciously. 'Aren't you going to tell me what's happening?'

'Now listen, this is rather delicate,' said Juliet, taking his arm and guiding him towards a bench. 'Carmen didn't want you to know about this, because she's too embarrassed, but I've decided to tell you. That woman in there . . . it turns out that she's Gideon's mistress.'

'Gideon's *mistress*?' echoed Duncan, looking suitably shocked. 'Oh, poor Carmen, that must be awful for her.' Then he frowned. 'But I thought Gideon had gone off with his mistress,' he said with a puzzled expression. 'Wasn't that why he'd gone away?'

'Well, maybe he's got more than one of them,' suggested Juliet, improvising rapidly. 'He might have gone off with someone else and told his mistress that he was down here with his wife. She's probably come to check him out. The thing is, we need your help to get her out of the way. Otherwise Carmen's going to be in huge trouble for what she's doing here, with you posing as her husband and everything. If that woman tells Gideon what's going on, it'll look as if Carmen's having an affair, too.'

'Oh dear,' murmured Duncan, a cloud of anxiety crossing his face. 'Maybe we shouldn't carry on with all this. I know Carmen's paying me and everything, but isn't it getting a bit risky?'

'Oh, come on, Duncan, surely you're not going to back out now?' Juliet swallowed. 'Surely you don't want to let Carmen down?'

'No, of course not,' he replied, too quickly for Juliet's liking. 'It's just that, well, I don't fancy my chances if Gideon turns up here and catches me pretending to be him.'

'He won't turn up,' said Juliet firmly. 'Trust me. Now are you going to help us?'

Duncan sighed. 'You always get your own way in the end, don't you?' he said with a smile. 'Go on then, tell me what it is that I've got to do.'

Leading him towards the car park, Juliet explained the details of the call she wanted him to make. 'We can use the carphone,' she added, opening the door of the Freeloader and motioning for him to get in. Picking up a tourist brochure she had obtained at the shipping office earlier, she searched through the hotel listings for the place that was furthest from Penzance. Then she looked up the telephone number of the Mount Imperial. 'She's called Angie, remember,' she said, dialling the number and passing the handset to Duncan. 'Say you need to speak to her urgently, and explain that she's the woman who's having her makeup done in the lounge.'

Craning her neck to look into the hotel from the car park, Juliet could see Mrs Mountjoy crossing the reception to answer the telephone. When Duncan had delivered his message, she strutted self-importantly back towards the lounge.

A moment later, Angie's figure appeared in the reception. 'Don't forget to tell her there's something urgent you need to discuss,' hissed Juliet. 'Arrange to meet her at this place tonight,' she added, pointing at the brochure. 'It's just off the A30. I think we must have passed close to it on the way down.'

Twiddling the controls, she switched on the hands-free speaker. 'Hello?' said a voice. 'Is anyone there?'

'It's Gideon,' began Duncan hesitantly. 'I need to talk to you.'

'And about bloody time, too,' interrupted Angie in an indignant tone. 'I've got quite a few things to talk about with you, too, as I'm sure you'll have guessed. I'll tell you right now, it's gonna cost you big time if you want me to shut up about *what I know.*'

'What does she know?' whispered Duncan, pressing the mute button.

'I haven't a clue,' hissed Juliet. 'Don't get involved in anything – just make the arrangements as quickly as you can and get off the phone.'

He gave her a nervous smile. 'If you're sure that's what you want, OK, let's go for it.' Taking a deep breath, he pressed the button so that Angie could hear him again.

'Now you just listen to me, you stupid bitch,' he snarled. 'I haven't got time for mindless gossip. I'll tell you where to meet me, right? If you can manage to find your way there without getting lost, I'll talk to you then.'

Juliet's mouth dropped open in amazement. He sounded *exactly* like Gideon. Glancing towards her, Duncan raised his eyebrows and gave her a questioning look. *Was that OK?* he mouthed. With a grin, Juliet held up two thumbs.

'Where are you?' asked Angie in a suspicious tone.

'Never mind that,' said Duncan briskly. 'Now listen, there's a place called Redruth, just off the A30. Do you know how to get there?'

The conversation continued, with various promptings from Juliet, until it was all fixed up that Angie would meet 'Gideon' in Redruth that evening, in the bar of The Buccaneer Inn. She was instructed to keep waiting if he was late, as he didn't know what time he would be able to get away. 'You just hang on in there, baby,' said Duncan in a faintly sinister tone. 'I'll be taking a room when I get there, so that we can stay overnight.'

It took some time to get her off the line as, each time Duncan came close to ending the call, she launched into a fresh bout of awkward questions. 'But why won't you tell me where you are?' she whined. 'Why can't I talk to you now?'

'Because I'm in a bloody hurry,' snapped Duncan eventually. 'You'll just have to take it or leave it. Now, for Christ's sake get off my back, I've got a lot of important calls to make.' Switching off the handset, he let out a sharp exhalation of breath. 'Blimey,' he muttered. 'I'm glad I don't have a girlfriend like her.'

'I wonder what she meant about *what she knows*?' murmured Juliet, fighting back the impulse to ask him what sort of girlfriend he would prefer.

'Search me,' said Duncan. 'Maybe he's got some dark secret that she's found out, like dressing up in women's underwear or something.' He paused for a moment, then turned to face Juliet with a look of alarm. 'Hey Jules?' he asked anxiously. 'You're not expecting me to actually *go* there, are you? I mean, I might be a brilliant actor and everything, but I'm not *that* good.'

'No, no, you don't have to worry about that,' said Juliet distractedly, staring towards the hotel. She had seen Angie coming back into the reception and it looked as if she was leaving already. 'Get down,' she hissed, dragging Duncan onto the floor of the Freeloader. 'She might recognise the car.'

Peering over the dashboard, Juliet watched anxiously as Angie paused in the doorway and glanced around. She seemed, however, to have more pressing things on her agenda than searching the hotel car park. Setting her blood-red lips into a determined line, she hurried purposefully down the driveway and disappeared from view.

Angie's pulse was racing with excitement as she made her way back towards the seafront. Things were really happening for her now. It had been a strange experience being made up by Carmen Bird, and she didn't know whether the electric thrill she had felt at her touch had been because she was so famous, or because she was Gideon's wife. Either way, it had given her a real buzz to sit there, quietly savouring the knowledge that she could blow the TV star's cosy existence to smithereens.

The telephone call from Gideon had been the icing on the cake. It made a change for *him* to be so keen to see *her*, she thought with a smile. In the past, it had always been the other way around.

When the call was over, she had sauntered back into the lounge and faced Carmen with a look of disdain. 'I think we've both had enough of this,' she had said, removing her hairband and tossing it carelessly on the floor. 'I'm afraid I've got a *much more important* appointment right now.'

If only she could have added some witty remark about faithless husbands who were also murderers, thought Angie, her happiness would have been complete. Unfortunately, as was often the case, the appropriate phrase failed to materialise on her lips. 'I'll be off, then,' she had concluded lamely. 'Toodleoo.'

Turning into the street where she had left the car, she brightened, remembering the surprise she had in store for Gideon. He was probably preparing to part with some small sum of money in return for the photographs. Just imagine what his reaction would be when he found out what she now knew. How much, she wondered, would he offer to pay for her silence? What kind of deal would he be willing to make?

The car seemed to be much as she had left it, apart from the fact that the local seagulls had been using it for target practice. She could also have sworn that it was equipped with wing mirrors the day before.

She was opening the door when she stopped, struck by a sudden fear. Gideon had been responsible for one murder already. Why should he hesitate to commit another in the interests of saving his skin? This whole rendez-vous thing could be a trap, she realised. Might he be luring her to a remote spot in order to bump her off as well?

But then, he wasn't aware that she knew about the murder. A hotel bar would be a safe enough place to meet him, she reasoned, getting into the car. She could make sure that plenty of people saw them together before she agreed to accompany him anywhere else.

The engine started with a loud rattle. It was totally inconsiderate of Ronco not to have warned her that he was selling it, she thought, adjusting the rear-view mirror so that she could keep an eye on her makeup. She had no other means of transport and, if she started splashing out on train fares, she would risk leaving herself without enough money for the journey home. She would just have to drive carefully and avoid drawing attention to herself, she decided. They were hardly likely to be searching for a stolen car as far afield as Penzance.

Narrowly missing a cyclist as she swung onto the main road, Angie pulled up outside the Harbour Lodge Boarding House and went inside to collect her things. She had thought it would be easy to slip out unnoticed, but the woman with the tattoo was waiting for her in the reception. 'You owe me for tonight,' she said flatly, blocking Angie's exit with folded arms.

'But I'm not staying here tonight,' she protested.

'You will be if you don't settle up,' growled a voice. Angie turned to see a burly man in a string vest standing behind her with a baseball bat. 'We don't like people who try to sneak out without paying,' he added, slapping his weapon menacingly against the palm of his hand. 'They often end up staying longer than they expected. We do a special rate for people with broken legs.'

Angie wasn't allowed to leave until she had paid for an extra night, two non-existent breakfasts, a 'booking' fee, and a charge for the electricity she would have used if she had stayed for the allotted time. 'I know how you feel, mate,' she muttered to the chained garden gnome as she fled the premises. If she had known they were going to treat her like that, she thought angrily, she would have made it a point of honour to steal the towels.

As she rumbled along the A30, she fell prey to a growing sense of insecurity. She had quelled her earlier fears with the assumption that Gideon would act rationally, but what if he had become completely unhinged? His moods were erratic at the best of times. What if he was planning to murder her anyway, making her the next victim in a bloodthirsty killing spree?

It had been a bright and sunny day when Angie embarked on her journey but, as she passed the turn-off to St Ives, the sky became suddenly dark with clouds and drops of rain began to spatter on the windscreen. She switched on the windscreen wipers as the rain became heavier, then immediately regretted it as they flapped ineffectually back and forth, emitting a high-pitched whining noise and achieving little more than smearing the seagull shit across the screen. And then another thought struck her. Where had Gideon been when he telephoned her? More importantly, where exactly was he right now?

She glanced nervously at the passing vehicles on the road, realising that she had only ever travelled in a taxi with Gideon, and had no idea what kind of car he drove. Might he be the shadowy figure in the grey four-by-four that was thundering alongside her? Or was he the driver of the sleek red sports car that kept tailgating her every time she slowed down?

With a clunk, one of the windscreen wipers died on her, falling limply to the bonnet. Before long, she could scarcely see a thing. The obvious solution was to pull over and fix it, but she wasn't so sure that she wanted to take that risk. It could be just what Gideon was waiting for – his chance to get his hands on her in an isolated spot. How long might it take before someone discovered her body concealed in a roadside ditch?

Flicking on the headlights, she was alarmed to find that they had no discernible effect on the encroaching gloom. Gripping the steering wheel tightly, she increased her speed as much as she dared and attempted to follow the hazy outline of the car in front. Blurred shapes roared past, strafing her with spray from the road, and Angie began to feel as if she was trapped on some kind of highway to Hell.

Closing her eyes briefly, she prayed for a turn-off to appear. She had no idea how much further it was to Redruth, but her only wish right now was to get out of this nightmare and find somewhere safe where she could stop.

Juliet and Carmen faced each other in the sitting room of Carmen's suite. A rhythmic snoring noise came from the bedroom, where Duncan was supposed to be getting changed.

'Do you think she'll come back again?' asked Carmen anxiously, when Juliet had finished explaining how Angie had been sent on a fool's errand to get her out of the way.

'I don't see why she should,' replied Juliet. 'She's been told to keep waiting until late, so I think she'll probably end up staying there overnight in the hope that Gideon might still turn up. When there's no sign of him in the morning, I reckon she'll just cut her losses and go home.' Taking a deep breath, Juliet hoped that she sounded more confident than she felt. 'We'll be gone from here in the morning anyway,' she added. 'I can't imagine she's going to follow us to the Scilly Isles.'

Carmen had started fiddling with her box of makeup, sorting containers of eyeshadow and blusher into separate compartments. 'Shouldn't we be getting ready?' she suggested, glancing at her watch. 'For dinner, I mean.'

'Don't you think we might be taking a bit of a risk by

having dinner in the hotel?' asked Juliet. She nodded towards the bedroom, where the sounds of snoring were getting louder. 'What happens if Duncan gets his story wrong?'

'But I thought the whole point of this was for people to see him acting as Gideon,' said Carmen, looking confused. 'Besides, it's going to look pretty odd if we don't turn up after all the fuss they've made. They'll think we've got something to hide.'

'I suppose so,' murmured Juliet uncertainly. Standing up, she crossed the room to the dressing table and stared at her reflection in the mirror. Did her reluctance stem partly from the fear that *she* would be the one to show them up, she wondered. She wasn't used to eating in smart hotels. What was she supposed to do to *get ready*, other than wash her hands and brush her hair? She had packed only practical clothes for this journey and didn't have anything remotely suitable to wear.

Picking up a stray eyeshadow compact, she clicked it open and examined the neat rectangles of pressed powder. Touching each colour with her fingertip, she transferred a little of each to the back of her hand and blended them to a warm purplish shade. It was just like mixing the colours in a paintbox, she thought. Was it really that easy to change the way you looked?

That afternoon, standing on the cliff top at Minack, there had been a moment when she had thought Duncan might be going to kiss her. She shivered, remembering the feeling of closeness. He had actually put his arm around her shoulder and briefly hugged her as they gazed at the view. But nothing further had happened.

What would it have taken, she wondered, to tip the balance in a situation like that? If she had looked a little more attractive, might it have prompted him to act?

Common sense told her that patches of colour on her eyelids were hardly likely to change the way Duncan felt about her. But then, common sense hadn't even got her to first base with him so far. Maybe it was time for a different approach.

'Er, Carmen,' she began hesitantly. 'Do you remember how you once suggested that I should be on *Makeover*? How you said you could do things to change the way I look?'

'I was wondering how long it would take you to come round,' said Carmen, appearing at Juliet's side with a smile. Placing her makeup box on the dressing table, she pulled out a chair. 'What are we waiting for, then?' she asked. 'Why don't you just sit down right here and let me make a start on your face.'

As Carmen set to work, Juliet decided that it was as good a time as any to broach the other subject that was bothering her. 'Do you think we ought to talk to Duncan yet?' she asked, lowering her voice so that she couldn't be overheard from the next room. 'About the murder, I mean. I'm starting to feel a bit guilty that we haven't told him the truth.'

She was hoping that Carmen would disagree, as she wanted to put off the moment of confession for as long as possible. How could she expect to inspire romantic feelings in Duncan once he knew that she had lied to him?

Their eyes met in the mirror as Carmen applied

a dusting of blusher, highlighting cheekbones Juliet didn't know she had. 'I thought you were keen to wait until we got to the Scillies,' she replied slowly. 'He might refuse to come with us if we told him now. Or he might even go straight to the police.' She fell silent for a moment, opening and closing different compacts in search of a particular colour. Then she looked up and smiled. 'It would be a shame to spoil things for tonight, wouldn't it? Especially now we've got Angie out of the way.'

With the new look that Carmen was giving her, Juliet couldn't help thinking that tonight might be her big chance with Duncan. An optimistic part of her clung to the idea that, if only she could get their relationship onto a less platonic footing, everything else would miraculously work itself out.

'You're probably right,' she said, closing her eyes to let Carmen brush her lids with shadow. She submitted meekly to eyeliner and mascara, and even allowed Carmen to tweeze her eyebrows into shape. When her lips had been finished in a soft plum colour, she gazed into the mirror with an expression of surprised delight. Why had she been so stubborn, she asked herself. Why had she fought against using makeup for all these years? Her face looked slimmer and more feminine than she had ever seen it before. She looked better than she had imagined was possible. And there was something else. With a tingle of appreciation, Juliet realised that she looked like a *real woman* for the first time in thirty-four years.

'That's only the beginning,' said Carmen. 'I haven't

started on your clothes yet.' She paused, picking up a leaflet from the dressing table, and regarded Juliet with an appraising eye. Then she flicked through the leaflet, looking up with a smile when she found what she wanted. Crossing the room to the telephone, she dialled a number.

'Yes, everything's fine, Mrs Mountjoy,' she said, pulling a face and grinning back at Juliet. 'Listen, I know this is rather short notice, but I see you advertise a professional hairdressing service in your brochure here. Is there any chance that someone might be available before dinner tonight?'

CHAPTER 15

When she saw Mrs Mountjoy approaching the table, Carmen realised belatedly that their decision to dine in public might not have been such a good idea. 'Don't forget that you're *Gideon*,' she whispered, nudging Duncan.

Mrs Mountjoy was wearing a pink trouser suit that looked disconcertingly like a pair of pyjamas, and her hair was puffed out even further than when Carmen had seen her last. 'Mr and Mrs Bird, how *delightful*,' she simpered, placing a leather-bound volume on the table in front of them. 'I was wondering if I could persuade you to sign our visitor's book.'

'Er, all right then,' said Carmen, taking the proffered pen. Glancing at the door, she wondered why Juliet was taking so long to arrive. She had left her in the hands of the hairdresser, who had whisked her away to another room with the promise of a radical restyling. With a pang of anxiety, Carmen hoped that nothing had gone wrong.

'And Mr Bird?' asked Mrs Mountjoy, smiling coyly at Duncan.

'I'll do it,' said Carmen hurriedly, filling in Gideon's name after hers. In the box reserved for comments, she added: '*Helpful and attentive service. If you're looking for privacy, give this place a miss.*'

'Oh, how charming, a little joke,' squealed Mrs Mountjoy, peering over her shoulder. 'I must get a copy made so that we can have it framed.'

'Hey, Carmen,' whispered Duncan, staring at the doorway with an expression of disbelief. 'Look at this!'

Carmen took a moment to realise that the attractive woman making her way towards their table was, in fact, Juliet. Seeing the finished effect for the first time, she was stunned by the transformation. The hairdresser had been true to his promise: he had drastically shortened Juliet's hair, shaping it into a stylish bob that accentuated her features. The clothes made a big difference, too. Instead of the usual chunky jeans, she wore a black Lycra skirt of Carmen's and a matching sweatshirt that had been restyled with a pair of scissors into a sleeveless, slash-neck evening top. She had also acquired an elegant pair of black shoes from an unknown source.

Heads turned, following her progress with looks of admiration. She's gorgeous, thought Carmen, feeling a burst of pride in her creation. Now that Juliet's previously dumpy-looking figure was revealed in its full, curvaceous glory, she embodied a powerful argument against the popular consensus that beauty couldn't exist in anything larger than a size ten.

'Hi,' she murmured, arriving in front of them with a self-conscious smile.

'You look great,' said Carmen softly. But Juliet's eyes were fixed on Duncan. Glancing sideways, Carmen saw an expression of amusement on his face.

'Hey Jules,' he said, laughing. 'What have you done to yourself? You look like something out of a fashion show.'

'What's wrong with it?' asked Juliet, her confidence visibly faltering.

'Well, nothing,' said Duncan. 'It's just that I hardly recognised you. Your hair's all different and I've never seen you dressed up like this before.' With a mischievous grin, he glanced around at the other tables. 'Is there someone you've got your eye on here tonight?'

Juliet sat down with a pained expression. It looked to Carmen as if she was on the verge of tears.

'Hey Jules, I'm sorry,' said Duncan quickly, reaching across the table and squeezing her hand. 'I was only joking, you know. You look great, really.'

Juliet gazed at him doubtfully. She was about to speak, when Mrs Mountjoy reappeared with a bottle of champagne on a tray.

'With the *compliments* of the house, Mrs Bird,' she announced, placing the bottle on the table. She glanced at Juliet, not recognising her, and leaned across the table towards Carmen. 'If you need an extra room for your *guest* tonight,' she added in a conspiratorial whisper, 'I'm sure it could *easily* be arranged.'

A waiter arrived with the first course. Mrs Mountjoy fussed around him like a demented bluebottle, hindering his progress as he attempted to distribute the items on his tray.

Carmen gazed into her bowl with dismay. An arrangement of beady-eyed crustaceans glistened pinkly on a bed of lettuce and *rose-marie* sauce. It was prawn cocktail. 'Oh Christ,' she murmured, as the image of an electric carving knife flashed into her thoughts. 'I'm not sure if I'm going to be able to eat this.'

The evening progressed awkwardly, without much conversation. Mrs Mountjoy finally took the hint and left them in peace, but one of the waiters kept hovering attentively, casting wistful smiles in Juliet's direction. Juliet didn't even notice, concentrating her attention on the food and maintaining a sulky silence throughout the meal.

As soon as the last course was finished, she stood up. 'I'll be back later,' she muttered, tossing her napkin on the table. She left the room at a brisk pace, too fast for the admiring waiter, who made an impulsive dash to follow her but was left stranded halfway across the room as she disappeared through the door.

'You shouldn't have made fun of her like that,' said Carmen, turning to Duncan.

'I'm sorry,' he murmured, refilling her wineglass. The lack of conversation had encouraged their consumption of alcohol and the champagne was long gone. They were now on the second bottle of red wine.

As he glanced up at her, Carmen felt a stirring of attraction. 'I'm sure she'll be OK,' he added. 'I didn't mean any harm. She must be used to me teasing her by now.'

Shifting his chair closer, Duncan held her gaze. The

look on his face made it clear that Juliet wasn't upper-most in his thoughts right now.

'I expect this is totally the wrong thing to say, with all that's happened today – but haven't you ever thought of doing something about the way that husband of yours treats you?'

Carmen looked away uncomfortably. 'What do you mean?'

'Well, leaving him is the obvious suggestion, I suppose. How can you stand it – knowing that he's having an affair? It doesn't seem right that you should have to put up with his mistress following you around like this.'

'Did Juliet tell you about her?' she asked, feeling a pang of distress at the thought of the two of them discussing her private life behind her back.

'Well, sort of,' he replied. 'She couldn't have explained that business about the phone call otherwise.'

'Maybe I will leave him,' murmured Carmen, won-dering how she could change the subject before it strayed into more dangerous areas. Then she was over-taken by a flirtatious impulse. 'I don't really want to think about Gideon at the moment,' she said, smiling. 'After all, *you're* supposed to be my husband tonight.'

'Then I must be the luckiest bloke on the planet,' said Duncan softly. 'You wouldn't believe how much I'm enjoying being here with you.'

Angie's nerves were in tatters when she finally arrived in Redruth. As soon as she had escaped from the A30 she pulled over to fix the windscreen wipers, but her efforts only resulted in one of them snapping off in her hand. Unable to see where she was going in the rain-spattered twilight, she had several near-misses with pedestrians, other vehicles, and a flower bed in someone's front garden before she eventually found her way to The Buccaneer Inn on the opposite edge of the town.

It was a rambling sort of building that might have been cobbled together by a drunken contractor with a job lot of bottle-glass windows and white-painted weatherboarding. To Angie, it looked like a place from the seaside that had been accidentally marooned inland. A whiff of deep-fried cooking from an open window conjured up the smell of candy floss and, as she entered through a creaky veranda festooned with coloured fairy lights, she was reminded of childhood visits to the haunted house at the local fun fair.

Bypassing the reception area, she followed a sign draped in fishing nets which directed her to Cap'n Hook's Bar. Installing herself at a table, she spent the next three hours sipping brandy and lemonade while she waited for Gideon to arrive.

By nine o'clock, she was starting to get worried. The Friday night after-work drinkers had gone home, to be replaced by darts players and sad-looking men with wet dogs, and there was still no sign of Gideon. Had she made some kind of mistake? It wasn't exactly his kind of place, she realised, glancing at the hand-lettered signs promising 'Karl's Karaoke Klub' later that night. Somehow, she couldn't quite picture Gideon belting out Abba songs for the entertainment of the beer-swilling locals who were now beginning to fill the bar.

Had he tricked her? Had he remained at his hotel while she raced all over the countryside on a wild goose chase? In an alcove decorated with somebody's collection of beer mats from around the world, Angie tried to get through to the Mount Imperial on the payphone. Each time she heard the receptionist's prim tones, however, the machine gurgled and swallowed her money, cutting her off.

She really ought to return to Penzance right now, she told herself, to be sure of being at the quayside in time when the boat left the following day. But what if Gideon had genuinely been held up? What if he had decided not to go to the Scillies after all? If she missed him now, she might never get another chance to make her blackmail proposition. *What should she do?*

The decision was made for her when she opened the door to the car park and found herself reeling dizzily in the fresh air. Counting the number of drinks she had consumed, she realised that she would be lucky to make it to the end of the street without hitting anything, let alone to Penzance. As she clutched the rail of the veranda and struggled to compose herself, the door swung open again and a man appeared beside her holding out a glass.

'I noticed you were on the brandy, love, so I thought this might hit the spot,' he murmured in a velvety tone. 'Go on, why don't you give it a try?'

Angie took a cautious sip of the sour-sweet liquid. 'What is it?' she asked, checking out his expensive-looking coat and chunky gold rings.

He raised his eyebrows. 'You never had a side-car before? Brandy, Cointreau and fresh lemon juice, shaken, *not stirred*, with cracked ice and strained into a chilled glass.' He flashed her a look that made her go weak at the knees and wonder what she had ever seen in Gideon. 'What do you think?'

'Mmm, very nice,' she replied, inspecting his craggy face and watery blue eyes. Early fifties, at a guess, she thought. A good few years of mileage left in him yet. Most likely married, but he looked the kind of man who could afford to keep a mistress.

'So what's a handsome girl like you doing in a dump like Redruth on a rainy Friday night, then?' he asked with a smile. 'You look to me like someone who's used to a more sophisticated kind of place.'

'Well, it's funny that you should mention that,' she murmured, allowing him to take her by the arm and guide her back towards the bar. 'Because I come from London, you see . . . quite close to Kensington, in fact . . .'

Upstairs in her attic room, Juliet stared into the mirror and tried to make an objective analysis of how she looked. Duncan's reaction had shaken her confidence badly. She had endured the meal in a state of embarrassment, scarcely tasting her food as she bolted it down. Convinced that she had made a complete fool of herself, she had escaped at the first opportunity with the intention of scrubbing off the makeup and changing her clothes.

But, after studying her reflection from all angles, Juliet had to admit that she liked what she saw. The new hairstyle made her face look slimmer and the clothes were flattering to her figure. The makeup, on careful inspection, was less startling than she had imagined. Carmen had simply used a subtle range of natural colours to highlight her best features and define the shape of her face. With a shock, Juliet realised that what she had often assumed to be natural beauty in others was, in fact, most likely to have resulted from the use of techniques such as these.

So why had Duncan laughed at her, she wondered. What was the point of being attractive if it had no effect on the man you loved? Did looks really make any difference to the way people felt?

Juliet had always maintained that they didn't – that it was the person inside that mattered. Now, however, she wasn't so sure. If you were unlucky enough to be repulsively ugly, she thought, what chance did you have of getting close enough to anyone to show them what your personality was like? A certain minimum quota of looks seemed necessary for getting to the stage where someone might start to show an interest. And looks weren't restricted to physical beauty; people made assumptions about you from the way you dressed and how you behaved.

Carmen had provided her with the looks and the clothes, and Juliet knew that Duncan liked her as a person. So where had she gone wrong? Sitting on the bed, she spent some time trying to answer this question and was eventually forced to conclude that he simply didn't fancy her. Sooner or later, she realised, she would have to come to terms with his indifference. Otherwise, she would waste her life holding out for the unattainable and risk ending up with nothing at all.

Duncan wasn't the only man in the world, she told herself. If she could acquire the necessary confidence to go with the new image, why shouldn't she meet someone who was genuinely interested in her? Why shouldn't she change her life?

In this more positive frame of mind, she decided to go back downstairs and be sociable. But when she arrived in the dining room, the meal was finished and the tables were all empty. Carmen and Duncan were nowhere to be seen.

She searched through the other public rooms, but couldn't find them anywhere. Her resolutions began to crumble as she struggled with a growing feeling of jealousy and disappointment. Why hadn't they waited, she asked herself, ordering a double whisky at the bar. Was there some reason why they didn't want her around?

'Cheer up, love,' said the barman, pouring two generous measures into her glass. 'It might never happen.'

'That's exactly the trouble,' muttered Juliet, half to herself, as she reflected on her crushed hopes for that evening. 'I'm beginning to think it never will.'

Things were hotting up in Cap'n Hook's Bar. Karl, an anaemic-looking youth in a glittery jacket, had arrived to set up his karaoke machine, and the empty tables were rapidly filling. Angie was on her second sidecar and was listening intently to her new friend, whose name was Ray.

'In my line of business,' he told her, 'you make a decision – you act on it fast. Before the competition gets a chance to move in.' He flashed her a disarming smile. 'When I came into this bar tonight, Angie, I could see straightaway that you were my kind of girl. I think we're gonna get along real fine.'

'And what *exactly* did you say your line of business was?' she persisted, having by now asked the same question several times and received no satisfactory reply.

A shadow crossed his face. 'I don't like mixing business and pleasure,' he said sternly. 'Let me level with you, Angie. There are plenty of women out there who would take advantage of me if they knew what I did for a living. I don't want any of that. I want to be liked for who I am, not for what I can do for your career.'

'But I wouldn't take advantage of you,' she protested, determined to uncover his secret. Was it possible, she wondered, that Ray was exactly the kind of big-time operator she had always longed to meet? A man who, unlike Gideon, could live up to his promises and deliver the goods.

'Listen, Angie,' he said in a more kindly voice. 'I really shouldn't tell you this, but I've got a feeling I can trust you.' Leaning close to her, he whispered softly into her ear. 'Let's just say that I'm in the music industry. Will that do?'

'The *music industry*?' echoed Angie in awe-struck tones. 'Do you know, like, rock stars and people then?'

'One or two,' he replied with an indulgent grin. 'But it's not as glamorous as it sounds, Angie, babe. It's a tough life, travelling around the whole time the way I do.'

Travelling round? Angie frowned. Why would a high-flying record company executive be travelling around to places like Redruth? What, for that matter, was he doing in a dive like The Buccaneer Inn?

Then the penny dropped. 'I know,' she blurted out excitedly. 'You must be a *talent scout*!'

'Sssh!' hissed Ray, clapping his hand over her mouth and glancing round to see if anyone had heard. 'Keep it down, for Christ's sake! If any of this lot get wind of who I am, they'll be wanting me to listen to their goddamn party pieces all night. Our cosy little chat together will be right off the agenda, believe you me.'

Angie let out a breathless sigh as her imagination began to work overtime, picturing herself as a chart-topping singer with Ray as her husband/manager. She could sing as well as the next person, she told herself. Why shouldn't she get her chance at fame? Glancing towards the door as some new arrivals entered the bar, she realised that it was becoming increasingly unlikely that Gideon would turn up. *Forget him*, she thought angrily. Why should she bother with a common murderer who didn't even have the decency to keep his appointments? Why get involved in the problems of blackmail when she had the chance of a respectable meal ticket with someone like Ray?

There was a howling whine of feedback as Karl switched on his microphone and announced that it was Karaoke time. Cheers and wolf whistles resounded through the room and a plump man with a shaved head got up to set the ball rolling with a rendition of 'Hi Ho Silver Lining'.

'Another sidecar?' asked Ray, wincing slightly.

Angie nodded vigorously, not trusting herself to speak. Several drinks later, after listening to a dozen or more hit songs being butchered by the regular clientèle, she boldly suggested that she might have a try.

'Sure, baby,' replied Ray with a shrug. 'Why not?'

After a hurried consultation with Karl, Angie elected to make her stage debut with 'Lovin' My Man Tonight', by Crystal Lee Jones. Fixing her eyes on Ray, she pushed out her chest and held the microphone close to her lips – injecting all the feelings that were welling up inside her into the song.

'Oh yeah, baby . . . I'm lovin' my man tonight,
Oh yeah, baby . . . I know it's gonna be alright,'

As she came to the final chorus, he looked up at her with tenderness in his eyes and she knew she'd hit paydirt. Eat your heart out Gideon, she thought triumphantly. I don't need you anymore.

'So come with me baby, 'cos I'm gonna be lovin' yoooo!'

She stepped down from Karl's podium to tumultuous applause and found herself teetering into Ray's outstretched arms.

'Hey, Angie,' he murmured softly. 'I can see you're a woman of the world, so I won't beat around the bush. I've got a room here for the night, so how do you fancy coming upstairs and getting yourself well and truly laid?'

Carmen emerged unsteadily from the bathroom, wondering what was happening to her. Once she had started flirting with Duncan, she hadn't been able to stop. They had somehow ended up back upstairs in the suite, at whose suggestion she couldn't remember. Returning to the sitting room, where Duncan was opening a further bottle of wine, she was aware of a strong current of sexual tension in the air.

'I've been waiting for a chance to be alone with you all day,' he said, holding out a glass. She moved to take it, but he set it on the table and reached for her hand with an impulsive gesture. 'How do you feel about picking things up where we left them last night?'

The intensity of his kiss surprised her, but she soon found herself responding with an equal passion. It felt as if her body was waking up from years of sexual slumber and launching itself on a mission to make up for lost time.

Before long, they were struggling to get out of their clothes. 'I think I've torn your shirt,' whispered Carmen, as several buttons flew across the room.

'I never liked this one much anyway,' said Duncan, ripping it off impatiently and throwing it aside. With a swift tug, he unzipped her dress and reduced it to a pool of material encircling her feet. 'Come here,' he murmured, taking her hand and drawing her into a fierce embrace. 'I've dreamt of this for such a long time.'

They made their way to the bedroom, shedding further garments as they went. 'Wait there a moment,' whispered Duncan, removing his trousers. 'I'll just go and check that the door's shut properly.'

Carmen stretched out on the bed in the darkened room, abandoning herself to fantasies of what was about to happen. She had almost forgotten what it was like to make love – a term she had never applied to the brutal couplings that had been forced on her throughout her married life.

'I'll take the phone off the hook,' called Duncan from the sitting room. 'We don't want Jules splitting us up again, do we?' he added with a laugh.

Carmen felt a twinge of guilt. Juliet had said something about meeting back in the dining room. What was she going to think of them for disappearing like this? With a stirring of unease, she remembered how unhappy Juliet had seemed that evening – how hurt she had looked when Duncan joked about her clothes. Then she sat up, jolted by a sudden realisation. She had been too absorbed in her own problems to register what should have been obvious from the start: *Juliet was in love with Duncan*. Why else would she have been so eager to submit to the makeover, if not to impress him?

Gathering the bedclothes around herself, Carmen contemplated her dilemma. She was strongly attracted to Duncan, but she certainly wasn't in love with him. Did her need for physical gratification outweigh the risk of spoiling everything for her friend?

As he reappeared in the doorway, she made a decision.

'Listen, Duncan,' she said, tightening her grip on the duvet. 'I've just been . . . well, thinking. I'm not sure that this is such a good idea, after all.'

His expression changed abruptly to one of disappointment. 'But, why?' he asked. 'What have I done?'

'I'm sorry,' she whispered. 'It's not your fault – it's mine. I shouldn't have let things go this far. I'm married, remember?'

'To a bastard who doesn't appreciate you!' Moving closer, he fixed her with a look of entreaty. 'I'm crazy about you, Carmen. I only want to make you happy. Won't you give me a chance?'

'But you hardly know me,' she protested, startled by this declaration. 'I mean, we might be attracted to each other, but you don't have any idea of what I'm really like. You can't judge me by what you've seen on TV.' She wanted to say something about Juliet – to wake him up to his blindness – but she couldn't find the right words. It also occurred to her that it might not have the effect she intended if she mentioned it just now.

'But I *want* to get to know you . . .' began Duncan.

'Look, I'm really sorry,' she interrupted. 'But I don't think we should take this any further.' She paused, wondering how she could soften the harshness of this remark. 'I'm sure it's the best thing to do,' she added, 'if we want to carry on being friends.'

'I suppose I'd better get dressed, then,' he muttered, glancing down in embarrassment at his now limp penis. Reaching for the hotel bathrobe, Carmen escaped to the sitting room and left him to recover his dignity. She was sobering up rapidly from the effects of the wine and felt as if she had been thrust into the morning after without being given a chance to finish off the night before.

Picking her way through her own discarded clothing, she sat down in front of the dressing table. Taking a long look in the mirror, she tried to see herself as other people did — as the glamorous and self-assured TV star. It was a trick she had often used in front of the cameras, thinking herself into the role until she *became* that person. But, somehow, it didn't work tonight.

Her makeup kit was spread out where she had left it earlier. Absent-mindedly, she began to gather up the compacts and brushes, stacking them neatly away. If she hadn't been so obsessed with keeping up appearances, she reflected, she might have been better equipped to deal with the problems of her marriage. She might have had the courage to leave Gideon and make a fresh start.

But she had been prepared to commit murder rather than destroy the illusion of her perfect life. And now that Gideon was dead, whether by accident or not, she no longer had anyone but herself to blame for the things that went wrong.

Slotting the final tubes of lip colour into their compartments, she closed the lid of her makeup box and secured it with a click. If she wanted to be able to live with the consequences of what she had done, she realised, it was time for a change of attitude. She would have to stop hiding behind her TV image and start taking responsibility for her own life.

CHAPTER 16

The next morning, Juliet, Carmen and Duncan break-fasted in silence. When Juliet saw that the other two weren't speaking to each other, she assumed they must be putting on an act to throw her off the scent. She had little doubt in her mind that Duncan hadn't slept on the floor the previous night.

She had waited in the bar for some time, checking the other rooms at regular intervals, but Duncan and Carmen hadn't returned. When she finally plucked up the courage to telephone their suite, the engaged signal had convinced her that they had something to hide.

The barman had tried to cheer her up, plying her with drinks and offers of further entertainment after he finished his shift. But when the bar closed at eleven, she had slipped away quietly to her room. She slept fitfully, her dreams troubled by recurring images of Duncan having hot sex with Carmen up against the trouser press.

While Juliet and Carmen restricted themselves to coffee, toast and cereal, Duncan opted for the *Full Cornish Breakfast*, tucking into a plate laden with *West*

Country Sausages, Cornish Bacon, Newlyn Kippers and something called a *Mount Imperial Fried Breakfast Slice*. The silence was finally broken when Juliet vetoed his request for a second pot of coffee. 'We haven't got time,' she hissed, pointing at her watch. 'We'll be late for the boat.'

A look of apprehension appeared on Duncan's face and he glanced down at his empty plate with dismay. 'I hope the crossing isn't going to be too rough,' he said anxiously. 'Perhaps I should have held back on the fried slice.'

After checking out of the hotel and depositing the Freeloader in the Harbour Garage, they made their way down to the quay. The pavements were still wet from the night's rain, and a dense covering of dark grey clouds promised more to come. As they crossed the main road and approached the *Scillonian's* berth, Juliet was relieved that there was no sign of Angie. With a bit of luck, she told herself, Gideon's mistress would have spent the night in Redruth. She would probably be waking up just about now and wondering why her lover had failed to appear.

When they reached the ship, boarding had already commenced. Joining the queue with Carmen and Duncan, Juliet watched carefully to check the procedures for the return journey. One man stood at the foot of the gangplank collecting tickets, while another issued each person with a boarding pass as they stepped onto the deck.

There were names on the tickets, noted Juliet, so there would be a record of everyone who had made the crossing. The boarding cards were presumably to give confirmation of the numbers actually entering the ship. Handing over her ticket, she made her way up the narrow gangplank. The crucial question yet to be answered was whether similar checks would be carried out when they disembarked.

As Duncan and Carmen joined her on the deck, Juliet noticed a woman in a bright yellow tracksuit pointing a camera in their direction. 'You'd better go downstairs,' she whispered, grabbing Duncan by the arm and propelling him through the door which led inside the ship. 'I'm told it's the best place to be if you're feeling seasick.'

'What are you talking about?' asked Carmen. 'Surely he ought to be out in the fresh air?'

'That's fine if you want him appearing in the background of everyone's holiday snaps,' hissed Juliet, pulling her to one side. Glancing through the door, she saw that Duncan was hesitating at the top of the stairs with a queasy expression. 'I suppose you'd better go with him and keep him out of trouble,' she added, realising that she had to stay on deck to watch out for Angie. 'I expect he'll be needing someone to hold his sick-bag.'

When Carmen had gone, Juliet stationed herself at the rail and watched the last few crates of provisions for the islands being hoisted into the front of the ship. Once this task was complete, there was a flurry of activity as the gangplank was lowered to the quayside and men in overalls busied themselves doing complicated things with ropes. Before long, the *Scillonian III* was moving slowly away from its moorings. Juliet felt a faint pang of disappointment that the moment of departure had passed with so little ceremony. By embarking on this journey, she felt as if she had crossed a boundary past which she could never return. They were committed to her plan now, she realised, gazing at the receding quayside. The next time she set foot in Penzance, she would know whether or not it had worked.

As they moved out into the harbour, a recorded tannoy announcement outlined the attractions of the forthcoming trip, promising spectacular views of Cornwall's Heritage Coast. Spare us the *son et lumière*, she thought irritably, glancing around at the camera-wielding tourists crowding the deck. She had imagined that this journey would be something of an adventure – an intrepid voyage to a far-flung outpost of the British Isles – but the reality was beginning to seem more like a fairground ride.

Once they had left the protection of the quay wall, however, gusts of wind and rain began to swirl across the deck. There was a token unfurling of pac-a-macs and kagoules, but it didn't take long for most of the passengers to abandon their viewing positions in favour of the comforts available inside. '*Tea, coffee and light refreshments,*' offered the tannoy in enticing tones. '*A wide selection of souvenirs and a fully licensed bar.*'

Juliet was left alone, clutching the rail and staring over the side of the ship at the cold grey waves. What would it feel like to fall overboard, she wondered uneasily. It would be a long drop before you even hit the water, a bit like jumping off the high board at the swimming pool. She shuddered, imagining the icy darkness of the waves closing over her head. It was one thing to theorise about the perfect murder, but quite another to go ahead and stage such a horrible death. How would she ever convince herself, let alone anyone else, that it had actually taken place?

'Juliet? Is everything OK?'

She looked round to see Carmen approaching, the collar of her designer raincoat turned up against the wind. 'Fine,' she muttered, still troubled by thoughts of what had happened the previous night. It didn't seem right that Carmen should be starting a new love life when Gideon still wasn't even officially dead.

'Look, Juliet. I need to talk to you.' Drawing her into a sheltered area behind a lifeboat, Carmen faced her with a determined expression. 'About last night . . .' she began.

Surely the woman wasn't going to have the temerity to brag about her conquest, thought Juliet in dismay. She certainly didn't want to hear the sordid details of what had taken place.

'It's only just dawned on me,' continued Carmen. 'I'd never have gone off with Duncan like that if I'd known . . .'

'Known what?'

'About you, of course. How you feel about Duncan. You care for him a lot, don't you?'

Juliet felt a hot rush of embarrassment. She didn't want sympathy, especially not from the woman who had compounded her misery by seducing Duncan right under her nose. With a shrug, she turned to stare at the passing cliffs. The tannoy started up again, droning on about artists' communities and smugglers' coves.

'Don't you?' repeated Carmen. 'Please, I wish you'd trust me, Juliet. I'm only trying to help.'

Eventually, something in her tone made Juliet weaken. She longed to share the burden of her secret with someone, and there seemed little point in denying it now that Carmen had worked things out for herself. 'Well, I suppose so,' she admitted reluctantly. 'But he's not interested in me at all, as you probably noticed last night.'

'I'm sure that's not so.' Juliet felt Carmen's hand touch her shoulder. 'I think he cares more about you than he realises.'

'Why did he laugh at me, then?'

'I expect he was just surprised. I mean, you looked different from the picture he has of you in his mind. But he'll get used to it, if you give him a little time.'

Juliet continued to stare at the cliffs, noticing that the Minack theatre – the place she had visited with Duncan the day before – was coming into view. If all this was true, she wondered, what exactly *had* happened in Mrs Mountjoy's best suite the night before?

As if reading her thoughts, Carmen began to speak. 'Listen, Juliet, I'm really sorry about what I did last night – leaving you on your own and everything. I had too much to drink and I kind of got . . . well, carried away . . .'

Glancing up, Juliet saw a seagull hovering above them, its fat belly clean and white against the dark backcloth of the sky. Floating on the warm updraft from the ship's funnel, it seemed unaffected by the surrounding weather and needed only to make an occasional flap of one wing to keep on course. If only her own life could be so uncomplicated, she thought, bracing herself for what she was about to hear.

'But nothing happened,' continued Carmen. She hesitated. 'Well, nothing more than a bit of a snog, anyway,' she added, shamefaced. 'It won't be repeated. The whole thing was a big mistake.'

Abruptly, the seagull swooped sideways and disappeared from view. Juliet stared at Carmen, wondering if she could believe what she heard. A tiny glimmer of hope began to form inside her, whispering that she might *still have a chance*.

'Carmen,' she asked anxiously. 'You didn't actually *say* anything to Duncan, did you? About me, I mean.'

'No, of course not,' she replied. 'But I will if you want me to. I think all he needs is a hint to push him in the right direction.'

'No, you mustn't do that!' said Juliet, alarmed. 'I'd feel such an idiot . . .'

'OK,' said Carmen. 'If you're sure that's what you want. But perhaps you ought to consider saying something to him yourself.'

'I don't know if . . .' Juliet's reply was cut short by the tannoy, which crackled into life to inform them that they were passing Land's End. A handful of passengers emerged from the shelter of the lounge, eager to catch a final glimpse of Heritage Coast.

'I can't see anything,' complained a woman, training

her video camera on the hazy outline of the distant cliffs. 'Where's the Lost Land of Lyonesse?'

'That's not on this trip, stupid,' said her companion, struggling to read a brochure in the wind. 'That's in the Legendary Last Labyrinth. It says here that you only get that included if you book for the End of England Experience as part of the Triple Theme Tour.'

The wind buffeted the ship with renewed force, driving Juliet and Carmen back into the shelter of the lifeboat. 'Don't you think we should go inside?' asked Carmen, looking slightly bilious. 'We really ought to make sure that Duncan's OK.'

'You're probably right,' replied Juliet, glad that she no longer had reason to be angry with Carmen. 'I can't see our plan working out too well if one of us gets swept overboard.'

When Angie opened her eyes, her first thought was to wonder why someone had jammed her head in a vice. Her second was to wish that they had wound it tighter to prevent her from moving, which was infinitely more painful than staying still. It took some time before she was able to focus on her watch, and even longer before she could understand what it said. When the information finally made it through the fog surrounding her brain, she sat up with a start. She was supposed to have been in Penzance looking for Gideon, but it was too late to get there now. She had missed the fucking boat.

Then she felt the delicious, throbbing soreness between her legs and remembered that she didn't need to worry about the boat anymore. She had Ray now – Ray, the demon lover who was going to make her rich and famous. They had been through every position in the book last night, and more. She couldn't remember much detail but, if the state of the room was anything to judge by, the earth had moved.

There was no one in the bed beside her. 'Ray, honey,' she called, watching for him to return through the bathroom door. There was no reply. When she eventually hauled herself out of bed, she found that the bathroom was empty. I expect he's gone down for breakfast, she thought, lowering herself stiffly onto the lavatory. Muscles she hadn't known existed were beginning to hurt.

Painfully, she dressed herself and headed downstairs. There was no sign of breakfast, however, and a notice on the wall informed her that it had finished at some godforsaken hour, when it was probably still dark. She was about to wander outside to see if Ray was on the veranda when a voice stopped her.

'Would you mind coming over here a moment?' Angie turned to see a stout woman with coal-black eyes and flaring nostrils standing beside the reception desk with her hand on her hip. 'If you wouldn't mind settling up now,' she said in a hostile tone, 'we're waiting to clear your room.'

'Settling up?' echoed Angie stupidly.

'Paying the bill,' explained the woman, extending her thumb and forefinger and rubbing them together. 'Your husband told us when he left that you'd be looking after it.'

Husband? Angie stared at the woman in bewilderment. 'When he *left*?' she asked, aware that her recently acquired dreams were crumbling around her. Where had Ray gone?

'Here, Caliban,' called the woman quickly. A huge Alsatian appeared beside her, letting out great steaming clouds of breath as it slavered into her hand.

'But I . . .' Angie was about to say that she had no money, but thought better of it. 'I'll just pop up and find my chequebook, then,' she said, forcing a note of brightness into her voice. Caliban growled his approval.

Upstairs, she examined the contents of her handbag and discovered that her demon lover had not only disappeared, but had also helped himself to a substantial fee for his services. Money, chequebook and card, Co-op savings book, and even her Sainsbury's Reward card — he had taken the lot. She searched the room from top to bottom, hoping that she had made a mistake, but the only sign that Ray had ever existed was a collection of torn-up betting slips in the wastepaper bin.

Sitting on the bed, Angie indulged herself in a brief spell of silent mourning for her lost hopes of fame and fortune in the music business. Then she pulled herself together. A setback like this could happen to anyone, she told herself. There was no point in wasting time feeling sorry for herself when there was still a chance that she could catch up with Gideon and pull off her blackmail plan. Picking up the telephone, she dialled the Mount Imperial, this time getting straight through. The receptionist confirmed that the 'Bird party', as she called them, had checked out that morning and taken the boat to the Scilly Isles.

Gideon couldn't stay on an island forever, thought Angie, hanging up. When he came back, she would be waiting for him. Meanwhile, she had to find a way to get out of this hotel and back to Penzance. She began to dial Ronco's number, then stopped, remembering that she had failed to keep her promise to call him the night before. She wasn't in the mood for recriminations and it would be embarrassing to have to admit to him what had happened. Besides, even if he was willing to send her money, it wouldn't arrive in time. There had to be a better way to handle this.

If it wasn't for the stolen car parked outside, she could simply have done a runner. She had little doubt, however, that the dragon on the desk had taken note of the registration and would be onto the police like a shot if she disappeared. There was also Caliban to consider. If she wanted to get out of this place without being eaten alive, it looked as if she would have to stay another night while she got together the money to settle the bill.

And there was only one way she knew of doing that. With a sigh, she sat down in front of the mirror and began to apply generous quantities of makeup. It was lucky she had brought her good underwear with her, she thought. It would be difficult enough to find clients in a strange town, without the extra hassle of trying to look sexy in old Marks and Spencer knickers that had gone grey in the wash.

*   *   *

As the *Scillonian* drew close to St Mary's, the wind died away and the clouds dispersed. Returning to the deck as they came in sight of the harbour, Juliet gazed around at a calm blue sea dotted with islands. It was as if the ship had passed through some invisible barrier and entered a charmed circle where everything was bathed in warm sunlight.

Her mood, always quick to be influenced by the weather, was further brightened when she discovered that nobody was checking the passengers as they disembarked. 'It's just as I hoped,' she whispered to Carmen as they collected their luggage on the quayside. 'I'm beginning to think our plan might actually work.'

'What happens now?' asked Duncan, whose state of health had been steadily improving since he parted company with the remains of the *Mount Imperial Fried Breakfast Slice* over the side of the ship. 'Where exactly did you say your aunt lives?'

'Old Town,' replied Carmen, glancing around anxiously. 'She said she'd arrange for a taxi to pick us up.'

Aunt Bridget hadn't let them down. A battered estate car with a sign on the roof saying 'Phil's Taxi' was waiting for them at the end of the quay. Phil, a good-looking giant with a mop of unruly black hair, drove them across the island at breakneck speed.

'Looks like we're in for a warm one,' he said chattily, as they hurtled into a narrow lane. 'It can be like the tropics out here sometimes, with temperatures in the nineties when they've still got snow and blizzards on the mainland. Hope you've all had your malaria jabs.'

He drove on in silence for a few moments, then

glanced round and burst out laughing at their puzzled faces. 'Only joking,' he assured them. 'But you'd be amazed how many people believe me. I had some Americans in the back last week who got themselves in a right panic because they thought their medical insurance would be screwed up.'

Aunt Bridget lived in a white cottage set back behind a row of trees and a rough stone wall. The well-kept garden contained an abundance of fleshy, tropical-looking plants with huge flower spikes.

'I'll be seeing you, then,' said Phil, depositing their luggage by the gate and leaping back into the car. 'Got a booking from the Tregarthen in ten minutes.'

'How strange,' murmured Carmen, as he drove away before she could hand him his fare. 'I've heard that the locals are supposed to be friendly around here, but this seems to be taking it to extremes.'

As they approached the cottage, Carmen's aunt appeared at the door. Despite having been told that she was only in her fifties, Juliet had formed a mental image of Aunt Bridget as an ancient, grey-haired crone. The woman who came out to greet them, however, didn't fit this picture at all. Looking more like she was in her mid-forties, she had a slim, girlish figure, and was dressed in jeans and an embroidered Indian top. Her face was pretty in a kittenish sort of way and she sported a short, stylish haircut that had been dyed a bright copper-red.

Standing awkwardly to one side while Carmen and her aunt exchanged tearful embraces, Juliet was intrigued by the glimpse of homely interior visible through the open door. Carmen had mentioned that her aunt was a widow. What had happened to her uncle, wondered Juliet ghoulishly. And what was it like for Aunt Bridget to live all alone in a place like this?

'I'm sorry, darling,' purred Carmen, turning to Duncan with a fond expression. 'It's just that Bridget and I haven't seen each other for over eight years.' Wiping her eyes on her sleeve, she reached out and took his hand. 'This is my husband, Gideon,' she announced, blushing. 'I only wish I'd managed to bring him over here before now.'

Nicely done, thought Juliet. It seemed that Carmen was getting the hang of this acting thing at last.

'It's great to meet you,' said Duncan, kissing Aunt Bridget on both cheeks and threatening to crush her in an enthusiastic hug. 'Carmen's told me all about you, Mrs . . . er, Aunt . . . er . . .'

'Call me Bridget,' she replied softly, regarding him with a look of interest. Before Duncan could respond, however, she turned to face Juliet. 'You must be this new friend of Carmen's I've heard so much about,' she said with a disarming smile.

'Oh, er, hello,' said Juliet, completely thrown by this statement. What exactly had Bridget heard, she wondered, flashing Carmen a questioning look. They were going to end up in a complete mess if the three of them couldn't manage to get their stories straight.

'Well, it looks as if we've all got some catching up to do,' said Bridget, leading them into the house. 'I think we'd better kick off with a cup of tea.'

Inside, while Carmen and Bridget discussed family

matters and Duncan made an effort to look as if he knew what they were talking about, Juliet gazed around the comfortable living room. In addition to the usual books and ornaments filling the shelves, there was a considerable collection of pottery and clayware. The items varied from simple bowls to elaborate figurines, but they all had a certain quirkiness of style that suggested they originated from the same hand.

'This is lovely,' she commented eventually, touching a shallow bowl with a sleeping dragon curled around the rim. 'Did *you* make it?'

Bridget broke off her conversation with Carmen and gave Juliet a warm smile. 'That's one of my best-selling designs,' she said, looking pleased. 'They go like hot cakes down at the craft shop whenever I manage to get a batch out.'

'You didn't tell me you did this professionally, Bridget,' exclaimed Carmen. 'I thought it was just a hobby.'

'Well, it helps keep body and soul together,' replied her aunt cheerfully. 'Your uncle left his financial affairs in a bit of a mess when he was struck by lightning on the golf course.'

'I'm sorry,' muttered Carmen, looking flustered. 'I wasn't thinking . . .'

'I wouldn't worry about it,' she replied in a matter-of-fact tone. 'I'm much happier without him, to tell the truth.' She turned back to Juliet. 'If you're interested in this sort of thing,' she said, indicating the dragon bowl, 'you might like to see my more recent work. If you've nothing else planned, I could show you round my workshop this afternoon.'

*　　*　　*

Ronco stood halfway up the fire escape, twitching with indecision. It was over twenty-four hours since Angie had promised to call him, but his telephone hadn't rung once. Anything might have happened to her. He really ought to do something, he thought, shuffling from one furry-slippered foot to the other. The only problem was that he didn't know what.

If Angie was still negotiating her blackmail terms, she wasn't going to thank him for interfering. She could easily have asked him, after all, if she had needed his help. If Gideon had already harmed her, however, any action he took was going to be too late.

Meanwhile, the thought of her empty flat upstairs was preying on his imagination. He had waited a long time for an opportunity like this. Padding silently up the remaining steps to her bedroom window, he extracted a screwdriver from his pocket and forced it open with a swift movement. It wasn't as if he was planning to take anything, he reassured himself. Glancing around to make sure that he wasn't being observed, he slipped noiselessly inside. Nobody would ever know that he had been here.

Half an hour later, his panting breaths were interrupted by the sound of his own telephone ringing downstairs. It must be Angie, he thought guiltily, jumping up with a start and struggling to untangle himself from the contents of her knicker drawer. He scampered across to the window, pulling up his trousers as he went, then realised that it would be much safer to use the internal stairs.

Returning through the bedroom, he had made it as far as Angie's hallway when the ringing stopped. 'Bugger,' he muttered, leaning back against the inside of the front door and letting out a sigh of frustration. It was almost as if the call had been specially timed to spoil his fun.

Then his eye fell on the pile of newspapers on the hall table. 'WOMAN FOUND STRANGLED IN SHEPHERD'S BUSH FLAT,' said the headline on the top front page.

'Blimey,' he gasped, recognising the picture of the woman who had been in the local pub with Gideon on Tuesday night. Leafing through the various reports, he quickly arrived at the same conclusion Angie had reached a few days earlier. It had to be Gideon who had killed her.

Angie was in danger, he realised with dismay. But what could have possessed her to continue with her blackmail plan once she knew what Gideon had done? It just didn't make sense. His illicit pleasures forgotten, Ronco stumbled downstairs in a daze. He had hesitated to do anything before, but now he knew that he must. Otherwise, it would be his own fault if Angie ended up dead.

But how should he go about it? The obvious course of action was to go to the police, but Ronco had serious reservations about this. Having spent much of his life avoiding them for very good reasons, it went against the grain for him to start doing their job for them. He was also anxious to avoid stirring up old enmities. As far as he was concerned, he had served his time and paid his dues. The filth tended to have long memories, however, and he had no intention of being made a scapegoat for all the unsolved local burglaries of the last few years.

There seemed little point in traipsing down to Cornwall to engage in a single-handed confrontation with a murderer. Gideon would most likely have moved on from the place Angie had mentioned long before Ronco could catch up with him. Besides, how would he get there? He couldn't afford the train fare, and had no transport of his own since selling the car.

Ronco hated decisions. Back in the sanctuary of his own living room, he slumped into the armchair next to the gas fire and stared at his feet in despair. His badger slippers gazed back at him with reproachful eyes.

'Eeny, meeny, miny, mo,' he murmured, reaching for the remote control. *I'll just watch a bit of telly*, he decided sleepily. *Then I'll think about it some more and make up my mind what to do.*

While Duncan took a nap upstairs and Carmen went for a walk on the nearby beach, Juliet spent the afternoon admiring Bridget's pottery. There was a whole series of items based around the dragon theme – bowls, plates, drinking mugs, and even a range of jewellery.

'Do you really make a living from this?' asked Juliet, greatly impressed that Bridget could support herself by doing something she enjoyed.

'How else am I going to pay the bills?' she replied simply. 'I wouldn't want to sponge off my boyfriend, would I?'

'Er, no . . . I mean, of course not,' said Juliet, flushing as she realised that she had unthinkingly labelled

Bridget as a lonely, single person like herself. At the same time, glancing through the window at the profusion of spring flowers in the garden, she felt a pang of envy at the contrast with her own working environment. The thought of going back to Castlemayne Insurance filled her with gloom. How could anyone endure the rat race of city life after spending time in a place like this?

Wistfully, she remembered the plans she had once made with Maggie to join her at Belfry Books. In an odd way, Bridget reminded her of Maggie – they both had the same type of independent spirit and quirky charm. Worcester might not be as idyllic a location as the Scilly Isles, thought Juliet, but it was a place she knew and loved. If only she had been less cautious – less reluctant to take risks – she might have achieved the kind of lifestyle that these women had.

But perhaps it wasn't too late. If she was prepared to risk the consequences of covering up a murder, she ought to be able to cope with a little financial insecurity without turning a hair. Picking up a dragon-shaped bracelet and trying it on, she made herself a promise. If she succeeded in carrying out the rest of her plan without ending up in prison, she would take some positive action to sort out her life.

'Do you like it?' asked Bridget, pointing at the bracelet. 'You can keep it if you want.'

'Are you sure?' Juliet pushed the dragon back on her wrist and held out her arm to admire it. 'That's really kind,' she said, blushing. 'But I ought to pay you for it . . .'

'It's a gift,' said Bridget firmly, patting her wrist. 'I'm glad Carmen's found a real friend at last.'

Later, when Carmen had returned from her walk and gone upstairs to get ready for dinner, Juliet offered to help Bridget prepare the food.

'You just sit there and keep me company,' she replied, handing Juliet a glass of wine and parking her at the scrubbed pine table in the centre of the spacious kitchen. Opening the oven door, she stirred a delicious-smelling casserole. 'Everything's under control.'

Juliet noticed that five place settings had been laid at the table, but didn't like to pry by asking who the extra guest would be.

'I get worried about Carmen sometimes,' said Bridget, arranging a garnish of anchovies and olives on a French onion tart with the same attention to detail that she applied to her pottery. 'I think she gets so wrapped up in that TV job that she loses touch with the real world. Have you known each other for long?'

'Um . . . quite a while I suppose,' muttered Juliet evasively, feeling that three weeks was too short a period of time to seem respectable. How long did you have to be acquainted with someone, she wondered, before you were allowed to qualify as a friend?

'And her husband?' asked Bridget.

'Well . . . er, the same, of course,' she faltered.

'Mmm . . .' Bridget slid the tart carefully into the oven. 'He's not at all like I expected.'

'How do you mean?'

'Well, I probably shouldn't be saying this to you behind Carmen's back,' said Bridget, glancing at the door, 'but I always got the impression from her letters that he was a bit of an ogre. She didn't actually say anything specific, but reading between the lines . . . well, you know.' Pouring herself a glass of wine, she joined Juliet at the table. 'What do you think? Are they happy together?'

'They, er, seem to get along all right to me,' said Juliet awkwardly.

'I know how hard it is to admit when things have gone wrong in a marriage,' murmured Bridget thoughtfully. 'There are a lot of things I never told Carmen about my own.' She sighed. 'Relationships are strange things, aren't they? You can live with someone for years and never really get to know them at all.'

'I'm not the best person to ask.' Juliet felt a unexpected pang of misery. 'I've only ever managed it for six months.'

'You don't know how lucky you are,' said Bridget firmly. 'There's more to life than men, though God knows it's taken me long enough to find that out. If you can't have them on your own terms, they're not worth getting involved with, believe me. Not if you want to be anything more than an unpaid drudge.'

It was all very well to say that when you were in a position to choose, thought Juliet bitterly. Right now, she would be happy to clean out the Augean stables with a teaspoon if it meant that Duncan would recognise her as a member of the opposite sex.

The doorbell rang. 'On the other hand,' added Bridget, with a twinkle in her eye, 'there are times when you simply can't manage without them.' She opened the door to admit Phil the taxi driver, who was carrying a large Tupperware container. 'I've never been any good at puddings, but Phil's cheesecakes are out of this world.'

'Hi Bridge,' he said, kissing her on the lips as he handed over his offering. Producing a bottle of red wine from each pocket, and a third from inside his shirt, he placed them in a line on the table. 'I'm not late, am I?'

At this moment, Carmen came into the kitchen. 'Oh,' she said, glancing at Phil with a look of mild surprise before turning back to Bridget. 'Do we need a taxi? Are we going out?'

'Not unless you're offering to drive,' said Phil with a laugh, picking up a corkscrew and starting to open one of the bottles. 'I'm strictly off-duty.' Pausing, he slipped his arm round Bridget's shoulders and gave her an affectionate squeeze. 'The only journey I'm planning to make tonight is upstairs and through the bedroom door.'

Carmen was momentarily flummoxed. 'Why didn't you tell me?' she asked Bridget in a whisper. 'I thought you'd been all on your own since Uncle Colin's . . . er . . . accident.'

'I wasn't quite sure how to,' she replied, blushing. 'Besides, I didn't really think it was such a big deal.'

'Oh blimey,' said Phil, letting go of Bridget. 'I thought you'd already told them about us. Have I gone and said the wrong thing?'

'It's all right,' she said, reaching for his hand and pulling him back towards her. With a smile, she wrapped her arms around his generous waist and gave him a hug. 'I don't think we need to get my niece's permission for you to stay the night.'

Dinner tasted as good as it had looked and smelled, and Phil's wine turned out to be rather better than the supermarket plonk that Juliet was accustomed to drinking. Duncan, who had by now fully recovered from the crossing, demolished two helpings of everything and spent much of the meal talking to Phil. As the wine flowed, Juliet became increasingly anxious that he was going to forget himself and slip up.

The only sticky moment, however, was when they strayed on to the subject of *Mangus* and Bridget revealed an unexpected interest in the minutiae of filming locations. 'Remember that sequence where he gets chased by lions?' she asked. 'You know, the one where they go through the safari park in an open-top bus? Was that done at Longleat or Woburn?'

'I . . . er, couldn't say for certain,' replied Duncan, looking confused. 'I remember the episode, of course, but I think my assistant must have handled that one. I was probably tied up at a broadcasting conference at the time.' Juliet smiled, impressed by his performance, but Carmen's face remained a picture of anxiety until the subject was changed.

Things improved when they went through to the living room and Phil produced a pack of playing cards. Discovering that it was possible to dispense with serious conversation by hiding behind the rituals of a game, everyone became more relaxed. A convivial atmosphere quickly developed and even Carmen began to enjoy herself. Before long, Juliet felt as if she was in the company of old friends.

Later, while Bridget was in the kitchen making coffee, Carmen took Juliet to one side and congratulated her on getting on so well with her aunt. 'Bridget's really taken to you,' she whispered. 'She told me so earlier.' Then, flushed with the excitement of winning three hands of poker in a row, she nudged Juliet and nodded towards Phil. 'I still can't believe it,' she added with a giggle. 'Aunt Bridget and the local *taxi driver*. Uncle Colin would be turning in his grave if he knew. He was such a snob.'

'We should think ourselves lucky,' murmured Juliet. 'On a small island like this, she might easily have ended up with the local copper instead.'

CHAPTER 17

When Carmen woke up the next morning, Duncan wasn't there. She had felt rather awkward about sharing a bedroom with him after what had happened in Penzance, but he seemed to have accepted her rejection without ill feelings and had even volunteered to sleep on the floor.

Glancing at the bedside clock and discovering that it was already mid-morning, she dressed hurriedly and went downstairs. 'Where's Dun . . . I mean Gideon?' she asked, finding Bridget in the kitchen rolling out the pastry for an apple pie.

'Gone for a walk,' replied her aunt, wiping her hands on her apron and facing her with a quizzical look. 'He left about half an hour ago.'

'And Juliet?'

'She went out earlier – said something about wanting some time on her own.' Returning to her pastry, Bridget gave it a final roll and nodded at the chair opposite her. 'Why don't you sit down? I think we need to have a talk.'

'What about?' asked Carmen uneasily.

'This husband of yours,' said Bridget. 'I find him a little . . . well, confusing.'

'How do you mean?' With a feeling of trepidation, Carmen pulled back the chair and sat down. Had Duncan got his story mixed up and said something incriminating to her aunt?

With an expert movement, Bridget lifted the pastry on her rolling pin and flipped it on top of the pie. 'He's not at all what I expected. From what you said in your letters, I mean. I know you never actually spelled it out, but I got the impression you weren't very happy. That he pushed you around a bit – kept you on a short leash.'

'We did have a few problems in the early days,' murmured Carmen, looking down at the table to avoid catching her aunt's eye. 'Things are much better now, though. We're getting along just fine. You shouldn't judge him on anything I might have said in the past.'

'Well, I'm glad to hear that you're happy,' said Bridget. She paused, crimping the edges of the pie with her fingers, then glanced up at Carmen with a curious expression. 'It doesn't really explain what's bothering me, though. I never mentioned this to you at the time, but I was getting a bit worried about you earlier this year. There was one particular letter, no need to remind you of the details, that made me decide to get in touch with your father. Just to reassure myself – to ask him if he thought you were OK.'

'He wouldn't have been likely to know much,' said Carmen, wondering uncomfortably where this was leading. 'I hardly ever see him.'

'Maybe not,' replied Bridget. 'Though I suspect that's more your doing than his. But the point is, he sent me some press cuttings – he's got quite a collection apparently – and there were pictures of you and Gideon at some awards ceremony . . .'

Carmen gazed at her aunt in dismay. Had she known all along that Duncan was an imposter? His disguise was scarcely good enough to stand comparison with a photograph. At the same time, she was aware of other feelings surfacing inside her. She was touched that her aunt should be so concerned about her well-being. And her parents – why hadn't she seen more of them? With a pang of guilt, she imagined her father in his study, carefully clipping articles from the newspaper. Why had she never realised that he took such an interest in her career?

'Are you sure it was Gideon?' she suggested weakly. 'I seem to remember some mix-up in the press about who I was with.'

'Don't worry,' said Bridget, smiling. 'I wasn't about to get out the pictures and call an ID parade. This is just between you and me. Now, are you going to tell me the truth about what's going on?'

'But I *am* telling the truth,' protested Carmen, with a feeling of desperation.

'Well, I'll have to make a little confession then,' said Bridget. 'I'm afraid I did something rather underhand last night, just to satisfy my curiosity. Remember those questions I was asking? The ones about Mangus and the lions in the safari park?'

'What about them?' asked Carmen, relaxing slightly.

Duncan had managed quite well on that front, she thought, providing perfectly plausible explanations for the gaps in his knowledge.

'I was rather surprised when he assured me that he remembered that episode,' continued Bridget. 'The one with the lions. You see, I made the whole thing up.'

'He must have got confused . . .' Carmen stared dizzily at the pattern of the woodgrain on the tabletop. Where on earth had her aunt learned a trick like that?

Bridget let out a sigh. 'You're missing the point here, Carmen. I don't really care if he's not your husband. It's your life, after all. I'm just a little hurt that you don't trust me. And I can't understand why you've been putting on this charade for *my* benefit. How can it possibly make any difference what *I* think?'

After a few more half-hearted attempts to insist that she didn't know what her aunt was talking about, Carmen burst into tears and gave up. She told Bridget the truth about her marriage to Gideon, about the violence, the betrayals and the unexplained desertions. 'Please don't tell anyone about this,' she pleaded. 'I'm going to get into terrible trouble if anyone finds out what I've done.'

'But I still don't understand,' said Bridget, frowning. 'If you've left him for this other man, whoever he is, why are you trying to pretend that he's Gideon?'

'I haven't finished,' Carmen said evenly. 'I haven't got to the worst bit yet.' Taking a deep breath, she described the accident with the gun.

Bridget looked stunned. 'You *shot* him?' she echoed in a voice of disbelief.

'I didn't mean to,' said Carmen with obvious distress. 'It's just that it would have looked that way if I'd owned up.' What was her aunt going to do, she wondered, trembling. Make a citizen's arrest with her rolling pin?

'If only you'd confided in me before,' murmured Bridget. 'It might have made all the difference. There *are* other ways of dealing with domestic violence, you know.'

'I'm sorry for getting you involved,' said Carmen. 'It was a stupid thing to do. But we can leave straightaway if you want . . .'

'Don't talk nonsense,' replied Bridget crisply. Then, to Carmen's surprise, she let out a soft chuckle. 'It sounds as if you gave him what he deserved,' she said, reaching across the table and patting her hand. 'I'd never have guessed you had it in you.'

Carmen dissolved into tears again. 'If you knew how he treated me . . .' she began.

'From what you've already told me, I can understand how you must have felt.' Moving her pie out of the way, Bridget came round the table and gave Carmen a hug. 'There were times when I was almost tempted to do something like that myself. If the lightning hadn't got to him first, your Uncle Colin might have ended up the same way.'

'Did he beat you, then?' asked Carmen in a shocked whisper.

'Not really, but there are other ways of hurting people that can seem just as bad. I know he was your father's brother and all that, but he wasn't a very nice person.

He spent most of his time over on the mainland, chasing skirt and trying to launch his various get-rich-quick schemes. The worst thing was that everyone on the island knew what he was doing. You'd be surprised how the gossip finds its way out here.'

She sighed. 'I was so naïve when I married him. I really believed all the rubbish he told me about how he was going to set the world on fire.' She paused, looking for a moment as if she was on verge of tears. 'But as it turned out,' she continued, recovering herself with a bitter laugh, 'the only things he ever set on fire were his golf bag and shoes. I'm told that if you look from the helicopter, you can still see the scorch marks on the fifteenth green.'

While Carmen reassessed her view of her late uncle's character, Bridget cleared away her pastry-making tools and put the pie in the oven. When she had finished, she returned to the table and faced Carmen with an interrogative smile. 'So how are you expecting to get away with all this, then?' she asked. 'Did I hear you say you had some scheme worked out?'

Carmen explained Juliet's plan at some length, skipping only the details of how they had persuaded Duncan to get involved. Bridget, however, homed in on this flaw in the logic with uncanny precision. 'Do you seriously expect me to believe that you've dragged this poor boy all the way down here without telling him a thing?' she asked, raising an eyebrow.

'Well, not exactly,' replied Carmen, blushing. 'We, er, had this story . . .' Reluctantly, she explained the fiction they had concocted about Aunt Bridget's will.

'If he's stupid enough to be taken in by a half-baked fabrication like that,' said Bridget eventually, 'then he deserves everything that's coming to him.' She let out a scornful laugh. 'Changing my will, indeed! I'll have you know I'm leaving everything to the local duck sanctuary, just in case you were getting ideas.'

'It was all we could think of,' said Carmen, embarrassed. She was relieved when the telephone started ringing in the next room.

Bridget went to answer it. When she returned, she was smiling. 'Well, it looks as if you're going to have to explain things to him pretty soon,' she said. 'That was Phil calling from the coastguard's office. Apparently we've got fog on the way and it's forecast to stay around for the next couple of days. If you're planning to have anyone disappearing off the side of a boat, then now's the time to do it.'

The dragon at the reception of The Buccaneer regarded Angie with suspicion when she announced that she wanted to stay on, but her scruples were eventually overcome by greed at the prospect of letting the room for another night. 'Check-out's at ten tomorrow then,' she said gruffly, opening a door in the counter to let Caliban out for another sniff. 'No takeaways in the room, and the front door gets locked at midnight.'

Walking the streets of Redruth, Angie swiftly realised that she was a long way from London and wasn't going to be able to pick up clients as easily as she could in Bayswater or Notting Hill. It was late afternoon before she found her first trick, an unemployed mining engineer who had just won with a 10 pence stake on the Trifecta in the local betting shop.

'If I'd only put down a fiver, you'd be looking at a rich man now,' he grumbled as she escorted him back towards the hotel. Resisting the urge to tell him that it served him right for being such a cheapskate, she smiled at him sweetly and tried to ignore his bad breath. As a girl who wouldn't normally even take off her coat for less than fifty quid, she felt that she had come down in the world.

The dragon didn't seem to be around when they arrived back at The Buccaneer, and Angie led the way upstairs. They had almost reached the first floor landing when their progress was halted by the appearance of Caliban. He loomed menacingly towards them in the dim light, showing off his gleaming fangs as he emitted a series of blood-curdling growls.

'Er, good boy,' suggested Angie hopefully. Edging past his demonic presence, she crept along the corridor and escaped into the sanctuary of her room. Her companion didn't fare so well, however, bursting through the door behind her with Caliban still attached to his ankle. When he finally managed to shake off the hell hound and eject him from the room, it became apparent from the blood seeping into his Crimplene trousers that he had suffered a nasty nip.

Angie spent the next half-hour listening to him grumble while she improvised bandages from the limited supply of towels in the bathroom. Eventually, realising that she was wasting valuable time, she was forced to cut her losses and offered him a quick freebie to get rid of him. She couldn't take the risk of him hanging around and complaining about his injuries to the dragon downstairs.

When she returned with her second client of the day, a retired schoolteacher with a penchant for spanking, she was ready for Caliban. 'Here, boy!' she called, hurling a film-wrapped package from the supermarket along the corridor. Caliban bounded after it with enthusiasm. There was an unpleasant crunching sound as his jaws closed around the offering and he wolfed down a family pack of lamb chops, complete with styrofoam tray.

'Your doggie's got quite an appetite there,' remarked the schoolteacher nervously, as they slipped into her room. 'I did make it quite clear, I hope, that I'm only interested in the mildest varieties of S&M.'

When she had finished pretending to be a naughty schoolgirl, Angie divided the evening between a plastic keyring salesman and an itinerant worker from a nearby theme park. She went to bed exhausted. After having forked out for two further meals for Caliban, she had just enough cash left over to purchase her freedom the following day.

In the morning, however, the dragon faced her from behind the desk with a look of triumphant disdain. 'I'm sorry, *madam*,' she said, glancing pointedly at her watch, 'but it's well past check-out time. I'm afraid I'm going to have to charge you for another night.'

'You're kidding!' said Angie in disbelief. 'It's only just gone ten!'

'Exactly,' replied the dragon, her nostrils flaring with

satisfaction. 'The latest check-out time is ten o'clock precisely.' Turning to a closely printed notice on the wall beside the desk, she tapped it with her pencil and let out a clucking sound. 'I think you'll find that it's all written down here.'

'I'm not paying for another night . . .' began Angie aggressively, then fell silent as she followed the dragon's gaze out of the window and into the car park. If only Ronco's bloody car wasn't stolen, she told herself in frustration, she would have been out of here long ago. As it was, however, she couldn't take the risk that the dragon might decide to call the police.

Overcome by a feeling of dejection, she realised that she would probably have to repeat the experience of the last twenty-four hours all over again. Could she be trapped in this hell hole for eternity, she wondered, with the bill clocking up faster than she could earn the money to pay?

She seemed to have made a friend of Caliban, however. Following her upstairs to her room with a look of slavish devotion, he watched her with hungry eyes as she changed back into her working clothes. 'Don't they feed you here, mate?' she asked him, as he wolfed down a tube of KY Jelly, complete with packaging, from the bedside table. Tentatively patting him on the head, she was rewarded by an insistent nuzzling at her groin accompanied by a low growl.

'Don't worry, mate,' she assured him, wondering if the local supermarket would be open on a Sunday. 'You'll be getting your cut later.' In spite of her misery, she smiled, struck by the absurdity of the situation.

She was probably the only working girl in the history of the oldest profession to find herself being pimped by a dog.

Duncan had been hoping for a chat with Juliet when he went downstairs that morning, and was disappointed to find that she had gone out. Not wanting to face Carmen when she woke up, he had left the house and walked down to the beach. He was still smarting with embarrassment at his behaviour in Penzance.

Kicking a pile of seaweed at the water's edge, he admitted to himself that he had been dazzled by Carmen's TV star image. What else could have prompted him to throw himself at her in such a gauche and inconsiderate way? And what had he expected? A one-night stand to boost his self-image, so that he could brag about having slept with Carmen Bird? Surely he hadn't believed that the fleeting intimacy of a drunken coupling could form the basis of a *relationship*?

Leaving the beach, Duncan crossed the road and turned down a path signposted as a nature trail. Carmen had been right to point out that they hardly knew each other, he realised. At the time, he had protested that he wanted to know her better, but now, he wasn't even sure that this was true.

Carmen was *married*, he reminded himself, clambering over a stile and following the path into a thicket of hawthorns and willows. She was also troubled by some-thing — something, his instincts told him, that ran deeper than her husband's infidelity. Piecing together the hints he had gathered from both Juliet and Carmen, he had glimpsed a dark tangle of secrets that he couldn't even begin to understand.

Why didn't Carmen leave Gideon, he wondered, instead of persisting with this strange charade? Skirting a muddy area, he pushed his way through the overhanging branches and emerged into a field of yellow irises. He was feeling increasingly uncomfortable about his own part in the proceedings. He liked Bridget and wasn't at all happy to deceive her in this way. There were also things that didn't add up: Bridget didn't seem old enough to be worrying about changing her will, neither did she strike him as the type of person who would blackmail relatives with promises of a legacy. Besides, surely Carmen had plenty of money of her own?

Taking a fork in the path, Duncan arrived at a small timber hut with a sign on the door inviting him to come inside. It was a bird hide, he discovered, entering the shadowy interior and peering through a horizontal slot at the reed-fringed lake beyond. Beneath the viewing window, an illustrated panel claimed frequent sightings of dozens of rare birds.

After spending twenty minutes staring across the water in search of Collared Pratincoles and Bridled Terns, he had seen nothing more exciting than a moorhen pecking at the floating remains of a Cornish pasty. It was a bit like his love life, really, he thought miserably. The exotic-looking creatures he fell for were usually happy enough to strut with him in their finery on a Saturday night, but never stayed around to keep him company the next day.

Duncan had never had any trouble finding women to go to bed with him, but it was in the sphere of everyday life that his relationships always started to go wrong. It was all very well having nights of wild sex — getting drunk on vodka and licking whipped cream out of each other's orifices — but his partners always became mysteriously unavailable when it was time to clean up. They would disappear with enigmatic smiles to count their false eyelashes, wax their nails and manicure their bikini lines, or whatever it was that women did these days, leaving him to scrape the goo off the sheets and take them to the launderette.

It wasn't fashionable to admit it, but Duncan secretly yearned for the domestic tranquillity of a stable relationship. Why was it easier to have sex with someone than to share a trip to the supermarket, he wondered gloomily. Sonia had been down to Sainsbury's with him once, but her idea of shopping for the basics was to pick up a few jars of hand-reared Tuscan olives and a packet of crispbread before heading off to the cosmetics counter. Later, she had the cheek to make fun of him for eating Pot Noodles and to lecture him about the importance of a well-balanced diet.

Friends made much better shopping companions, he had decided. Take Juliet, for example. In their Worcester days she used to speed through the aisles with military efficiency, finishing before he was halfway round. But she always returned to help him, assisting him in his search for those difficult items, like tissues and eggs, that never seemed to be shelved in the same place. She would also entertain him with her observations on the other shoppers, speculating on their lifestyles from the contents of their trolleys. With a smile, he remembered the time she had spotted a shoplifter; they had followed the woman through the meat department, giggling as they watched her slip packets of fillet steak under the waistband of her voluminous jogging suit.

Duncan frowned for a moment, considering the sudden change in Juliet. She had surprised him in Penzance, with her new attitude to her appearance. When she came into the dining room that night, it had been the first time he'd ever seen her dressed up in the same kind of clothes and makeup that other women wore. For a moment, he had scarcely recognised her as the Juliet he knew.

Why had she done it, he wondered. Was it the effect of Carmen's influence? Looking out across the lake again, Duncan saw a flash of blue reflected in the water. A kingfisher, perhaps? Checking the information panel, he was mildly disappointed to find that this bird didn't feature on the list.

He left the hide, blinking in the sunlight, and continued along the path until he came to a road. Turning left towards Hugh Town, he contemplated visiting a pub and chatting to some of the locals. But he would have to pretend to be Gideon again, he realised. He wasn't in the mood for play-acting right now.

In the town, he glanced at the Sunday papers in the newsagent's, but was discouraged by their bulk. He wasn't in the mood for reading, either. Instead, he turned to a local guidebook, flicking through the pages until he found a map, and planned a route back along the coastal path. Something was nagging at the back of his mind, but he couldn't quite place it. He needed fresh air and more time to think.

When he reached Peninnis Lighthouse, he was forced to sit down on a rock to recover his breath. It had been a harder climb than he had expected. Groups of walkers kept passing him, nodding greetings in the self-conscious manner of tourists uncertain of the local etiquette. Duncan grinned back at them, wishing they would go away and leave him to his thoughts. He hadn't yet pinned down exactly what was bothering him, but he was gradually beginning to work out that it was something to do with Juliet.

Continuing along the path, he thought back over the events of the previous day. Juliet had reverted to her normal clothes and hadn't appeared to be wearing any makeup, but she had looked different. The new hair-style suited her, he realised – it accentuated her features and made her look younger and more feminine.

Over dinner last night, she had caught his eye and smiled at him in an unfamiliar way. It had affected him strangely, and he remembered feeling the momentary tingle of excitement that always came when he was attracted to someone new.

In the past, when he had enjoyed a good evening of drink and companionship with Juliet, he had often felt the urge to go to bed with her, almost as a way to prevent the fun they were having from coming to an end. He had always resisted, on the assumption that it would ruin their friendship. But now, looking back, he was beginning to wonder if his pride in their platonic relationship had blinded him to something more crucial.

Then it dawned on him. The one thing he had entirely failed to appreciate. Juliet's 'makeover' had been for him.

Duncan stopped in his tracks, cursing himself for his stupidity. No wonder she had rushed off like that when he had laughed at her. He had scarcely acknowledged her distress – had even been glad to be rid of her – all because he was caught up in his fantasy of getting into bed with Carmen Bird. He had behaved like a complete brute.

You're a stupid bloody idiot, Swayne, he told himself, quickening his pace. He needed to get back quickly and find out where Juliet had gone. Maybe it wasn't too late to put things right.

Instead of facing up to his dilemma about Angie, Ronco watched his way through a selection of Saturday night quiz-shows and then fell asleep in the middle of a Clint Eastwood film. Waking at midnight with a raging thirst and a fuzzy head, he decided that the best thing to do was to go to bed and sleep on the problem. There would be plenty of time, he told himself, to sort things out the following day.

On Sunday morning, he resolved to get the essential household chores out of the way before he settled down to any serious thinking. By lunchtime, he had scrubbed the kitchen floor twice and had resorted to activities such as ironing his best anorak and combing his badger slippers to put off the dreaded moment of having to make up his mind. He was busy cleaning the fluff out of the telephone keypad when he remembered that he had left Angie's bedroom window open the previous night. He would have to return upstairs, he realised, to make sure that she hadn't been robbed.

Her flat was just as he had left it, and he found himself drawn once again by the lure of the knicker drawer. But he had more important things to do, he told himself guiltily. If anything happened to Angie, it would all be his fault.

He needed to act while the impulse was upon him. Making sure that the window was secured, he collected the newspapers from the hall table and took them downstairs. An anonymous tip-off would do the trick, he decided, dialling the number of the local police station. Identifying himself as 'just a friend', he explained that the Shepherd's Bush murderer was the husband of TV star Carmen Bird, and that he was about to strike again in Penzance.

'I'm sorry, but you'll have to give your name and address, caller,' replied a voice blandly. There was a pause, during which Ronco could hear a muffled conversation taking place in the background. Then the voice came back again. 'Excuse me, but *what* was it that you just said?'

'You heard me,' muttered Ronco, breaking into a sweat as he slammed the receiver down. The filth always had this effect on him, making his pulse accelerate and his brain spin. He would have to careful, he told himself, or he would end up having one of his fits.

But he had done his duty by Angie. It was now up

to the fuzz to see to the rest. They were always quick enough to pull their fingers out over minor cases of burglary, he reflected gloomily. They ought to find it relatively easy to track down someone as important as Gideon Bird.

He was just about to start cleaning the keypad again when the telephone began to ring. *Angie!* he thought, snatching up the receiver. But there was nobody there, only a crackling sound and a hum of background noise that he recognised from earlier. With a sinking feeling, he realised that he'd forgotten to dial 141, to prevent the call being traced, when he'd called the police.

After a moment, he heard a series of clicking noises and a voice came on the line. 'This is Sergeant Cowley from Notting Hill Police Station. I was wondering if you'd mind answering a few questions about a call we've just received . . .'

Ronco dropped the receiver in alarm. As he stared at it, spinning on its cord, a dizzy sensation began to overtake him. Clutching at the table for support, he sank back into a chair. The next thing he knew, a flashing blue light was intruding into his consciousness. There was a loud thumping sound coming from the hallway, as if someone was trying to break down the door.

Half an hour later, he found himself at the police station, incarcerated in a windowless cell described euphemistically as the 'interview room'. He knew it well from visits several years earlier, but it had been redecorated in a new colour scheme since he saw it last. Probably to cover up the bloodstains, he thought unhappily. He had hoped never to set foot in this place again.

He was subjected to intense questioning by officers of varying rank and, although he managed to avoid any mention of blackmail, he was forced to reveal far more than he had intended about Angie and her affairs.

'So why was she following this guy around Cornwall if she knew he'd killed somebody?' asked a poker-faced Detective Inspector called Longbridge. Pacing frenetically back and forth, as if he was starring in an episode of *NYPD Blue*, he turned and confronted Ronco with a menacing look. 'Withholding information in a murder case is a serious offence, as you know.'

'I'm . . . er, not sure,' stammered Ronco. 'I mean, why should she have known anything about it? I expect she just wanted to . . . well, see him again.'

Waiting for seemingly interminable stretches while rozzers came and went, he realised that he was missing the last episode of the Sunday afternoon rerun of *Badgerwatch Special*. How long was it going to take to convince them that he hadn't committed the murder himself?

Eventually, however, they started to believe him enough to check out some of his facts. At six o'clock, in the middle of a second grilling by DI Longbridge, they were interrupted by a knock at the door.

'Sorry to disturb you, sir,' said a fresh-faced constable, bursting into the room. 'It's just that we talked to the barman at the Slug and Ferret, sir, as you suggested, and he recognised the picture of Louise. He says she was there on Tuesday night, and that she left with this tall guy wearing a moustache.'

'Get him down here to make a statement, then,'

snapped DI Longbridge. 'Do it straightaway. And get on to the BBC and see if they can come up with a mugshot of this Bird character for him to identify. What was the programme he was supposed to be involved in? *The Sweeney*, did you say?'

'It was called *Mangus*, sir,' murmured the constable. '*The Sweeney* was on ITV.'

'Ah, *Mangus*. Of course, I remember it now.' DI Longbridge smiled for the first time. 'Well, it can't be too often that fact and fiction come together like this,' he added, rubbing his hands together in a gesture of anticipation. 'If this Bird man turns out to be our killer, we ought to get a nice bit of publicity from this case.'

Juliet had risen early that morning and taken an invigorating walk along the coastal path as far as Pelistry Bay. She had hoped to focus her mind on the next part of their plan, but instead spent most of the time worrying about how Duncan would react when she told him about Gideon's murder. What would they do if he decided to go to the police? She had delayed her confession for as long as she could, but there were no more excuses left for putting it off.

It was a warm, sunny morning with the gentle hum of birdsong in the air. Returning to Old Town via a series of footpaths and winding lanes, she admired the vivid colours of the wild flowers in the hedge-rows and found herself wishing that the whole sordid business was over. It seemed such a waste to have travelled all the way to this beautiful place when she was too preoccupied with her troubles to appreciate it.

Arriving back in the village, she felt disinclined to join the others straightaway and instead went to the café opposite the beach. Sitting at a table outside with a mug of coffee, she felt an inexplicable pang of homesickness. Not for London – a place she was beginning to dislike more and more – but for Worcester, and the happy years she had spent growing up in her parents' pub.

Back then, it had seemed as if the future stretched interminably, with endless scope for trying things out and making mistakes before you had to settle down to the grown-up business of organising your life. Now, it felt as if everything had sped up. In a few months' time, she would be thirty-five, probably half-way through her life. Glancing down at her dragon bracelet, she reminded herself of her promise. If she didn't start chasing her dreams right now, she would soon be lost in the wasteland of middle-aged regret.

Just then, she looked up and saw a figure coming around the headland. It looked remarkably like Duncan. Watching as he drew closer, she was surprised to discover that it *was* Duncan. She had scarcely expected him to be out of bed at this hour, let alone walking the cliff-tops. Feeling impatient to get things sorted out, she left the café and set off along the beach to meet him. He looked completely wrapped up in his thoughts and didn't notice her until they were only a few yards apart.

'Juliet,' he said, hurrying towards her. 'Are you all right?'

'Of course I am,' she replied, feeling slightly confused. 'Why shouldn't I be?'

With a swift and unexpected movement, Duncan put his arms around her. 'I'm so sorry, Jules,' he murmured, hugging her tightly. 'I've been rotten to you lately. You looked beautiful the other day – I mean, you still do – and I never said anything. I've taken you for granted all this time.'

Stunned by this sudden change in his behaviour, Juliet pressed her cheek against the fabric of his shirt, luxuriating in the feeling of closeness. It took a moment before she found the courage to look up and meet his gaze.

'But, Duncan . . .' She paused, not knowing what to say. She wasn't at all certain who made the first move but, a few seconds later, they were kissing. Overwhelmed by a dizzy sensation of pleasure, she responded eagerly to the pressure of his lips.

When she finally drew back for breath, she was laughing with happiness. The miracle had taken place at last. Now, all she needed to do was unburden herself of her guilty secret and everything was going to be all right.

'Duncan,' she whispered, sliding her arm around his waist. 'There's something I have to tell you . . .' There didn't seem to be any way of breaking it gently, so she launched into a straightforward account of what had happened, starting with the circumstances of Gideon's death.

But it wasn't long before Duncan interrupted. '*What* did you say?' he asked suddenly, drawing back with a horrified expression. 'You can't be serious! Are you telling me I'm impersonating someone who's *dead*?'

'Well, yes,' admitted Juliet reluctantly. 'But if you'd let me explain . . .'

'But don't you see what that means? You've made me an accessory to *murder*, for Christ's sake.' He paused, looking thunderstruck, and glanced nervously up and down the beach as if he expected the entire Scillies police force to come leaping out from behind the sea wall. 'They might even think that *I* did it . . .'

'But Duncan, it's not like that at all. If you'd only listen . . .'

But he turned and walked rapidly away from her, heading in the direction of the cottage. 'No, wait!' she cried, running after him. 'Duncan, please!' Catching up with him outside the café, she seized him by the arm. 'You mustn't say anything to Bridget,' she pleaded. 'She doesn't know about this.'

'Well, she'll be getting a bit of a shock then, won't she?' he snapped, shaking her off and continuing along the road.

Bridget was sitting in the garden with Carmen when they arrived at the cottage. The two women started nervously to their feet as Duncan crashed open the gate and strode across the lawn towards them. Juliet followed in anxious pursuit.

'You haven't . . .' Carmen's eyes darted nervously from Duncan to Juliet and back again.

Walking straight up to her, Duncan glared at Carmen with a scornful expression. 'Do you think I'm a complete fool?' he burst out angrily. 'Did you expect me to be so besotted with you, so pathetically grateful for the attentions of the great *TV star*, that I'd take the rap for killing your husband?'

Panicking, Juliet turned to Bridget. 'This isn't what it sounds like,' she gabbled, frantically trying to think of an explanation for Duncan's behaviour. 'We were just having an argument on the beach about this murder game we sometimes play, and . . .'

'She knows,' hissed Carmen, jerking her head in Bridget's direction.

Juliet glanced anxiously at Bridget. 'Don't worry,' whispered the older woman calmly. 'We'll sort this out somehow. I'm on your side.'

'So you're all in this together, are you?' asked Duncan in an icy voice. Juliet had never seen him so angry before – not even when she trod on his pet caterpillar at his seventh birthday party.

Carmen took a deep breath. 'Duncan, this isn't what you think. Besides, it was an accident . . .'

'An accident? You expect me to believe that after all the lies you've told me?' He paused, shaking his head. 'I've got a good mind to call the police right now,' he added. 'I'm sure they'd love to know just what you're really like.'

'Look, you don't know anything about what really happened,' interrupted Juliet. 'If you'd just calm down and listen to us, you might understand.'

'Understand?' Duncan turned to face her with an angry expression. 'What I don't understand is how you, of all people, could do this. Do you really care so little for me, Juliet? I thought you were my friend.'

'But I . . .' Juliet faltered and fell silent. This was all going horribly wrong.

'If you're going to blame anyone,' said Carmen quietly, 'you should blame me, not Juliet. I'm the one who actually did it, whether it was an accident or not.'

Juliet stared at Duncan, willing his features to soften into a smile. She could hardly believe this sudden reversal in her fortunes. A short time ago, on the beach, she had felt as if she were the happiest woman alive. She had even thought, for a moment, that Duncan might have been about to say something further – to tell her that he loved her, even.

But that wasn't ever going to happen now, she realised, blinking back tears. The worst thing about it was that it was all her own stupid fault.

CHAPTER 18

'He'll come round,' said Bridget, as the three women sat in the kitchen drinking tea. 'Just give him time.' She gave Juliet a thoughtful look. 'I'd guess that he's actually rather fond of you, underneath all this.'

'I doubt it,' said Juliet with a sigh. 'Not anymore, anyway.' Glancing through the window, she could see Duncan's solitary figure pacing back and forth at the end of the garden. 'I just can't believe how stupid I've been,' she added unhappily. 'How on earth did I manage to make such a complete mess of this whole thing?'

'But you haven't made a mess of it,' protested Carmen. 'You've been brilliant. If it weren't for you, I'd probably be in prison already.' Standing up, she went over to the window and spent a moment contemplating the scene in the garden. 'I'm sure we'll be able to convince him if we try hard enough,' she murmured, drumming the tips of her fingers on the windowsill. She turned back to face Juliet with questioning look. 'Surely you're not going to give up now?'

For the rest of the afternoon, Carmen and Bridget

took turns talking to Duncan, keeping him constantly occupied in the hope of distracting him from his threat of calling the police. Eventually Carmen sat down with him for over an hour, speaking to him in a low voice that couldn't be heard from the kitchen window. Juliet watched anxiously from behind an arrangement of dried flowers, trying to guess what was passing between them from their looks and gestures. The memory of Duncan's kiss kept surfacing in her thoughts, taunting her with suggestions of how things might have been.

Carmen returned to the house just as dusk was beginning to fall. 'He'll do it!' she announced, appearing at the kitchen door with a look of triumph. 'He's changed his mind.'

'How did you persuade him?' asked Juliet with a puzzled frown.

'I told him everything,' she said, flopping into a chair with exhaustion. 'The whole works about Gideon and the way he treated me.'

'Was that all?' There had been something in their body language, thought Juliet, that suggested the exchange of some other kind of secret.

'More or less,' replied Carmen in a guarded tone. 'It wasn't easy, you know. It still hurts to admit to all that stuff from the past. But by the time I was finished, he was right there with me on my side.'

Juliet opened her mouth to question her further but, at that moment, Duncan came in.

'OK, Jules,' he said, sitting down opposite her at the kitchen table. 'It looks as if you win, as usual.

You'd better explain exactly what you want me to do, though there's one condition I'm going to have to make.'

'What's that?' asked Juliet, taken aback by his friendly manner. She had expected that he would still be angry with her.

Duncan grinned. 'Dressing up as a dead man and pretending to get drowned is OK up to a point, but I don't want to take any chances. I'm not doing anything that involves me actually getting wet.'

As she became caught up in explaining the details of her plan, Juliet quickly forgot how miserable she had been feeling. A thrill of the old excitement ran through her – the very same feeling that had inspired her to dream up the idea for the perfect murder in the first place. She glanced around the table, glad to be taken seriously at last. Now they were all working together as a team, she believed there was a real chance that they *could* get away with it, especially with the fog coming. If it was thick enough the next day, the conditions would be ideal for them to carry out their plan on the afternoon crossing to Penzance.

'How exactly are you going to make it look as if he's fallen overboard, then?' interrupted Bridget with a frown. 'That part sounds a bit dangerous to me.'

'No, listen, it's not dangerous at all,' said Juliet. 'The whole point is that he doesn't actually pretend to fall over, he simply changes out of his disguise. He spends the first part of the journey in the bar as Gideon, making it clear that he's a bit drunk and talking to people so that they remember him. Then he says he's going up for some air but, instead, goes down to the lavatories and comes back out as himself.'

'So what happens then?' asked Carmen. 'How will anybody *know* that he's supposed to have fallen overboard if he doesn't pretend to do it?'

'Think about how it might happen in real life,' said Juliet. 'Gideon falls over the side because he's drunk, but you're down in the lounge and don't notice that he's missing. You assume that he's in the bar. When the boat arrives in Penzance, you start getting worried. You look round the ship and can't find him. *That's* when you start raising the alarm.'

'Wait a minute,' said Carmen. 'What about the boarding cards? Aren't they numbered? Won't somebody realise there's one less person on the ship than there should be?'

'But that's the beauty of doing it this way, can't you see?' Juliet glanced round the table, smiling. 'They might count the people getting *on* the boat, but they don't count them getting *off* again. I made sure of that by watching very carefully when we arrived here. When you raise the alarm, the other passengers will already have started disembarking. Duncan will be gone, and nobody will be able to prove a thing.'

'Hey, I see what you mean,' said Duncan, after a moment's thought. 'If we faked the falling overboard, someone might see us. But if we don't fake it, then nobody can prove it didn't happen. Everybody will assume it was while they were looking the other way.'

'At last,' murmured Juliet with a sigh of pleasure.

'Someone appreciates my idea.' Feeling more cheerful and confident than she had for a long time, she gave Duncan a look that was almost flirtatious. 'I was wondering when you were all going to realise that I'm more than just a pretty face.'

The following morning, Phil materialised at the breakfast table, though he hadn't been around when they all went to bed the previous night. 'You'd better get your sunbathing in quick, before the fog gets here,' he warned them, clearly relishing the opportunity to play the prophet of doom. 'We get some real pea soupers down here. Sometimes it comes in so thick that you can't see your own hand in front of your face.'

Carmen and Juliet exchanged glances, unsure whether or not he was joking. By mid-morning, however, thick tendrils of mist were swirling round the cottage. 'It looks like this is it,' said Juliet, peering out of the window. 'Are you ready?'

'OK,' replied Carmen nervously, picking up the telephone. 'I'll call the travel office and get our tickets arranged.'

'Oh shit,' muttered Duncan, putting his hand to his mouth with a queasy expression. 'Talk about bad timing – I've just gone and eaten half of one of Bridget's pies.'

Angie had done a brisk Sunday trade in Redruth, working her way through a lorry driver, a computer programmer and a travelling hot-dog vendor – who got a special discount as he brought his own bribe for Caliban. The ex-schoolteacher from the day before also came back for a second helping, bringing with him a school uniform and a cane.

Exhausted from a hard day's work, Angie had overslept slightly on Monday morning. She made it to the reception desk with only seconds to spare before the clock ticked ten. As she handed over her cash, the dragon stared at her with undisguised disappointment. She must have imagined herself to be on to a great new money-spinner with her late check-out clause, thought Angie gloomily. No wonder there weren't any clocks in the rooms.

Caliban was also disappointed to see her go, howling mournfully from the veranda as she carried her bag out to the car. The dragon had tied him there that morning, she learned from another guest, as a punishment for eating the chef's mobile telephone.

'Cheer up mate,' she murmured, starting the engine. 'Look on the bright side – at least you don't have to turn tricks to pay for your keep.'

Leaving Redruth behind her as quickly as she could, Angie drove back to Penzance and parked in a side street near the harbour. Making her way on foot to a pub opposite the quay, she sat down to review her options over a brandy and lemonade.

She was reluctant to waste money travelling to the Scillies herself, as she had no idea which of the islands Gideon was on. There was also a chance of missing him, as he might come back to the mainland at any time. It was better to remain in Penzance, she decided, and meet the boat as it came in each evening. She now had enough money to keep her going for a few days.

Glancing out of the pub window, Angie winced at the distant sight of the Harbour Lodge. She would probably need somewhere to stay, but she wasn't going back to that place under any circumstances. She decided to wait for the arrival of the seven o'clock boat before she made a decision. If Gideon was on it, she wouldn't have any reason to remain in Penzance overnight.

A few drinks later, Angie started to feel bored and in need of conversation. There were no likely prospects in the bar in the middle of the afternoon and she found herself wondering what Ronco was doing. She had scarcely given him a passing thought for the last three days, but he was sure to be wondering what had happened to her. Making her way to the telephone in the lobby, Angie dialled his number. It would be nice to hear a familiar voice, she told herself. Hadn't she promised to call him when they last spoke?

'Angie?' He didn't sound his usual placid self. 'Thank God you're all right! Where the hell are you? I've only just got back from talking to the police again . . .'

'The police? But why? What are you supposed to have done this time?'

'It's not so much what I've done,' said Ronco. 'It's . . . er, more to do with a certain murderer we both know.'

'What do you mean?' she asked, with a sudden premonition that all was not well. 'What are you talking about?'

After much to-ing and fro-ing, Ronco owned up about how he had found the newspapers in Angie's flat and gone to the police. 'I wouldn't normally play the nark,' he added plaintively. 'I only went upstairs to check that everything was OK, but then I started getting worried that something might have happened to you.'

Angie was momentarily speechless with anger and confusion. How dare he break into her flat and interfere with her plans? At the same time, she felt oddly touched that he should care enough to do something. No one, not even the closest of her relatives, had ever worried about her like this before.

'So what's going to happen, then?' she asked eventually, struggling to hide the panic in her voice. 'Surely no one believes that a man in Gideon's position would kill someone?'

'Oh, but they *know* he went home with that woman,' babbled Ronco excitedly. 'The barman saw them leave together, and he identified an old photo that they got biked across from the BBC. They've just been in touch with the police in Penzance, about half an hour ago. Apparently he's moved on from that hotel you told me about, and gone across to the Scilly Isles. They're flying over there this afternoon to pick him up.'

'You fucking idiot!' screamed Angie, forgetting about everything except how she was going to miss her big chance to get rich. 'What in hell's name did you have to go to the police for?' Slamming the receiver down in anger and frustration, she glanced around the pub and realised that everyone was staring at her. 'Sorry,' she mumbled, heading back towards the bar. She badly needed another drink.

After indulging in a double brandy and a short bout

of black despair, Angie made an effort to pull herself
together. Nothing was ever achieved without persever-
ance, she told herself sternly. Borrowing a timetable
from the barman, she checked the boat and helicopter schedules. The daily sea crossing left St Mary's
at four-thirty, but the last helicopter flight to arrive
on the island before then had already departed. If
the police had missed this flight, she reasoned, there
was a chance that they wouldn't think of looking on
the boat. They were unlikely to know about Gideon's
fear of flying and, besides, criminals fleeing from the
law were usually expected to do so by the fastest
route.

She didn't know if Gideon would be on the boat, but
an instinct told her that the odds were good. She would
wait on the quayside, as planned, she decided. There
was still a possibility that she could get to Gideon before
the police did.

As Phil drove them into Hugh Town for the four-
thirty sailing, Juliet stared out of the window at the
fog and wondered what had happened to the place
that had seemed so welcoming when they arrived.
Now that the sunshine had gone, the character of the
island was transformed. It seemed to turn in on itself,
wrapping up its secrets in a blanket of fog and making it clear to outsiders that they could never belong.
Groups of disconsolate tourists wandered aimlessly in
the town, deprived of their fair-weather activities. The
gift shops and tea rooms were making the most of the
increased trade and it looked, to judge by the crowd

gathered outside the church hall, as if the *Shipwrecks of Scilly* slideshow was set to break box office records that day.

'It's a shame you're all leaving so soon,' commented Phil, swerving to avoid a group of damp hikers outside the Bishop and Wolf pub. 'I was looking forward to another game of poker tonight.'

'Don't worry,' whispered Bridget, who had come along to see them off. 'I told him that Carmen's been called back by the TV company to make a special programme. He doesn't suspect a thing.'

When they had collected their tickets from the travel office, they made their way to the *Scillonian*. Staring at a newspaper under a man's arm as they queued to go on board, Juliet wondered if Gideon's death by drowning would make the front page. A few people had already recognised Carmen, whispering excitedly to their companions and nodding in her direction. What would they think if they knew just how newsworthy this crossing was going to be?

Boarding the ship, they waited on the deck to wave goodbye to Bridget and Phil. There were several delays, as last-minute items of cargo were loaded and someone's dog made a break for freedom down the gangplank. Eventually, when everything was on board, the ropes were untied and the *Scillonian* moved away from the quay. Bridget and Phil disappeared into the mist and the island slid quickly out of view.

Arranging to meet Carmen and Duncan in the bar, Juliet lingered to check out the situation on deck. It was the ideal weather for an accident, she decided. The cold and damp would keep most of the passengers inside, and visibility was so poor that anyone who ventured on deck would find there was nothing to see.

They had decided to spend the first part of the journey in the bar. The idea was for Duncan to pretend to get drunk, making an impression as Gideon and also providing a possible reason for his falling overboard. Watching him as he downed several large whiskies, however, Juliet began to worry that he might have forgotten about the 'pretending' part.

'You look like death,' giggled the barmaid, handing him another drink.

'Feel like it, too,' replied Duncan with a slight slur in his voice. 'So would you if you'd been up half the night writing a screenplay.'

'A screenplay?' she asked, looking interested. 'Are you in the movies or something, then? What's your name?'

'Gideon Bird,' declared Duncan ostentatiously. 'But I don't imagine you'd hear of me much outside Soho these days.'

Retreating to a table in the corner with Carmen, who was trying to avoid being recognised again, Juliet watched as he continued to talk to the barmaid. Leaning against the bar in a crumpled suit and tie with Gideon's Burberry draped over his shoulders, he looked heart-breakingly attractive. The barmaid obviously thought so, too, judging by the amount of attention she was giving him.

Juliet couldn't imagine why Duncan had finally agreed to go along with the deception, but she loved him for it. It showed that, somewhere deep down, there had to be some kind of imaginative spark that they shared. With a pang of sadness, she remembered that this was the last time she would see him properly for what might be several days, or even weeks. They had decided that it would be safest not to meet up again in London until they were certain that everyone believed Gideon was dead.

At the appointed time, just under an hour into the journey, Duncan blurted out some drunken apology and lurched away from the bar.

Watching him leave, Juliet was seized by an impulse she couldn't control. 'Don't worry,' she told Carmen. 'I'll be right back.' Dodging her way through a group of beer-swilling hikers, she left the bar and followed Duncan downstairs.

She caught up with him on a deserted landing. 'Dun . . . er, Gideon,' she hissed. 'Wait a moment.'

'What's wrong?' Duncan looked round with an expression of alarm. 'Is there a change of plan?'

'I just wanted to say goodbye,' she whispered. Feeling greatly daring, she leaned forward and kissed him lightly on the cheek. 'I want you to know that I really appreciate what you're doing,' she added softly. 'I don't want you thinking that I'm taking you for granted, either.'

'This isn't the best time . . .' he began, looking embarrassed.

'I know,' said Juliet quickly, backing away. She held her breath, hoping that her words might have somehow reminded him of what happened on the beach.

'Perhaps I ought . . .' He paused uncertainly. 'I wanted to say . . .'

A door banged open somewhere above them and footsteps began to approach. 'I'd better go,' he said anxiously. Turning his back on her with a swift movement, he hurried down the stairs.

Juliet went back to the bar to find Carmen, and they both went down to the lounge to establish alibis for the rest of the journey. The seats Juliet chose for them were in full view of the door to the men's lavatories and she was able to get a good look at Duncan when he finally came out.

He was dressed in lightweight, casual garments that he had been wearing under Gideon's suit. The moustache was gone, and his hair was rumpled into an approximation of its original style. A nylon rucksack on his back, which had earlier been hidden in the lining of his Burberry, contained Gideon's clothes, together with the Burberry itself. This item, they had agreed, was to be dropped discreetly overboard on the off chance that it might be washed up and found.

Seeing Duncan as himself again, Juliet found it hard not to acknowledge his presence and couldn't resist giving him a friendly smile. But he looked straight through her, turning away and heading towards the stairs. Watching him disappear, she felt a pang of anxiety. She knew he was acting, of course, but there had been a coldness in his eyes that disturbed her. What had he been about to say to her, if they hadn't been interrupted on the landing? How was he going to respond to her when they next met?

The rest of the journey passed slowly. Irritated at having nothing further to do, Juliet circled the lounge reading the information panels on the walls. She learned a lot of information about the islands which might have been of some interest if she had been on her way there. Now that she was going home, however, it merely served to point out how much she had missed.

As they approached Penzance, Carmen grew increasingly nervous. 'I don't know how I'm going to cope with this acting bit,' she whispered uneasily. 'How on earth are you *supposed* to behave if your husband's just drowned?'

'I'm sure it'll be much easier than you think,' said Juliet in a reassuring tone that belied her own anxieties. 'Come on, I think it's time we went up on deck and pretended to look for him.'

On the stairs, they passed the barmaid, who was crossing the landing with a box of salt and vinegar crisps. 'How's your friend?' she asked, seeing Juliet. Then she saw Carmen as well and gave a start of recognition. 'Hey, just a minute,' she said excitedly, 'aren't you Carmen Bird?'

'Pleased to meet you, too,' said Carmen coolly. 'I think that must be my husband you were asking about. We're just going up to find him on the deck.'

'See, you're doing fine,' whispered Juliet, as they continued on their way.

'I don't know about that,' muttered Carmen. 'I think I've just used up my entire reserves of inner strength in one go.'

Reaching the deck, the two women wandered around

both sides of the ship, pretending to be looking for someone. The fog was beginning to clear and the Penzance townscape was rapidly coming into view. 'I'm scared,' whispered Carmen. 'I really don't know if I'm going to be able to pull this off.'

Juliet's reply was drowned by a blast on the ship's horn as they rounded the end of the quay and entered the harbour. 'What's wrong,' she asked a moment later, seeing Carmen's face turn pale. 'Are you OK?'

Carmen leaned forward with a terrified expression and clutched at Juliet's arm. 'Look,' she yelped, pointing over Juliet's shoulder and nudging her to turn round. 'Can't you see?'

Juliet looked. A row of police cars were waiting on the quayside, their flashing blue lights reflecting in synchronised patterns in the water. Fear clutched at her stomach. 'Oh Christ,' she mumbled, realising that something had gone horribly wrong. Had they found the body in the landfill site? Had somebody identified Duncan as an imposter? There was no time to come up with another plan. Their only way forward was to try and bluff it out.

'What are we going to do?' whimpered Carmen, eyeing her with a hysterical look.

Juliet had intended to let Carmen take a background role, but saw that she was now frightened enough to put on a convincing performance. 'Start acting,' she replied grimly. 'Just go for it. Stick to our plan and pray that Duncan does the same. It's our only hope.'

*   *   *

The brandy-and-lemonades consumed during the course of the long afternoon had left Angie with a warm glow of optimism. Waiting for the *Scillonian* to arrive, she had been too busy thinking about how she was going to spend the blackmail money to notice the first patrol cars that turned on to the quay. It took a few moments for the meaning of the flashing blue lights to sink in. When she finally realised that the police had beaten her to it, she was overcome by a rush of anger and frustration. She had spent the best part of a week trying to track Gideon down, she thought bitterly. How dare they show up at the last minute and cheat her out of her hard-earned reward?

Looking up, she saw the *Scillonian* looming in the harbour. It seemed to take forever to manouevre into its berth and there was a long wait before the passengers were allowed to disembark. After lengthy discussions between the police and a uniformed ship's officer, the gangplank was opened up and people began to surge onto the quay. Angie rushed forward, hoping to catch a final glimpse of Gideon before they took him away.

Several policemen stood at the foot of the gang-plank, inspecting the departing passengers with suspicious glares. Would Gideon succumb meekly, wondered Angie, or would he put up a fight? For a moment, she imagined herself visiting him in prison, bravely standing by her lover while his wife abandoned him to his sufferings. But what did she stand to gain by doing that? She still had the photographs, and she could scarcely put them to good use if she was supposed to be on his side.

Suddenly, a commotion broke out on the ship. Screams

could be heard on the upper deck and Angie saw a hysterical-looking woman making an exhibition of herself. With a shock, she recognised Carmen Bird. Stupid cow, she thought irritably. Trust her to lose it in a crisis.

But what was she saying? Straining her ears, Angie caught the words *fallen overboard*. A likely story, she thought scornfully. Gideon was probably hiding somewhere on the boat, shitting himself with fear. She was going to wait here until they found him, Angie told herself with determination. It might be small consolation for the disappointment of her plans, but she would enjoy seeing the look of humiliation on his face when he was brought out.

'We'd better get some reinforcements in to carry out a search,' crackled a voice from a nearby police radio, echoing her thoughts. 'Sounds like they're claiming he panicked and jumped ship.'

Before long, the rest of the passengers had departed and Angie was one of the few people remaining on the quayside who wasn't a member of the Penzance police force. Positioning herself discreetly behind a forklift truck, she watched a police dog handler go on board with a distant cousin of Caliban's. When they came out again, half an hour later, and there was still no sign of Gideon, she felt a pang of concern. Surely he wouldn't really do something as foolish as trying to drown himself?

More police began to arrive on the quayside, together with a gaggle of people who looked like reporters and others who had come simply to stare. After another long wait, there was a flurry of activity on board. Carmen Bird appeared at the top of the gangplank, accompanied by a policeman on one side and a plain-looking woman on the other. As they descended to the quayside, the reporters went wild, rushing forward with popping flashbulbs and microphones thrust out at arm's length.

'How does it feel to discover that your husband's wanted for murder?' yelled a woman in a bright green suit who had arrived at the last moment with a TV camera in tow.

Carmen stared at her, looking completely stunned, while her friend tried to shepherd her into a waiting police car. 'Murder?' she echoed in a trembling voice. 'I don't know what you're talking about.'

'How do you rate the chances of his body being found?' shouted a man with a dictaphone, pushing his way through a cordon of policemen.

Body? thought Angie in panic. *Were they serious?* As Carmen disappeared into the police car, the green-suited woman turned to her camera and launched into a spiel about helicopter searches and coastguards on alert. It was the usual stuff you heard on the TV news when someone had drowned.

Could Gideon really be dead? Stumbling out from behind her forklift truck, Angie found herself staring through the window of the police car, straight into Carmen's face. They held each other's gaze for a few seconds before the police car sped away. 'Stuck-up bitch,' muttered Angie, making her way slowly back towards the harbour front. Why couldn't it have been Carmen, instead of Gideon, who had fallen over-board?

Returning to the car, she let herself in and cried for a good half hour over her lost hopes of wealth. Then, with a shudder, she began to absorb the full significance of what had happened. Gideon was *dead*. That was something final. It didn't just mean that her blackmail plans were thwarted, but it also meant that he would never, ever fuck her again. It was a bloody tragedy, she thought, letting out a noisy sob. Just think of it, that throbbing six inches of manhood that had given her so much pleasure, reduced to nothing more than a teatime nibble for the fish. It really was enough to choke you up.

Her grief was interrupted by a tap on the window. 'Excuse me, madam,' said a voice. 'Do you think I could have a quick word?'

'Fuck off!' she snapped, then fell silent as she saw that the voice belonged to a policeman.

'I'd like to have a look at your documentation,' he continued, unruffled. 'Then I'd like you to come to the station with me. I have reason to believe that this is a stolen car.'

CHAPTER 19

When they were finally shown to the door of Penzance police station and told that they were free to depart, Juliet experienced a curious feeling of dislocation. It was just like leaving a cinema at the end of a film — abandoning the characters to their fictional resolutions and facing up once again to the harsh reality of the world outside. With a shock, she realised that her plans extended no further than this point. Caught up in the excitement of plotting the perfect murder, she hadn't once stopped to consider what would happen if they got away with it.

Glimpsing a phalanx of reporters and photographers waiting outside, Juliet stopped helplessly in the doorway, unable to go forward or back. It was Carmen's turn to take over, organising a taxi to pick them up from the back door and booking them into a hotel. The following day, she drove them both back to London in the Freeloader and insisted that Juliet stay at her house until things quietened down.

Their escape still seemed little short of a miracle. Expecting to be arrested as soon as the *Scillonian* docked, they had been stunned to discover that it was Gideon whom the police were after, and that he was wanted for murder. Hauled off for questioning, Juliet had stuck to their prepared story and hoped for the best. It wasn't until she pieced together what had happened that she worked out quite how lucky they had been.

The beauty of the whole thing was that the police, by the very act of pursuing Gideon, had reinforced the assumption that he was still alive when the *Scillonian* left St Mary's. They had also been watching for him when the passengers disembarked in Penzance, establishing proof that he hadn't sneaked away before the alarm was raised. All the evidence pointed to Gideon's having fallen overboard, whether by accident or design. The search would eventually be called off – as there was no body to find – and they would end up with a verdict of either suicide or accidental death. It didn't look as if it was going to occur to anyone that Gideon had never been on the boat at all.

Poor Louise Cooper, thought Juliet. In one sense, Carmen had avenged her death; in another, she had benefited from it by getting away with a murder of her own. The whole thing had worked out by chance, but Juliet knew just how close they had come to disaster. Imagine how things would have looked for Duncan if the police had caught up with them any sooner than they did.

Thanks to Carmen's celebrity status, Gideon's death hit the tabloids in a big way. Pictures of Carmen filled the front pages, accompanied by headlines such as 'CARMEN'S KILLER SPOUSE FLEES JUSTICE IN SUICIDE

BID' and 'MAKEOVER MURDER HUSBAND IN DROWNING SHOCK'.

Much to the disgust of Carmen's Holland Park neighbours, who had their own secrets to hide, the press set up camp on the pavement outside the house. If this was what fame was like, then they could keep it, thought Juliet, glancing at a full-colour spread of herself putting out the milk bottles the day before. She couldn't even sit in the back garden without being spied on by paparazzi. A clutch of them had broken into next door's tree house and were perched there, smoking and drinking like bored guests in a nightclub waiting for the floor show to begin.

What were they expecting to happen? Were they waiting for Carmen to crack under the pressure and dance naked in the garden with a teapot on her head? Or did they seriously think they would be invited in for an exclusive interview with the widow of the Shepherd's Bush Strangler?

Unable to leave the house, Juliet spent her time working out her plans for the future. After a series of long telephone conversations with Maggie at Belfry Books, she was finally in a position to make the decision she had been moving towards for some time. She would leave Castlemayne Insurance and return to live in Worcester. Maggie, whose fortunes seemed to have improved since she started implementing some of Juliet's suggestions, had agreed to employ her on an experimental project. Her task would be to develop an idea they had discussed many times in their late-night sessions – setting up a new, Internet-based side to the business, which would specialise in crime and mystery books.

Now that she had convinced herself of her need to get out of the rat race, Juliet would have been happy to work for nothing. Maggie, however, had just received a windfall from an unexpected source.

'Remember that insurance policy you persuaded me to take out all those years ago?' she said. 'Well, it's just matured, and it turned out to be worth a lot more than I expected. I can use the money to pay you a salary until things get off the ground.'

The salary would be modest, but they made plans for Juliet to receive a share of any profits, eventually buying into a partnership if the scheme took off. In the meantime, if she budgeted carefully, she would have just enough money to live on after making the mortgage payments on her flat.

Once all this was settled, Juliet began to feel happier and more carefree than she had for a long time. It was highly appropriate, she thought, that Castlemayne Insurance should unwittingly be funding the launch of her new career. She wrote a short letter, confirming her resignation from their London office, and bribed the milkman to post it for her. '*Goodbye Lemon-Lips*,' she murmured, watching from a window as he rattled away in his milk float. It was hardly likely to be a surprise for them, she reflected. Her appearance on the television news while she was supposed to be at home with food poisoning had probably given Rowena the excuse she needed to fire her anyhow.

The press continued to lurk outside the house until

the weekend, when a politician was caught having gay sex in a telephone box on Parson's Green and Gideon was pushed off the front page. As soon as their persecutors had decamped to SW6, Juliet prepared herself for action. The only thing left for her to do in London, once she had squared things with Mrs Billings, was to pay a visit to Duncan. This time, she resolved, there would be no misunderstandings. She would simply tell him how she felt about him and find out where she stood once and for all.

Juliet made her way to Hammersmith by a circuitous route, anxious to avoid any of the more persistent newshounds who might still be hanging around. As far as she could work out, the fact that Duncan hadn't been challenged by the police in Penzance had left him more or less in the clear. There was nothing to prove that he had impersonated Gideon, or that he had even been to the Scilly Isles. His friendship with Juliet was the only thing linking him to the whole affair.

Not wanting to tempt fate by making a special effort, she had dressed in her usual clothes. She hadn't been able to face wearing makeup since that night in Penzance, and didn't think she could bear the humiliation if Duncan laughed at her again. Arriving at his flat early on Sunday afternoon, she found him lunching on what looked like the cold leftovers of a Hammersmith Tandoori takeaway from the night before.

'So, it's you,' he said in an impassive voice. 'I was wondering if you were going to turn up.'

'I thought we'd better be careful,' she said, anxiously

searching his face for some hint of his mood. 'I hope I'm not interrupting anything,' she added, remembering her unscheduled meeting with Sonia the last time she had visited unannounced.

'Only my lunch,' he replied, depositing his half-empty plate in the kitchen. 'I wouldn't worry though, it wasn't very nice.' Leading her through to the living room, he sat down, avoiding her eyes.

Positioning herself opposite him, on the sofa, Juliet glanced around at the empty beer cans and coffee mugs that littered the room. An assortment of the previous week's newspapers were strewn on the table – the now-familiar tabloids with their headlines about Gideon, together with the usual dog-eared copies of *The Stage*. 'What's wrong, Duncan?' she said eventually.

'I'm surprised you need to ask,' he muttered. Picking up a copy of *The Daily Dog*, he thrust it towards her with an angry gesture. 'You've read all these, haven't you? What kind of friend are you, Juliet? Why didn't you tell me Gideon had *murdered* someone?'

'But I didn't know . . .'

'Imagine if they had found out any sooner,' he continued. 'Just think what could have happened to me. Things are bad enough right now as it is – I missed an audition for a big TV commercial while we were away. I could do without thinking that my so-called best friend was trying to get me put in prison.'

'I'm so sorry, Duncan,' she said helplessly. 'But we really didn't know anything about this other murder. How could we have done? Surely you must believe that? I mean, we'd never have taken such a risk . . .'

She fell silent, realising how inadequate her apologies must sound. How could she even begin to explain her real motives?

'I don't know what to believe after all these lies, Juliet,' he said, facing her with a hostile expression. 'You took me all way the down to the Scilly Isles, letting me think the whole thing was just some harmless deception, and then you turn round and tell me that I'm mixed up in a murder. Then I find out that Bridget was in on it as well – that the three of you were planning to use me as some kind of scapegoat.'

'But it wasn't like that. I tried to explain it to you on the beach, remember? Bridget didn't know until . . .'

'Ah yes . . . on the beach,' he said in a mocking tone. 'That was where the real deception started, wasn't it? That was when you knew you had me dangling on a piece of string – all ready to be sucked into the next stage of your convoluted little plot. You should have been an actress, Juliet. Faking it seems to come naturally to you.'

'I don't understand,' said Juliet in confusion. 'I was telling you the truth then, Duncan. I know I shouldn't have held it back for so long, but I was scared of how you'd react – scared you'd be angry with me.'

'Oh come on, Juliet. Why don't we have the *real* truth for a change? You had it all worked out, didn't you? Right down to the details of the timing – how you'd leave me in the garden to let off steam, and then send Carmen out to set me up with another pack of lies.'

'But she told you about Gideon, didn't she? About how it happened? I thought that was why . . .'

'You know perfectly well that's not what I'm talking about. All this murder business was quite bad enough, Juliet, without messing around with my *feelings* as well. I should have seen right then what a ridiculous idea it was, but – like a fool – I *wanted* to believe it.'

'Believe *what*? What did she tell you?' Remembering Carmen's secretive expression when she returned from the garden, Juliet began to wonder if there was something she had missed.

'As if you didn't know,' he muttered with contempt. 'I expect the two of you had a great laugh at my expense, watching me make a complete fool of myself trying to please you with that ridiculous charade on the boat. Throwing common sense to the wind, all because I thought . . .'

'Because you thought . . .'

'Thought I was *in love*, of course,' he snapped. 'Wasn't that what you had intended?'

'In love with Carmen?' asked Juliet, feeling a rush of the old jealousy. 'So *that* was how she talked you into it.'

'Not with *Carmen* – you idiot!' he said angrily. 'With *you!*'

'With *me*?' Juliet stared at him in disbelief. 'But how . . .'

'You thought it was the only way to convince me, didn't you? Making me think that you cared about me so that I'd risk my neck to help you out. I know I was a bit slow to cotton on at first – when you did all that dressing up in Penzance – but Carmen spelled it out to me clearly enough. It was a clever touch, that kiss on the boat, just when I was starting to wonder if I'd imagined the whole thing. You really had me taken in.'

'But wait, Duncan, you've got this all back to front. I didn't even *know* that Carmen said anything to you about . . .' Juliet paused, struggling to grasp the implications of what she was hearing. 'And if that's what Carmen *did* tell you,' she added, 'why are you assuming that it was a lie?'

'Well, it's obvious, isn't it? As soon as I got back here and had time to think about it, I saw straightaway that it couldn't be true. We've been friends for years, Juliet. How could you possibly have felt like that without me noticing something? I know you too well.'

Juliet took a deep breath. There was a straightforward solution to all this, and that meant telling him exactly what she had come here to say. But even now, with her cue set before her, she felt the familiar signs of approaching panic — felt a constriction in her throat and a dryness in her mouth as she attempted to summon the words to her lips. Why was the truth always the hardest thing to admit?

She took another breath, clenching her fists with the effort of remaining calm. 'I'm sorry, Duncan,' she said quietly. 'But I'm afraid that's where you're wrong. You *don't* know me well enough. What Carmen told you was completely true. You see, I *do* love you.'

She closed her eyes, feeling a shudder of insecurity at having finally exposed her secret. What was he going to think of her now? There was a moment's silence, then she heard his footsteps crossing the room and felt the movement of the cushions as he sat down beside her.

'Do you really mean that?' he asked in an incredulous tone. 'You're not winding me up?'

'Of course I mean it,' she said, lowering her head in embarrassment. 'I've loved you for years.'

'Then why on earth didn't you . . .' There was a long pause. Juliet sat completely still, not daring to move a muscle. She could hear the distant sounds of the world outside – the rumble of a passing train and the hum of the traffic on Chiswick High Road. But the world outside didn't mean anything to her right now. The only thing that mattered was what Duncan was going to say next.

The sofa gave a creak as he shifted his position and let out a long sigh. 'Oh hell, Juliet, I'm so sorry . . . it sounds like I'm the one who's been an idiot. Will you ever forgive me?' With a shock, she felt his arms around her. 'Is it *really* true?' he asked. 'Have I really got the whole thing the wrong way round?'

'Of course it's true,' she whispered, moving instinctively towards him and burrowing into the warmth of his embrace.

'I think all this complicated plotting of yours must have rubbed off on me,' he said slowly. 'I've been sitting here all week – my thoughts going round and round in circles – and haven't been able to see anything for what it really was.' He paused, hugging her tighter. 'Why didn't you tell me before all this happened, Jules? If only I'd known . . . things might have been . . .'

'But I didn't think you could ever . . . ever feel that way about me. I'm so sorry, Duncan . . . all the stupid things I've done . . .'

'Well, I've done some pretty stupid things as well,' he said softly. 'And the biggest one was not realising how I felt about you until it was almost too late.' Putting a finger beneath her chin, he tilted her face towards him. 'Look at me, Jules.'

Juliet opened her eyes and gazed at him, hardly daring to believe what was happening.

'I love you, too,' he said, kissing her on the lips. Then he reached out and gently undid the top button of her blouse. 'Why don't we forget about all these misunderstandings,' he murmured, stroking his finger against her bare skin. 'I think we've got an awful lot of catching up to do.'

Learning that Gideon had committed a murder of his own had been a huge shock for Carmen. Nobody seemed to have worked out why Gideon had been with Louise Cooper that night; some said it was a random pick-up, others that they had been involved in some kind of relationship. It wasn't clear whether there was any solid proof that Gideon had killed her, but the fact that he had been with her at the time of her death appeared to have been enough to satisfy the police.

Whatever the details, the nature of the murder had thrown things into perspective for Carmen. She felt less troubled about her own guilt now that she knew Gideon had strangled an innocent woman with his bare hands. How could she be sure that he hadn't been planning to do the very same thing to her?

She shuddered to think how close she and Juliet had come to being caught – parading their ersatz Gideon around Cornwall while the police had been on the verge of launching a manhunt. They had been incredibly fortunate that this Ronco character hadn't raised the alarm any sooner, she realised, glancing at a report in *The Daily Dog*. The press were making a big fuss about the way the Shepherd's Bush Strangler had been identified, claiming that the truth might never have come out if Angie's quick-witted neighbour hadn't recognised Louise's photograph. The man was now being hailed as a latter-day Sherlock Holmes, and there was even talk of his being put forward for some kind of award.

Seeing Angie, both on the quayside and in the police station, had also been a shock. She hadn't known anything about the murder, according to *The Daily Dog*, and had been involved with Gideon for some time without even realising that he was the husband of a TV star.

She skimmed through the article: *'He had even talked about us getting married,'* claimed unemployed Angie Potts, 43, a petite blonde from Notting Hill. *'I never suspected that he was lying to me, even though he was away for much of the time. He told me he had to travel a lot in his line of work.'* The article went on to explain that Angie had only recently discovered the truth about Gideon's domestic situation, and had followed him to Cornwall in the hope of patching things up after a quarrel. *'All I wanted was to tell him I forgave him,'* said grief-stricken Angie, on learning that her lover was dead. *'I can't believe that he killed someone. He will always be special in my memory – nobody can ever take that away from me.'*

Remembering how Angie had looked in the police station, dishevelled and crying as she was being led away for questioning, Carmen felt a pang of sympathy. The irrational jealousy she had felt earlier was now completely gone and instead she felt an urge to do something for this woman – to help her straighten out her life. Hadn't Angie been just as much a victim of Gideon as herself?

As soon as the news of Gideon's death broke, Carmen's producer Kevin had been on the telephone with talk of spin-doctors and damage limitation. She had expected some sympathy for what had happened to her, but it soon became clear that Conquest TV were more concerned about protecting their image.

'Just think of the associations,' Kevin had said. 'Murder. Suicide. Drowning. Rape, as well, if you believe what *The Daily Dog* says he did to that poor woman. The average punter's going to take one look at you on the screen and start feeling depressed about what an awful world they live in. It's hardly going to endear us to our target audience – we're talking prime-time quality programming here, not the fucking *Jerry Springer Show*.'

'Er, Kevin,' Carmen ventured. 'I don't want to sound insensitive to your problems, but my husband's just been drowned, you know.'

'I know, I'm so sorry, baby,' sighed Kevin, completely unruffled by her remark. 'Hang on a minute, someone's chewing my ear . . . what was that, sweetheart?'

Carmen had to wait for several minutes before he came back on the line. 'Listen, honey,' he said. 'We might need to do a bit of rescheduling, but you just hang on in there and don't worry about a thing. The PR people will fix it for us. You put your feet up and relax.'

There was a pause. 'Kevin?' asked Carmen. 'Are you still there?'

'Shit, Carmen,' he said eventually. 'I don't know how you're handling this stuff. It must be really freaking you out. Did you actually know about . . . oh hell, forget it, it's none of my business. Just remember that I'm here if you want to talk.'

'Kevin, I . . .'

'You take it easy, honey. I'll call you again next week. Just keep away from *The Daily Dog*. They've been looking for an excuse to drag us into the gutter with them for years.'

The only other person who contacted her from Conquest TV was Barry.

'Listen Carmen, I know Gideon and I didn't really get on,' he said, 'but I wanted to let you know how sorry I am about what happened. It must be awful for you. If there's anything I can do, whether it's putting in a word with Kevin, or helping out with the chores while you recover, just let me know.'

'Thanks, Barry,' said Carmen, smiling. It was nice to know that at least one person would be friendly to her when she returned to work.

Deep down, she couldn't wait for all the fuss to blow over. She had never been able to enjoy her job properly in the past because of Gideon, but there was a chance for things to be different now. There were aspects of

Makeover she didn't like, and she now felt that she had the confidence to suggest some changes. She wanted to see the programme move away from its obsession with beauty queen looks and focus on issues that were relevant to real women. It was time to use her fame to some positive effect, she told herself – time to do something worthwhile instead of living her life as just another self-serving media type.

At this, she had an idea. Angie was a real woman – someone who had suffered, like herself, and who was currently unemployed and struggling to survive. What if she befriended her – gave her some kind of assistance? What if she offered her a job?

Carmen knew that one of the Amandas from the research team would soon be leaving to have a baby. The timing was perfect. Someone like Angie could bring a real breath of fresh air into the way the programme was made. She might have no experience of television, but Carmen felt sure she would be a fast learner. She probably had a far better grasp of street fashion than the middle-class career girls who currently dominated the *Makeover* production team.

Hadn't there been a telephone number on the back of that photograph Juliet had found? She hoped it hadn't been thrown away. Glancing at her watch, Carmen felt a stirring of impatience. Juliet had been at Duncan's for most of the day now. How long was it going to be before she returned?

When Juliet woke up in Duncan's bed later that afternoon, she was glowing with contentment. At last she knew that he cared for her; the long years of hoping and waiting had all been worthwhile. Looking down at his sleeping face, she felt a rush of affection towards him. This was coupled with an erotic thrill as she remembered all the things their naked bodies had done together in the last few hours. She pressed herself close against him, fitting the curves and hollows of her body into his and luxuriating in the sensation of intimacy. Planting a kiss on his sweaty forehead, she reached between her legs and felt the hot wetness on her fingers. The air was heavy with the smell of sex.

Then, suddenly, it all seemed rather frightening and grown-up for two people who used to play at Cowboys and Indians when they were ten. Shivering, she got up and wrapped herself in his dressing gown. There was something faintly sordid about being in bed in the afternoon.

Hunting for tea bags in the kitchen, she was unnerved to find a photograph of Sonia on the pinboard behind the door. Were they still in touch with each other? And who else was Duncan involved with in London? For all she knew, he might have dozens of other girlfriends that she had never met.

There were no tea bags to be found, and the milk bore a distinct resemblance to cottage cheese. After an extensive search, she unearthed a jar of coffee and some individual portions of UHT that looked as if they'd been stolen from a café. Waiting for the kettle to boil, she noticed that the remains of Duncan's lunch were beginning to give off an unpleasant smell.

When she returned to the bedroom with the coffee,

Duncan was beginning to stir. 'There's something I have to tell you,' she said, perching on the side of the bed. 'I'm going back to Worcester. To live there, I mean.'

'You're what?' he asked, sitting up and rubbing his eyes. 'But why? Don't you want to stay here with me? I thought we could move in together, or something.'

Juliet had dreamt of hearing these words for as long as she could remember. She had spent many lonely hours imagining the pleasures of sharing a home with Duncan – of spending time with him every day and knowing the security of a proper relationship. But she had woken up to some painful facts about herself in the last few weeks. She could now see how empty her life had been – how devoid of any real purpose or ambition beyond her perpetual yearning for Duncan's affections. If she hadn't been drifting so aimlessly, she realised, she would never have even considered getting involved in Gideon's murder. What kind of sad case had she been, to need to do something so outrageous to manufacture some interest in her life?

She had also used Duncan's apparent indifference as an excuse for everything that was missing, telling herself that *if only* Duncan would care for her, her other problems would magically resolve themselves. But she now knew that this wasn't true. She had wasted most of her life by letting her choices be determined by other people. What she really needed was to have the courage to make her own decisions – to take some positive action to improve her own life.

If Duncan really loved her, she told herself, they would somehow find a way to be together. Picking up the dragon bracelet from the bedside table, she slipped it onto her wrist and turned to face him with a confident smile.

'I've got a new job,' she said. 'With Maggie at the bookshop, remember? I've already given in my notice at Castlemayne.'

'But why . . .' Duncan frowned, looking confused. 'Why did you come to London in the first place, then? If you weren't intending to stay.'

'I didn't know what I was intending to do,' she said quietly. 'But I've realised that I don't belong in London. I'd never be happy here.'

'But surely you can't expect *me* to go back to Worcester?' he said, looking crestfallen. 'Look how hard I've struggled to get this far with my career.'

'Why not?' asked Juliet. 'You always used to tell me there were plenty of openings for actors outside London. And besides, you don't seem to be getting much work here.'

'There's no need to remind me of that,' he said sharply, reaching for his underpants and putting them on. He faced her with a look of reproach. 'I thought you said you loved me, Juliet. If you really meant it, surely you'd want to stay here with me?'

Juliet struggled to hide her disappointment. She had somehow hoped that his reaction might have been less predictable — that he might have welcomed the chance to get out of the rut he seemed to be in. 'I *do* love you, Duncan,' she said. 'But I've got to think about my life, too. Would *you* want to stay in the kind of job I had — office fodder from nine to five for the rest of your days?

You know how much I wanted to work with Maggie — you told me so yourself. This is the first chance I've ever had to do something I might actually *enjoy*. Surely you don't expect me to sacrifice that?'

Duncan gazed at her with a hurt expression. 'Well you can't expect *me* to sacrifice everything, either,' he said. Climbing out of bed, he reached for his shirt and pulled it on. 'Don't you realise how important it is for me to stay here now? If I don't keep on trying, I'll never stand a chance of getting a big break.' Buttoning his cuffs, he went into the living room to look for his trousers. 'Besides,' he called back to her. 'Didn't I tell you? I've got another audition for *Southsiders* next week.'

After a few moments, Juliet heard him clattering things in the kitchen and realised that he wasn't going to return. Removing his dressing gown, she retrieved her clothes from the floor and began to put them on.

If all this had happened a short time ago, she would have jumped at Duncan's offer – would have abandoned all her plans without a second thought. But things were different now. Staying here in London, even if she found another job, wasn't going to change anything for her. She could never be happy in Duncan's twilight world of sleazy lodgings and uncertain employment, eating takeaways from the Hammersmith Tandoori and living out her life against a constant background of noise and traffic fumes.

If she stayed, she would end up working all hours to support him while he waited for his 'big break' to come along. She would be forced to entertain all manner of dubious acquaintances who might further his career, and then to wait patiently at home while he was out 'networking'. If he was successful, he would spend even more time away from her. And eventually, in the predictable way that things happened in the acting world, she would come home one afternoon and find him making out with some young actress right here in their bed.

When she had finished dressing, Juliet swallowed the rest of her coffee, which was now cold, and took the mug through to the kitchen. She found Duncan scraping the remains of his lunch into an overflowing plastic bin. 'I'm sorry,' she said, watching him from the doorway. 'But I've already made up my mind. If it's such a big deal for you to get a part in some lousy soap opera, you'll just have to stay here and manage on your own.'

Duncan swung round and gazed at her, dripping a trail of luminous red sauce on the cracked linoleum floor. 'But Jules . . . wait a moment . . .' he said in an unhappy voice. 'We need to talk . . .'

'I think we've talked enough already,' she said firmly, surprising herself with the strength of her resolve. 'You know where to find me in Worcester,' she added, turning to leave. 'I just hope you'll get in touch with me if you change your mind.'

It had been a bad week for Angie, what with being caught drunk at the wheel of a stolen car and having her blackmail plans scuppered by Gideon's death. But it could have been worse, she realised. At least she hadn't been dragged into the murder case. Her explanation for being in Cornwall had been a spur-of-the-moment inspiration that was based, like many good stories, on an element of wishful thinking. Imagine if Gideon *had* actually proposed marriage, with the intention of divorcing Carmen. He might have changed his will and left everything to her.

The thing that really rankled was how little Carmen Bird had been touched by the whole affair. She was left with all her wealth and fame, and would now be free to look for a new husband who was as big a celebrity as herself. Angie, meanwhile, needed money more desperately than ever. The next month's rent was due at the end of the week and the remains of her earnings from Penzance were rapidly dwindling away.

She still had her photographs of Gideon, but doubted that she would be able to use them to blackmail Carmen, now that the details of the affair had been made public. Eventually, she had been forced to the conclusion that blackmail wasn't really her forte. Far simpler, she had decided, to keep things legal and sell the pictures directly to the press.

Taking a deep breath, Angie pushed her way through the revolving doors that led into the marble foyer of the *Daily Dog* building. A series of telephone calls had swiftly established that this was the best, indeed the only place, to come with the particular kind of material she was offering for sale.

'I'm here to see Ron Lurcher,' she told the receptionist, feeling somewhat intimidated by the polished grandeur of the surroundings. 'I spoke to him on the phone yesterday.'

'Got some pictures for him, have you, love?' asked the receptionist in a bored whine. Nodding, she indicated a waiting area populated with sad-looking people clutching brown paper envelopes. 'Better join the queue, sweetheart. Looks like Ron's in for a busy morning.'

'No, listen,' insisted Angie, getting out her Fotorola packet. 'He said he'd see me straightaway if I really had what said I did.' Selecting a picture, she slid it across the desk with a shy smile. 'He said that I was to show you one of these.'

'Blimey!' murmured the receptionist, dropping her nail file in her coffee. 'Isn't that the bloke who came a cropper last week? *Star's Shame as Strangler Spouse in Suicide Shock*? And who's the . . .' She paused and glanced up at Angie, as if to check that she hadn't imagined the resemblance, then turned her eyes back to the picture with an expression of disbelief. 'This won't do Ron's blood pressure any good,' she said eventually, picking up the telephone. 'Go easy on him, ducks, he had his first heart attack last year.'

After a short wait, Angie was escorted upstairs to Ron Lurcher's office – a partitioned-off cubicle at one end of a busy newsroom. She was met by a view of his huge, polyester-clad buttocks as he bent over the combination lock of what looked like a safe.

It turned out, in fact, to be a small refrigerator. 'Just fixing my elevenses,' he grunted, heaving himself around to face her. He proffered a half-empty pack of individual pork pies. 'Fancy a growler?'

Angie shook her head, watching queasily as he squeezed one between a fat thumb and forefinger and inserted it into his mouth whole. 'So who do we have here then?' he asked, challenging the suspension of a defeated-looking adjustable chair as he lowered himself into position behind his desk. 'Angie Potts, eh?' He tapped at the crumb-strewn keyboard of his computer with greasy paws. 'Ah yes . . . *Makeover Mistress Misses Boat*,' he murmured, flashing her a lecherous glance. '*Forlorn Fiancée Fell for Felon's Fibs*. So what have you got for me today?'

'I've got pictures . . .' began Angie eagerly.

'Pictures?' he asked, suddenly businesslike. 'What kind of pictures? This story's pretty much on its last legs, you know – our readers aren't interested in see-ing snapshots of little-girl-lost holding hands with her boyfriend anymore. You'd have to be offering a whole new angle – *I Carried Killer's Love Child*, for example.' He licked his lips. 'Or *Sold into Sexual Slavery*? *Secret Sex Syndicate*? You get the idea?'

'The pictures are very explicit,' murmured Angie, sliding one out of the Fotorola envelope and offering it to him.

'Blimey!' he spluttered, his eyes popping. Snatching the envelope from her, he flicked greedily through the stack of photographs, glancing up from time to time to fix her with a disbelieving stare. 'How did you . . . never mind. Have you shown these to anyone else?'

Angie shook her head. 'I was wondering how much . . .'

'We could even be talking five figures here,' he gasped, picking up the telephone. 'Listen, Bas,' he whispered excitedly. 'I've got the tart in the Bird murder here with pix of the killer with his kit off.

Don't worry, I'll get a story to go with them. Can you give me clearance for an upper four or low five? OK, great. I'll send her over to see Tony when I'm done.'

Replacing the receiver, he reached for another pork pie. 'OK, darling,' he continued breathlessly. 'You and me are going to have a little chat about what happened. We're going to have to come at it from a more sophisticated angle – not so much the jilted fiancée as the kinky sex kitten. Naughty things you used to get up to together, know what I mean?' Cramming the pork pie into his mouth, he took out a notebook and a grubby pad of carbonless forms. 'I'm going to need a signature, too – exclusive rights, you understand?'

'He used to do quite a lot of coke,' offered Angie, scrawling her name across the bottom of the form.

'*Drug Fuelled Sex Orgies*,' wrote Ron.

'And he liked a bit of bondage . . .'

'*Tie Me Up, Tie Me Down*,' he scribbled, salivating. '*Sex Slave Tells Tales of Torture*'. His chair let out a series of squeaking noises and there was an embarrassed pause while he adjusted his position. 'Now listen, Angie,' he went on, pocketing the Fotorola envelope. 'This is a bit delicate, but I'm sure you'll understand. Our readers have a right to know. Did he ever say anything about his, er, wife? Carmen Bird, that is. Anything special he might have mentioned that they did together? Sexually, I mean.'

'Not really,' said Angie. 'I don't think they did it very much, actually.'

'Oh, come on, darling,' said Ron impatiently. 'We need you to use a bit more imagination here. What do you think would have turned her on? Bit of B&D like you, maybe? Swedish culture? Body piercing? Golden showers? Coprophilia?'

'Copro *what*?'

'Messing around with shit and stuff.'

'Blimey,' murmured Angie. 'Well, yes. If you say so.'

'This is great,' panted Ron, scribbling furiously. 'I'll just need another signature here and then I'll send you over to Tony for a few tasteful shots in your *lingerie*. There's, er, just one more thing . . .'

'Yes?'

'Are you free for a drink later, darling?' His tongue slid insinuatingly around his fat lips. 'If you were interested, I could teach you one or two other words that you might not know.'

After being shunted around various departments for the rest of the day and fighting off Ron Lurcher in the lift, Angie went home as the proud owner of an official-looking receipt promising payment of a five-figure sum. She was slightly disappointed when she saw the actual amount, having assumed, in her earlier excitement, that the five referred to the number of noughts on the end. It wasn't exactly going to set her up for life.

But she could still have some fun with it. 'Drinks are on me tonight,' she trilled, banging on Ronco's door.

To her astonishment, Ronco came into the hallway wearing a smart-looking jacket in place of his usual anorak. 'I'm sorry, but I've got to go out this evening,' he said quickly, looking embarrassed. 'It's the local wildlife society. They got in touch after reading that article about me in the newspaper. I've promised to give them a talk about my special badger-watching techniques.'

Alone in her flat, Angie started planning how many copies of *The Daily Dog* she would buy the next day. Just think of it – she was going to be famous! Imagine how jealous everyone at the local pub would be.

The telephone rang, and she snatched it up eagerly. 'Yes?' she asked. It was probably just Ronco changing his mind about going for a drink, although part of her was busily fantasising that her story might have grown into something big and filtered through to other newspapers. For a brief moment she pictured headlines spinning towards her – just the way they did in old films – as she rocketed to fame and fortune overnight.

'Is that Angie? I'm sorry I don't know your last name . . .'

With a shock, Angie recognised the voice. It was Carmen Bird. 'Er, hi,' she said awkwardly. 'I mean, yes. This is me.'

As Carmen introduced herself, Angie's mind was racing ahead, trying to anticipate what was to come. Had *The Daily Dog* leaked the details of her story? Was she after some kind of revenge?

'I was hoping we could meet up,' suggested Carmen. 'There's so much we have to talk about.'

'What do you mean?' asked Angie suspiciously. 'Why should you think I've got anything to say to you?'

'I thought, well, perhaps you might want to talk about Gideon. Get things out of your system. I know you must be feeling pretty terrible, and I was wondering if it might help to share things . . .'

'How do you know what I'm feeling? What business is it of yours?'

'Please don't get the wrong idea,' said Carmen quickly. 'I just thought, well, it just seems pointless to be enemies after all that's happened. When we could do so much for each other . . .'

'What are you going to do for me, then?' demanded Angie in a petulant tone. 'Talking's all very well when you're rich and famous, but people like me have to worry about paying the rent.'

'I know,' replied Carmen, sounding slightly taken aback. 'I was . . . er, just coming to that. I know how hard it is finding work these days and I thought . . . well, there's a job coming up here at Conquest TV that you might be interested in. I could put your name forward. It wouldn't be a huge salary, I'm afraid, but there would be prospects for promotion once you'd learned the ropes. Obviously we'd need to talk things through first to see if it's going to be a feasible option but . . .'

'Hold on a minute,' said Angie, unable to believe that she'd heard correctly. 'Did you say a job at *Conquest TV*?'

'That's right. It's only in the research team, but you don't really need any previous experience if you've got good people skills . . .'

'Oh, but I'm extremely good with people,' said Angie in an eager voice. 'Especially men.' *Conquest TV!* she thought excitedly. *She was going to become a somebody after all!* For a moment, she pictured herself in a new life – caught up in a heady whirl of parties and free lunches, wearing designer clothes and carrying a clipboard under her arm. It would only be a matter of time, she told herself dreamily, before they recognised her potential in front of the camera. She would start off in a small way with weather reports and filling in while people were out at lunch, then move on to co-presenting in a daytime slot for a series or two before she was given a show of her own. Forget Ron Lurcher with his five-figure sums, it wouldn't be long before she was pulling that in every month.

Then, with a horrible, sinking feeling, she realised that she couldn't forget Ron Lurcher. She had signed his filthy piece of paper and it was now too late to turn back. Her exposé of Carmen Bird's sex life would be published in the morning for all the world to see, together with photographs – teasers, Ron had called them – of herself in her underwear.

'Angie? Are you still there?' Carmen's voice was anxious. 'I hope I haven't offended you by mentioning this . . .'

With a whimper, Angie dropped the receiver. She didn't know why Carmen Bird had made this offer, but she could be certain that it would be swiftly withdrawn after tomorrow's *Daily Dog* hit the newsstands.

For once, Angie's sense of optimism completely deserted her. She had fucked up – seriously fucked up in such a big way that she was going to regret it for the rest of her life. Every time she switched on the TV, she would be reminded of her failure. She would be reminded of how she had missed her chance to belong to that privileged elite – that inner circle of people who mattered.

It was enough to choke you up. Slumping into a chair, Angie abandoned any pretence of toughness. Bursting into tears, she began to cry in great, racking sobs, just like a little girl.

CHAPTER 20

Carmen was baffled by Angie's reaction to her offer. She could understand if Gideon's mistress had been offended – angry, even – but she didn't think she had said anything to warrant the heartbroken sobs that were just audible before the line went dead.

Was everyone suffering from some kind of madness that prevented them from acting in their own interests? Juliet seemed to be doing exactly the same, disappearing back to Worcester when she was right on the verge of getting what she had always wanted.

But at least Duncan had finally admitted to his feelings, she thought, reflecting on the brief details Juliet had imparted about their afternoon together. It sounded to Carmen as if her talk with Duncan in Bridget's garden had produced the desired result.

The following day brought a telephone call from Kevin. 'Good God, Carmen – are you stark raving mad?' he bellowed in an outraged voice. 'Have you seen *The Daily Dog* this morning? Didn't I warn you to keep away from them?'

'But I haven't . . .'

'We've been having crisis talks all morning,' he went on, ignoring her. 'I doubt if we're going to be able to absorb another scandal of this size. It's one thing being unlucky enough to have married a murderer, Carmen, but it's quite another to parade your bedroom secrets all over the tabloids. We're a channel with family values, for Christ's sake!'

'But Kevin, surely you don't think I . . .'

'To be honest with you, sweetheart, it's not going to make a lot of difference whether it's true or not. I'll put in a good word for you, of course, but if you want my advice you'd better start thinking about your next career move.'

'But I don't even know what they've said about me!'

'Look, I've got to go, honey,' he said quickly, sounding embarrassed. 'I've got a meeting with the top brass in a few minutes. I'll call you later and let you know how it turns out.'

Carmen was forced to take the embarrassing step of going down to the local newsagent and purchasing a copy of *The Daily Dog*. One glance at the front page was enough to tell her that she could forget about going back to work at Conquest TV. 'CARMENGATE SCANDAL': trumpeted the headline. '*Sex Secrets Exclusive*, by top investigative journalist Ron Lurcher. *Makeover Mistress Shares Pillow Talk.*'

The woman behind the counter fixed her with a hostile glare. 'You ought to be ashamed of yourself coming in here after all what you've been doing,' she muttered darkly, taking her money. 'I shan't be watching that programme of yours anymore, for one.'

Back at home, Carmen surveyed the damage. She was accused of having all kinds of perverse sexual habits, including some she had never even heard of. No wonder Angie hadn't wanted to talk to her on the telephone, she realised, gazing at a picture of the 'Makeover Mistress' spreadeagled on a tiger skin in skimpy underwear. There were even photographs of the bloody woman in bed with Gideon, carefully cropped so that they stopped just short of obscenity. Why on earth had she done it? Didn't she realise how ridiculous it made her look?

Well, she could forget about that job offer now, thought Carmen blackly. Thanks to Angie, she was no longer in a position to help anyone get a job at Conquest TV.

She spent most of the afternoon feeling sorry for herself. Her job had been the one thing that gave her some kind of self-respect. In the absence of anything else to hold on to, she had depended on it to keep her sane. At the same time, however, she was beginning to realise just how shallow her life had been. There had to be something missing if her only pleasure came from staring at herself in the distorted mirror of the television screen.

Surely she hadn't escaped Gideon only to be tyrannised by the superficial values of the TV world, where things were judged by how they looked rather than by what they actually meant? This was the underlying premise of *Makeover*, that appearance was the only thing that mattered. Remembering Hazel from Sunbury and countless others like her, Carmen felt a huge pang of guilt. She had been personally responsible for screwing up their self-image – brainwashing them into spending their hard-earned money on clothes and cosmetics in pursuit of an unattainable ideal.

The whole concept of *Makeover* was based on the assumption that all women were unhappy with their looks. It could never work otherwise. Who would buy the beauty products if everyone was content to stay as they were? If only she had more courage, she thought, she would love to expose the whole 'makeover' business for what it was – a formula for exploiting women based on intimidation and commercial greed.

But what was stopping her? She had plenty of time now, and money wasn't an immediate problem. She certainly had no further allegiance to Conquest TV, and she had a famous name, a valuable commodity that could now be employed in the interests of whatever cause she chose.

Sitting at her dressing table, Carmen tied back her hair and scrubbed off her makeup with tissues and cold cream. She scarcely recognised the person underneath – but it was the real Carmen Bird, not the shallow creature who had married Gideon and worked for Conquest TV.

Then she telephoned Kevin – not to argue about her job, but to ask for some information. He gave it to her eagerly. 'I'm glad you've decided to be sensible about this, sweetheart,' he said, sounding greatly relieved. 'There's really no point in fighting against the weight of popular opinion. If you want my advice, you'd be better off steering well clear of TV for a few years.'

The telephone rang as she put the receiver down; it was Barry calling to ask if she was all right. 'Don't worry about *The Daily Dog*,' he assured her. 'Nobody with any sense believes a single word they print. The whole thing's bound to blow over in a few weeks.'

'I wouldn't be so sure about that,' said Carmen, touched by his concern.

There was a pause while Barry cleared his throat. 'It can't be much fun for you at the moment,' he added. 'I was wondering if you might like some company this evening to cheer you up.'

'That would be lovely,' said Carmen, smiling. 'Let me warn you, though, I've changed a bit since you last saw me. You might be a little surprised.'

A few days later, Carmen took a taxi to Foccaccio's restaurant in Soho to meet the renowned agent and PR guru, Montague Large. He wouldn't have been Carmen's first choice for a literary agent – dealing as he did with disgraced politicians, topless models and celebrities with armies of ghostwriters in tow – but Kevin had pulled strings to arrange the meeting for her, assuring her that he was the best.

He was waiting at a well-positioned table on the mezzanine level. 'Charmed to meet you at last,' he murmured, extending a plump, well-manicured hand and making a slight movement with his body in lieu of getting up. 'Do join me in some *antipasto*,' he added, gesturing with a torn-off hunk of bread. On the table was an array of dishes containing different kinds of olives, anchovies, and sun-dried something-or-other drenched in oil. 'I'll just call for some menus, nothing like a good meal to put you in the mood for business.'

Carmen sat down, watching in amazement as he demolished an entire ciabatta. 'This is terribly exciting,' he continued. 'Kevin tells me that you've decided to turn your hand to a little writing. Autobiographical, I venture to presume. Your life with the murderer, details of your luxurious lifestyle, famous friends and so on?' He faced her with a quizzical smile, his chin glistening with extra-virgin oil. 'We could be talking a seriously *large* amount of money here.'

'Um, actually,' said Carmen, 'that wasn't quite what I had in mind.'

'How so?' he asked, raising a disapproving eyebrow. 'It seems the most obvious route, wouldn't you say? In the circumstances?' He let out a gentle sigh. 'A terrible shame, of course – the fiasco with that stupid woman in *The Daily Dog*. Now if only she'd had the sense to come to me . . .'

A waiter arrived with menus. 'I might not be much of a literary man,' he continued, scanning the list of specials, 'but I do know how to get you the best deal. Just give me a rough idea of what you were planning. Cookery books are selling well at the moment – secrets from the stars' kitchens and all that. Or perhaps you were thinking of a new dieting idea?'

'Not exactly,' said Carmen. 'It's more like . . .'

'The wild avocado and mozzarella salad is particularly good here, by the way,' he added, spearing the last anchovy with a toothpick and sliding it into his mouth. 'Are you ready to order?'

'Maybe we should get this out of the way first,' said Carmen, handing him a piece of paper. 'It's just a rough summary, outlining the main points.'

Glancing at it, Montague Large began to cough violently, regurgitating bits of anchovy into his aperitif. 'But nobody's going to want to publish something like this, let alone *read* it,' he spluttered. '"*The Makeover Myth? Why the media want to make women feel insecure?*" This is heresy! Biting the hand that feeds . . .'

'Fed,' interrupted Carmen emphatically. 'Past tense.'

'And what's . . . what's this?' he continued in an outraged tone. '"*The Fashion Conspiracy? Why manufacturers want you to keep changing your look?*" But what . . . what about the merchandising tie-ins? Surely you want to capitalise on your position? As your agent, I would have to advise you . . .'

'You're not my agent yet,' said Carmen firmly. 'I haven't made up my mind. Now listen carefully. I'm not doing this for the money. I'm doing it because I want to. And I'm going to go ahead and do it anyway, whatever you say.'

'But you can't . . .'

'Oh yes I can. You might be forgetting that I've got a name. A name that will sell. As Kevin so eloquently put it the other day, I could probably get into the bestseller lists if I copied out the first hundred pages of the London telephone directory. I hardly think it matters whether or not *you* approve of what I'm going to write.'

'But have you considered your viewers — what they would expect . . .'

'It's precisely *because* I'm considering my viewers that I'm doing this,' said Carmen. 'Now do you want to join in with me? Make a bit of money for yourself by finding me a reputable publisher? Or do you want me to take this to one of your rivals?'

Montague Large opened and shut his mouth several times – which wasn't a pretty sight when viewed from close range – and let out a sigh of defeat. 'Very well, my dear,' he said eventually. 'I'll get my secretary to send you one of our standard contracts. We can sort out the details later on. You might always reconsider your options when you've had time to think.'

Turning back to the menu, he clutched at it with the expression of someone seeking consolation from an old friend. 'They do a very nice roast beef here,' he announced with a note of desperation in his voice. 'With a garnish of Dijon mustard and green peppercorns – I recommend it cooked rare so that the blood still runs red . . .' He paused, staring at her. 'Are you all right?'

Carmen's appetite disappeared abruptly as she was confronted by a sudden vision of the electric carving knife. 'I'm sorry,' she muttered queasily, standing up. 'I'm going to have to leave you to it. I've just remembered that I'm supposed to be somewhere else.'

Once she was out in the fresh air, she felt much better. There were bound to be moments like that, she told herself. You could scarcely expect to kill your husband and get away with a completely clear conscience. But she now had the chance of a new life ahead of her. Hopefully, the flashbacks would become less frequent as time passed.

As she went to meet Barry for a drink that evening, Carmen wondered if he might ever become part of her future. It was too early to be certain whether his interest was romantic or not, but she felt very comfortable in his company. He was far less committed to the world of Conquest TV than she had imagined, and had confided that he was thinking of giving it up to pursue a long-held dream of running an antique shop.

Carmen wasn't going to rush into anything. She had wasted over eight years of her life by letting that happen with Gideon. But she couldn't help trying to imagine what it would be like to be involved in a proper relationship – one that was built on trust and mutual respect instead of violence, hatred and fear. She would wait until she had finished her book, she decided. By then, she might have a clearer idea of how things were working out.

When she arrived at the pub, she gave Barry a big kiss on the cheek. 'What was that for?' he asked, looking pleased and surprised.

'Just for being there,' said Carmen, smiling. 'Or if you felt like reading something into it, you could take it as a hint that I don't want you to go away.'

Juliet's parents, contrary to her expectations, had been delighted to learn that she was returning to Worcester.

'You don't mind, then?' she asked her mother on the telephone. 'About me leaving the insurance job, I mean?'

'Goodness no, not if that's what you want,' Mrs Jennings had replied. 'As long as you're happy, that's the important thing. I always used to wonder why you stuck at that Castlemayne place. They never sounded much like your kind of people to me.'

Juliet had been glad to take up her parent's offer of temporary accommodation, especially when she discovered that her carefully chosen tenant was refusing to leave her flat until the full term of his lease had expired. The letting agents assured her that they would find a way to speed things up, but she eventually told them not to worry. The extra money was useful, and she was enjoying her stay at her parent's pub much more than she had expected. It was comforting to be surrounded by her childhood memories. She felt as if she was purging herself of the horrors of the recent past, clearing the way to make a fresh start.

Resurrecting her old bicycle from the cellar, she cycled the three miles to Belfry Books each day and devoted her energies to her new project. It was a relief to be out of London – to be able to measure the gradual shift from spring into summer by the blossoming of the different species in the hedgerows, instead of by turning the pages of a calendar. If it wasn't for the absence of Duncan, she would have been completely happy.

They spoke on the telephone at regular intervals, having long, awkward conversations in which a lot of things were left unsaid. They both admitted that they missed one another, but were unwilling to suggest any compromise that might overcome the difficulties keeping them apart.

But eventually, after a month had passed, Duncan announced that he was making a visit to Worcester.

'I've got a surprise for you,' he told her, in a voice that sounded more positive than usual. 'But you'll have to wait until I see you.' He refused to elaborate further, despite her entreaties. 'I'll come over on Sunday afternoon, if that's OK,' he concluded. 'I just need a few days to sort out some things down here.'

The rest of the week passed slowly. When Sunday finally came, Juliet found it hard to conceal her impatience. The morning seemed to go on forever as she helped her mother with the chores and served behind the bar. In return, her parents had agreed to make themselves scarce for a few hours while the pub was closed in the afternoon.

As soon as she was alone, Juliet took a long bath and washed her hair. Then, wrapping herself in a towel, she went into her old bedroom and opened the wardrobe.

Her new dress was waiting on a hanger. It looked good on her, she thought as she slipped into it and admired herself in the mirror. The thing that had surprised her most was the fun she'd had choosing it. She had thoroughly enjoyed her shopping trip to Worcester the previous day.

She was reminded of the excitement she used to feel as a teenager getting dressed up for a party, back in the days before she gave up on that sort of thing. Was it possible, she wondered, that this was the reason women went in for clothes and makeup in such a big way. Maybe it *was* nothing to do with commercial pressure, or subservience to men. Maybe they did it simply because it was *fun*?

Might as well go the whole hog now, she decided,

checking that the door was closed. Opening the top drawer of the dressing table, she took out the rest of her purchases – a selection of cosmetics and a *Carmen Bird Makeover Video*. Slipping the last item into the video machine she had borrowed from her parent's bedroom, she sat herself in front of the mirror and prepared to follow its advice.

As the train drew close to Worcester, Duncan sneaked a final look at the letter from Wyvern FM. It might not be offering the dizzy heights of theatrical stardom he had once dreamed of, but he had to admit that it still sounded pretty good. '*We were most impressed by . . . would like to offer you the position of . . . presenting the morning show, as discussed . . .*' and, possibly most importantly, '*at a starting salary of . . .*'

Duncan had never had an actual salary before, and found it hard to imagine what it would be like to be able to pay the bills in the same quarter that they arrived. He hoped it wouldn't turn him into a middle-class bore overnight.

It was the *Southsiders* audition that brought about his sudden change of attitude. Arriving at the venue, along with hundreds of others, he had been dismayed to learn that the 'major role' his agent had spoken of was, in fact, the part of a milkman. True enough, it was a speaking part, but the speech consisted of five lines spread over three episodes, if you counted the repetition of 'Morning, Mrs Mallory', as two of them. The total air time was something in the region of twelve seconds, and the character wasn't even involved in the storyline.

To add insult to injury, the casting director had laid down a whole set of finicky requirements, including height, build, regional accent, and even the ability to drive a bloody milk float. Gazing around at the assembled hopefuls, many of whom he recognised from his last audition, Duncan had felt a chill creep down his spine. Even supposing he had a chance against all these others, what if this was as far as he ever got? How would he feel, in years to come, if his one contribution to TV posterity was a twelve-second cameo delivering the milk?

For the first time in his life, Duncan broke faith with his creed of *never, ever, giving up*, and walked out of the audition. He spent the whole journey back to Hammersmith brooding about his career prospects in London. Was it worth sacrificing his happiness to stay and chase the ephemeral rewards of fame? Wouldn't he be better off spending his time with the woman he loved and setting his sights on a more realistic goal?

When Juliet had first returned to Worcester, Duncan had been of the opinion that she had given up on London too easily. Now he could see that she had, in fact, been brave enough to make a harder choice. She had held out against other people's expectations in order to do what she really wanted, and he admired her for it. Was there any good reason why he couldn't do the same?

When he saw the advertisement for a local radio presenter in Worcester, everything seemed to fall into place. The audience ratings might be small compared with the likes of *Southsiders*, but he would reach a lot more people than he could on the stage. It would also mean that he could use his talents on a daily basis, instead of leaving them to wither away in the long periods of 'resting' that currently dominated his life.

Finally, and most importantly, it would mean that he could be with Juliet. Her absence had become more painful to him every day since her departure, and he was now determined to put an end to their separation once and for all.

Duncan had wasted no time in making an application for the post. He had been through a gruelling selection procedure, which had made him blush to think that he once considered such employment beneath him. It wasn't until he had suffered over a fortnight of nail-biting and been called back for a further interview that he finally received the call to say he would be offered the job.

Taking a last look at the letter, he folded it away in his pocket. He hadn't dared make any promises to Juliet before he had it in writing. He was only too familiar with the tricks fate could play on those foolish enough to celebrate good fortune in advance.

The train arrived in Worcester. Leaving the station, he bought flowers and chocolates from a kiosk before hailing a taxi. If he was a proper romantic hero, he thought wistfully, he would be turning up armed with champagne and an engagement ring. But, again, he was reluctant to tempt fate. He didn't want to seem too sure of himself, which could easily lead to more misunderstandings. This time, he told himself, he wasn't going to screw things up by jumping to conclusions. He was going to make sure he *listened* to what she said. The time for extravagant gestures could wait until he was certain that her answer to his proposal was a 'yes'.

Juliet finished applying her foundation and blusher, then turned her attention to the selection of eyeshadows she had chosen the day before. They all had names like flowers – foxglove, lavender and lupin. If she looked into the garden she could see the originals flourishing in the warm sunlight.

What was Duncan's surprise going to be, she wondered, dabbing colour onto her eyelids. She had been thinking about it constantly since he called, conjuring up fantasies of him whisking her away for a night of romance, or even that he might be returning to Worcester for an extended stay. But it was hard to be sure with Duncan. It might just be his way of telling her that he had been cast in the lead of some play – that his 'big break' had finally come along.

She frowned, blending in the colour with the tips of her fingers. The video had said to use a special kind of sponge, but she hadn't thought to buy one. It was best not to set her hopes too high, she told herself firmly. It would be enough to know that Duncan still cared for her – to be reassured that he hadn't shacked up with another Sonia as soon as she was out of the way.

She abandoned the eyeliner as the instructions were impossible to follow. It looked as if you needed hands as steady as a brain surgeon's and eyes that never blinked. The mascara was difficult enough for a beginner, but she managed a couple of sweeps of the brush without blinding herself. Not bad at all, she decided, peering into the mirror at the results.

Just the lipstick now. She had purchased several colours as she hadn't been able to make up her mind which one she preferred. Twisting open the shiny tubes, she still found it hard to reach a decision. The names weren't much help; faced with choices like *Shimmering Burgundy* or *Dusky Claret*, she felt like a novice at a wine-tasting class.

Eventually, picking one at random, she poised herself at the mirror. But as she made contact with her lips, the doorbell rang, making her start so violently that she ended up with *Spicy Mulberry* all over her nose. Surely Duncan couldn't be here already? But she could hear his voice outside, negotiating with a taxi driver. Surveying the damage in the mirror, she felt a strong impulse to lock herself in the bathroom and scrub her whole face clean.

But she didn't. Her thoughts circled wildly. Would Duncan kiss her, she wondered, or would there be misunderstandings again? What was his real reason for coming here?

All she knew was that she still loved him as much as ever. Wiping the lipstick from her nose with a tissue, she covered the traces with some more foundation and steadied her hand for a second attempt. She applied the colour carefully, blotting her lips as instructed, and smiled at herself in the mirror. Then, with an effort to muster some dignity, she made her way slowly downstairs to answer the door.